Take Me to Another Place

ROTUNDA WRITERS

Copyright © 2016 by the Authors

All rights reserved.

The moral right of the authors has been asserted.
No part of the publication may be reproduced, stored in a retrieval system or transmitted any form or by any means without prior permission in writing of the publisher; nor be otherwise circulated in any form of binding or cover other than that in which it is published and without a similar condition including this condition being imposed on the subsequent purchaser.
All characters and events in this publication, other than those clearly in the public domain, are fictitious and any resemblance to real persons living or dead is purely co-incidental.

ISBN-13: 978-1535470377
ISBN-10: 1535470372

Published by Rotunda Writers 2016

Rotunda Writers

was founded

in September 2002

The Authors 2016

LIZ BIGGINS	RITA CHEMINAIS
JOHN COLLIER	MICHAEL CREAN
JOHN J CULKIN	M DAINTY
ROS EMERY	LORAINE FELCE
ANN GALLAGHER	EDNA GRIFFITHS
PETER HEATH	ERIC McEVOY
JIM McGUIRK	PAT McGUIRK

"Reading and Writing set your imagination free,"

Anonymous

CONTENTS

LIZ BIGGINS	3
SOMETHING NICE	4
THE UNDERTAKER	8
THE LOCKED DRAWER	13
THE RAG TRADE KING	22
THE FIRST HUSBAND	33
WITHOUT PROBLEMS	44
RITA CHEMINAIS	49
MURDER MYSTERY WEEKEND FROM HELL	50
ONLY THE LONELY	56
ONE OF THOSE NIGHTS AT THE HOTEL CALIFORNIA	58
JOHN COLLIER	64
RUNAWAY *OR*	65
HOW SCOUSE MOUSE GOT HIS NAME!	65
FLIGHT OF FANCY *OR*	71
SCOUSE MOUSE'S DAY OUT	71
THE NEW FRIEND	74
"YOU'RE SO VAIN" *OR*	78
HOW MAGPIE BECAME MAXIMUS	78
FOR THOSE IN PERIL ON THE SEA *OR* HOW SETH GOT HIS NAME	88
IT'S NOW OR NEVER *OR* HOW SCOUSE & FRIENDS SAVED JIMMY DREW	94
THE DOCUMENTS IN THE CASE *OR*	100
ALL IN A DAY'S WORK	100
THE FORTUNE TELLER	107
ROUGH JUSTICE	109
LEFT OUT	112
SPARKLING CYANIDE *OR*	114
ALL THE TIME IN THE WORLD	114
INSIDE THE LIBRARY	119
MICHAEL CREAN	121
ENCAPSULATED PHRASES FROM THE BARD	122
A FEMALE'S NATURE	123
JOHN J CULKIN	124
MILES TO GO BEFORE I SLEEP	125
M DAINTY	171
LEGACY OF CAIN	172

A CHILD'S PRAYER	208
ANOTHER PLACE	209
BROKEN BOTTLES AND BROKEN BONES	210
IN MEMORANDUM	211
IRIS	212
ODE TO THE GRAFTON ROOMS	216
SONNET	217
ROS EMERY	218
A DICKENSIAN TALE	219
A FAIRY TALE	233
COLIN AND BILL	243
ALL'S WELL THAT ENDS WELL?	248
Sequel to "COLIN AND BILL"	248
MEET THE FAMILY	254
THE VALENTINE	259
LORAINE FELCE	264
THE STATEMENT	265
NEW BEGINNINGS	270
DYING TO LIVE	273
ANN GALLAGHER	290
SNOWBOUND	291
CHILDHOOD MEMORIES	295
POSTCARD HOME	301
SECOND CHANCE	303
THE CONFESSION	305
TITANIC - SHIP OF DREAMS, QUEEN OF THE SEA	307
FIRST FOOTING	308
LAST OF THE MOHICANS	309
ENDLESS NIGHT	311
THE BOOK CLUB	314
GHOSTS	316
THE JOURNEY	318
FIRST LOVE	319
THE BOSS'S DAUGHTER	320
THEN AND NOW	323
EDNA GRIFFITHS	324
CHARLIE TED	325
LADY IN RED	327
JUST LIKE OLD TIMES	329
LONG LOST FRIENDS	332

THE NIGHT BEFORE CHRISTMAS	334
CINDERELLA	336
BLACK COFFEE	339
A NIGHT ON THE TOWN	342
EYE WITNESS	345
MAKING DO	347
PETER HEATH	349
JENNY McCRACKEN	350
GIRL UNSEEN	369
ONE FINE DAY	386
ERIC McEVOY	393
AMSTERDAM IMPRESSIONS	394
THE TRUTH WILL OUT	398
THE RIDE	420
WAR	427
THE PHOTOGRAPH	430
WHAT'S GOING ON IN THE SLEEPY TOWN OF STORFAIRY?	435
THE LAW AND THE LADY	440
JIM McGUIRK	442
ROBERT FROST –	443
WRITING BETWEEN THE LINES	443
THE FUSTARD BIRDS	445
by Colonel Oblivion, RSPB, BTO, WWT	445
THE TIME MACHINE	448
HITCH HIKER'S GUIDE TO THE LOONEY BIN	454
PAT McGUIRK	458
A QUIET PLACE	459
ANOTHER FINE MESS	461
BROTHERLY LOVE	466
GONE!	469
RESOLUTIONS	475
ON THE MOUNTAIN STANDS A LADY	478
TIME'S ARROW	491
ROUND ROBIN COLLABORATIONS	503
IN THE WOOD	504
LIZ BIGGINS & PETER HEATH	504
THE 10.40 a.m. TO OBAN	510
JOHN COLLIER, ERIC McEVOY & ROS EMERY	510
GILVIN	517
JOHN J CULKIN, LORAINE FELCE & ROS EMERY	499

THE SCHOOLMASTER 525
ROS EMERY, PETER HEATH 525
& JOHN J CULKIN 525
THE SCHOOLMASTER 547
ANN GALLAGHER, ROS EMERY 547
& JOHN COLLIER 547
THE SCHOOLMASTER 554
PAT McGUIRK, ERIC McEVOY 554
& ROS EMERY 554

ACKNOWLEDGMENTS

Rotunda

"Community-led Rotunda is for everyone; for all of us . . above all and everything else, Rotunda is a place for you."

109-115 Great Mersey Street, Kirkdale, Liverpool L5 2PL.
Tel: 0151 207 2176   Website: www.therotunda.org.uk

Workers' Educational Association

"A better world – equal, democratic and just . . the WEA challenges and inspires individuals, communities and society."

North West Region, Suite 405 Cotton Exchange, Old Hall Street, Liverpool L3 9JR.
Tel: 0151 243 5340   Website: www.nw.wea.org.uk

WEA tutor: June Davies

Cover photography: Eric McEvoy

Cover design: Steven Ingley

Editors: Liz Biggins, John J Culkin, Peter Heath

LIZ BIGGINS

SOMETHING NICE

Liz Biggins

Olivia and Frank sat companionably, watching television, as they did most nights. She glanced over at him and thought. *"How did we turn into a pair of old fogies?"* Without a trace of vanity she thought, *"The years have been good to me but his hair has receded so far it's almost all gone. His beer gut has gotten larger by the week since, well since, I don't know when!"* Frank, perhaps sensing his wife's gaze looked over and asked *"Want another cuppa, darling?"*

Soon he returned with a tray, presenting two cups and saucers, a milk jug, sugar bowl and a large pot of tea. He liked to do things properly did Frank, why have a tea set and only use it for visitors he reasoned. As an extra treat Frank had laid out a selection of biscuits on one of their best tea-plates. Explaining as he laid everything out on the coffee table. *"Thought you deserved a little treat."*

Olivia smiled graciously, grateful that they were able to enjoy such simple pleasures together. Relaxed the watched the evening news while sipping their tea and dunking biscuits.

Her thoughts slipped back to her youth, meeting Frank at University was the single most thrilling event of her life. It was a Sunday afternoon, she was making her way passed the halls of residence after attending Mass, something her father insisted upon. She knew he would check with Father Goggins.

Frank was athletic, tall with brown eyes and lovely curly dark hair, in fact the most handsome man she had ever met and the fact that he seemed to be interested in her almost blew her mind. Frank called her lovely, beautiful, gorgeous, feminine and sexy, but instead of believing him she remained convinced that what her father had told her over the years was the truth.

Her childhood was a dark place, she resisted all thoughts of it. No way did she want to revisit those days. As she considered that time, the nightmares returned, a flood of horrible recollections rushed in. Dave's voice, harsh and unyielding, the name calling, the insults, the fear. Dave's fists beating her, but only where the bruises would not show. These were the fear and pain that punctuated her days and nights, only relieved when at school. Olivia learned to expect nothing from her mother.

She knew that any courage her mother possessed was used up in getting through her own dark nights. She had been battered for years, her voice begging her husband to stop, trying to deflect his attention, would never leave Olivia. She knew her mother had done all she could to protect her, it was never going to be enough, until she managed to get a cleaning job at the local University.

Their companionable silence was shattered by the insistent ringing of the telephone. It was Jennifer. Frank happily exchanged a few words with his little girl, as he still thought of her, despite her being grown up and married. After a short chat they exchanged 'goodnights' and 'love you's' passing the phone back to his wife, Frank blew her a kiss and signalled that he was going up to bed. Leaving Jennifer and Olivia to finalise arrangements for the week ahead.

As his head touched the pillow, normally Frank would go fast asleep, tonight thoughts flooded his heart and soul. Throughout the years they had managed to keep secret the facts about Jennifer's conception. His beloved daughter was born only 7 months after their wedding. Frank and Olivia had convinced everyone that their daughter was premature, thankfully she was a small baby so their lies were accepted.

It was vital that Olivia's father believe them. The birth had been long and difficult and thanks to his abuse, Olivia could never have a child together. Frank didn't just love his wife and daughter, he adored them. Over the years Olivia had found it cathartic to talk to Dave but he never ever asked questions of her, even to the present day.

Olivia's love for her husband was deeply rooted in his being diametrically opposite to her father. As she sat, after talking with her daughter she reflected.

"Frank is a thousand times a better Dad to Jennifer than her own Dad had ever been to her, in fact her Dad really did not deserve the title." involuntary shivering at thoughts of the man who had cast a shadow over her childhood.

Thankfully the man who had fathered her was no longer in their lives, Dave as she always called him, had died many years ago. It was such a pity that Mum had missed out on her grand-daughters life while serving time for dispatching this evil from their lives forever. In Olivia's mind her mother should have been awarded a medal.

Delighted that Mum would be coming home and Frank insisted that she make her home with them, at least until she was able to manage on her own. He had made it clear that Maria would always be welcome in his house, correcting himself, in our house. Their smiles had been infectious as they'd made plans together.

In a few days Jennifer would drive her Mum to collect Maria from prison. On the return trip the three women would enjoy a leisurely afternoon tea at the new hotel on the by-pass, before bringing Grandma home to meet the rest of the family. After all this time, she more than anyone, deserved something nice!

THE UNDERTAKER

Liz Biggins

Evelyn's concern was bordering on frantic. After all John was seldom this late. He had phoned to say he was on his way home but perhaps, as occasionally happened a mate had waylaid him. He'd have kept to his usual 'soft drink' she felt sure.
"He's likely gone to the pub with Tom. Though he's not had a drink since the drink-driving conviction." Evelyn reasoned. *"Gosh"*, she thought *"that's years ago now, he'd served the ban and made reparation. Would he have broken his vow to her? Is it likely? No! No! No!"* Evelyn asked and answered herself.
She picked up the receiver, dialled, thinking. *"I'll phone the office to see if he's got caught up in work!"* The ringing goes on and on until she has to accept that no one is going to answer! *"Should I try his mobile? What if he's driving and tries to answer, he'd get done for illegal use of a mobile phone and I'd be to blame."* Finally, she decided to call Tom, but that call went to voicemail. She left a short cryptic message and asked him to call her as soon as he could.
Talking to herself had become part of her life since the catastrophe that had changed their family lives only five years ago. John's career had stalled, his income was a lot less now but thankfully, no one

had been hurt. However, on a night like tonight, the events of the past haunted her. *"Really"* she admonished herself, *"I shouldn't let my imagination run away with me, after all he's rarely late home, in fact no more than once or twice a month. It's inevitable in his line of work, but he had phoned to say he was leaving."* Anxiety heightened as she heard the wind moaning outside the windows. November temperatures were definitely at winter levels and it had been extra cold recently. Earlier the forecaster had announced there was be a threat of snow tonight and winds would be gusting strongly from the North East. On top of that the wind chill factor was making the dark night icy cold and potentially dangerous.

"What if he's crashed?" Unwillingly she followed her imagination, in which she saw John lying in a wrecked car, the windscreen broken, an icy wind chilling his comatose body. *"Oh Lord!"* She exclaimed *"Don't let anything terrible happen to him, please keep him safe."*

She pleaded silently with a god she had no real faith in, no real belief. After all, she reasoned if there was a god why does he/she let all these vile things happen, murder, rape, terrorism, floods, it's not right, not fair. Taking a deep breath, she struggled to bring herself back to the present moment.

"He's just been held up in traffic, someone else has had an accident and he's stuck behind them. That's all it is!" She reassured herself aloud, aware that she lacked

conviction. Swiftly followed by self-recrimination for being relieved it might be someone else who had been involved in an accident.

A voice that resembled her deceased mothers' advised *"Have a nice cup of tea! You'll feel better after a nice cuppa."* Much to her own astonishment, she put the kettle on and was soon sitting at the kitchen table sipping the scalding liquid. The house was silent. Outside, darkness deepened as the minutes ticked on relentlessly, and became an hour, and then another half hour passed.

Thankfully, their teenage son and daughter were upstairs sound asleep; she could not have coped with their incessant questioning. Evelyn was getting tired now; anxiety was beginning to wear her out. Lost in thought, tea rapidly cooling, Evelyn wondered what to do. Should she phone Tom again? Should she try John or the office?

Several loud raps on the front door, followed by a doorbell ringing, abruptly interrupted thoughts about what she should do. Rushing to respond, heart in her mouth, she gasped as she spied the police uniform.

She missed the first part of the Sergeant's explanation, hearing only *"Mrs Smythe, I can assure you your husband will be alright! He's being monitored for concussion and treatment of minor cuts. He'll likely he'll be discharged tomorrow. He asked us to let you know that this was nothing like the last time, and there is no need to wake the children, nor any need to come to the hospital."*

Constable Brady enquired *"Do you want to call someone to come round to sit with you?"* Evelyn responded by asking for further explanation, she just could not get the sequence of events clear in her head. The Sergeant obliged.

"A collision occurred when a van shot out of a side street, striking the vehicle your husband was driving in the nearside rear end. The contents of the hearse, a certain Mr Davidson was propelled out of the back door, and slithered along the street being ejected from the body bag. Your husband, though stunned by the impact, managed to stagger to the rear of his vehicle before he was overcome and collapsed on top of Mr Davidson."

Muffled titters from Constable Brady were silenced by a stern glare from Sergeant Anderson, who continued. *"When the ambulance arrived there was further confusion as it seems the van driver, while trying to get away, tripped over the bodies. Collapsing he hit his head on the road knocking himself out. He was found lying on top of your husband."* He went on to explain, *"As the paramedics endeavoured to extricate the bodies from each other, there was initially some consternation that one of the bodies was in fact dead."* By this time, the Sergeant was himself having some trouble with his own facial muscles.

He endeavoured to continue, clearing his throat; he continued in as serious a tone as he could muster. *"Then someone recognised your husband. They recalled he had been done for driving while under the influence some time back and this further confused the situation. However we can assure you tests showed he was, in fact, sober."*

Constable Brady recognised your husband, and arranged for him to be taken to A&E for medical attention while a fellow undertaker was called out to remove the deceased. *"Oh yes and the van driver was also taken to A&E but under arrest for causing an accident while in commission of a crime. He was fleeing the scene of a jewellery break-in. Empty handed as it turns out."* Evelyn's tears were real and copious, though accompanied by hysterical laughter. Realising this the officers, who could restrain themselves no longer, joined in. After a while, Evelyn managed to splutter, *"And I thought being an undertaker would keep John out of trouble!"*

THE LOCKED DRAWER

Liz Biggins

Staying in a large country house was turning out to be an exciting experience for Timothy, what puzzled him was that his mother had told him that one day the house and estate would be his. He found this very confusing, as everyone knew it was Uncle John & Aunt Hilary's house. To him they were very old, therefore could not care for him themselves but they employed a Nanny and a nursery nurse. At just seven year old, he revelled in his new surroundings which were so very different from his home in the suburbs of the historic and bustling city of Coventry.

Timothy missed his father greatly; he knew his Papa was a very brave man. His mother had spoken in detail about how his father had volunteered to go to another country to fight the enemy and that he would lead his men to victory. Timothy wished he could have gone with his father as it sounded like it was a great adventure.

Natural curiosity compelled Timothy to listen to the servants conversations even though he wasn't sure what they meant. The war was their main topic of conversation. Many discussions took place in hushed tones, sometimes using words he had never heard before. Timothy found it exciting that they did not realise he was listening to them. Being the only person in the house under four foot tall and of slight build, he could linger undetected in the shadows and hiding places that abounded throughout the house.

Having been evacuated almost as soon as hostilities began, Timothy thought living with his aunt and uncle was good fun though he missed his mother greatly. She had remained in the city despite the bombs, Timothy did worry about what might happen to her if one of these devices falling from the sky hit her, he would not want her to have a sore head. Today, however, his mother was coming to visit. Timothy was very excited but also bewildered, as the atmosphere among the adults of the household seemed charged with tension.

To fill the time till his dear mother's arrival Timothy secreted himself in his Uncle's study, hidden in the folds of the drapes that festooned each of the tall windows along the east wall. These windows gave him a vantage point as they looked out on the views of the enormous gardens stretching down to the lake. It was home to all sorts of birds and wild life that he enjoyed watching, enthralled as they went about their daily business. Uncle John strode into his study, closing the door firmly behind him. Surprized by this turn of events, as his uncle rarely used his study in the mornings, Timothy stood as still as a statue barely daring to breath in case he was found. He did not want his uncle to be angry with him. Uncle John sat at the desk for some time studying a number of papers. Timothy was struggling to keep quiet, he prayed his Uncle would go away as he needed to move, apart from anything else, he was getting quite bored.

Just as he thought he would need to burst out of his hiding place, he heard the voice of Alice, the nursemaid, calling his name; it was time for luncheon. Fortunately, his uncle must have heard this also, as he proceeded to gathered the papers into a pile on top of his desk and swiftly stuffed them into a drawer, which he then locked. Not only that, but he took the key and put it in the inside pocket of his jacket. He saw Uncle John turn towards his hiding place and immediately withdrew deeper into the recess. He sighed with relief when he heard the door close as his uncle left the room, only to be shocked when he thought he heard the key turning in the door.

He came out from his hiding place and ran to the door, confirming his worst fear, it really was locked; how on earth was he to get out of this room without his Uncle knowing. Timothy ran back to the window. He wondered if he might catch sight of his favourite maid, Maria. He knew she was fond of him and would keep his secret. His eyes scanned up and down the path as far as he could see until saddened he lowered his head. His eyes focused on something that caused a broad smile to spread across his little face as he saw that the window was open. Just a fraction but it was open, *"Oh golly gosh I'm going to have to get this window up a bit more"* He struggled with all his strength to lift the heavy sash window without effect. Suddenly he remembered something. He and Alice had been out walking in the woods when he had gone over to pick some early pretty wild flowers. He saw a scuttling beastie disappear under a large stone and tried to move it with his hands. When Alice saw what he was trying to do she had shown him how to use a stick to lever it up, but only to have a look she'd told him.

He looked around the room, *"Ah! The poker, it's metal and strong, the maids use it to poke the fire"*. Lifting the poker from its stand Timothy almost dropped it, he had not realised how heavy it would be. Dragging the tool behind him, he hurried back to the window and just managed to fit it into the small gap widening it sufficiently to get his hand under it. Whoosh! The window shot up! Timothy, not stopping to think further, climbed out and ran like the wind, only stopping momentarily when he heard a loud thud as the window fell back into place. His only thought was *"Thank goodness, now no one will know I opened it."*

As he rounded the end of the house, he saw a large black car had drawn up to the steps leading to the front door. Climbing out of the vehicle was the most wonderful sight a young boy could hope for; there was a tall brown haired woman dressed in warm colourful clothing with a huge fur colour; a woman he recognised immediately. His feet took wing as he sprinted towards her, his mother, Lady Sarah Fordham.

Stunned at his unexpected appearance from the side of the house, she joyfully declared *"Oh my darling Timmy."* Delight brightening her strained features, she opened her arms to receive her beloved son *"Come here darling boy, give your Mama a big hug!"* She continued without pause, *"Oh my little soldier, how lovely to see you. My goodness have you come running from play in such haste, just to see me?"*

Elated as much by relief about escaping from his Uncle's study as with delight at seeing his dear Mama, Timmy soon found himself lifted into the air. His mother reciprocated his delight, bending over and with one smooth movement raised him, kissing his face and hair while holding him close to her. Timothy's happiness was complete, not only had he had an adventure and had not been caught in his Uncle's room but his mother was here. *"Oh Mama, how wonderful. Mama have you come to stay for a while? Oh have you come to take me home?"*

"Questions; questions; questions let me get inside darling boy." his Mama responded. With this she placed him back on his own two feet, taking his hand in hers, Timothy held onto her much as a shipwreck

mariner might hold onto some jetsam, they made their way into the main hall of the house. Timothy couldn't resist asking *"Is Papa coming home from the war?"* His question was not answered, as Aunt Hilary and Uncle John were most effusive in welcoming their visitor.

After Lady Fordham had freshened up, the party met up again in the dining room, were a simple but delicious lunch awaited them. In the meantime, Alice, the nursery maid, was relieved to see Master Timothy, having searched high and low for him and been on the verge of confessing that the young master was missing, hurriedly spirited him away to the nursery.

The pair climbed the stairs in silence. Once inside the nursery Alice closed the door behind them and looking down at her young charge, she enquired. *"Now then young Master Timothy, where in the world have you been?"* Alice continued, *"You know you are not to leave the house without me, you have been told many times."* Timothy started to explain but Alice cut him short. Timothy felt hot tears sting his eyes and on seeing this Alice relented her harsh stance and gently asked *"You're not in any trouble, I was worried about you, now tell me what you've been up to?"*

Timothy took a deep breath wiped his cheek and recounted his adventure. *"I was hiding as Uncle locked the drawer, then I could get out because of the locked door. I had to open a window to get out and then it shut behind me, so I ran."* Touched by her charge's tearful countenance Alice decided to ask no more questions. *"Well, never mind, your here and in one piece, let's have lunch you must be starving."* At that moment, Lady Sarah popped into the nursery to say goodnight to her son, she only stayed a short time before; in a small voice Timothy said, *"I am but I need the toilet!"* His Mama smiled and indicated that she must leave, offering her cheek to her son for a quick goodnight kiss.

Alice smiled and instructed her charge to do just that, adding for him to be sure to wash his hands and be quick about it. Meanwhile she put fresh crumpets onto the toasting iron and placed them on the grid in front of the nursery fireplace.

Downstairs his mother was duly entertained by her brother & sister-in-law. After sharing a tasty meal in the elegant dining room, they moved to the withdrawing room and were relaxing with aromatic coffee. Sarah took the opportunity to update them on the welfare of her husband Lord George Timothy Fordham, now promoted to Brigadier. Finally, she came to the matter which had occasioned her journey, the issue that was most important to her.

"John dear" she addressed her brother-in-law *"Have you found the missing papers yet?"* John grimaced, he was well aware of what Sarah was referring to.

The codicil to George and John's grand-father's will!

"*It's complicated,*" he began. Interrupting him without apology Lady Sarah continued, "*There can be no excuse for papers going missing, they should be held by the family solicitors Harkens & Ellison. You know it's ridiculous to claim they are gone; lost, you claim; they've always been locked in the study safe.*"

John was annoyed at her attitude and responded brusquely "*It is something for myself and George to discuss when he returns, you should not be troubling your pretty little head with these matters.*"

"*Don't you dare speak to me like that!*" Sarah's voice rose sharply in indignation, and would have continued but was interrupted by her sister-in-law Hilary. "*Sarah no one is trying to prevent George receiving his inheritance in due time, as you say the originals must be with the solicitors. Why not leave it till your husband comes home, why upset yourself over this now.*" She sighed, "*There is so much going on with the war and everything.*" Sarah responded sharply "*Exactly because of the war, and everything, George and I need to be absolutely sure that everything is in order.*"

Later, in the privacy of her bedroom, Sarah took out the packet of letters from her husband. Despite her protestations, George was disinterested in these matters, he simply wanted to know that she and Timmy were safe and well. He couldn't refer to the battles, but she knew from his last visit they were somewhere in Belgium, an area of high casualties. Distressed she turned her face into the soft downy pillows and wept till sleep overtook her.

Waking in the early hours, Sarah had an unclear recollection *"Didn't little Timmy say something about a locked drawer?"* And she had mentioned important papers should be kept in a safe, in front of John and Hilary and they had neither confirmed nor denied this. *"Was John hiding something from everyone, was their really something to worry about, how could she get into that drawer, or even into the study."* Her thoughts spun out of control. *"Was her husband legitimate, did his Grandfather really leave everything to him and not John? What is in that codicil? I must see it and see it tonight, now."*

The surreptitious trip down to John's Study was stressful, in the dark, on creaking floors she crept very carefully. Sarah had been surprised to find the door open as well as all but one of the drawers in the huge oak desk which dominated the room. Using a letter-opener, she was amazed how easily it gave way. There in front of her was the codicil; there was her husband's birth certificate together with his parents' marriage certificate. All her fears were allayed in those moments, when she realised that there was no problem. Great Uncle John had a lifetimes interest in the estate and then it was to be inherited by George and ultimately by their son. She breathed a satisfied sigh of relief.

THE RAG TRADE KING

Liz Biggins

"Hey Tom! What have you been up to recently? How is your business doing, still making money?" Tom turned and looked bewildered as he realised it was Dave Spencer. Seeing he was not going to give up unless he responded Tom, expressing surprise replied with false cheerfulness *"Oh Dave, hello how are you, it's been years."* Thomas intuitively felt that he should not confide in this old school friend, recalling Dave's unsavoury reputation from those days. Yet he went with him to a local hostelry for a few drinks.

A few pints and whisky chasers later Tom whispered conspiratorially *"You know how the crash has affected every business; well our accounts are going to be audited soon. I admit we're over extended and I've been a complete chump. I found a way to cook the books and I'm worried sick they'll see through it. I know it's illegal, I'm terrified of the consequences."*

Dave listened carefully, nodding in agreement while Tom continued to relate his sorry tale. *"It's no different from what everyone's been doing, you know. I am not any more guilty than the banks and corporate institutions, Dave, you know that don't you? The thing is Dave I'm in dread at the very idea of prison."* Tom drunkenly continued all but murmuring to himself.

"I was led into temptation I know it, I wish I had been stronger, now I could pay with my life."

In the following week Tom increasingly regretted that he had spilled his guts in this drunken disclosure. He fought to suppress the inner voice nagging at him that he would pay for this error. He would have to wait till Dave got in touch with him again.

Tom recalled how just a few months back that he and Monty had been discussing their partnership, focusing on how well business was progressing. Monty's focus was on the management side, while Tom dealt with the sales and he had proved himself very capable at drumming up business. *"Business is booming, we are on the up and up!"* Tom rubbed his hands gleefully, in a characterisation of Fagan. *"It's only ten years since we set up our own business; we've got a lot to celebrate."* Monty agreed, *"Yep it's been hard work but it is been worth it."*

Tom had persuaded Monty into taking advantage of the increasing interest in vintage fashion. Consequently, their business had joined the blossoming Retro industry. Drinking a cup of coffee from the newly acquired percolator, they chatted about how in the past four years the business had gone from strength to strength and congratulating themselves on their foresight.

Well aware that only true vintage brings in real money, they kept their eyes open for garments with links to a famous individual. Monty and Tom had since ventured into reproduction vintage underwear. In the meantime, they felt content that they were meeting a need in the market place and were pleased with the profits so far. Gulping down the last of his coffee, Monty got up from his desk, *"See you later mate."* Lifting the production list, he made his way down onto the shop floor where the clackety clack of the machines was quite deafening. The daily routine was comforting as row upon row of machinists assembled the flimsy pieces of material, while threads and cut off scraps littered the floor.

Noting this Monty called out to one of the charge hands as he passed *"Iris, will you please make sure the floors are kept clean, that lot are a fire hazard, I need you to keep on top of this."* Approaching the shop floor manager Percy, he enquired. *"Afternoon Percy, Everything going well? Where are we up to on these figures?"* Monty became engrossed in discussing production issues with Percy. It was a normal day at Vintage Clothing Ltd.,

After a short telephone conversation with his erstwhile friend, Tom found himself approaching the offices of Reeves and Benton. Dave had advised him to look the part so he had dressed in a tailor made silk shirt, Savile Row suit & tie to match, highly polished leather shoes, together with a briefcase from Aspinal of London, he may have gone overboard but he considered it a necessary expense, one he could write off against tax.

All the same, his nerves were on edge, the company's financial situation was getting dire, and it was his fault. He could not let Monty or anyone else know just how bad things were. He reasoned *"Every business is experiencing the effects of the down turn in the world market."* He totally ignored the fact that he was burying his head in the sand, in denial about the fact that his business problems were exacerbated by his foolish decision to borrow funds against the business for his mistress.

"Ah though!" Tom thought *"Cynthia is adorable, so tempting I just could not resist her."* Ruefully he considered her a necessary expense. She needed fine clothes, shoes and fur wraps if her ambition to act, to get on the stage, was to be fulfilled; though it was costing him dearly. Now for the umpteenth time he assured himself. *"When her career takes off she will start paying me back, there won't be a problem."*

In the meantime, Tom had a serious cash flow crisis. Time was of the essence as the auditors were due in next month. Living in hope was not enough, he needed to secure this deal and knew that he could if he just deliver his selling 'spiel' with confidence. Tom needed to make sure that strong new partners would commit financially and give the company a much needed boost. Tom straightened his tie and cleared his throat. In his briefcase were the company's books and other documents, well the adjusted versions. With a sense of trepidation, he tentatively knocked on the office door.

After the introductions Tom handed over the accounts and weighed into his proposals with gusto. There was a moments silence, then things took a sudden and inexplicable turn. This meeting on which he had hung all his hopes, all his plans, was now going pear-shaped. Stunned, he sat staring as Mr Benton rose from his huge chair, leant forward menacingly across the immense desk separating the two men. *"Reeves and Benton's are a respectable company, you do understand this! We don't want anything dodgy, your figures just do not add up."* He proclaimed indignantly.

Tom's stomach was in knots; his nerves were on edge as the reality of the situation he had gotten into was dawning on him. It appeared he had misread the situation, his sources had told him that R & B were top dogs in the area, something akin to the Mafia. Dave Spencer had assured Tom they would get him want he wanted, but at a price; Tom was prepared to pay the price, whatever it was. He would do anything to get his hands on the money he needed to keep his company going, anything to stop Monty finding out what he had been up to.

Rob Benton roared with laughter, loud and long. *"Got you going there, didn't I?"* he paused drawing deeply on a huge Cuban cigar. *"I want you to understand me, clearly. If you want me to bale you out I want half your business and I want you to do a little job for me. Do you agree to these terms?"*

"I only own half of the business, I can only give you half of what is mine."

"That's where your figures don't add up, I won't take less than half and if half is all you own then I'll take your half. Capice!"

"What! No! I cannot do that! It's too much! And what about the little job you want me to do?" Tom's earnestness made Mr Benton smile extra widely.

"Would it not be enough that I do this job for you? I mean along with half of what I own. Please I need an income. I'll do anything you ask but please don't make me hand over my share in the business. I have a family to feed." Tom pleaded.

"So you'll do anything I ask?" Rob Benton mused, staring at the terrified young man, he had this guy by the short and curlies and they both knew it. *"Even........ ?"* Rob paused for effect. *"Well just how far would you go to placate me? How much do you want me to rescue your company, for that there has to be recompense. I need this job doing immediately."* Tom looked down, stared at his shoes, shifting them back and forth, uncomfortable, dreading what he might hear next, simply nodded.

Returning to the office, trembling, his hands shaking like jelly, Tom held the gun tightly, hidden in a deep pocket of his overcoat. Despite the warmth of his coat he was shivering uncontrollably. *"How the hell can I get through this?"* His throat closed over, chocking him, he coughed and coughed again trying to clear his airways.

Monty entered the office busily sorting some papers, glancing at this friend he became concerned. *"Are you well Tom? You look a tad pale, how did the meeting go? Will Mr Benton agree to purchase stock from us for his shops?"* Tom just couldn't find the words to reply, his mouth was dry and his mind blank. He felt like a man on the edge of a precipice. What was he going to do?

Taking a deep breath Tom spoke in a croaking voice. *"Oh Hello there Monty, thought you were out of the office today, weren't you taking a day off, or was it a dentist appointment?"* Aware that he was wittering, Tom lifted the mug on his desk. Unthinking he gulped a mouthful of cold tea then grimaced at which Monty let out a splutter. *"No mate I don't know what you're talking about"* he paused looking curiously at his friend. *" Anything wrong? I mean that tea's been sitting on your desk since yesterday, must have tasted awful eh!"* Moving towards Tom Monty continued. *"You look deathly pale, what's the matter, are the family all right? No one injured or sick is there?"*

Silence hung between them as Tom sought a reply. Finding his voice Tom adopted an air of nonchalance and responded, voice croaking. *"No all's well, just a bit of a cold, I think I might need some time off."*

"Of course Tom, do that, you work all hours as it is, but before you go tell me did Mr Benton agree to purchase our stock for his shops? Did he give you an answer?" Tom's quick thinking brought an answer to his lips. *"Oh yes, he's interested but you know he is a canny businessman and wants to look at the figures again. I'll get back in touch with him in a day or two. Give him time to think."* Monty seemed pleased with this information and Tom soon found himself driving home.

At least that is where he told Monty he was going. He knew that his lies could easily be uncovered. All it needed was for Monty to call him at home or for their wives to speak to each other and the 'cat would be out of the bag'.

He drove with unusual care, yet trying not to draw attention to himself. If the police stopped him now with an unlicensed gun in his possession he would be in deep trouble. Indeed he realised his life would never be the same no matter what. However he decided it was best to pull over and hide the package in the spare wheel well in the boot. Supermarket car parks have CCTV so he opted to drive into a housing estate and park in one of the quieter roads.

He had no sooner slammed the boot lid down than he heard his name called. Stunned he could not believe it was his sister! *"Hello! Tom what a surprise to see you here!"* It had never entered his head that she could have clients in this area, but as a social worker she did visit people all over the town.

"Oh hi Moira, err hello what are you doing here?" Tom nervously enquired hoping to deflect her interest in why he was there. Moira raised her eyebrows disdainfully, he realised she couldn't discuss her work with him. Tom hurriedly chipped in *"Well, I suppose you're very busy so I won't keep you chatting. See you at the weekend, Okay. Bye then!"* He was in the car, started the engine before Moira could reply. She stared after him concerned as this was not her usually garrulous brother. Thankful that Moira had come upon him after the package was safely out of sight.

Tom wondered, not for the first time *"What the hell have I got myself into?"* He drove out of town and along the coast road, keeping religiously to the speed limit. No one was treated to any hand signals from him today; nothing must make him stand out. Then he suddenly thought that maybe just driving too carefully would draw unwanted attention.

He prayed for the first time in many years. *"Oh God I cannot do this, yet if I don't it I will be the one killed! What am I to do?"* The silence was deafening.

Reaching his destination, he rang the door-bell and breathed deeply. If he could only get back some of the money he'd invested in his 'girl-friend's' career. His thoughts drifted into how he might be able to put it back into the business and at least prop it up, if the inevitable did happen. If he was in prison, well the thought was unthinkable!

Cynthia exclaimed *"Oh erm, what are you doing here today, I mean I wasn't expecting you till Friday."* Tom might be distraught himself but he noted her flustered appearance, her cheeks were pink with a glow similar to those he had seen post-coital.

"Who's in there with you?" His voice rising. *"Don't try to fool me, I know you're up to something, you've got someone in there with you!"* Tom pushed her aside and stormed into the bedroom to have his suspicions confirmed, in the most surprising way.

"Dave! What in the name of god are you doing? No forget that, you're coming with me, come on get up out of that pit. Get dressed now, come on you bastard."

Then turning to Cynthia, spitting out his venom *"As for you, you're finished, I want every penny back that I invested in your bloody so called 'career'. What a mug you took me for. You're nothing but a whore!"*

Tom had known better than to ask Mr Benton why Dave had to be *'taken care of'*. At the time he considered it an interesting concept, care was the last thing he was being asked to do with regard to his old school chum. Now Dave had made the 'taking care' a whole lot easier for him. Now he knew he was capable of saving his business.

Dave, not realising the reality of his situation was waiting beside Tom's car. *"Listen mate, I didn't know she was your bird, I never thought......"*

"That's your problem Dave, you never did think, did you?"

THE FIRST HUSBAND

Liz Biggins

"Hey Tom! What have you been up to recently? How is your business doing, still making money?" Tom turned and looked bewildered as he realised it was Dave Spencer. Seeing he was not going to give up unless he responded Tom, expressing surprise replied with false cheerfulness *"Oh Dave, hello how are you, it's been years."* Thomas intuitively felt that he should not confide in this old school friend, recalling Dave's unsavoury reputation from those days. Yet he went with him to a local hostelry for a few drinks.

A few pints and whisky chasers later Tom whispered conspiratorially *"You know how the crash has affected every business; well our accounts are going to be audited soon. I admit we're over extended and I've been a complete chump. I found a way to cook the books and I'm worried sick they'll see through it. I know it's illegal, I'm terrified of the consequences."*

Dave listened carefully, nodding in agreement while Tom continued to relate his sorry tale. *"It's no different from what everyone's been doing, you know. I am not any more guilty than the banks and corporate institutions, Dave, you know that don't you? The thing is Dave I'm in dread at the very idea of prison."* Tom drunkenly continued all but murmuring to himself.

"I was led into temptation I know it, I wish I had been stronger, now I could pay with my life."

In the following week Tom increasingly regretted that he had spilled his guts in this drunken disclosure. He fought to suppress the inner voice nagging at him that he would pay for this error. He would have to wait till Dave got in touch with him again.

Tom recalled how just a few months back that he and Monty had been discussing their partnership, focusing on how well business was progressing. Monty's focus was on the management side, while Tom dealt with the sales and he had proved himself very capable at drumming up business. *"Business is booming, we are on the up and up!"* Tom rubbed his hands gleefully, in a characterisation of Fagan. *"It's only ten years since we set up our own business; we've got a lot to celebrate."* Monty agreed, *"Yep it's been hard work but it is been worth it."*

Tom had persuaded Monty into taking advantage of the increasing interest in vintage fashion. Consequently, their business had joined the blossoming Retro industry. Drinking a cup of coffee from the newly acquired percolator, they chatted about how in the past four years the business had gone from strength to strength and congratulating themselves on their foresight.

Well aware that only true vintage brings in real money, they kept their eyes open for garments with links to a famous individual. Monty and Tom had since ventured into reproduction vintage underwear. In the meantime, they felt content that they were meeting a need in the market place and were pleased with the profits so far. Gulping down the last of his coffee, Monty got up from his desk, *"See you later mate."* Lifting the production list, he made his way down onto the shop floor where the clackety clack of the machines was quite deafening. The daily routine was comforting as row upon row of machinists assembled the flimsy pieces of material, while threads and cut off scraps littered the floor.

Noting this Monty called out to one of the charge hands as he passed *"Iris, will you please make sure the floors are kept clean, that lot are a fire hazard, I need you to keep on top of this."* Approaching the shop floor manager Percy, he enquired. *"Afternoon Percy, Everything going well? Where are we up to on these figures?"* Monty became engrossed in discussing production issues with Percy. It was a normal day at Vintage Clothing Ltd.,

After a short telephone conversation with his erstwhile friend, Tom found himself approaching the offices of Reeves and Benton. Dave had advised him to look the part so he had dressed in a tailor made silk shirt, Savile Row suit & tie to match, highly polished leather shoes, together with a briefcase from Aspinal of London, he may have gone overboard but he considered it a necessary expense, one he could write off against tax.

All the same, his nerves were on edge, the company's financial situation was getting dire, and it was his fault. He could not let Monty or anyone else know just how bad things were. He reasoned *"Every business is experiencing the effects of the down turn in the world market."* He totally ignored the fact that he was burying his head in the sand, in denial about the fact that his business problems were exacerbated by his foolish decision to borrow funds against the business for his mistress.

"*Ah though!*" Tom thought "*Cynthia is adorable, so tempting I just could not resist her.*" Ruefully he considered her a necessary expense. She needed fine clothes, shoes and fur wraps if her ambition to act, to get on the stage, was to be fulfilled; though it was costing him dearly. Now for the umpteenth time he assured himself. *"When her career takes off she will start paying me back, there won't be a problem."*

In the meantime, Tom had a serious cash flow crisis. Time was of the essence as the auditors were due in next month. Living in hope was not enough, he needed to secure this deal and knew that he could if he just deliver his selling 'spiel' with confidence. Tom needed to make sure that strong new partners would commit financially and give the company a much needed boost. Tom straightened his tie and cleared his throat. In his briefcase were the company's books and other documents, well the adjusted versions. With a sense of trepidation, he tentatively knocked on the office door.

After the introductions Tom handed over the accounts and weighed into his proposals with gusto. There was a moments silence, then things took a sudden and inexplicable turn. This meeting on which he had hung all his hopes, all his plans, was now going pear-shaped. Stunned, he sat staring as Mr Benton rose from his huge chair, leant forward menacingly across the immense desk separating the two men. *"Reeves and Benton's are a respectable company, you do understand this! We don't want anything dodgy, your figures just do not add up."* He proclaimed indignantly.

Tom's stomach was in knots; his nerves were on edge as the reality of the situation he had gotten into was dawning on him. It appeared he had misread the situation, his sources had told him that R & B were top dogs in the area, something akin to the Mafia. Dave Spencer had assured Tom they would get him want he wanted, but at a price; Tom was prepared to pay the price, whatever it was. He would do anything to get his hands on the money he needed to keep his company going, anything to stop Monty finding out what he had been up to.

Rob Benton roared with laughter, loud and long. *"Got you going there, didn't I?"* he paused drawing deeply on a huge Cuban cigar. *"I want you to understand me, clearly. If you want me to bale you out I want half your business and I want you to do a little job for me. Do you agree to these terms?"*

"I only own half of the business, I can only give you half of what is mine."

"That's where your figures don't add up, I won't take less than half and if half is all you own then I'll take your half. Capice!"

"What! No! I cannot do that! It's too much! And what about the little job you want me to do?" Tom's earnestness made Mr Benton smile extra widely.

"Would it not be enough that I do this job for you? I mean along with half of what I own. Please I need an income. I'll do anything you ask but please don't make me hand over my share in the business. I have a family to feed." Tom pleaded.

"So you'll do anything I ask?" Rob Benton mused, staring at the terrified young man, he had this guy by the short and curlies and they both knew it. *"Even........ ?"* Rob paused for effect. *"Well just how far would you go to placate me? How much do you want me to rescue your company, for that there has to be recompense. I need this job doing immediately."* Tom looked down, stared at his shoes, shifting them back and forth, uncomfortable, dreading what he might hear next, simply nodded.

Returning to the office, trembling, his hands shaking like jelly, Tom held the gun tightly, hidden in a deep pocket of his overcoat. Despite the warmth of his coat he was shivering uncontrollably. *"How the hell can I get through this?"* His throat closed over, chocking him, he coughed and coughed again trying to clear his airways.

Monty entered the office busily sorting some papers, glancing at this friend he became concerned. *"Are you well Tom? You look a tad pale, how did the meeting go? Will Mr Benton agree to purchase stock from us for his shops?"* Tom just couldn't find the words to reply, his mouth was dry and his mind blank. He felt like a man on the edge of a precipice. What was he going to do?

Taking a deep breath Tom spoke in a croaking voice. *"Oh Hello there Monty, thought you were out of the office today, weren't you taking a day off, or was it a dentist appointment?"* Aware that he was wittering, Tom lifted the mug on his desk. Unthinking he gulped a mouthful of cold tea then grimaced at which Monty let out a splutter. *"No mate I don't know what you're talking about"* he paused looking curiously at his friend. *" Anything wrong? I mean that tea's been sitting on your desk since yesterday, must have tasted awful eh!"* Moving towards Tom Monty continued. *"You look deathly pale, what's the matter, are the family all right? No one injured or sick is there?"*

Silence hung between them as Tom sought a reply. Finding his voice Tom adopted an air of nonchalance and responded, voice croaking. *"No all's well, just a bit of a cold, I think I might need some time off."*

"Of course Tom, do that, you work all hours as it is, but before you go tell me did Mr Benton agree to purchase our stock for his shops? Did he give you an answer?" Tom's quick thinking brought an answer to his lips. *"Oh yes, he's interested but you know he is a canny businessman and wants to look at the figures again. I'll get back in touch with him in a day or two. Give him time to think."* Monty seemed pleased with this information and Tom soon found himself driving home.

At least that is where he told Monty he was going. He knew that his lies could easily be uncovered. All it needed was for Monty to call him at home or for their wives to speak to each other and the 'cat would be out of the bag'.

He drove with unusual care, yet trying not to draw attention to himself. If the police stopped him now with an unlicensed gun in his possession he would be in deep trouble. Indeed he realised his life would never be the same no matter what. However he decided it was best to pull over and hide the package in the spare wheel well in the boot. Supermarket car parks have CCTV so he opted to drive into a housing estate and park in one of the quieter roads.

He had no sooner slammed the boot lid down than he heard his name called. Stunned he could not believe it was his sister! *"Hello! Tom what a surprise to see you here!"* It had never entered his head that she could have clients in this area, but as a social worker she did visit people all over the town.

"Oh hi Moira, err hello what are you doing here?" Tom nervously enquired hoping to deflect her interest in why he was there. Moira raised her eyebrows disdainfully, he realised she couldn't discuss her work with him. Tom hurriedly chipped in *"Well, I suppose you're very busy so I won't keep you chatting. See you at the weekend, Okay. Bye then!"* He was in the car, started the engine before Moira could reply. She stared after him concerned as this was not her usually garrulous brother. Thankful that Moira had come upon him after the package was safely out of sight.

Tom wondered, not for the first time *"What the hell have I got myself into?"* He drove out of town and along the coast road, keeping religiously to the speed limit. No one was treated to any hand signals from him today; nothing must make him stand out. Then he suddenly thought that maybe just driving too carefully would draw unwanted attention.

He prayed for the first time in many years. *"Oh God I cannot do this, yet if I don't it I will be the one killed! What am I to do?"* The silence was deafening.

Reaching his destination, he rang the door-bell and breathed deeply. If he could only get back some of the money he'd invested in his 'girl-friend's' career. His thoughts drifted into how he might be able to put it back into the business and at least prop it up, if the inevitable did happen. If he was in prison, well the thought was unthinkable!

Cynthia exclaimed *"Oh erm, what are you doing here today, I mean I wasn't expecting you till Friday."* Tom might be distraught himself but he noted her flustered appearance, her cheeks were pink with a glow similar to those he had seen post-coital.

"Who's in there with you?" His voice rising. *"Don't try to fool me, I know you're up to something, you've got someone in there with you!"* Tom pushed her aside and stormed into the bedroom to have his suspicions confirmed, in the most surprising way.

"Dave! What in the name of god are you doing? No forget that, you're coming with me, come on get up out of that pit. Get dressed now, come on you bastard."

Then turning to Cynthia, spitting out his venom *"As for you, you're finished, I want every penny back that I invested in your bloody so called 'career'. What a mug you took me for. You're nothing but a whore!"*

Tom had known better than to ask Mr Benton why Dave had to be *'taken care of'*. At the time he considered it an interesting concept, care was the last thing he was being asked to do with regard to his old school chum. Now Dave had made the 'taking care' a whole lot easier for him. Now he knew he was capable of saving his business.

Dave, not realising the reality of his situation was waiting beside Tom's car. *"Listen mate, I didn't know she was your bird, I never thought......"*

"That's your problem Dave, you never did think, did you?"

WITHOUT PROBLEMS

Liz Biggins

The icy wind blasted into the slim figure, inappropriately dressed for this type of weather. Lucy had left home only an hour since, when the sun was warming the earth, with only a smattering of white cloud meandering across the blue skies. Now she pulled her light-weight jacket tightly around her, holding her large shoulder bag to the front as a shield. *"Brrr, where has the sun gone, I should have realised it would be colder in the city."*

Her thoughts chased each other like hobby horses on a merry-go-round *"How could the weather change so suddenly, and why did I not even think of bringing at least a scarf or a heavier jacket."* Lucy shivered as responding to new text message she removed her mobile phone from her pocket, typed a hurried response while continuing to plough on through the crowded streets. Intent on her purpose she still managed to avoid colliding with others while staring at her phone. Aware she had to arrive early so she could catch her breath before going in for the interview, she dodged to the left then right. This interview meant so much to her. She glanced up as she progressed, noticing many people like her intent on their own business, several also peering into the brightness of their small hand held screens. Distracted people yet determined to reach their particular destination as quickly as possible.

Lucy turned another corner and a sharp wind tugging at her thin jacket, she found herself unable to proceed for another reason. Looking up from her all-important messages, she found her path blocked by a relatively tall, broad, solemn looking, dark haired man.

Her first thought was *"He could be a Rugby player."* however she addressed this Atlas of a man politely asking. *"Excuse me, could you please let me pass?"*

"Why should I? You can walk round me! I don't see why you expect me to move for you." he muttered menacingly, looking down at her with distain. This wasn't easy as Lucy was six foot tall herself, although she surmised that he was at least three inches taller. Still feeling uncomfortable at his intimidation, Lucy found the courage to spit out indignantly *"You're no gentleman!"* as she side-stepped the muscular edifice before her, pocketing her phone. Aware of the clattering of her inch heals as she attempted a quick getaway, although some may have described it more a quick totter. A safe distance away she glanced back to give the man a look of disgust but he was not looking in her direction, instead he was engaged in a tussle with someone more his own height.

The two men seemed equally matched as they pushed each other back and forth. As she stood in shock, she observed the exchange though she couldn't clearly make out what was being hissed by one to the other. She had just selected the camera function on her phone when she realised that something was gleaming, something the other man held tight in his fist, threateningly. She gasped as she saw the man, she thought of as her adversary, quickly grab his opponents arm, forcing it away from his body and twisting the man's wrist. As he did so, the weapon fell to the ground. All this time she was snapping picture after picture, she could not be sure how clearly she had captured the action.

Along with several others, Lucy looked on as punches were exchanged. From somewhere behind her, two police officers appeared, and speedily took control of the situation.

They advised both men to 'cease and desist' while removing their truncheons threateningly. The complete stranger to Lucy started to throw a punch at the officers, which one of the them deftly caught, forcing the flying arm behind the perpetrators back. Grabbing the man's other arm he lithely joined them together with handcuffs. Meanwhile the other officer did the same to the other perpetrator. Speaking sternly to both men the officer advised them of their rights.

Lucy was impressed by the efficiency of movement that had resulted in two rather large men being contained, particularly as one had a weapon.

She turned to go on her way feeling extremely relieved, when she felt a hand on her shoulder. *"Excuse me, I understand you saw everything and I need to ask you for a statement."* Lucy started to explain that this was impossible as she was already late for an appointment, she deliberately did not volunteer that she may have caught the whole incident on her phone. The officer replied, *"That's no problem. Now, could you just give me a quick resume of what you saw, and I will need your full name and contact details in case we need to talk to you again or ask you to come in to make a full statement."* Having satisfied the officer's demands Lucy, breathing a sigh of relief, was able to go on her way, unharmed.

As it turned out her appointment went extremely well, in fact, within a few hours of the demanding interview she received a phone call on her parents land line. She was absolutely thrilled; they were actually offering her the job. The call had interrupted her as she related the exciting tale from the morning's adventures to her parents, now she could add her own very good news. Delight spread across all their faces, not least because this job was effectively a promotion.

Lucy had spent 8 years studying, university had been thoroughly exhilarating, and particularly the PhD studies, ironically enough in Conflict Resolution. Now she was on track for the best job of her life. Now she was going to be the

Humanitarian Information & Communications Officer. She'd be based in London but that wasn't a problem she was sure her parents will be happy for her.

It had been a humiliation to have to move back home after a messy divorce. A passing thought of disdain for her ex filled her mind but she pushed this aside and joined in the celebration. Her parents Gerry and Alice were also relieved that she had emerged unscathed from the traumatic events of the morning.

With this happy new development Lucy's dreams could start to come true she knew her parents also felt good that they would again have their home to themselves, not that they didn't love her, nor was her presence a problem, but they had to acknowledge that this had not been an ideal situation for any of them. This news would lead to changes, not that the future would be without problems but there were none they could not face as a family.

RITA CHEMINAIS

MURDER MYSTERY WEEKEND FROM HELL

Rita Cheminais

Pete and Anne were good companions. They fancied a weekend experience with a difference. Pete booked a murder mystery weekend at the Old Swan Hotel in Harrogate. The scenario was a country house gathering of family and friends, to celebrate a birthday.

Pete and Anne arrived at the Old Swan Hotel to check in for two o'clock, on Saturday afternoon. They went up to their room, unpacked, and made their way downstairs to the lounge, for afternoon tea at three o'clock. This was the first part of the murder mystery experience. Pete and Anne mingled with the other guests, some of whom were actors. They began to listen and look out for clues. Anne had a small note pad and pen in her handbag. When she or Pete thought they had discovered a strong clue, Anne made a note of it, for later reference.

"This is fabulous Pete," remarked Anne enthusiastically, as she tucked into her afternoon tea.

"Good. Have you spotted who the actors are yet Anne?"

"I think I've identified two or three of them. Have you observed anything Pete, when you scanned the lounge?" "I noticed the old chap sitting by the bar, passed a note to a tall young man, wearing a bright blue jumper. Don't know whether that's significant?"

"Well, I'll jot it down Pete."

The murder mystery weekend coordinator, Dan Johnson, suddenly appeared in the lounge. "Good afternoon ladies and gentlemen. You are welcome to go off now and enjoy some free time in Harrogate. We meet again tonight in the Library restaurant at seven thirty sharp, for dinner. It will be formal dress."

Pete and Anne walked in the Valley Gardens. On their way back to the hotel, they went into the art gallery. Pete spotted the tall young man in the bright blue jumper. "Oh look Anne. It's that young man I saw in the lounge at the hotel taking the note from the old chap at the bar. Shall I ask him what was in the note, just in case it's a vital clue?"

"If you really must Pete."

Pete went over to the tall young man. "Excuse me. I saw you earlier at the afternoon tea at the Old Swan Hotel. I don't know if there was anything relevant written in the note, that the old chap at the bar passed to you?" The young man turned around to face Pete and replied: "I'm not at liberty to discuss any action you may have observed earlier, with you now." Anne apologised. "Sorry. Pete thinks he's Hercule Poirot, and he does have a tendency to take his powers of detection too far." "No worries. See you later this evening."

The tall young man walked quickly to the art gallery exit, where he promptly made a call on his mobile phone. He appeared rather agitated. "I wonder who he was speaking to Pete," remarked Anne inquisitively. "I don't know my love. Let's make our way back to the hotel." "OK Hercule," joked Anne.

Pete and Anne made their way downstairs to the Library restaurant. They were shown to their places at the dinner table by Dan Johnson. Pete sat next to the old chap he had seen at the lounge bar, during afternoon tea. Anne was sitting next to a blonde haired woman, in a skimpy black dress. When Dan Johnson, introduced the main murder mystery characters, the old chap was Lord Haversham, and the young blonde was Susie Manning, girlfriend of Ralph Haversham, the youngest son, who just happened to be the tall young man.

As dinner progressed, and the wine flowed endlessly, the conversation became more animated between the guests and actors. Pete was like Hawkeye, never missing a move, or an aside, from any of the murder mystery characters. Anne thought the maid who was waiting on, resembled someone she knew. Just at that moment, Pete slumped face first into his dessert. Everyone stopped eating and turned towards Pete. Anne gave Pete a nudge, but he didn't stir. "Oh my God," uttered Anne. "What has happened to my boyfriend? He can't be dead. Surely not?"

The maid waiting on table dropped the empty dessert plates she was carrying. One of the waiters rushed to help her rescue the fragments of crockery, strewn across the carpet. Ralph Haversham, the tall young man, got up and left the room. Dan Johnson was mortified. He asked everyone to go to the Library bar. Anne insisted on staying with Pete, until the police, the doctor and the paramedics arrived.

"This wasn't supposed to happen," explained Dan Johnson to the diners. "Lord Haversham was to be the murder victim. I must ask you all to remain here, as the police will want to ask you some questions, about the evenings events." Anne was still sitting next to Pete in the Library restaurant. She was traumatised by what had happened. Anne suddenly remembered who the maid waiting on reminded her of. It was a long lost acquaintance called Rachel. Anne had heard she was working as a film extra. Perhaps she might know something? If only she could catch Rachel's attention, to speak to her. This had turned into the weekend from hell for Anne.

Anne was moved to a smaller private lounge. Close examination of Pete's body by the doctor and the police inspector, revealed the cause of death as poisoning. Pete's body was taken away to the police mortuary. Witness statements were taken from all present, including Anne. The hotel and grounds were searched extensively for the missing actor, Ralph Haversham. He wasn't found.

When Anne eventually returned home and entered the house, sitting before her in the lounge was Rachel and the tall young man, who played Ralph Haversham. "Hello Anne. We thought you wouldn't want to return to an empty house. So sorry your twit of a boyfriend got Lord Haversham's poison by mistake. He really was becoming a threat, going on about the note," remarked Rachel.

The tall young man pointed a gun at Anne. "We can't let you live either. Goodbye Anne." He shot Anne. She fell down on to the lounge floor. Taking Anne's notepad from her bag, removing all traces of finger prints and the gun, Rachel and the tall young man vacated the house, via the back door. "Phew! Those amateur sleuths nearly blew our cover. If they had found out what was written on that note, we would both be doing time now, at Her Majesty's pleasure," remarked Rachel.

The note written by the old chap at the bar, which he handed to the tall young man said:

I'm watching you and your girlfriend, playing the maid. I should have informed the police a year ago, about how you murdered that wealthy old lady, at Sunnyside Mansions. Don't let history repeat itself tonight.

ONLY THE LONELY

Rita Cheminais

Oh! How I loathe the coming of Valentine's Day.
No sooner is Christmas and New Year over
The shop shelves begin to fill-up, three times over
With lots of tacky Valentine's trash
Encouraging loved ones to splash their hard-earned cash.
Everywhere you go there's another gaudy pink Valentine's display
Even in the local bookshop there's no escape, to my dismay.
Red heart-shaped helium balloons
Tempting all the love-sick buffoons
To buy expensive pink fizz
To give them the romantic whizz.
Heart-shaped chocolates filled with sickly gooey pink gunge,
And a pink heart-shaped cake, made of sponge.
A dozen red roses
To tempt ardent lovers, one supposes.
A cute little teddy bear, wearing a red bow
A romantic over-priced meal, with the lights turned down low.
How about a romantic seaside weekend away?
Battling the storms in the bay.

Attempting to keep their feet, the lovers, stroll hand-in-hand
Along the wind-swept promenade, to listen to the band.
Oh! And don't forget,
To buy the over-priced, over-sized Valentine's card,
With its computer-generated,
Nauseating message of love and regard.
Heavens above!
Please spare me from this commercial con.
Yes, I'm alone, with the love of my life gone.
Another February the fourteenth passes me by.
But hey! I don't have to pretend to love, and live the lie.

ONE OF THOSE NIGHTS AT THE HOTEL CALIFORNIA

Rita Cheminais

The 'Eagle' had landed. Tay Alan, hired assassin, walked over to the bar at the Hotel California. Heads turned to admire the good-looker. "What can I get you?" said the barman. "A tequila sunrise with ice would be just perfect." As Tay Alan got out some cash to pay for the drink a photograph of a young man fell out on to the bar counter. The barman glanced at the photograph. "Have you seen this guy recently?" enquired Tay Alan.

"No, not recently, but he does drink here on occasions," replied the barman. Tay Alan slipped the barman a twenty dollar note. "Let me know when he next appears. I'd like a word with him."

"Will do," replied the barman.

It was Friday the thirteenth. Unlucky for some, but not for Tay Alan, whose horoscope foretold, *Hitting a lucky seam on Friday the thirteenth enables you to take several steps forward in following your intuitive hunch to make a significant move. This will lead to an all-important breakthrough, with you calling the shots, to reach the goal within your grasp.*

Tay Alan fancied a bit of 'afternoon delight' before the evening kicked in. However, on looking around the bar, no one appealed enough for Tay to want to fulfil that desire. After leaving the bar Tay Alan moved outside to the poolside and admired the lithe, tanned bodies of the lazy sunbathers. Nothing special there, either. Just the rich and famous enjoying the American dream . . . while it lasted.

Suddenly, at that moment, Tay Alan's mobile phone rang. On pressing the answer button Tay immediately heard the gruff voice of Frankie Owen, former big time war hero (and now a small fry private eye) asking for an update on progress. "Not a lot of action here at present," said Tay Alan. "Got the barman on the lookout for the target. Will let you know once the mission is accomplished."

Tay Alan strolled over to an empty table near the poolside and sat down. After taking out a cigarette and lighting up Tay Alan surveyed those swimming in the crystal-clear pool. One guy in particular, who was wearing a pair of tight red Speedos, was of particular interest to Tay. *It can't be? Surely not? It is the assassin's target,* marveled Tay. This assignment was certainly looking like an easy kill – providing Tay could get the target on his own, away from the glitzy crowd.

The target, Monty Scott – desperado, and the most wanted international drug baron – was still enjoying his afternoon swim in the hotel pool. As he swam over to the side of the pool where Tay was sitting he shouted to Tay, "Hey! Could you pass me a towel?" Tay did as requested. "Thanks," spluttered Monty Scott as he rubbed himself down with the towel. "What's the food like in the restaurant?" enquired Tay Alan.

"I've heard it's pretty good. Maybe see you later for a drink?" remarked Monty Scott. "Maybe," replied Tay Alan.

When Tay eventually got back to the hotel room there was a note pushed under the door. On opening the note Tay read,
TONIGHT'S THE NIGHT DON'T FORGET THE DUTY-FREE. SEE YOU AT EIGHT THIS SUNDAY FOR DINNER.

Tay took a shower, changed for dinner and transferred the lighter and cigarettes to the jacket hanging over the back of the desk chair.

After dinner in the hotel restaurant Tay strolled through to the hotel bar and sat down at a table. Sitting at the bar was none other than Monty Scott. Tay Alan noticed the barman looking closely at Monty Scott as he took his drinks order. Tay got up from the table and sat on the bar stool next to

Monty Scott.

"Hi there. How are you doing? Let me buy you a drink," said Monty Scott. "I'm doing fine, thanks. I'd like a tequila sunrise with ice, please," replied Tay Alan. "I was supposed to be meeting my brother here tonight but for some reason, at the last minute, he couldn't make it," remarked Monty Scott.

"Oh . . . I'm sorry to hear that," said Tay Alan. "Listen, it's a lovely warm moonlit night tonight. Why don't we continue our conversation outside, on the poolside terrace? Hey, barman, can you bring the drinks outside?" requested Monty Scott.

Tay Alan and Monty Scott both made their way outside to sit at a table on the terrace. There were no other guests sitting outside. Tay offered Monty Scott a cigarette, which he accepted. Monty Scott leant forward to accept a light from Tay. Tay Alan discreetly pressed the hidden button on the base of the cigarette lighter. This promptly released a shot, which directly hit Monty Scott right between the eyes. He slumped forward, his head hitting the table top.

Tay got up. There was no time to spare. After walking over to the other side of the swimming pool Tay walked out of the open side gate, started up the getaway car and drove out of the Hotel California. Los Angeles Airport was a thirty-minute drive.

On arrival at the airport Tay Alan checked in and proceeded through security. After purchasing a couple of items in the duty-free shop Tay went to relax in the airport lounge. Sky News was on the big screen television. Tay glanced at the subtitles as they flashed across the screen. One subtitle of interest reported that Jerry Scott, a Los Angeles city banker – *and identical twin brother of Monty Scott, desperado and international drug baron* – had been found dead on the terrace at the Hotel California. The death was being treated as suspicious.

Tay Alan sat motionless. Friday the thirteenth was certainly one of those nights Tay would never forget. Failing to know that Monty Scott had an identical twin brother was definitely a major oversight on the part of the British intelligence service.

How was Tay Alan, hired assassin, ever going to live this mistake down? More to the point, Monty Scott, the desperado drug baron, was still at large somewhere in the USA. Tay Alan had failed miserably in completing the assignment. This would inevitably result in a permanent foreign posting to some godforsaken outback.

What made the situation so much worse for Tay Alan was the fact that her career – as the only female assassin working with British intelligence – was well and truly over. Right now, Tay Alan would welcome a cushy little administrative job in the City of London.

As the London Heathrow flight was called Tay Alan walked casually over to the boarding gate.

If you have enjoyed these two short stories by Rita Cheminais, you may wish to read her book entitled: *Twelve Thrilling Tales.*

JOHN COLLIER

RUNAWAY *OR*

HOW SCOUSE MOUSE GOT HIS NAME!

John Collier

Mouse was having a bad day. His long term riverside shelter under the rafters of the Sugar Warehouse had become too dangerous. The company who owned the warehouse had hired the notorious Mouse Hunter. Super Mogg had a really hot and big reputation for cleaning up any building anywhere on Liverpool's miles of Merseyside Docks.

Poor Mouse found himself wandering up unknown alleyways, scuttling across wide busy roads, dodging lorries, cars and bicycles. Mouse had never heard so much noise in his life. His only home and memories were the Sugar Warehouse. His only friends were there, so he was beginning to feel very lost and lonely.

Mouse felt he had been trudging uphill for hours away from the River Mersey, he had always lived so close to. He was beginning to feel very tired. Night was beginning to fall, so Mouse knew he had to find somewhere safe to sleep.

Mouse crossed yet another busy road, and found himself in a quiet leafy square. It seemed safer here. The lights were glowing from the windows of a big double-fronted building. It seemed a rather welcoming and probably warm place to spend the night. Mouse saw a crack of light from under a basement door, and squeezed underneath.

The basement rooms were all lit up, but there seemed to be nobody about. Mouse felt puzzled, where were all the people gone? Mouse found a warm corner in a dark cupboard , which was full of paper, paints and brushes. He was so tired, that he was soon asleep. The lights in all the rooms gradually all went out, and Mouse was left sleeping peacefully.

In the morning, Mouse woke up in his strange new surroundings and began to explore all the strange new rooms and new smells. It was still quite dark, but slowly the morning light began to creep into the rooms of the big house. People began to arrive so Mouse darted back into the warm cupboard, that was to become his new home.

Mouse began to get used to the daily routine of people arriving, then going home. At night he had the whole building to himself. Mouse felt really secure here. The only frightening thing that ever seemed to happen, was the sudden daytime bells that regularly sounded.

Mouse got used to them after a while, and all the noises of people moving about. Then it all became quiet again. At regular intervals, Mouse noticed that suddenly a bell would ring for a long time, and all the people in the building would leave and stand in the street outside.

One day the bell went on longer than usual, and the people outside seemed to be there for hours. Mouse then saw from his view under the crack in the basement door a big red vehicle arriving. Men in uniforms searched the building and then went off again. All the people outside came back, and the life in the building seemed to go on as usual.

Mouse, after several months, learned to know every wire and every pipe in the building. When the bells went off, Mouse had begun to notice the wires to the bells seemed to vibrate. Mouse also heard the word Fire being used by all the people, who left the building.

Even for Mouse the word Fire means fear. Mouse had heard stories of the 'Great Fire in the Rum Warehouse' when many of his family had been killed. Mouse had never seen a Fire, but had listened to stories from his family of heat, bright flames and terror for all involved.

Mouse patrolled the big house all night. Mouse began to feel that at night it was his house. One downstairs room, the kitchen, always seemed to have a few crumbs of waste food etc left on the floors or in the waste bin.

One fine summer evening Mouse was on his usual patrol. He came to the waste bin in the kitchen, but there was smoke billowing out of it. Mouse began to worry, no food tonight. Then he thought of the old stories of fire and death that his family had always told.

Mouse ran through the house in some panic. Why didn't the bells ring? Mouse looked at the wires that usually began to shake, but there was nothing happening. Mouse was beginning to feel desperate.

Mouse found the bell on the ground floor. He started to chew at the bell wire, in some desperation, trying to get his small teeth into the thick plastic cover. He chewed so hard, that suddenly his teeth got through to the metal wire inside. Mouse bit harder and harder into the next plastic cover running alongside.

Suddenly Mouse was thrown violently across the room by a savage spark. All the bells throughout the house began to ring. Mouse had been so stunned by the electric shock, that he was left unconscious on the floor.

Mouse was found later that evening still unconscious, by the Firemen, who finally arrived to deal with the kitchen fire. He was taken off to the PDSA for loving care and attention.

Somehow after several hours of investigation, the raw wires to the downstairs bell were seen. It became very clear to all that Mouse had saved the building from destruction.

Mouse was unconscious for several days. When he finally woke up, he found himself in strange surroundings. The Staff at the PDSA were so proud of Mouse. Mouse was now a local Liverpool Hero.

Mouse finally fully recovered. All the local news was full of stories about Mouse. All Mouse wanted to do was to go home.

Mouse's journey home was a spectacular one. Along the whole route, he was cheered and cheered by thousands of school children.

At Liverpool Town Hall, the Lord Mayor came out to meet Mouse.

Mouse was hailed as a Hero by the Lord Mayor. In a long speech Mouse was given the Freedom of the City. The Lord Mayor told Mouse and the Cheering People. "From this Day Mouse, you are to be known as 'Scouse Mouse'"

The Bells of the City Churches began to call out to each other in joy. The people all cheered, 'Scouse Mouse', 'Scouse Mouse', 'Scouse Mouse', 'We love You, You've Come Home !'

From that day onwards, the people in the College where Mouse lives, leave food out at night for him. Whenever a scratching noise is heard behind the woodwork in June Davies class, June looks up and says to her class, "That's 'Scouse Mouse' he has come back to join us again."

FLIGHT OF FANCY *OR*
SCOUSE MOUSE'S DAY OUT

John Collier

Scouse Mouse wasn't happy !
The Rotunda's busy bustling rooms were all quiet. No sounds of clattering feet on the old wooden staircases. No scraps of food left out for our Liverpool legend.

The old house was filled with a dismal hush. Scouse wondered what he had done to be left so alone and so hungry. Since his celebrated return to the Rotunda College, through the shouting joyful crowds, Scouse had become used to being pampered and well fed.

"Where has everybody gone?" Scouse whimpered into the silence. Scouse scratched feverishly at the woodwork of June Davies's classroom, but there was no familiar response. "Why have all my friends left me here alone?" Scouse was now crying quite loudly. He was feeling so alone and so very afraid.

After hours of endless wandering, Scouse ventured out into the Rotunda's Gardens. You must understand Folks, that Scouse Mouse had become very dependent since the Great Rotunda Fire Scare on his new Human Friends. So leaving the security of the great old house was another new adventure for our heroic friend.

Scouse was very aware of the dangers of Mouse Hunters like Super Mogg, so he sniffed the fresh air outside with some trepidation.

"What are you doing here on my vegetable plot?" a croaky voice screamed out! Scouse, shaking with some alarm, peered around warily into the morning sunlight.

There was nobody to be seen, apart from a jaded old magpie perched high up on a silver birch tree. "Don't mess with me!" the same voice bawled out.

Scouse was now more puzzled than frightened. There was nothing to be seen, apart from the movement of the vegetable plants in the gentle breeze. It was a really beautiful day, and even the sunlight seemed friendly to Scouse!
The voice screeched again "Don't Mess with me Matey!"
A bewildered Scouse could see nothing in the gardens apart from small groups of vegetable plants, and some seedlings under glass covers. "There are

no Humans here, or even Mouse Hunters" Scouse whispered to the balmy sunlight.

Even the gentle breeze whispered back "Have no fear Scouse, we will look after you".

The voice was croaking louder and louder "You defy me at your peril, you foolish mouse, this is my plot, my garden.....get out now or you will be whooshed away forever........"

Will Scouse be 'whooshed away" ?   Who is the Voice ? What powers does he have?

THE NEW FRIEND

John Collier

Scouse was terrified ! The croaky voice was getting louder and louder. Scouse cowered under a large cabbage plant, but the voice wouldn't stop croaking "this is my garden, get out now".

Suddenly Scouse noticed an old sort of hat flapping in the grass. It was bright red, with odd tassels hanging from it. Clearly the hat had seen better days

"Now I've lost me hat" the same voice croaked, but more feebly this time. Scouse looked up again, and noticed a tall pole with a human type figure fastened onto it. The face looked down at Scouse, and whispered gently "sorry I shouted at you Mouse, see little fellah I'm here to scare off the birds from damaging all our vegetables."

Scouse was so relieved, and chuckled back " Hi, I'm called Scouse, wot's your name ?" "They call me Worzel, well the local kids do" Scouse thanked the gentle breeze for being there, and asked Worzel "Look Worzie, can we be mates now ?".

Worzel croaked out quite loudly "Listen Mousie, just because I've lost me hat, don't you take no liberties with me name, I can still whoosh you away".

Scouse felt quite lonely again. All his human friends were away. Worzel seemed rather aloof and Scouse really wanted to be Friends with Worzel.

"Hi Mister Worzel" Scouse whispered "Would you like to me try and help you find a new hat ?" Worzel smiled in the sunlight, and croaked "that would be wonderful Scouse, do you really think you can help me ?"

Scouse was suddenly filled with a new found happiness. "Worzel has called me by my proper name" he whispered to the gentle breeze. "Maybe we can be mates after all !"

Suddenly a new voice was heard echoing across the Rotunda Garden. "Where's yer Hat Worzel, you look right silly without it". All Scouse could see was a shock of blond hair and a cheeky looking face peering through the railings.

The same face shouted at Scouse "Who you looking at you silly mouse ?" Once again Scouse was trembling with fear, but the gentle breeze just murmured back "Have no fear Scouse, we will look after you".

"Jimmy leave my new Friend Scouse alone" Worzel croaked towards the railings. "Wot" Jimmy shouted out "you can't be dat Scouse Mouse, me Mum read about in der Echo, you really him, wow, wow, wow !" Scouse proudly nodded back, and Worzel just bowed his head in amazement.

" Oh Matey, I'm just made up to meet you, wait, I must just tell me Ma and Dar" A breathless Jimmy ran home through the streets shouting "Its Scouse Mouse, Scouse Mouse, I've seen him, I've seen him..........."

"You really that Scouse Mouse, which saved the College" Worzel croaked. "I've heard so much about you from him up there". Scouse and Worzel both stared up at the jaded Old Magpie in the birch tree high above them. Even the leaves of the tree seemed to shake more energetically, when they realised who was in their garden.

"I've got one for yer" a voice shouted, as a bright yellow straw hat flew across the railings towards Worzel's pole. Jimmy then explained, more quietly, how "Me Dar was so thrilled when I told him about you Scouse Mouse, that he gave me his gardening hat for you Worzel."

The Yellow Straw Hat lay awkwardly on the ground, but suddenly out of nowhere came the Jaded Old Magpie strutting importantly across the grass. "I'll help you" he squawked. Then without any more words the Old Magpie grabbed the hat in his beak and gently lowered it onto Worzel's Head. With a bit of pushing and sitting on it, the Old Magpie got the hat well and truly fixed onto Worzel's Head.

Jimmy was jumping up and down in excitement against the railings. He could hardly believe what he had seen. Neither could the Rotunda Students as they returned back to College, when they all stared, amazed, at Worzel's wonderful new hat.

Scouse was overwhelmed, and exhausted by all that had happened. He had found several new friends, and knew he would never feel alone again. Jimmy's mates too were stunned, amazed and delighted that Worzel now looked so splendid.

"YOU'RE SO VAIN" *OR*

HOW MAGPIE BECAME MAXIMUS

John Collier

The Old Magpie was always strutting around rather importantly in what he regarded as his garden. Worzel too regarded the Rotunda Garden as his personal domain, whilst Scouse Mouse saw the Garden just as a friendly space to come and meet his new Friends in.

On this brisk November Morning there were the usual muddle of pigeons squawking their boring gossip around Worzel's' ears. The Old Magpie had given up driving them off 'his Garden', as they came back in droves within minutes.

The pigeons' tittle tattle, on this Autumn day, was all about how Captain Birdseye had not been seen out that morning to feed them in his New Brighton backyard. "He is out regular as clockwork at 7am with scraps for us", one rather manky old pigeon kept screeching. "It aint right" another screamed. "Does he want us to starve ?"

Worzel shook himself vigorously in the morning wind, hoping these boring birds would go away and bother somebody else. Scouse was thinking deeply about what he had heard. "Maybe the Captain has gone away" he whispered to the Gentle Breeze. One darker and rather unusually handsome pigeon squawked "he aint gone away, he never goes away nowadays".

Scouse was beginning to worry, as he had heard much about Captain Birdseye and his legendary Mersey Ferry exploits from his former friends in the Sugar Warehouse. "What if he has been taken ill.." Scouse murmured to the Gentle Breeze. "If only Jimmy was around, he would know what to do"

Scouse looked up towards the Old Magpie perched half asleep in his Birch Tree. "Magpie, Magpie come on down we need you now". The Old Magpie was startled, "who needs me" he replied feeling rather surprised, and then filling up again with his usual sense of self importance.

Scouse explained in detail his concerns to the Old Magpie, and that "We need to somehow get over to New Brighton now and see what has happened to the Captain". By this time the now curious more Handsome Pigeon was listening intently to what was being discussed. "I know where he lives, I can show you the way".

Scouse explained that the only way he, Scouse, could get across "that River" was via the Ferry. "Magpie, can you carry me as far as the Ferry on your back?" The Old Magpie was a bit nonplussed. "Carry you down, and onto the Ferry ! I've never flown that far for years, and with a Mouse on me back! Don't be so ridiculous !"

Eventually the Old Magpie was persuaded by Worzel's pleadings "Go and help them two, please Maggers" "Maggers, who are you calling Maggers you cheeky old idiot of a scarecrow ".

The three finally took off, with the Handsome Pigeon leading them over the rooftops and down towards the Mersey. Scouse was perched precariously on the back of the Old Magpie, who was by now filled up with so much pride about the importance of his mission, and the fame he dreamed of.

All three Scouse, the Old Magpie and the Handsome Pigeon managed to find a comfortable spot on the roof of the Royal Daffodil's Bridge. "you are all so brave" the Gentle Breeze whispered.

As the Ferry crossed the River, Scouse explained in great detail that they must stay on board until they reached the Seacombe Terminal, as this was nearer to New Brighton than Woodside. Scouse said "Somehow you will have to assist me onto the 411 bus at Seacombe, as Maggers can't really carry me as far as New Brighton. really."

By now the Old Magpie had accepted his new nickname with some pride, and felt really involved in his first real adventure for as long, as he could remember.

Scouse also described in some detail how the original Royal Daffodil in 1940 had assisted at Dunkirk, and evacuated over 7,000 people to safety. Maggers and the Handsome Pigeon were amazed at all the information Scouse seemed to have. "Where did you learn all that stuff" sniffed the puffed up Magpie. "Well see, where we lived in the Old Sugar Warehouse, tales from our great mice ancestors were handed down to us."

Finally they arrived at the Seacombe Terminal, and Maggers gently carried Scouse up over the Landing Stage and dropped him gently off by the Bus Terminal. Scouse had already told the other two how the Handsome Pigeon must fly ahead with Maggers towards New Brighton. "Then when you see the Bus getting near to Captain Birdseye's Street, I want you Maggers to tap on the Bus Window, and make sure I get off at a nearby Stop."

The Handsome Pigeon was now in his element, as he was the only one of the Three to know where they were all going. "I'll show you the way he proudly squawked".

Fortunately the Arriva Driver had left the Bus Door open, and seemed to be having a wee nap. Scouse was easily able to climb aboard and hide comfortable on an empty seat. The 411 Bus on its journey towards New Brighton attracted some attention. Its Passengers and passers-by were amazed to see the Two Birds continually circling over the moving Bus, and occasionally peering through the Bus Windows when it stopped. The Handsome Pigeon and Maggers just wanted to make sure Scouse was safe and still hidden.

AS the 411 neared the end of Seabank Road, the Handsome Pigeon got really excited. "We are nearly there" he squawked loudly "Do your stuff now Maggers". The Old Magpie began a frenzied attack on the windows of the Bus, and the frightened passengers began to shout out to the Driver to stop, which he did. Scouse slipped out of the open Bus door and scampered off towards his waiting friends nearby.

"That's his house over there" the Handsome Pigeon explained. Maggers was by now gasping for breathe after his frantic tappings on the Bus Windows. Scouse scurried across Seabank Road to a small side street, where Maggers and the Handsome Pigeon were waiting.

All three were standing outside a small end of terrace house with a lovely blue painted door. "Maggers lift me up to that small open 1st floor window" Scouse pleaded. The Old Magpie now breathless whispered "Climb aboard" .

Somehow Scouse clambered and dropped through the small window into a very dated bathroom. He scuttled downstairs, and found an elderly man lying down near a phone, which had fallen onto the floor. The man seemed to be gasping for breath, and seemed asleep to the little Mouse.

Since the Rotunda Fire, Scouse had learned about how humans use 999 for emergency calls. Scouse knocked the receiver off the phone and heard a loud dialling sound. He jumped several times on top of the no 9 button.

A Human Voice was shouting "Fire, Police or Ambulance." All Scouse could do was to squeak as loud as could down the phone. The Human Voice said, "What is happening there ?" Mouse just carried on squeaking, and squeaking until the Human Voice said "I'm sending the Police around to assist you".

After breaking the Front Door Locks, the Police arrived to find Scouse still squeaking madly into the Receiver. One of them recognised the Mouse from Newspaper Pictures, and shouted out excitedly "That's Our Scouse Mouse, how on earth did he get here?" Seeing the old man on the Floor, an ambulance was summoned. The Police Officers made the Elderly Man as comfortable as could be, until he could be taken on a Blue Light to the nearby Arrow Park Hospital's A & E Dept.

By this time Scouse was totally exhausted, and was virtually collapsed on the floor. Maggers and the Handsome Pigeon were wandering around the helpless Mouse with some concerns, and in a distressed state themselves.

A storyline had begun to break, as amazed passengers told the Police about "That half-crazed Magpie, and that Bluey Black Pigeon swooping around their 411 Bus".

Finally PDSA Staff, summoned by the Police, arrived with a Merseyside Police Escort from

Liverpool. Scouse and his worn out friends were gently placed in comfortable warm surroundings in the PDSA Vehicle, and then escorted by the Police on a Blue Light back through the Wallasey Tunnel.

After a week of PDSA rest and recuperation, our Three Friends were desperate to return home to their Rotunda surroundings. Like before, it was not a silent journey home. Crowds lined the City Centre as Our Three Heroes were yet again escorted by a Police Vehicle with sirens blazing and Motorcycle Outriders. "Scouse, Scouse, Maggers, Maggers" the Crowds shouted".
Yet again, the cavalcade stopped outside Liverpool Town Hall to be greeted by the Lord Mayor of Liverpool, the Mayor of Wirral and the Chairman of Merseytravel. The Mayor of Wirral told the Cheering Crowds that Maggers, the Old Magpie, would be renamed Maximus, and all three would be invited to another grand ceremony at Wallasey Town Hall to be offered the Freedom of the Wirral.

The Chairman of Merseytravel declared all Three as "Our Mersey Ferry Heroes. You are now given the Freedom of Mersey Ferries to travel whenever you want to, anytime on our Beloved Mersey".

Radio Merseyside and Local Newspapers avidly reported every day about how Captain Birdseye had been rescued by the intrepid trio. They also recalled, that this was the same Captain David Peters, who all those years ago had rescued three children drifting out to sea in a rubber dingy.

Jimmy and all his Mates were waiting outside with another smaller Crowd to welcome Scouse and his Friends back to their Rotunda. News had filtered through to their local School, and a wise Head had allowed them all out early.

Worzel, who had heard all the gossip from the other pigeons was shaking with excitement. Maggers flew gratefully back to his beloved Silver Birch Tree, which too was waving its branches in excitement at having such a distinguished guest back home.

"Maggers" screeched Worzel "even I missed you that little bit". The Old Magpie filled out his Chest with some pride, and said "Don't you ever call me Maggers again, I'm now called Maximus, but if you are very polite, I will let you call me Maxi". The Gentle Breeze whispered "Welcome Home My Friends !"

Life in The Rotunda Garden was quiet again. It had been discovered at the PDSA, that the Handsome Black Pigeon was indeed a retired rare Belgian Blue

Chequered Racing Hero called Pompey. His grateful Owner willingly allowed Pompey out freely as the Local Merseyside Pigeon Hero.

Captain Birdseye was greeted every day in his Hospital Room by Maxi and Pompey tapping gently on the window. Both travelled back and forth on the Ferry to report back to Scouse, how the elderly Captain was recovering.

Good News my Friends, our Captain did finally return home to feed his Friends again.

FOR THOSE IN PERIL ON THE SEA *OR* HOW SETH GOT HIS NAME

John Collier

There was great excitement in the Rotunda Garden. Worzel had a captive audience "He has got the most amazing black head and tail. He arrived here this morning, and perched on top of my head"

"Stop exaggerating" Silver Birch shook his leaves angrily. "He perched on my branches first, so there! You never saw him, it was too misty for you over there to know what was happening"

A bemused Scouse had been suddenly woken up from his afternoon siesta by all the row and wandered into the Garden. "Guys what's all the fuss about?" Scouse asked as he tried to peer through the autumnal mist. "I saw him first, yes I did" Silver Birch hissed loudly. "Saw whom ?" the puzzled Scouse enquired.

"He told me all about that yellow empty boat floating alone out there in the Bay" Worzel, the Garden Gossip and scarecrow shouted. "You didn't know that Birchie ! Did you" "Stop flailing about there Silver Birch" Scouse told the angry Silver Birch "Lets get our facts together first, and see how we can help, if needs be". That was always Scouse's first ever thought.

Maxi, the Rotunda Magpie, was all puffed up and interrupted them. "Dat Bird was a Black Headed Gull, they are rare around here. I've spotted him down the Dock Road before. That one is the leader of his flock" "Maggers, can you find this particular Gull, and bring him back here to us". "I'm not Maggers, you silly Mouse just remember my new name. Its Maximus and Maxi to my Friends" the Magpie screeched out.

"OK Maxi, just please help us to see whether we can get more details about this boat, There may be somebody injured out there in it!" the thoughtful Scouse pleaded. Maxi flew off into the afternoon mist, all inflated up with hopes of more fame.

After an hour or so the handsome Black Headed Gull arrived with a breathless Maxi in tow. The Gull bowed slightly to the amazed Mouse. "I've heard all about you Mister Scouse. You are famous right along the waterfront". "Call me Scouse" the Mouse replied. "Please can you tell us some more details about that empty yellow boat floating out there in the Bay."

"We spotted it early this morning in Liverpool Bay, about two miles out. We woz returning from a feeding trip out to some local trawlers out there. There was no signs of any Humans aboard. It was a type of sailing craft we thought, as the sails were still flapping".

Scouse was immediately alert and ready for action. "Can you get me out there somehow?" Scouse entreated the puzzled Gull. "Maxi carries me around in emergencies like this, and you are much bigger and stronger". "Me carry you, the amazed Gull" screeched "It would be my greatest privilege to assist the Great Scouse. It's very cold and misty out there, you need to wrap well." The Gull seemed to have similar leadership qualities to Scouse's, and seemed excited and moved to be doing something he sensed was worthwhile.

The Black Headed Gull's amazing sense of direction and powerful speed through the darkening misty skies soon brought Scouse onto the bobbing Yellow Boat. Luck seemed to prevail, as there was now a quiet calm all around. Scouse scuttled round the topside, and then into the small cabin space below. "There's a young Human down here!" he shouted to the Gull. "He seems asleep, but I cannot rouse him, we must get him some assistance."

"Calling Swallow, do you read me Seth" a voice shouted from a black box in the corner. "Come in please" Scouse was puzzled by the Box, and knew it was a radio device of some kind. Before the Great Sugar Warehouse Fires, all those years ago, Scouse had heard about something called Morse, from the shipboard mice, who regularly landed and sought shelter within the Warehouse. But this was a Human Voice. Scouse only knew about the sounds SOS made, as he had been taught that too by the Seafaring Mice.

Scouse saw a handle by the Radio, pushed it once out of curiosity and it bleeped. Scouse shouted to the Gull "I am going to try and get some urgent assistance via the Radio here." The wise Gull, who knew all about sea rescues from many years of observation, screeched "I will go and get some other Black Headed Gulls to assemble at the Hoylake Lifeboat Station, so that when the lifeboat is launched we can lead them back to you here".
From out of the darkness Scouse started tapping SOS slowly and rhythmically, and ignored all the Voices from the Radio. The SOS was picked up by the Liverpool Coastguard, who decided it was quite local from the bearings they could roughly make.

A swift decision was made to request RNLI assistance from the Hoylake RNLI Station. The

Hoylake Boat Crew were startled to see a Colony of Gulls encircling their vessel with one, who kept tapping onto the Lifeboats wheelhouse windscreen The Coxswain was certain something unusual was happening, and said to his mates "we will follow them, as in this mist we cannot see much anyways"

A small bleep on the Lifeboat's radar screen began to enlarge. The Lifeboat proceeded very slowly thorough the thickening mist. Suddenly all the gulls started to screech loudly, flying around in crazed circles of noise. The Lifeboat immediately slowed down, "Boat ahead shouted one of the crew" as he spotted the bright yellow 'Swallow.' Once aboard the Lifeboat Crew were amazed at what they saw.

"Believe me or believe it not" John Smythe the Lifeboat coxswain radioed to the Coastguard. "There is a Mouse here tapping away, plus we have an unconscious lad, who needs urgent medical assistance. It looks like he has some head injury from the bruise on his scalp". "Stay where you are John" the Coastguard replied. "We are sending the NW Air Ambulance out to you, now that we have an exact position for you. Once the lad has been evacuated, maybe you could tow the Yacht back into Liverpool. Also you need to know that your Mouse has to be the famous Scouse Mouse. There is none other, who would be out there in the middle of the night like this".

The now fully recovered Seth Thomas stood proudly with Scouse and the Black Headed Gull outside St Nicks Church. They had heard, during the Thanksgiving Service, from the Rector about another man, centuries ago, who had preached about the value of Nature and God's animals.

"You seem to have no name Gull, so I am naming you Seth in memory of what you did for me that misty night". Scouse smiled gently, all the Rotunda Folks now had a proud new Friend called Seth. In the skies above a colony of Black Headed Gulls swooped down and hovered gently over the strange group.

IT'S NOW OR NEVER *OR* HOW SCOUSE & FRIENDS SAVED JIMMY DREW

John Collier

A great December sadness lingered over the Rotunda Garden.
Gentle Breeze whispered to Worzel "where's our Jimmy gone. we have not seem him for over a week now". Even Maxi seemed quieter than usual and had even stopped arguing with Worzel. The Silver Birch was sad too, losing all his leaves was one thing, but not hearing Jimmy's regular cheerful voice shouting out "Hi Guys, I'm off to work" was really upsetting him.
Scouse Mouse shivered on the freezing ground. The frosty cover may have been magical to peer at out of the misty College Windows, but once outside was another thing altogether! "What's the matter folks ?" he shouted out as loudly as he could "Why you all sulking?" A very dejected and cold Worzel stuttered "Scouse its allll right for you in there in your warm college, but out heeere it's very cold and even lonelier than ever without our Jimmy's visits. We have not seem him for over a week now!"

Scouse was now very upset too! "We must organise an immediate search party" "Maggers you go and check with all your pigeon cronies. Try and find Pompey, that Prize one, he has more intelligence than the others." The Magpie was not happy, as he had been renamed Maximus by the Lord Mayor after his heroic efforts in saving Captain Birdseye.
"How dare you ?" the indignant Magpie croaked "I'm Maximus to you, and Maxi to my special Mates "!
"Oh whatever......" Scouse shouted "This is an emergency, so let's all work together..." The ruffled Magpie calmed down and croaked "I know where to start". and flew off into the cold morning mist.
"Worzel, you must be our intelligence gatherer and keep us all updated about any news you hear". Worzel the Scarecrow shook himself importantly "Sure Scouse I won't let any of you down, you know how much we love our Jimmy ! We have watched him grow from a young boy to man, and he has never forgotten any of us"
Pompey arrived suddenly dropping out of the gloomy sky. "I've just seen Maxi and the talk on the street is that Jimmy has disappeared following a pub stabbing. He used to feed all us Pigeons every night in the Penny Car park on his way home. That's all we know"
"We must find our Jimmy, he may be needing us" the now weeping Scouse shouted. The Gentle

Breeze whispered "don't weep Scouse we will all assist you!" "You are right my friend" Scouse said "let's get moving, and as Elvis said, It's now and or never! Let's start at The Royal, as Jimmy may be in Hospital""

"Worzel keep all the other pigeons updated, and as they arrive tell them to meet Pompey. Maxi and me are off down by the entrance to the Royal" "Sure thing Scouse"!

"Maxi are you prepared to carry me again as you did before ?. I need to get inside the Royal and see if I can find Our Jimmy"

Maxi was again puffed up with pride and self-importance at the thought of another mission and maybe more fame!

Jimmy was in a bad way emotionally, and had been placed in a side room to recover from his chest injury. Neither friends or family visits seemed to penetrate the dark emotional gloom, which had descended upon him.

Scouse had somehow found his way onto the surgical floor, having escaped from the well intentioned efforts of shouting porters and terrified nurses to delay him. Nobody stopped Scouse, once he had made up his mind. Scouse saw a big 'JD' on a door, and waited patiently for somebody to open it. A nurse bustled out, and left enough space for Scouse to scuttle into the room.

"Scouse wot the effing fuck you doing here? Ure not allowed up here, but am I effing glad to see you mate. You had better be off now, before somebody tries to hurt you"

An hour or so later Jimmy was suddenly aroused by the sound of mass tappings on his Hospital room window. A dozen or more pigeons just hovered there led by Maxi and Pompey.

Every Morning and Evening the Birds all arrived and just gently tapped and hovered by Jimmy's window. The Medical & Nursing Staff noticed a remarkable change in their patient's mental well-being. Jimmy had begun to smile again. His wound seemed to begin to heal more quickly, and Jimmy was able to breathe more easily again without needing any oxygen.

A wearied Mr Fairclough with an entourage of other Medics and Students marched into Jimmy's Hospital Room. "Hello Jimmy, we hear you are really doing well now! I think we could send you home later tomorrow, if you like". "What's fascinating me is how or why you suddenly seem to have recovered so well after such a long malaise". "Sister seems equally puzzled!"

"Have you heard about Scouse Mouse Sir ?"

"Scouse who ?" the tired Surgeon queried.

Suddenly all attention was diverted to the tirade of noise coming from the Hospital window.. "See Sir, that's Scouse's friends coming to visit me " All the

Medics and amazed Students stared at a gaggle of Pigeons hovering and pecking at the window led by a frenetic Magpie.

"I may be tired Sister, but what was all that about ?"
"Seeing is believing Mr Fairclough ! Maybe recovery has a lesson here for us all, and specially your Students! Security have noticed the last few days that a swarm of pigeons and that magpie have been appearing regularly at 8am and 8pm every day near our Ward Windows."

Jimmy was overwhelmed by the Echo Press awaiting his discharge. "Yes that was Scouse Mouse again, and Yes he is one of my Dearest Friends. If it wasn't for him and his Friends I would never have found the will to recover".

Another Press Story broke in the Local Media the following day. It was how some lad called Jimmy Drew had stopped a Thug from stealing the takings from the Local Penny Bar in the City Centre, and how he had been stabbed in the Chest. Jimmy's Courage had been highlighted by the Trial Judge, and his bravery rewarded from Court Funds. Scouse Mouse and his courage was reported too in the legal despatches.

Peace has now returned to the Rotunda Garden. Worzel has now recovered from all the excitement, and is back to square one arguing with Maxi.. The Silver Birch is proudly flourishing and shaking his new spring leaf buds, when Jimmy calls by again each morning.

Pompey has confirmed that Jimmy still visits the Penny every evening to see the other feral pigeons and feed them. His nickname amongst the Penny Regulars is now 'Birdman'.

There are rumours that a certain Elvis song has all the pigeons jamming in the Penny car park to 'It's Now or Never' whenever it's played on the Karaoke screen. Tourists claim to have seen it all too. As Sister said "seeing is believing!"

THE DOCUMENTS IN THE CASE
OR
ALL IN A DAY'S WORK

John Collier

"Me case, me case, me case" were the shouts I heard as the Front Counter Bell rang, rang and rang in my small Office in St Ann's Street Police entrance Hall. Billy was incoherent at the best of times, but now his words were strident, indignant and clear. His weathered unkempt face was crying, and very unexpected. We usually only saw Billy coming in via the custody suite entrance, and this was when he was brought in, mainly as a gesture of humanity on really freezing nights.

Every Northern City probably has a Billy somewhere within their City limits and this one of ours is our beloved 'Bold Street Billy.' Nobody really knew Billy's age or where he was from. I am not sure Billy really knew himself!

Billy's name was derived from his usual pitch down the side of Oxfam. Local shop staff tended to feel sorry for Billy, and give him the odd sandwich, hot cuppa and even the odd few coins. Billy had been there, as long as most people could remember, and he always had a ready "Tah mister, God Bless Ye" for any donation received.

Many a young zealous Merseyside Officer had tried to engage Billy in conversation, or take him to local Hostels and homeless projects, yet Billy just walked straight out again. Billy wasn't part of any of the usual groups of regular street drinkers, and how he survived had always been a mystery. Billy carried no paperwork, and seemed to have no DHSS support.

Billy's cries of "Me case, me case" were becoming more and more plaintive. The usual queue of the restless public grew, so I decided to take Billy into the small interview room off our main lobby, where he could be well away from curious eyes and ignorant comments.

As a Civilian Assistant at St Annes Street my role was mainly to deal with random inquiries, maintain the Lost Property Register and record details of Driving Documents when produced for inspection.

"What case ? " I gently asked the sobbing face across the table. "Me case, me case" was all I could elicit from the now bowed head in front of me. Billy's long straggled locks seemed younger looking than I had expected. I was left with a blank piece of paper. Was this lost property or a legal case this unfortunate man was on about ?

I stood up and wandered into the adjoining corridor, where I bumped into PC Dell Foster. Dell was acting up as Custody Sergeant for the day. "How busy are you today Dell " I asked. "Cells are 80% empty , after the usual Mondays offload to the Courts" he replied. Young Dell was known as a thoroughly decent Police Officer with strong views about treating Folks " as I would expect my family to be treated".

Dell also knew 'Our Billy' well, so it was agreed we would let Billy stay, with some steaming breakfast from a local Cafe, for a few hours in a an empty cell, with the door left ajar. Billy seemed a bit consoled with this but was still muttering "me case, me case" under his breath.

The Bell rang again ! I had hopefully settled down with my own steaming cuppa . Yes that "Damn public" I hissed "are always out there."

Trying to peer over the Counter was what we Scousers would call a 'Young Scally". "Hey Mister" he shouted out, "look wot I got ere". His shock of blond hair, was all that was visible at first. "Where's me award?" At his feet was a very battered looking brown leather case with surprisingly all the locks intact. The Lad couldn't quite lift it up onto the Counter, so I leant over and grabbed it. "I want me award now" he kept demanding loudly.

His whole situation seemed a bit beyond my simple civilian remit, so I asked PC Diane Brown to lend me a hand. By this time our Scally was importantly seated in the Interview Room, with the Case on the table in front of him. Diane and I sat facing him. "Ure a pretty lass" he stuttered, "wot you doing working with this lot ere". "when do I get me award ?"

Diane's gentle questions elicited that our Scally was known as Jimmy Drew, 10 years old from Anfield Road. Jimmy was on a legitimate half-term break. He had been playing with his mates in Stanley Park, when one of them had produced the very same battered case, which was on our table in front of us. Jimmy maintained it had been found on a previous evening by one of his school mates in a semi-derelict house off Anfield Road. Jimmy had persuaded them of a probable "big award etc" so they had trusted him with his mission to the Police.

Jimmy claimed he had been taught to always hand anything of value, which he found, into the Police. This apparently followed his Mum losing her wedding ring, and somebody handing it in. His

Mother's weeks of tears had somehow so impressed the young lad, that when he saw her joy at having her ring found and handed into the Police, he had sworn to do likewise.

The leather case seemed quite heavy for such a young lad to have carried so far. As its two locks didn't yield to WD40, or any other sort of persuasion, it was decided to force them. By now Jimmy was shaking with excitement.

Inside were two photos, and what looked like a pile of legal papers. Also there was a plain wooden cross on a short rather tattered piece of dark cord. Jimmy was encouraged to accept an interim paper receipt with the promise of further real rewards to come.

The legal paperwork contained the Death Certificate and Copy Will of a Dorothy Lorringer, and details of some Bank Accounts in the same name. The Plain Wooden Cross was still a mystery. The photos showed a smiling young man with black hair wearing what looked like some religious garb.

An immediate search of the address shown on the Bank Accounts was made. The house was as Jimmy said "semi-derelict", though it was clear somebody had been regularly sleeping there over many years.

A detailed search for the name Lorringer was carried out through various databases. Then a Trevor Lorringer was found to have been reported missing from a Welsh Franciscan Friary 15 years earlier.

"Me case, me case" was still reverberating in my mind, so Diane and I agreed to see if the impossible idea we had about Our Billy now happily snoring in Cell 2 was even tenable. With some trepidation, and with PC Dell Foster gazing at us rather unbelievingly, we took the old case in to Billy's Cell.

Billy's reaction to seeing the case was incredible. His reactions on seeing the contents were even more powerful.

Loss of memory is often reported, as our Missing People. Our Billy was found to be the missing Rev Trevor Lorrington. A few days in Hospital quickly recalled how Trevor's Mother's Death had affected him. The house had been bequeathed to Trevor, but the conflict between his vows of poverty and his sudden apparent wealth had confused the young 23 years old Friar. None of his Mother's Bank Accounts had ever been touched.

Jimmy's got his reward, once Father Trevor learned more about how his Case had been returned to him. This Father's faith and beliefs in his Vows were reignited.

Jimmy's reward was to be driven with PC Diane and PC Dell Foster in a Merseyside Police Car to visit the now recovered Fr Trevor in his Welsh Friar. All were warmly welcomed, and though Jimmy's reward was never to be a cash one, he could always now proudly claim to his friends about his "popo drive award" and his lifelong friendship with Fr Trevor.

Fr Trevor was allowed by his Order to donate his Mother's House, and all his cash inheritance to build an Anfield Youth Club, which Jimmy and his Mates proudly used as their coveted "award, Our Club". A plaque there reads 'In Memory Of Jimmy Drew's Honesty' !

THE FORTUNE TELLER

John Collier

Wordsworth Words haunt you still
Wafting Winds with Daffodil
Waving, Shouting Calling Me
We waited, now we'll bloom for thee

In Morning light bright yellows glow
Pushing through the Winter Snow
Waving, Shouting , Calling Me,
As you run shouting to the Sea

Shimmering lights from Winter Sun
Gentle murmuring, Spring will come
Waving, Shouting, Calling Me
Always here whatever will be

The Mirror darkens, That house is sold
Their Song is waning, going cold,
Waving, Shouting, Calling Me
We will wait for you in Eternity

Daffodils in your Backyard
Remind you still of memories charred,
Waving, Shouting, Calling Me,

We are waiting still to bloom for thee

Hunched Old Lady with Crystal Ball,
Gently Smiles I've told you All !

ROUGH JUSTICE

John Collier

"This was my Tree, my Friend I can still feel you heaving against my breast." The Old Man's words were blown away into the dusk.

"Mama Mama, look Mama the leaves are falling. Why Mama, my Tree will feel all cold and undressed" My Mother reminded me of my words later in my teens. But even then, my solid Oak Tree was still the first thing I wanted to run to, see and hug on my holidays, from that Boarding School.

Yes that Boarding School, where only excellence was expected, demanded and where failure was beaten into you. Yes that Boarding School, where bullying was accepted, and where less sporty types of boys were sneered at by both Staff and fellow boarders. I hated and feared the place. Its awesome Rugby Football reputation covered its darker deeds.

My Tree was my Best Friend, and my only Holiday companion. It shared all my sorrows, hopes and tears. Its powerful boughs sheltered many long summer hours of play and fantasy games.

In later years it was still there, waiting and waving to me, as I drove up the long gravel drive. My parents were now quite frail and elderly, and the Old House was becoming quite demanding and too expensive to maintain for their limited needs. For me, even if their welcome was somewhat cold and rigid, my Tree was there to welcome and console me.

After the Move to that Place, unwittingly called a Nursing Home, they both rapidly deteriorated. They seemed to lose hope and just gave up living. Maybe it was fortunate they died within a few days of each other.

My Mother's dementia lapsed into total incontinence, and the unkindly ministrations of the Liverpool Care Pathway ensured her rapid demise. Their care was abysmal, and I cannot forgive that Place ever for taking my Parents and then My Tree from me.

"It's time to leave Sir," a kindly voice says. The National Trust Uniformed Guide gently points me towards the long gravelly driveway. "We know it was your Tree Sir, but times have changed here, you know that. It will always be here for you to visit."

I look back wistfully. Again I see the leaves falling in the gentle evening breeze.

Soon it will be Winter time, and I will think of my Friend there cold and forlorn. I too will be sitting cold, old and alone in my unheated tiny terrace living room. But I have my memories, your picture and your strength always with me. For us both, Time and Rough Justice have prevailed!

LEFT OUT

John Collier

The darkness never goes, the fear of the unknown and the fear of fear itself fills every corner of my mind. I wake up with it, I go to bed with it. It stalks me like a malevolent spirit that has never found a refuge. I read in my youth, about the how the Christ from the Bible could exorcise men possessed with 'evil' spirits.

Once upon a time there was a boy, named Joe. Joe knew he must have been a boy once, as "Boy, come here, Boy go there !" was all he seemed to remember. Joe, had a birth certificate that proved somebody called Joe Boswood did exist. Joe had vague memories of various houses, schools and faces, some even had names.

Joe doesn't remember any happiness. Joe doesn't remember any kindness. Joe doesn't remember any laughter. Joe remembers the ridicule. Joe remembers the fear of nightfall. Joe desperately wants to remember. Joe desperately wants to be a Man.

Joe dreams of the truth-juice flowing gently into his vein. Joe imagines gently floating above himself. A soothing voice gently leads him back back into that wasteland of buried memories. Joe's degradation and desperate recollections are clearly visible. Joe sees the confused boy squirming desperately to make some sense of his body, mind and spirit. Joe hears the compassionate voice reassuring the boy, that he is safe and unassailable now. Joe desperately wants to lead the boy to safety, and into the open daylight.

The cold winter daylight filters across this keyboard. I feel its heartless fingers tearing yet again into the entrails of my brain. Maybe Joe and the boy will one day be allowed to meet up, chat and laugh together. I know that neither deserve to be left abandoned, bereft of hope and emotions out there in their darkness.

(Written as a literary effort to break into hidden repressed memories, yet to be unshackled & released.)

SPARKLING CYANIDE *OR*
ALL THE TIME IN THE WORLD.

John Collier

It's boring sitting here. My lawyer came to see me again this morning, and explained that my warrant for execution had been signed off and I should be on my way to the Chamber within days. Seth is a decent man, and tries his best to reassure me that it will all be over quickly and with no pain. Then I have Jim Tomlinson too, he's in the Cell next door to me. We chat and walk around together in the Yard. Jim is much older and wiser than me, he reads my Sister's letters out for me, and then answers her in me own words.

I keep telling Jim, "Why did that Southern man have to keep trying to feel me up. The bastard wouldn't leave me alone, so he got what he deserved!" I tried to tell this at the Court Hearing, but the DA tied my words up in knots. He made it sound as if it was all my effing fault.

The Chaplain came around again this afternoon and we chatted about my early years, when my Step Dad used to beat me regularly for nothing. I told the Rev "He was an effing drunk" and how they then sent me off to Reform School. There they beat us with a leather strap just for not saying "Sir". The Rev then told me about Jesus, and how he had lived and died for us all, and that we could pray together now if I wanted it. I began to cry, as nobody had mentioned Jesus to me, since me Mam used to teach me to pray to Jesus every night and morning.

This evening the Warden came around and explained that what he called my Execution Warrant was now signed, and I would be taking the 'Long Walk' as we call it here, tomorrow morning. He said I could have whatever I wanted for a Final Meal. All I could think of was ice cream, my favourite childhood treat. I told the Warden I had no Family, who would be coming to visit me for that last day as my Sister was really too scared of travelling to San Quentin. He explained to me in some detail how I would spend my last day with 3 guards, who would be allowed to play board games etc with me, and that my lawyer Seth and the Rev would be with me some of the time too.

They gave me something to get me to sleep. I dreamt of me Mam and happier times, before my

Step Dad came along. Cas, me younger brother and me were fishing happily in the local stream when I was rudely awakened by voices "Come on Sam it's time to go Son".

The Guards seemed somewhat kinder that morning, and there were a few shouts from other lads of "Keep smiling, weel be there for you Sam". Somehow I began to realise that maybe others were more on my side than I had ever thought about before.

Today seems to have gone really fast. I was allowed to chat for over 30 minutes with my Sister on the phone, and we cried together, as we remembered happier times. "Sammie, Sammie" she kept saying "Our Mam will be waiting for you on the other side".

The Chaplain has been again, and we prayed together, and he told me "Sam I will be there with you, and so will be Our Lord be there and waiting for you." This all seems strange to me, why will all these people be waiting for me. I don't want to go there, wherever it is yet, I am only 35 years old.

Seth and the Warden came to see me together this evening, which the Guards told me told me was very unusual. They all called me "Sam", which was kinda of nicer than being shouted at as "Bradden".

The Warden explained that at 11.55am I would be taken to the Chamber where I would be strapped into a metal chair. He advised me "Sam, take 2 or 3 deep breaths when you feel the gas rising up towards you, then you will just fall asleep easily". It all sounded much simpler and less scary than I had imagined it would be.

I've just enjoyed that Ice Cream, and we listened to some really wonderful jazz on the radio,. That Louis Armstrong has always been my favourite. "We have all the time in the world" says all I want now.

"Come on Sam, it's time to go" the Warden's Voice seemed to say. I am feeling very drowsy already, and they have all stood up and are walking me slowly towards the Chamber. It's narrow door is a bit of squeeze for me. Then they strapped me into this tight chair, but I just don't feel scared now, I will soon be meeting me Mam and that Lord Jesus the Rev has promised me. Somewhere I can hear a phone ringing........

The Guards are shaking me hard "Sam, Sam it's all over Son, you have been granted a Reprieve". "Where's me Mam, they promised me" I whimper, as I am led gently back towards my old cell. All the Lads are cheering wildly. They laid me down, and whatever they had given me sent off into a deep sleep.

Next Morning I was taken to the Warden's Office. "Sam, you have been granted a complete Reprieve of your Death Sentence by the Supreme Court, as Doctors have now Certified you as Mentally Retarded. You will eventually be taken to a State Hospital where you will be treated for your illness." What illness I wondered, and where's me Mam , but now it seems "I have all the time in the world too......................

INSIDE THE LIBRARY

John Collier

Books, books everywhere ! No, not in our more modern Libraries.

Is this Sainsbury's or Tesco's with all these automated self-service check out machines ?

Is this a public Office with these lines of desks with computer screens, with men, women, and children and all ages with some hands tiptoeing clumsily, others dancing with speedy dexterity across the keyboards ?

Is this an Airport ? A section marked 'Latest Arrivals' has many varied colourful Titles on the shelves ?

Is this some kind of zoological mystery tour ? A section marked 'Large Print' demands attention.

Is this place the auditions showcase for X factor ? A section marked 'Local Talent' has names like Rotunda Writers, Joan Lewin, John Culkin, Scouse Mouse etc. gazing excitedly from the shelves.

Is this a drop in for all the lonely people ? A section marked 'The Beatles' has a bustle of tourists and foreign languages buzzing in the air around it.

Is this some kind of Local Government Church ? A notice marked "Silence Please" outside a large room labelled 'Reference Library' frightens the unwary away!

Is this a Coffee Bar ? Outside the entrance are tables and chairs with all human shapes sipping various odd shaped cups.

Is this a Railway Station ? "CENTRAL LIBRARY" stares out across the Street, and outside the entrance, is what looks like an automated Ticket Issuing Machine.

Is this formidable Building really My Local Library ?

But where are all the Books ?

MICHAEL CREAN

ENCAPSULATED PHRASES FROM THE BARD

Michael Crean

When I was young and 'fancy-free,' I thought,
'Forever and a day,' meant every day,
'Be-all and end-all,' nothing more to come,
Yet such sweet childish notions were as naught.
I never dreamed of me when I was young,
Then me, and us, the family, we were one:
And 'all our yesterdays' were far away,
With mother, brothers, sisters, one among.
Those visions crowd my misty dreams at night,
I wake and 'wear my heart upon my sleeve':
'In my mind's eye,' we sit with 'bated breath,'
While mother sings or one of us recite.
In times that were, now all those people dead,
Still come alive when I'm asleep in bed.

A FEMALE'S NATURE

Michael Crean

A female's nature is to propagate,
Her life's chief purpose but to find a he,
Entice the male, their lust to satiate,
Produce a boy or girl of like degree.
We men and women, beings of higher race,
Conceal intentions of ensuing hunt;
Young women pout and smile, allure with grace,
While men, poor things, may row milady's punt.
Yet men must play their part and too, pretend,
They only come to dress-up and to dance;
Wear evening suit with dicky bow and end,
With just a kiss, a promise, sans romance.
The tango, wine, compelling, senses led:
A house, a mortgage, children, Madame's bed.

JOHN J CULKIN

MILES TO GO BEFORE I SLEEP

John J Culkin

1

It is the twenty seventh of December in the year of our Lord 1896, my name is Jeremiah Whitby, but I cannot tarry.

Drifting snow tugs at the wheels on my wagon and slows it to a crawl. My good horse staggers under the strain of pulling its mysterious cargo.

Let me try to explain why I am in this Godless part of England.

Back at the dockside of Column Bay, a Cornish village which I have called my home for more than thirty years, a ship's captain had found his way into the tavern that I spend some of my time and most of my dwindling supply of money in.

The Captain was looking for a willing soul to transport part of his cargo to the house whose candle lights glow in a window about half a mile ahead from where I am now, struggling through deep snow to complete this task.

The sallow faced Captain had offered such a man one hundred guineas to perform this task. And if the said task was completed before dawn the following day, then there would be another hundred guineas paid to this man by the person who lives in the sprawling stone built house that I can see before me.

The amount of money is of no small consequence. It represents what I have probably spent in Harker's tavern over the past five years. In fact ever since my own ship had foundered on the rocks below the cliffs at Column Bay.

My ship, The Osprey, had been lured in the darkest hours of the night by wreckers, who had taken advantage of a heavy fog that had draped itself over the English Channel.

They had used lanterns to tempt my ship closer to the shore than she would have normally been. It was a foul deed, perpetrated by foul people, who had no thought for the good men who might perish on the jagged grinding rocks. The Osprey was wrecked on those rocks, and looted.

I Jeremiah Whitby, captain of the Osprey was the only survivor of that foul deed, and I have been drinking myself into an early grave ever since, with only the occasional respite from the alcohol, being provided by the Marston sisters.

Daisy and Rosie Marston are the comely daughters of Noah Marston, the village baker, and who would for a shilling; keep my bed warm at night. But even that rare and delicious treat was losing its appeal, as the ever increasing amounts of Harker's rum are dulling my ardour.

The Captain's reward has given me another chance at salvation. With the money I can buy myself a small craft which I will use for fishing, and hopefully become a sailor once again. It is the remnants of a dream that has been lost to me these last five years.

But now as I strain through the snow, and my goal is in sight, ill fortune has befallen me. A wheel on the port side of the wagon has become trapped in the deep snow, and I fear that as close as I am to completing the task, it is now doomed to failure. I have checked the watch in my fob, in one hour the dawn will break, and all of my efforts will have been to no avail.

Still, I manage a weak smile; at least I am one hundred guineas to the good. I have a leather thong tied around my neck, and attached to it is the captains pouch containing the guineas. That pouch rests snugly against my chest. Not enough money to buy the small boat that I yearned for, but plenty enough to keep me in Harker's tavern's good ale and rum for a few years yet. Then with any good fortune I will die before the guineas are gone. The feel of the leather pouch comforts me in the biting cold, but the wicked ice laden wind that screams across Dartmoor is weakening my resolve.

I slump exhausted onto the frost hardened snow; my efforts to dislodge the wheel have come to nought. Lifting my head I can see the red streaks of dawn breaking in the eastern sky. I turn in frustration to look at the house, and I can see that the flickering candle lights are being snuffed out, probably by an overzealous housekeeper. Those same snuffed out candles signal my failure.

The baying of dogs can be heard coming from the direction of that bleak looking house. My good horse rears up at these sounds, and breaks free of the shafts. With eyes wide in terror, the horse panics and bolts back along the tracks in the snow that we laid over an hour ago. I am alone.

Despite the brutal frost that is numbing my fingers, a river of perspiration trickles down my spine. Fear clutches at the pit of my stomach. I fear that I will not be alone for much longer.

Then a beast such as I have never encountered before in my miserable life, rears up in front of my startled eyes.

My brain begins to swim in a fog which might have drifted in from across a chilled sea. Just before I slip into the fogs stifling embrace, a scent of lavender creeps into my clouded brain. Then strong arms enfold me. I am being carried across the snowy waste, and I can hear booted feet crunching against frosty snow. Then a cold blackness claims me.

2

'Mister Whitby, can you hear me sir, are you alright?' A woman's voice finds its way into my drowsy mind, and I can hear the crackling of burning sticks. My eyes blink open. Flickering shadows dapple the cold grey walls. The room feels icily cold despite the fire that blazes in the hearth.

She is leaning over me, hair pulled back severely from her face, and fashioned into a style that resembles a baker's bun at the back of her head. She is grinning through worn down teeth. Her breath is rancid, and I jerk my face away from the foul miasma. A scrabbling snuffling noise is coming from behind the huge closed oaken door at the far end of the room.

I stare at the door, and I tremble a little, fearing whatever it is that scratches at that door, has come to end my miserable life.

'Have no fear sir.' She changes the smile to a full laugh. 'It's just Belial, the master's dog, wanting to greet you mister Whitby sir.'

She walks to the door, but really it's more of a shuffle, and the woman slowly lifts the latch on that sturdy door. My heart seems to falter. The dog, if that's what it is, pushes past her, and pads slowly across toward the large fireside chair that holds my shaking body.

It regards me with sad bloodshot eyes. Then a low rumbling growl emits from its huge slobbering jaws. It is the beast that I had encountered out in that cruel icy night. An animal of huge dimensions rolls back its top lip and snarls at me through a jaw full of terrifying, jagged teeth.

I am reminded of a blood curdling incident concerning a feeding Timber Wolf that I had stumbled on in the frozen wastes of North America. The animal had obviously perceived me as a threat to its bloody meal, turned to attack me, and only the quick reactions of Thomas Scully, the first mate of the Osprey, who shot and killed the savage beast, saved me from what would have been a fatal mauling.

That same fear freezes my heart now; once again I slip into a sleep full of nightmarish visions.

3

Weak rays of winter sunshine filter through spider webbed window panes, my eyes blink open, and I use a cold hand to blot out the harsh sunlight. The fire, which was well backed up with logs that are now blazing in the huge grate, has caused the stone walled room to shimmer in a searing heat. A heat I welcome, for my bones are still brittle with the freezing cold from last night's exertions in the frost and snow.

'Would you care for some hot broth Mister Whitby sir?' She stands over me, a plump woman of some fifty years. Her smile is warm and kindly. She reminds me vaguely of the old woman who roused me from my earlier slumber. But here the resemblance ended. For this lady has a beatific smile. Her teeth are clean and even, and a faint aroma of lavender surrounds her. It is not hard to compare this woman with my long deceased and sainted mother.

'My name is Eleanor McKnight, and the master of the house has urged me to tend to your needs sir.' She places a serving tray onto the table that stands next to my seat. The wooden tray has a bowl of steaming broth in its centre, accompanied by a wedge of freshly baked bread. There is a large silver spoon alongside the broth. My mouth waters at the sight and smell of this little feast, and I reach for the spoon. That movement triggers a growl from behind the chair, and my hand freezes above the spoon. The nightmarish vision from earlier slips into my mind, and I wait trembling, for the snap of the dog's jaws.

'Stop that Belial.' Mrs McKnight's voice admonishes the beast, and the growls that are emitting from the darkened corner of the room cease.

My heart is pounding in a tight chest. I sit in silent terror, listening as the beast begins a slow but purposeful padding from behind my chair. The dog sits down; its big brown eyes stare at me. A meaty red tongue lolls from a gaping mouth. I smile in relief. The wolf like beast from earlier has gone, before me sits a large but not threatening Red Setter. The dog's tail wags furiously, and it places huge paws onto my lap. The animal's red tongue laps across my face. My relief is plain, and the housekeeper smiles reassuringly at me.

My brain accepts the strangeness of the animal's change, and I venture a question to the housekeeper. 'Belial, Mrs McKnight, what a strange name for this beautiful creature?'

'It is Mister Whitby, the master has a wicked sense of humour, but old Belial there wouldn't hurt anyone.' Again she smiled at me. 'Just push him away sir, and enjoy your broth.'

I put my hand on the dog's chest and shoo him away. He stares at me with those big brown eyes. I tremble slightly as those same eyes reflect the beast. The dog's top lip curls back to reveal huge canine teeth. A growl rumbles from deep within the dog's chest and a little squawk of fear leaps from my slack mouth.

Mrs McKnight grins at me and then she growls at the dog, Belial whimpers and tucks a bushy tail between shaking hind legs, then the animal slinks away, and curls up by the roaring fire.

'Thank you Mrs McKnight.' I try to put a little bravado into my words, but I'm not sure that I succeed.

As I raise a spoonful of soup to my mouth; I am aware that Belial is staring balefully at me. My ravenous hunger deserts me, and the spoon clatters noisily to the stone floor.

'Lost your appetite Mister Whitby?' Mrs McKnight retrieves my fallen piece of cutlery. 'Never mind sir maybe you will eat it later, or would you prefer some cooked meat mister Whitby'

'Your master, Mrs McKnight?' my words are paper dry. 'When will I meet him? For I need to be on my way soon. I have business back at Column Bay, and,' again my voice fail's me, just scratchy words squeak out of my mouth. 'Your master owes me one hundred guineas madam.'

'Ah! Mister Whitby, the master won't be back until late this evening sir, but be assured that you will be paid in full for your efforts during last night's grim weather.' Her stare is unflinching and cold. 'It will be near dark when he gets here sir, but as you can see,' Mrs McKnight jabbed a pointing finger in the direction of the bookcase that filled up a wall in the darkened corner of the room, 'there are plenty of books to keep you occupied during your wait.'

'But madam I have urgent business back at Column bay.' My words are lies, but I need to be gone from this place. Images of the wolf like creature filled my mind, and even Mrs McKnight was beginning to worry me a little. The features of her face seem to be misty, as if there is another person hiding behind that comely smile.

'As you wish Mister Whitby, but if you leave before the master gets here then I fear you will lose the rest of your remuneration. How much was it sir, a hundred guineas? That's a princely sum to give up Mister Whitby, are you a rich man? I think not sir.'

She grinned through small white teeth. 'I'll just fetch your coat and scarf. Also good sir can I remind you that it snowed heavily again last night, so beware, you don't want to slip and break a leg, you could die out there and no-one would find you until the spring.' She smiled sadly. 'Or you could spend the day here, take warm sanctuary from the weather, and if the snow relents, you can be on your way tomorrow morning.'

Belial sent another rumbling growl in my direction, and my intention to leave this place takes a jolt. I think about the hundred guineas, Mrs McKnight is right, the money owed, along with the hundred that I'd already secreted in a pouch around my neck, represents a small fortune to me. Subconsciously my hand goes to my throat and I breath a small sigh of relief, the pouch feels warm to my touch.

She is also correct about the weather. I wander over to the solitary window and take in the desolate landscape. A fresh carpet of snow had indeed fallen, and reached to a height just below the window sill, and I remember the desperate toil from last night. A fleeting memory of my horse bolting in the darkness causes a small sob to issue from my throat. That sad thought forces a change of mind. I whisper a little prayer for the animal's safety.

'Yes I agree with you Mrs McKnight, I am not a wealthy man, and can ill afford to forgo a sum that I have worked hard for. And the weather has most definitely taken a turn for the worse.' I clear my throat nervously. 'So I will take up your kind offer of sanctuary, and be on my way on the morrow's sun rise.'

'Very wise sir, now you just make yourself comfortable by the fireside.' She points to the pile of logs next to the open grate. 'There's plenty of fuel Mister Whitby. Now why don't you take one of the master's books to pass the time away?'

She brushes past me. The scent of Lavender is now so strong that it makes me baulk, it seems to roll in waves from her body. She disappears through the oak doorway, and I sidle over to the large bookcase.

After spending twenty minutes browsing through a myriad of leather bound ancient volumes, I make my choice, and retire back to the comfort of the armchair. I jab the logs with an iron poker, sparks scatter up the wide chimney, and I feed the hungry flames with two more logs.

The broth, which is still hot, is spooned into my grateful mouth by a surprisingly steady hand. It tastes wonderfully sweet, as does the wedge of bread, which is far superior to the offerings of Column Bay's baker, a mister Noah Marston, who coincidently was the father of the comely lasses Rosie and Daisy Marston. My lips smack in appreciation as the last spoonful of broth slides down my throat.

A decanter of red wine seems to have appeared on the mantelpiece above the fire, and a piece of fried meat that covers a large plate, lies tantalisingly on the large oak table. At first this shocks me, but I smile my thanks, Mrs McKnight must have put the wine and food there whilst I was perusing her master's library.

Using the dagger like knife that is on the side of the plate, I cut into the meat. The blade glides effortlessly through the beef. My mouth waters at the sight and smell of the freshly cooked meat. I have not been able to afford such fare since my days as the captain of the unfortunate Osprey. The meat, barely cooked, and pink with the animal's blood, melts in my mouth. I cannot remember such a feast, even those exotic meals served to me on my travels as a seaman pale in comparison.

I help myself to a schooner of wine, it is delicious. Smiling I raise the glass in a silent toast to Mrs McKnight's absent master. I am also grateful to her for the many candles that are dotted around the room.

The flickering light that they give off remind me of a long ago childhood Christmas, when my father had returned from a long sea voyage. My family had rejoiced in that happy time. Within minutes, that memory had flown, and two more glasses, full of the enticing wine have sluiced down my greedy throat.

Belial the Red Setter curls up at my feet, and we bathe in the fires benevolence. I am happy now, though slightly lightheaded. The wine is dulling my brain ever so lightly.

I choose book. It is a leather bound first edition. The author intrigues me, Mary Shelley. I smile conceitedly; it is probably a tale of lost love and betrayal, typical of the female authors of her time. I wonder what this book is going to offer. The title leaves my inquisitive brain a little puzzled. "Frankenstein" It was a book published in the year 1818.

I begin my quest, and turn the page. Then I enter another world, and two hours later, as the midwinter sun blinks through muggy windows, I slide into a terrifying sleep filled with a monstrous being that is born of a madman.

Somewhere even deeper in the dark unconsciousness of my mind, another unholy monster is waiting for me. Bloodshot eyes stare back at me from the abyss, and sharp teeth glint, a teardrop of crimson blood drips from an exposed fang. Belial roams the dark crevices of my mind.

4

My eyes flicker open, and parts of me tremble uncontrollably in the room's iciness. There is only the guttering light from a solitary candle on the mantelpiece to cast dancing shadows around the stone walls. A few faint embers glow amongst the dying ashes in the huge grate, and a sound like laboured breathing emanates from the darkest corner of the room.

'Mrs McKnight, are you there?' My teeth chatter in the cold, and the breath from my mouth drifts away in the cellars freezing cold.

'No Whitby.' The voice's owner grunts with the effort of speech. 'Mrs McKnight is busy; you have me for company now.' Then a low guttural growling that seems to echo from a long distant and Godless past, fills the room. I can hear a painful gasp as whatever it is that speaks to me, is rising from their seat, and I am filled with stomach churning fear. Is this to be my fate, confined in a darkened room with only God knows who as a companion? Surely I am still sleeping, and what is happening is probably just the outcome of the decanter of wine?

'Who are you?' I am shivering, not with just the room's chill, but from an increasing terror that has gripped the depths of my stomach. The candlelight shows him, or it. I try to shrink myself into the depths of the armchair.

'My name, Whitby, is Orlok, Count Orlok, but Mrs McKnight calls me the Master.' His laugh is more of a dry sarcastic cackle, something that a witch might utter whilst conjuring up a spell. 'You may choose either, but I do have another title.' His voice drops to a conspiratal whisper. 'I am also called Nosferatu.' His eyes close and the man appears to be in a trance. Then he speaks again, softly, cajoling. 'The food Jeremiah, did you enjoy it?'

'Yes s... sir I mean Count.' My own voice is full of trepidation. Then for a reason that is not apparent to me, my fear begins to drift away. Maybe this poor soul has some terrible affliction, and is looking for the company of another lonely man. I continue my conversation with the Count. 'The broth was excellent. You have an excellent cook in Mrs McKnight good sir, and the beef was better than any meat that I have tasted in my miserable life.'

Again that hideous laugh rumbles through the near blackness of the room. 'We have no cattle Jeremiah, the flesh you ate came from a horse. Mrs McKnight found a stray animal in our barn. She butchered it earlier today. A woman of many talents is Mrs McKnight, don't you think so Jeremiah?'

My stomach rebels against the food that I have eaten and I baulk at his casual words. 'Please God good sir; tell me she has never killed my horse?' Tears flow freely down my face.

'It is just meat Whitby. We all need such food if we are to survive in this world.' Again he laughs at my obvious discomfort. 'I am from the Carpathian mountains in Transylvania Mister Whitby, a place where food and especially meat of any kind is scarce. People from that land would fight for such a meal that you have dined on this day. So please do not fret over the animal that provided you with sustenance.'

The single candle's bare light casts a shadow over me, and with more than a little trepidation I raise my eyes up.

He looks down at me, and smiles. He is beautiful. I try to tear my eyes from him, but his voice, now like warm honey, draws me closer. An arm reaches from beneath the black cloak that covers his body from shoulders to below his knees. He cups my face, and I feel his power and something else, a dark pulsating evil emanates from this creature, for surely it is not a man, but I am snared by his eyes, they draw me like a moth to a flame.

'Mrs McKnight informs me that you wish to leave once I have paid you for your labour, is that true Whitby?'

Before I can answer he smiles at me. A smile that turns into a lip curling snarl, and my body trembles. 'Do not be afeared Jeremiah.' And once again his voice changes from a lingering threat to a pleasurable tone. 'Once I have thanked you properly for delivering my cargo, I will give you the promised amount, and you can find your way back to Harker's Tavern.' His voice is now heavy with sarcasm. 'And you can drink yourself into oblivion sir. Or,' he pauses, and I am transfixed, waiting on his next words. 'You can stay until morning, and over another decanter of my good wine we can plot both our futures Mr Whitby.' He looks balefully at me. 'Will you stay with me tonight Jeremiah? And if you agree to the offer I make, then you will learn everything about Nosferatu, but more importantly you will know the secret of life itself sir.'

I am intrigued by Orlok's words, and I nod my agreement. Tonight I would drink Orlok's wine, and tomorrow with the promised guineas filling up the leather pouch beneath my shirt, I would make my way back to Column Bay, and with my future already planned, a small fishing ketch, and a bench in the corner of Harker's Tavern, the misery I have endured during the last few years, was coming to an end.

Perhaps Count Orlok might even be persuaded to part with a flagon of his excellent wine for my journey home. Again I turned my face to him, his lips showed a thin smile, but the coal black orbs that were his eyes, glinted sharply at me, and a disconcerting thought enters my mind. This man can read my thoughts.

Nevertheless it would appear that my run of ill luck is coming to an end. I was to be proved right in this opinion, but not in the way that I thought.

I stare dreamily the fire's dancing flames, and my mind is being bent to his will. Then my eyes are drawn back to the shadowy figure of Orlok. He is a wraith, drifting around the room like a sea fog.

'Mrs McKnight.' Orlok's voice is urgent. 'Bring my guest another flagon of wine.' I hear the door that led from the kitchen creak open.

Mrs McKnight's voice seems to crawl through the icy blast of air that preceded her. 'Yes master, will that be all?' She stares at me through eyes that contain an animal's hunger, and my earlier fear tumbles its dreadful way back into the pit of my stomach.

Orlok, sensing my discomfort, puts a soothing hand on my shoulder, and the fearfulness slips away like a retreating tide.

Mrs McKnight disappears through the door, and what seems like just seconds later, she reappears in the doorway. A flagon of the wine hangs limply from her right hand. She walks over to where I sit and fills my glass to the brim. The wine has a slimy appearance; it looks like blood. I ignore the roiling in my stomach, and swallow a mouthful of the liquid. It is sweet and heady; I drain the glass, and hold it out to the woman again. She grins through those same stubby teeth. 'Ah, Mr Whitby the master said you would like the special wine.'

The wine glugs into my glass, and I watch mesmerised by the liquids slowness as the glass is once again filled to the brim.

This time I sip at the liquid, determined to enjoy its magic. Mrs McKnight nods her pleasure at Orlok, who speaks softly to her. 'That will be all Mrs McKnight, Mr Whitby and I have much to discuss before morning.' He smiles at me and I am smitten with his obvious charm. We discuss nothing, he speaks, and I listen.

I sit listening for what seems like hours. His voice laboured many times, and it is as if I am hearing a man's last words, but his meaning is abundantly clear.

'I have been here on this world since man crawled out of the ancient swamps at the dawn of time.' He hears my snicker of disbelief. 'No Whitby, please do not doubt my words.' There is just a trace of anger in Orlok's tone.

The flickering light from the candle shows his darkening face. He is old and decrepit. Then, just occasionally, I glimpse a man with the fire of youth in his eyes. It was probably the wine causing the brightness in his eyes; at least that is my hope. I thought to interrupt him about his ridiculous age, but his intense glare, warns me to hold my tongue.

'I am coming to the end of my time Jeremiah; you were selected by the ship's captain, to deliver the package, and to be my successor. You are a man with no future Jeremiah, with no one to depend on you. In short sir, you are the perfect Disciple to follow me, to live into the millennia. Will you accept the challenge?'

I stare in disbelief. This man is speaking madness, and I am tempted to ask for my money, and be gone from this insanity.

He feels my incredulity and stands up. His eyes regard me with disdain. There is a rustling of his cloak. Then Orlok moves toward the door, not in strides, he appears to glide across the stone floor. I shake my head, convinced the wine has stolen my reason.

'Come with me Whitby, I will banish your doubts.' His words are magnetic.

The door opens without him seemingly touching it. I try to remain in my chair, but this man's power over me is immense, and I follow him, through dark brooding passages.

Once I thought Mrs McKnight was stood there, a beckoning smile upon her face. I blink, and she is gone like a sea breeze. In stark contrast, Belial has now appeared, to lead us along dark passageways where candles mysteriously flicker into flame as we approach them.

Orlok is standing by an open trapdoor; he smiles thinly at me. The Count descends into a stygian blackness, I follow him, willingly.

I gaze around the cellar. It is not a room that I would normally associate with a cellar, the walls are covered in purple drapery, and the floor is wooden. Flickering candles brighten up the darkest of corners, and the opulence of the Counts residence is not lost on me. Maybe there are more than just a hundred guineas to be had here, I smile behind splayed fingers.

My gaze is drawn to two large caskets in the middle of the cellar floor. One of them is a rotting ruin, the other a polished wooden box that could be a coffin. I shudder and turn to the Count who is pointing to a large chair. 'Sit down Jeremiah.'

I obey him whilst stifling a smile; surely this is the house of a fool. Relieving him of more guineas would be a pleasure.

'No Whitby, I am not a fool, I am your saviour. Now listen to me or I will end it all now, and Belial will take great pleasure in tearing the flesh from your bones.'

Now I am convinced, he can read my thoughts, and perspiration bathes my face. I nod my acquiescence, and fear rises in my throat like an incoming tide.

The dog is huge now, and it is beginning to change shape, just like the wax that ripples down the sides of a burning candle. There is a threatening snarl, and I am faced with something that resembles a fiend from hell. Belial bares yellow fangs at me.

'I came into being many millions of years ago, in the shadow of the eastern European mountains, Whitby.' His voice is becoming weaker, but he commands my full attention. 'I was little more than a beast, and I eked a meagre living, eating the seeds and vermin which covered the fields. Then Belial came to me whilst I slept, and he offered me what I am offering you, to live forever. Will you take the journey Jeremiah?'

The thought of forever filled me with sorrow and joy in equal measures. To spend the rest of my life sitting on a hard cold bench in Harker's tavern drinking ale until my maker calls me, was losing its appeal. My head nods agreement to the Counts offer, and my mind is filled with swirling images of bloody scenes from a future battle. Orlok smiles through sharp teeth.

Belial is standing on his hind legs now, and the dog's face is beginning to take on a human shape. But he is not like any human that I have ever seen. His snout has flattened, and the once brown eyes are now a muddy yellow. The teeth, of which there are many, are all pointed, like a daggers blade. There is no fur on his body now, just a taut brownish skin covering a bony frame. Then a gasp of dread leaves my mouth. Satan's horns are protruding from a head that now resembles a serpent. I tremble in fear, and remember an old preacher from my time as a child in Column Bay.

The horror before me fitted the old preacher's description of Satan. It was an incarnation of the Devil who feasted on the souls of sinners.

I try to rise, but Orlok's bony fingers hold my arm in a vice like grip. 'You have made a pact with me Whitby. Now you must honour the agreement, else Belial will feast on your flesh.'

The snake like creature sways mesmerizingly above me, and Orlok's iron grip forces my head to one side, exposing my throat. Orlok whispers to me. 'Be still Whitby, your puny life is about to change.'

A dry rasping laugh is expelled from his mouth, and his next words tear at my soul. 'You have been chosen Whitby, In the next century, which is just three short years away, your world will be plunged into constant warfare; you will travel unnoticed through the carnage. Blood will flow in rivers, and you will feast on human frailty.'

My struggle is useless, and a spine tingling hiss blots out all other sound. Huge yellow fangs pierce my throat, and pain that could only come from the bowels of hell itself, explodes into my brain.

My back arches and then twists itself into a tortured shape, until I feel that it will break; such is the scalding pain that shreds my mind.

Then the nightmare shrieks throughout my body. My brain is invaded by the beating of a million tiny wings. I keep my eyes tightly shut fearing what I might see, but it is to no avail. Black wasps, biting flies, and leeches crawl across my skin. I watch transfixed as streams of alien blood are being squeezed through my veins.

I can see clearly into the veins under my skin. My own life's blood is being drained away; it is replaced with a thick oily black liquid.

The pain is reaching a crescendo, sweat drenches my face and I feel that I have been mistaken in putting my trust in Orlok, but that thought, like my blood, is being washed away, and now my body is set on a strange journey.

Bars of spangled lights surge across my skin, and the agony ceases, to be replaced with blinding ecstasy.

I can feel what must be a smile on my face. I have chosen well, that is my final rational thought, before my spirit is torn from the body that was once Jeremiah Whitby. Then that soul begins its terrifying journey, through black canyons and into a morass that leads surely to the gates of mans eternal nightmare, Hell.

5

The cellar is bathed in a cloying blackness, which is chokingly claustrophobic, but for just a few final moments, the creature sees with perfect clarity.

Orlok, Mrs McKnight's terrible master has slipped onto the wooden floor. His flesh is dripping from sallow cheeks, and the gleam from those dark flashing eyes is dimming.

At the entrance to the cellar, Mrs McKnight is weeping for the master who is leaving her. Belial is sitting close to the failing Orlok. The dog thing's brown eyes stare at the gruesome demise of Nosferatu, the entity into which it had breathed life, many thousands of years earlier.

Mrs McKnight tenderly lifts the dying body of Count Orlok from the cellar floor and carries it over to the ancient coffin. She places him amongst its rotting timbers, and then pours oil from a lantern over the body of her beloved master. With a mournful cry she drops a lighted candle into his casket.

A terrible shrieking sound reverberates around the walls of the cellar, and a plume of oily black smoke rises from the flames. That smoke becomes a wispy image of Nosferatu, who was once Count Orlok. Tortured screams emanate from the entity's mouth.

Slimy black fumes hug the cellar's grey walls, and then disappear through the open door. Mrs

McKnight's wail of sorrow drowns out Orlok's terrible scream.

The flames from Orlok's funeral pyre die away, and Mrs McKnight opens the lid of the newer coffin, which the unsuspecting Whitby had brought to the house on the wagon pulled by his unfortunate horse.

Then the Housekeeper carries the seemingly lifeless body, which was once Jeremiah Whitby. She places him tenderly into the caskets purple silk lined interior.

She kisses the seemingly dead lips of the creature and makes it a sobbing promise. 'Soon my new master, soon you will awaken, and all human kind will be at your mercy. You have crossed the dark river, and in a few short months you will be unleashed on this unsuspecting world. I will be here when you awaken, to serve you all my days.'

She covers the waxen face with a cloth of silk. Then she slides the wooden lid onto the coffin. The distraught woman hammers in four wooden pegs, one in each corner of the coffin, securing it tightly. Then she promised her new master that she will return in the spring, and free him from his incarceration.

The door of Orlok's cellar slams behind her, and Mrs McKnight produces a large iron key from beneath her apron, and puts it in the keyway. The key is turned three times, and she grins as the doors internal levers click into place. She swiftly ascends the staircase, and begins her vigil.

Eleanor McKnight has served one master for many years; she looks forward to Orlok's successor. Her love for Dracula will be pure and unconditional.

The world is getting ready to greet a new century. It will belong to her Master.

6

It is early May of the year 1897, a little more than five months since the demise of Nosferatu.

Abraham Stoker has completed his novel. He lays a worn quill to one side, and bangs his foot down on the attic floor. A noise, he hopes will summon his housekeeper up the three flights of stairs to the attic.

He can hear her footfalls on the wooden steps as she puffs her way up the stairs.

She opens the attic door, and stops to draw in a welcome gasping lung full of air. 'What can I do for you Mister Stoker sir?' She scowls at his back.

'Ah! Mrs Mannion, I have finished the book.' He beams a smile in her direction. 'Will you go around to Michael Egan's bar and get a quart pot of Porter. I think it is time for a celebration drink, don't you Brigit?'

'Congratulations Mister Stoker, would you like something to eat with your Porter sir? Maybe a piece of my beef pie sir?'

'That would be most welcome Brigit, your beef pies are legendary, and a fitting tribute to the finished book.' He grinned at the breathless woman. 'And Mrs Mannion, ask Mister Egan for a bottle of his very best whisky. We must celebrate this book with Ireland's finest spirit.'

Again he smiled at the woman. 'And would you also tell him Mrs Mannion, that I will be settling my substantial bill on receipt of a cheque from my publishers.'

Brigit Mannion smiled behind a grimy hand and thought she deserved a very large whisky from this man who had had her running up and down these flights of stairs for the last three months, bringing him food and Porter, and listening to his howls of disappointment whenever something went awry with the storyline.

She had only managed one downward step of the stairs when she turned and asked the self-satisfied author what the book was about.

'It is the story of a vampire Brigit, a creature of the night that drinks the blood from poor unsuspecting people. I have created the perfect nightmare Brigit. People just love to be frightened before they take to their warm beds, and my creation will do just that' Then he added with a sly grin, 'I think all of the problems surrounding my finances are about to be solved Mrs Mannion.'

Brigit Mannion shivered and fled as fast as she could down the stairs. 'Jesus Mary and Joseph. May the good Lord have mercy on Mister Stoker's soul?' How, she thought, could a God fearing man like Mister Stoker, write a story about such an ungodly creature that fed on the blood of poor Christians?

Then a smile creased her face. Maybe Mister Stoker would give her a small bonus if his book was successful. But for now at least there would be a couple of whiskeys in it for her. She increased her pace to Egan's bar.

Two hours later, after Stoker had drained the contents of the quart pot which had contained Egan's finest Porter. Brigit Mannion had consumed more than her fair share of Michael Egan's Irish whisky. Stoker spoke, 'Mrs Mannion.' He slurred. 'Would you take a little walk to Egan's, and ask him for another quart of Porter.' His grin was lopsided. Abraham Stoker had decided that his book was worthy of another jug of Porter.

Brigit Mannion left the smiling author to his self-congratulations, and sped down the stairs in the sure belief that there was much more drinking to be done before this night was over. She was to be proved right in this assumption.

'What did you say the book was called Mister Stoker sir?' Brigit Mannion burped, and held out her glass, her lopsided smile begged a refill.

Stoker splashed the ale into her empty glass. 'Ah Brigit,' he smiled slyly at the woman. 'My book is called Dracula. Do you like it Mrs. Mannion? I think it will sell many thousands of copies,' Stoker leaned back in the battered old chair, and smiled a drunken smile, his finances were about to take an upturn. He slumped across the little table. The Author burped loudly, and fell into a fitful sleep. A slumber, which was interrupted by loud snoring.

Brigit's hand trembled slightly as she fumbled with the manuscript. The housekeeper spent a terrified hour reading the story of Dracula.

After placing the manuscript next to the sleeping Stoker, she made the sign of the cross, and whispered a prayer to the blessed Virgin. 'Mary, Mother of God, please keep Mister Stoker's soul safe while he sleeps.'

She drained the last of the ale from the jug, and turned her head in the direction of the still snoring Stoker. Dark incantations emanated from the sleeper's mouth, and Mrs Mannion made another sign of the cross.

Brigit's own crowded mind was of a dark sky filled with the beatings of a thousand wings. The whisky was having a strange effect she thought. The housekeeper was terrified. Her heart thrummed behind pendulous breasts.

She didn't remember descending the stairs, but as she left the house, a distinct smell of decay invaded her nostrils. Brigit swore under her breath, and vowed that she would never return to that place. However much money Stoker received for that blasphemy, he was welcome to it. She wouldn't climb these stairs again, not for all the whisky in Ireland.

Abraham Stoker's housekeeper fled along O'Connell streets rain sodden pavements, not daring to glance over her shoulder. The beating of wings accompanied her all the way to her own cold house. But Brigit Mannion's house felt snug and safe in comparison to Abraham Stoker's chilling house of horrors. Once inside of her home, Brigit prayed earnestly to her God, 'Please keep this poor sinner safe through the night.'

7

As the distraught Brigit Mannion was fleeing along Dublin's streets, Eleanor McKnight was making her way through oily dark passages in the stone house. She had no need of the many unlit candles which were dotted along the passageway, or of the old ships lantern which she carried. The housekeeper knew every footstep of the one hundred and seventeen strides which took her from the huge living room, into the blackness of the cellar, and eventually, to her new master's crypt.

She lit the wick of the lantern. In its eerie flickering flame; an onlooker might see that Mrs McKnight's lips were set in a thin smile. But there would be no witness' to this smile, except the creature who had been entombed in the solitary wooden coffin for the past six months.

She placed the lantern on the cellar floor, next to the coffin, and produced a flat iron bar from beneath her skirts. She inserted the bar between the coffin lid and the sides of the casket. Then with a grunting effort, she prised the lid away from the wooden walls of the coffin, and then she let the lid slide noisily to the cellar's wooden floor.

A sound, much like a sigh of relief drifted up from the newly open casket, and then Eleanor McKnight held the lantern up as she tentatively looked into the coffin's opening.

The creature's eyes already open, stared directly into the housekeepers adoring gaze.

Dracula's irises were blood red, with pinpricks of jet black pupils.

Her trembling voice was filled with love for the gift that Belial had bestowed upon her. 'You are entering a new age my sweet bird of death, and I will be here to serve you always my master.'

The creature moved and the woman drew back startled. Her hand rested on the coffin lid. She felt the flesh of her fingers burning and in the dim light cast by the lantern; she could see letters being scorched into the coffin lid. An unseen hand was scrawling a name in fire. Mrs McKnight smiled her appreciation. The searing pain ebbed away, and she craned her neck again into the open casket.

8

Count Dracula.

The housekeeper gazed lovingly into those blazing red orbs. Tears of pure happiness formed in her misty eyes. The tears slipped easily down her cheeks.
Dracula raised his head from the purple silk pillow where he had rested for the past six months.
Blue tinged lips parted revealing four shiny pearl fangs, which were set in a jaw full of jagged teeth.
Her smile turned into a shriek of terror as bony fingers grasped Eleanor by her tied back hair. Dracula sank his teeth into her exposed throat, and in a blur of sprayed blood, he rip's the woman's throat away from her flabby white neck.
Eleanor's eyes widen in blank shock, as precious life began to ebb from her body. She was cast aside by Count Dracula. Her beautiful bird of death had

claimed its first victim of that spring evening, and the woman gasped a dying sob from deep within a heaving breast.

There was a ferocious beating of leathery wings in the cellar's black humidity, and the body that once housed Jeremiah Whitby's spirit, is now carried aloft on the wings of death. Then the creature was gone, gliding into that warm spring night on a sultry breeze.

Count Dracula flew low over moonlit fields, causing farm animals to bolt in terror, as they glimpse those terrible red eyes which scanned the earth below. Then the bird of death soared high into the night sky.

On wings of death, an ancient evil swept toward the Cornish coast, and the village of Column Bay.

Back in the grim darkness of the cellar, Belial leapt onto Eleanor McKnight's body, and huge wolf like teeth tore the flesh from her bones. A lifetime of agony seared through her dying mind, and she wonders how a gentle woman such as she, is destined for the bowels of hell.

Belial has transformed into what he always was, a demon from another world. He drags the housekeeper's remains across the cellar floor, which splits open to reveal a black marbled stair case.

Those ebony black steps lead to even blacker canyons, and eventually to a gaping pit that boils with a tarlike substance.

Eleanor McKnight's screams echo against the walls of Satan's pit. Belial has torn the eyes from her head, but she can still see an uncountable multitude of sinners waiting in a blood spattered queue.

Amongst those sinners waiting for their final judgement, is the soul of Jeremiah Whitby; he welcomed the woman who had saved him from the iciness of the night, only to condemn him to an eternity in a fiends embrace.

The housekeeper's welcome to hell is Jeremiah Whitby's toothless grin, it gaped at her from a black mouth.

It is the beginning of an everlasting agony, and not the future that Nosferatu had promised her.

9

Daisy Marston scurries across the muddy road that leads from Zachary Harker's tavern. She slips silently through the back door of her father's bakery. Daisy's voice is an urgent whisper. 'Rosie, Rosie where are you?'

Rosie Marston adjusts her threadbare dress and steps from a shadowy corner of the bakery. 'What is it you want Daisy?' Her smile is broad, showing small white teeth. She holds up a shiny sixpence for her sister to see.

Will Harker, Zachary Harker's fifteen year old son moves slowly from the same darkened corner which Daisy had just vacated. Harker is struggling to pull up his breeches. The smile on his grubby face is sly, and he exits quickly through the hayloft's open door. Rosie's mouth is set in a pout, and she takes slow pleasure in explaining to her sister how she had earned the sixpence.

'See Daisy, look how much that Will Harker has paid me for his education.' Her laughter fills the loft. Rosie holds out a dirty palm that has the silver coin at its centre, hoping to make her sister jealous. 'He didn't last more than a minute Daisy, quickest sixpence I've ever earned.'

Daisy puts a silencing finger to her lips. 'Shush Rosie, we don't want father coming to see what all the noise is about. She leads Rosie back into the darkness of the bakeries storeroom. 'Remember that old sea captain Rosie, Jeremiah Whitby I think his name was?'

Rosie's brow furrows in thought, and then she nods sulkily. She had expected Daisy to be really excited about the sixpence that she had cajoled out of Will Harker. 'Yes Daisy, I do, he would give us girls a shilling for spending the whole night with him.' Then she pouted. 'I've just got sixpence from Will Harker, and from drawers off, to drawers back on again it didn't take more than a minute.' She plonked her ample bottom down onto a sack of grain and scratched idly at a scuffed knee.

Daisy grinned at her sister. 'We don't need to worry about young Will Rosie, because that Whitby fellow is in the tavern, and he's got money lass, lots of it.'

Rosie Marston gave her younger sister a superior look, and sniffed. 'Well I don't fancy spending a night with an old man for just another sixpence each.'

Again she showed her sister the coin that Will had pressed into her palm a few minutes earlier. 'This will get us plenty of ale Daisy love, and a couple of tumblers of good gin. I'm happy with that lass.' She shifted herself down from the sack of grain, and marched purposely to the Bakery door.

'Rosie love.' Daisy's stern voice stops her sister's departure before she reaches the door. 'I mean real money lass.'

Rosie turns and places her hands defiantly on sturdy hips. 'How much money has he got then Daisy?' Rosie's eyes narrow to thin slits.

Daisy lifts her skirt and takes out the coin that she had secreted into a little seam. She holds it up for her sister to see. It draws a gasp of disbelief from Rosie.

'It's a golden guinea Rosie, and it's for me and you lass, if we spend tonight with him. What about it eh

Rosie love, a night in the old wheat loft diddling some old bugger? An' he said there's a lot more where that came from girl.' She laughs. 'He'll probably be asleep after ten minutes with you and me.'

Rosie is still gawping in wonder at the gold coin. She nods her head slowly; a greedy smile spreads across her face. 'For that kind of money Daisy I'd stay with him for the next month.' The sight of the coin causes Rosie to drawl her words.

'He's changed a fair bit since he left Column Bay last Christmas time Rosie. He's a lot thinner and a bit sickly looking, but I think that we can give Jeremiah Whitby a night that he'll remember.'

'I don't care what he looks like Daisy, If Whitby's got money, well then it's our duty to make him happy isn't it?'

The Marston sisters leave the bakery's store room all the while giggling at their good fortune. The sisters climb the wooden steps up to the village wheat loft and wait expectantly for their benefactor to fill empty pockets with gold.

After an hour of tortuous waiting Rosie gives her sister a sneering look. 'Ha' so much for rich old men then eh Daisy? I should have known it was all just wishful thinking lass.' She made her way toward the wooden steps. 'C'mon Daisy let's get ourselves over to Harker's Tavern and make a start on that Guinea.'

Daisy nodded her head. Instead of bemoaning the loss of future guineas, she felt the weight of the gold coin in her hand. Then the youngest Marston sister let out a whoop of delight. 'We should be able to drink for a month with this Rosie.' She puts a loving sisterly arm around Rosie's shoulder. 'Dya think old Zach Harker will have change for this Guinea Rosie?'

Rosie laughs scornfully. 'No worries there Daisy love, that old bugger Harker has got a chest full of money, young Will told me that before I let him peel my drawers off.'

A sudden gust of wind and a flurry of what sounded like beating wings halted their joyous conversation. Clouds of dust swirl in the loft.

Rosie stares into the darkness. She shivers involuntarily as two red eyes blink back at her.

Count Dracula steps out of the shadows and smiles at the trembling sisters. A leather pouch dangles from bony fingers.

Rosie lets out a gasp of relief. 'Everything's alright Daisy it's him, Captain Whitby.'

The sisters beam expectant smiles at him and dart over to the man who apparently has more money than they would ever see in their lifetimes. Daisy is already stepping out of her drawers.

10

Will Harker has filched another sixpenny piece from his father's old sea chest. He skips lightly across the muddy road, his thoughts firmly on a night of lust with the Marston sisters.

He climbs the steps up to the wheat loft, his young body already aroused at the thoughts of the sisters. 'I've got another sixpence Rosie.' His eager voice penetrates the loft's gloominess.

Will tumbles onto the straw covered floor. He puts a hand out to break his fall, and grasps onto something wet and sticky. He holds the object up to inspect it. The sight that greets him freezes the blood in his veins. It is Rosie Marston's severed head, and the scream that should have erupted from his throat is strangled in terror.

All thoughts of a carnal nature are driven from his frightened mind. Will tries to drop the thing of horror, but his trembling fist holds Rosie's blood matted hair in a vice like grip.

The young man's body is rigid in shock. His frightened eyes turn to the sacks of wheat that are stacked in the corner of the loft. Rosie's severed head falls from his hand.

In stark contrast to her sister's mutilated body, Daisy Marston lies stark naked on the bags of cereal. Her skin is pure white like alabaster. Will

Harker thinks she is beautiful and stumbles over to her lifeless body.

There are no thoughts of lust in the young man's head, just an admiration for her loveliness. He brushes stray hair from her forehead, and looks for her dress. The young man wants to cover her nakedness, and then gasps in horror.

On the right side of her exposed neck there are two small punctures. From each incision there is a thin crimson trickle of Daisy's blood.

The scream of anguish that comes from the young man's throat finally releases him, and he turns to run from this place of horror.

From the rafters of the loft's roof, the beating of huge wings invades the boy's ears. The bird, if that's what it is falls at the boy's feet, and then in a single beat of Will's heart, a man wrapped in a black cloak materialises in front of his eyes.

In the gloominess of the loft, the young man can see the man's fiery red eyes. His bladder releases.

'Do not be afeared young sir.' Dracula's voice is warm like honey, and the room becomes bright. Dracula is bathed in startling silver light. 'I will not harm you.'

Will slips to the loft floor. Before blackness claims him, he recognises the man's face. It is the old drunk, Jeremiah Whitby. The boy slips into the blessed relief of sleep.

In that disturbed slumber, Will is trapped in a soap bubble, and no matter how hard he fights to escape, the bubble just stretches against his frantic struggles. Will's terrified screaming can only be heard deep inside of his own head.

When he awakes, dawns light is streaming through the cracked and broken boards of the loft.

The man who looked like the drunken Whitby stares at him. 'Will you come with me young sir? I have use for a man with a strong back.' Before Harker can refuse, Dracula points to the remains of the sisters. 'If you refuse my offer William, I will drain your body of every last drop of blood, and you will join your would be lovers in everlasting death.'

The sweet smell of blood makes his head swim in nausea, and he heaves the contents of his trembling stomach onto the loft's dusty floor.

His eyes sweep around the room looking for a way out, but he is careful not to let his eyes rest on the scene of bloody savagery. The man in front of him grins through bloody needle like teeth, and Wills resolve deserts him. He nods his agreement to "Whitby!" For whom else can this creature be?

'A wise choice young sir, now come to me, I would speak with you.'

Will Harker walks dreamlike toward Dracula's hypnotic gaze. The man, who is both Jeremiah Whitby and Dracula, dangles a leather pouch tantalisingly in front of the boy's greedy eyes. 'I need a friend just like you William Harker, someone that I can trust. And if you are that person then your rewards will be great.'

Dracula throws the pouch which contains the guineas, at the boy's feet. 'I can offer you much more than gold young sir. I am offering to you a new world. It will be a world which gives you everything your heart desires. You will have the company of women eager to please you, and my young friend; you will visit all the lands of this world.' Then in a low whisper, 'there are other lands not of this world. I will show you my kingdom William Harker.' Dracula watches in sly amusement at the young man's face, as his words drip into an eager mind.

Will looks around the wheat loft. He stares dispassionately at the bloody head of Rosie Marston, whose warm flesh he had enjoyed for the briefest of moments. Then he turns back to face Count Dracula. He embraces the man who has promised him an escape from the dreary reality of village life that is broken only by the occasional romping with one of the village girls who would help him through his powerful sexual urges, for a sixpenny piece.

Will's mind is inundated with a landslide of promises, all of which Dracula assured him would be kept.

His eyes reluctantly absorb the carnage of the wheat loft. It becomes clear to him that the creature in front of him is more than just a man. The blood red eyes, and the teeth, which terrify him, convince the young man that he should follow this powerful creature, to the end of life if need be.

The boy's thoughts recall the Reverend Aldridge, the vicar who had warned all of the people in his village about evil beasts sent by Satan to tempt them with the sins of the flesh and the pursuit of mammon.

During a powerful lectern thumping sermon, Aldridge had assured his parishioners that an eternity of hellfire and damnation awaited all weak men and women who looked to the Devil for comfort. The only true way was abstinence, poverty and endless hours spent begging God's forgiveness for the multitude of sins that found a way into their everyday lives.

It seems to Will Harker that he had spent most of his young life in poverty, on his knees begging the Lord's forgiveness for sins real and imagined. Now here is a seemingly equally powerful being, promising him everything he desires.

He whispers his promise to Count Dracula. 'Whatever it is that you require from me master, I will give it willingly.' There are tears of gratitude filling his eyes. He knows without a doubt that this creature will fill his young life with all things wonderful.

Will makes his choice, and he thinks that he can live with it. Somewhere deep in his mind, words that his father had spoken to him many years ago when he made some mistake or other, came back to him, "You have made your bed lad, now you must lie on it." He tries, and fails to push those prophetic words away.

Count Dracula folds his cape around the young man, and they are gone, soaring through Dartmoor's early morning mist.

Count Dracula accompanied by a dazed Will Harker, appears on the stone steps that rise up to the heavy oaken front door. The ancient hinges creak in protest as the door is pushed open. Dracula glides through the opening, followed by the dreamlike figure of Will Harker.

A Red Setter greets the unlikely companions. Will Harker reaches down and pats its handsome head. Dracula smiles at the scene.

The boy stares at the dog's friendly brown eyes, and then the animal's eyes become deep black pools. Will Harker is being sucked into a bottomless black canyon.

Once again he is trapped in the soap bubble from which there is no escape. He hears the unrelenting screams of condemned souls, but then he smiles. It is just a dream, and soon he will awaken to a new life.

Jeremiah Whitby's soul has long since gone. Belial had ripped that spirit from a body which was eager to be someone else. Now that "someone else" was Count Dracula, reborn. There would be endless rivers of blood to feast on.

William Harker would be his confidante, and when Harker's time was done, another would take his place. There were always others. But Harker would become more than a confidante; Harker would be his friend, someone that he Dracula could depend on to protect him during the hours of daylight. Someone who would protect him when they came baying for Count Dracula's blood, and they would come for him, he knew that, they always did.

For now the miles had been covered. He was ready to sleep, until the song of the night called to him.

M DAINTY

LEGACY OF CAIN

M Dainty

Jonathan Cain sat on the comfortable, blood red leather settee deep in thought. The chesterfield, at least as old as he himself, was in excellent condition for its age, a mark of its obvious quality and the care that had been bestowed on it over the years. Not for the first time that afternoon he glanced towards the antique clock that resided on the mantle of a rose marble fire surround. A large Malus wood, proverbial plaque, ornately carved with ophidian, leaves and fruit hung on the wall above the clock and bore the legend "blood will tell".

The décor and other furnishings about him were as equally tasteful as they were expensive. The audible ticking of the precision timepiece was interrupted by the voice of an elegant and quite striking looking woman of around the same age as Jonathan but who still held some trace of the bloom of her youth and if anything had become more beautiful as she had aged.

Herodias Clayton-Cain, the wife of Jonathan's brother, had stopped what she had been doing in another part of the large open-plan home in an attempt to get his full attention and as she approached him now she addressed him by her husband's name.

"Abel, you've not listened to a single word I've said, have you? ...Abel!"

Jonathan shook himself from his trance "Sorry 'Dia', what was that?"

"I've been chatting away to you Abe' and you haven't been paying me any attention. You still haven't got those things I asked for earlier from your den. Honestly! I want to prepare everything tonight, ready for the twin's birthday tomorrow; I have no desire to be cooking sausage rolls first thing in the morning. Also, be a darling, would you, and write out Hermione and young Saul's birthday cards, your handwriting is so much neater than my own and don't forget to include their full titles 'including' their middle names. I know you dislike them but it was my only input into naming them and I only use them once a year on their birthdays. It's a tradition. Their cards are in our bedroom, top draw of the dresser, next to your father's safe".

Although, like the chesterfield Jonathan sat upon, many of the larger items of furniture that filled the opulent detached home had at one time belonged to her father-in-law, the large, imposing, key locking Yale safe was the one item that, all be it in name alone, still retained some slight ownership to its past master.

Herodias winced a little as she realized that the mention of her father-in-law would be a reminder of his recent demise but old habits die hard and to not call the safe by its full title with the omission of "your fathers" would have been incongruous. Besides she felt sure her husband had probably just been thinking about him anyway which was why his attention had been firmly elsewhere. It seemed of late she had always to say her husband's name at least twice to get his attention he had become distant and indolent even his sexual nature had changed, and not for the better, becoming selfish, more demanding and far rougher to the point of scaring her a little. All in all, he was just not himself. She knew Abel had been close to his father but his rapid ill health and subsequent death had, she felt, hit Abel hard.

Jonathan Cain took in what was said, "Yes 'Dia' I will do it shortly. I will write out their cards first, including their middle names, and then fetch what you asked for earlier. Just give me a few minutes".

Jonathan smiled, outwardly. "Of course" Jonathan thought to his self, "I don't know the twin's middle names, but I know where I can find that information out. All the documents are in father's safe right next to their birthday cards". He sneered, inwardly and the thought of his father's safe again set him to thinking.

Saul Solomon Cain a stern but loving patriarch was not the sole reason his son Jonathan had returned to his home town of Eden Falls after a long absence of almost fifteen years or rather it was not just the news of his father's recently discovered terminal illness that had lured him back, not just the hope of getting a share of his estranged father's wealth. There was also the matter of a debt he owed to some very unsavoury characters, a drug deal gone wrong, and the repercussions of what may happen to the debtor if said nasty people had caught up with him that had helped him make up his mind to execute a moonlight flit and return to the home of his youth.

Cain still had friends in Eden Falls, well one friend, and via him was kept up to date on all matters relating to his family. He knew when several years previous his parents had moved to a smaller property, a bungalow, to accommodate his ageing mother's lack of mobility. He knew that his father had had given 'Telluric', the family home to his younger brother, (younger by only four minutes, but still Jonathan felt his brother, Abel, to be lesser to himself). He knew too, of his mother's death several months ago. He had not attended her funeral as there was nothing in it for him; it was his father who had all the money.

He had not dared to approach his father directly. He had crossed the old man too many times and as way of a parting shot had cleaned out the very safe that had set him on his present train of thought when he had left Eden Falls on the night of his brother's wedding all those years before. His bother

Abel Cain, he felt, was a far softer touch and despite Jonathan bullying his brother throughout their childhood and spoiling his siblings wedding party by getting paralytic drunk and causing a huge fight on the night he had left, he felt sure he could use Abel to smooth the way with his father and return like a prodigal son, before reaping his unjust rewards.

His parents, Saul and Hermione Cain, after whom his own brothers fraternal twins were named, where already quite old when they themselves had monozygotic twin boys, identical in every detail, save one. While they may have shared an identical strain of DNA their personalities were as different as chalk and cheese. While Abel was placid and loving his elder twin Jonathan was wilful and narcissistic, high of testosterone and low of serotonin.

Abel Cain's twins, young Saul and little Hermione, or Small Saul and Minnie Moinnie as they had affectionately been called as toddlers were fraternal twins, a trait that had, coincidently, ran down from Herodias family line and being the more common twin type, the result of around one in every eighty or so births.

Jonathan and Abel's birth however was the product of a much rarer event, the splitting of a single maternal ovum fertilized by a single sperm and occurring just once in approximately every two hundred and fifty deliveries.

Monozygotic twins are in effect clones of each other and genealogy has shown that even when raised apart these twins often share freakishly similar traits. However external environmental factors can and do play their part. How they are treated in infancy, how and what they learn, their diet, childhood illnesses, even their relative positions in the womb and their birth order may have an effect sometimes to the point that although always of the same sex as each other their appearance itself may be radically different even if they themselves are scientifically identical. While paradoxically non-identical dizygotic siblings can often by sight be extremely difficult or near impossible to tell apart.

Jonathan and Abel Cain, had not only shared DNA but had been identical looking and sounding to each other, their upbringing parallel, with no early favouritism shown to either son. Therefore it could only be a fault in the unseen regions of Jonathans brain that bore any difference between the two. The misfiring of his neurotransmitters maybe, a misbalance of Nor epinephrine or some other unheard of or as yet unknown and unnamed hormonal chemical, perhaps an injury caused by a knock or inflammation to his inmigula while in the womb or in early childhood before his emphatic capacity could fully develop? Even the most skilled neuroscientist, if they were honest, would admit that when it comes to the workings of the human mind and despite great advancement, neuroscience is still in its dark ages.

Whatever the problem with his pre-frontal cortex it meant that Jonathan already in a percentage group due to the rarity of his birth joined yet another exclusive band, the one percent club, the percentage of the population who are thought to be psychopathic.

Now being a psycho in its self is not necessarily a bad thing. Many psychopaths live and walk amongst us without ever feeling the need to dress up in their mother's clothes and repeatedly stab people through a shower curtain, but in Jonathans case and despite having a stable and loving upbringing he had won many of the badges of merit that placed him high in the echelons of this particular fraternity. Jonathan was a bad apple, a snake in the grass.

Jonathan relaxed deeper, into the deep red, of the viscousesque hide that he had made his own over the last few months and replayed the events that had brought him back to Telluric.

It had been a week or so before Christmas and the prospect of an influx of cash due to the selling on of a large quantity of the white stuff was eagerly anticipated to aid in the lubricating of the Christmas period. 'The white stuff' not being a seasonal reference to snow, although it sometimes went by that name as it did by many other names.

Jonathan was, as arranged in a vacant car park, there to meet with other nefarious characters. There was that evening something about the clearness of the night sky that unnerved him, too bright to be doing shady dealings or perhaps it was the frequent shooting stars, the Geminoids, an annual meteor shower that peaks in mid-December that rattled his usually calm nerves. Jonathan Cain was a risk taker, but be it intuition or divine heavenly signs he just felt that something was awry. He was right to feel wrong; the law had been tipped off and they were awaiting the action.

Perhaps due to the extra caution he took but mainly from the confusion that followed, Jonathan, and not for the first time in his life, managed to escape arrest, but he did so without the large bag of drugs he had brought with him and without any payment for them in the way of the filthy lucre he had been expecting. The problem for Jonathan was that he was a middleman and the people who had given the drugs to him did so in lieu of payment and they were not the type of businessmen whom you could reason with, "sorry the police have your shit" or "could I possibly give you an I.O.U." were not phrases that would go down well with the type of people Jonathan mixed with. The word was out, 'Jonno was a marked man'.

Cain laid low for a couple of weeks and managed to keep out of the way. It meant he missed both the

Christmas and New Year's festivities, no eggnog for him, no whores, no lap-dancing clubs, no fun of any kind. If he had even shown his face at any of his regular haunts he would probably have seen in the New Year at best from a hospital bed and at worst on a mortuary slab. Even so and knowing the risk, he was tempted to 'party on' such was his sense of self grandeur.

Keeping out of the way was only a temporary fix, he either had to find a very large amount of money or else 'get out of Dodge'. It was at this point that fate played its part; the news came of his dying father from an old accomplice in crime, Fredrick Frink, his only friend in Eden Falls whom he had known since childhood and who was someone he had always been able to manipulate to his own ends.

Saul Solomon Cain had been diagnosed with a terminal illness, the old codger had apparently ignored his symptoms and had now been given just a few weeks in which to get his affairs in order. He had been told that he would be lucky if he made it to the end of the month.

So on a cold January evening, Jonathan boarded a late train that would take him to Eden Falls. His plan was simple; talk his brother into paving the way for a deathbed reunion with his dying father. He would be apologetic, full of remorse, he would act the part. Jonathan could even cry on cue if he needed to.

Along with high risk jobs like high finance and roles that require leadership and the willingness to 'stick your neck out' acting has, historically, always been a profession of choice for the psychopath, the need to be the center of attention, the ability to slip into a role. It's not that a psychopath doesn't know how another person feels, it's just that they don't feel it themselves, and they just don't care. Empathy is an essential human trait for most people for the psychopath they compensate by acting emphatic. A psychopath may appear to be listening to you with genuine interest while imagining what you would look like with your throat slit. It is strange to think that an unequal proportion of the people who govern and control our lives, who rule our business and financial interests, who we allow to lead us into war and who we turn to for leadership in those times of need, those who wield the surgeon's scalpel or don the wig and gown, who police us at the highest level and even some of those we look up to as our role models are drawn from that tiny unfeeling percentage.

Even if Cain's plan of becoming the prodigal son did not bear fruit he would sponge off his brother and be out of the way of his creditors until such time he could steal enough money from Abel to return safely and pay off the debt he owed.

The train Jonathan rode on actually passed by the rear of Telluric which along with the buildings occupied some acres of land and although the house itself was not close to the electrified track, Jonathan could make out lights were lit.

The station at Eden Falls was, as the crow flies, not that far from Telluric. Unfortunately the road network did not follow the same route as those large black birds of omen and would if used have made the journey home an epic one as no single bus route passed the house directly and it was in any case so late that the last bus would have already gone. Cain also had no money for a taxi so he took the direct route back along the tracks to enter Telluric via the rear of the property.

The tracks, being electrified, were a dangerous place for the unwary and were for the most part fenced off but there were places where access could be gained for those who took the risk.

The live rails had long held a morbid fascination for Jonathan as he had not just witnessed but been party to the death of a young friend of his when they had been children. Jonathan had not been directly responsible for the young boy's death but he had coerced the youth into crossing the tracks in the first place. He remembered being enthralled as he watched the electricity surge through the boy's body as the sparks flew and hair skin and clothes singed and blackened before finally catching fire. Jonathan could smell the burn and feel the electricity all around and it excited him. His friend,

Frederick Frink who had been feeding him the 'Eden Fall news' for all these years had also been present, later for the benefit of the adults they had both cried on cue, Freddy's' tears slightly more genuine than his own full on crocodile tears. The boy who died had been almost two years younger than Jonathan at the time but was in the same academic year as Frink, their first year of an all boy's senior school, and as both were just a scholastic year below Cain it was simply put down to a tragic accident. For the most part it was but that did not stop Cain and Frink returning to the area several times more to submit a found dog, some cats and other small animals to the same fate as had befell their young friend. They even perfected a way to get the smaller animals to be in contact with both the fatal rails at the same time and so it became a favourite pastime and one of a list of macabre hobbies for the young friends.

Jonathan knew too of the effect a speeding train had on a soft body. Smaller animals would completely disappear into a red mist of atoms. He had also seen, first hand, the results of such an impact on the human form, at certain times of year especially; the call of 'one under' at stations and some stretches of rail is far more common than the general public are aware of. Train drivers should expect it and a large part of the job of the British

Transport Police is picking up what pieces, they can find, that are left.

On his train journey home Cain could not help but notice a discarded free sheet newspaper, any headline no matter how small that contained the words death and railway sure to catch his eye; it told of an all-time high in the death toll on UK railways in the last twelve month period with 332 fatalities. Just over a score of these were the result of trespass on the main line but the bulk, 293, were suspected suicides. All without a fatal train crash for eight years in a row. Cain had reread the article several times.

Jonathan felt now or imagined that he could feel the electrical charge thicken the air about him and with that feeling came the memory of the smell of burning flesh as he approached the fence that separated the tracks from Telluric herself.

The old openings that Cain himself had made years before had long since been repaired and it took some searching in the dark and quite a bit of effort to find and to pull apart an entry point. Beyond this outer barrier he came across another smaller fence actually on the property itself. This wooden structure was a new addition to him and obviously erected by the property owners themselves as an extra safeguard but he had no trouble in scaling this second fence. Having passed through a copse he was soon approaching the rear of the house and as he drew level with some outbuildings which included a large double garage a security light blazed into life illuminating both him and the outbuildings. Jonathan paused in his stride for just a moment but then reminded himself that he was not on a job and was planning to be noticed, he strode on across a tidy lawn in a carefully landscaped and neatly manicured garden. He was still some yards from the main house when a substantial glass patio door noiselessly slid open and a male figure came outside to confront the stranger who was casually crossing his lawn while the powerful security light backlit the interloper.

The two men stopped several feet apart and to say that they were a mirror image of each other would be untrue as a reflected image shows simply a reversal of what truly is. Even their hair styles seemed to be the work of single barber and apart from their attire and the expressions they bore, Jonathan smiling broadly and Abel Cain's that of surprised horror, they were in effect not a reflection of each other but the very same entity split this time not as an ovum in the womb but as grown men separated by several feet of lush green grass. Like Adam in the garden of delights facing the god in whose image he was created and, bathed in the light of the world, Abel Cain was pierced and powerless. The bizarre halogen lit scene seemed frozen in eternity until broken with a single syllable.

"Bro'" It was Jonathan who spoke. The word shattered the inertia that had transfixed Abel Cain and the sound was like a clarion call to his senses. His expression changed from shock to pure anger, his eyes widened, his teeth clenched and he ran at his twin with outstretched arms grabbing his throat and knocking him backwards to the neatly mown turf.

To say that Jonathan was surprised by the attack would be a vast understatement, Able was in nature pacificatory, throughout their lives it had been his younger brother's policy to eschew violence and as far as he was aware Abel feared him. Jonathan had regular hit his weak willed brother from frequent unsolicited solo slaps to the more severe occasional beating. His twin had never retaliated, never informed on him for fear of reprisal and he had certainly never instigated aggression. The pre-emptive strike had knocked the wind out of Jonathan but the surprise of having his brother astride him, hands around his neck, trying his best to choke him had really knocked him for six. It was working too as he was struggling to breath.

It was now that the malevolence surfaced, it was not a red hot mist that ascended but a cold dark clarity. Jonathan Cain easily gained the upper hand, pulling his brother off him by his hair, he had laid a knee to his twins groin even before getting upright and when he had done so kicked viciously at his brother's torso several times. Dragging Abel upwards he held him in a classic headlock with which hold he could have easily restrained his brother but the thought to do so did not enter his mind. Instead Jonathan ran his twin into the centre of the lawn and towards a large stone sundial, letting go of him at the last moment with an extra push onwards and into the heavy igneous rock. The back of Able Cain's head connected soundly with the monolithic structure as he half somersaulted into its solid embrace and although the air vibrated with the snapping of cervical vertebrae and the very ground itself shook the granite remained unmoved and unmarked by its abetment in the act of fratricide. It's very demeanour remained as stone cold as that of Jonathan Cain who now stood looking at his dead twin, without pity for him or his brothers family, without fear for himself and totally without remorse for the crime he had committed.

Leaving his brothers broken body where it laid Cain entered the house via the open patio door and took stock of his surroundings. It would be a cliché to say that the house looked bigger to him especially as he had not been a child but in his mid-twenties when he had last stood where he stood now but he had forgotten just how spacious Telluric was and had become accustomed to more humble accommodation. He took the tour, remembering what he knew and making mental notes of any new addition. He stood over the sleeping children in each of their rooms for several minutes and also that of his brother's wife where he lingered for much longer watching her quietly breathing. Lustful thoughts filled his head briefly pushing away any new plan he was trying to formulate.

The fray on the lawn had not disturbed a soul and he carefully weighed his options. His father's safe did not go unnoticed and he wondered what was in it and where his late brother now kept its key. He considered waking up Herodias and making her reveal its whereabouts but this was not sure to produce a satisfactory result and it would also mean that she would then have to be taken care of. He thought of the possibility of swopping places, taking his brothers corpse to where he lived and faking his own death but the logistics of moving the body made this plan impossible.

After going through the house Cain located the spare keys for the outbuildings which were in the same place they had always been kept years before. On entering the double garage he noticed that its usage had changed somewhat and it now appeared to be his brothers man-cave complete with small carpentry workshop and utility areas. His eye line fell towards a large chest freezer and at once the new plan that he had started to construct reached fruition.

Cain spent the next few hours in preparation and refinement of his idea. Bringing the lifeless body of his twin into the den he removed his clothing and redressed him in several lightweight layers including gloves and woollen hat, he also fully covered the body in Saran wrap to reduce freezer burn, this he had found in the den on a packing roll so he did not have to resort to kitchen grade cling film. The freezer having a fair amount of space already due to the Christmas fare having only recently been used would easily accommodate its new produce, he had only to take out some frozen gateaux and boxes of finger foods to allow enough space for his brothers body. He had no need to worry about DNA evidence, his own DNA being an exact duplicate of the deceased.

His plan was as always a simple one; wait the couple of weeks for his father's death and the inevitable reading of the will , after which withdraw any money in the guise of Abel Cain, defrost the body and hide all evidence of its being frozen by electrocution and subsequent obliteration by a high speed train. An apparent suicide brought about by the grief caused through the loss of both his parents in such a short period of time. He would visit the doctor with warnings of his suicidal tendencies and could even write the suicide note as he could mimic perfectly Abel's handwriting.

His father's imminent death would account for any slight discrepancies in his acting ability but he had always been able to pass himself off as his brother when younger, so why not now? Herodias had never been physically able to tell them apart, so much so, that she and his brother had to use a password to make sure it was not Jonathan she was being intimate with. He had tried several times to fool her and had on one occasion only been successful. This had been two weeks before their wedding on his brother's stag night. Able had insisted it be held two weeks prior as he did not want to be hung over on his wedding day and had said that he did not want to drink too much anyway. Jonathan however had made sure that he did get very drunk and while heavily under the influence he had made his brother divulge the password to him, some mamby pamby phrase of her choosing. Then leaving his drunken and sleeping brother at home he took Abel's car and drove to Herodias's apartment. She had been mad at her pseudo lover for driving while under the influence but he spun a line about rather being with her than staying out with his drunken friends and loutish brother (a nice touch he thought). She had that evening consumed a little wine herself and despite some protests about an agreement to temporarily abstain from sex until after they were married, readily took the bait, of course she asked for the password but Jonathan was able to give it and so Jonathan Cain bedded his brothers fiancé just two weeks before they took their vows. The last time he had seen her prior to having just been watching her sleeping was on a hot, late August night, the night of her wedding party, she had been in tears after Jonathan had destroyed her big day, coked up and causing trouble.

Cain was looking forward to renewing his acquaintance with Herodias in the guise of his now dead brother, she was still a very attractive woman and he thought it would be an added bonus to his father's estate, but that would have to wait, the morning was almost upon him and he had much to prepare.

The following morning Herodias unbeknown to her found her husband's murderer sitting comfortably on the blood red chesterfield, dressed in the clothes he had taken from his dead brother just a few hours before. Abel's doppelganger claimed that he had been too mixed up to sleep and that he needed some time off work to get his head straight. He made Herodias phone Abel's work for him casually noting the number she dialled and asking whom it was she had spoken to so as to learn the name of a work college. He used many other ruses to glean any further information he lacked. His father's ill health was brought into play whenever it seemed he was in a spot but within a few days he had pretty much nailed his role as stand in for his brother. He even managed to effectively pass for Abel when he returned to his brothers workplace and although it was at first a little tricky getting his bearings he soon had his underlings doing his work load as well as their own. The old man was a different proposition almost right from the start and although he was heavily medicated and close to deaths door Saul Solomon felt a definite unease, something he could not quite put his finger on.

Quietus came to Saul Solomon Cain and he died in mid-March, fighting till the very end and lasting two full months more than the two weeks that had been granted to him by the doctors. His grandchildren were devastated having lost both grandparents within a year of each other. Herodias too having lost both her own parents when she was still quite young deeply felt his passing but she kept it together for the sake of her children and her husband whom it seemed had been the worst affected.

With the reading of the will there came a huge surprise. Saul Solomon Cain had without any explanation changed some of the stipulations of his will in the last weeks of his life. There were of course the usual charitable donations and minor offerings to more distant relatives remained unchanged. However the family home 'Telluric' which had remained in his estate was to be given in its entirety to his daughter- in- law, Herodias Clayton-Cain and in the event of her passing to that of her children. The other bombshell was that the remainder and bulk of his estate would be held in trust to be shared equally between the two grandchildren on their twenty first birthdays. Hermione and Saul would receive the lot.

His sons were both mentioned in the will but rewarded only with words; "To my loving son Abel I leave only what he would wish for himself. The knowledge that in him lies all that I was. To my son Jonathan I leave nothing bar regret". In life, Saul Solomon Cain had been a barrister of note, and this new will was without doubt a binding legal document.

Jonathan Cain seethed but did not display his anger he had seen in the eyes of the old man that he had suspected something and that had been enough for him to act on his intuition and change his will.

Although at the present time and by all standards, he had a cushy life, he was bored to death by pretending to be nice all the time. It was only on the odd occasion when he could sneak out to have a drink with his sycophantic friend Freddy Frink, who had been informed of his deception, that he could indulge in boasting about how clever he was and exactly what he was doing with and to his brother's wife. He could trust that Freddy would not reveal his deception; he could work him like a glove puppet and knew too much about him, secrets that Frink would never want revealed. Cain would often use this power over him to force Frink to do whatever he demanded.

One last option remained open if Cain wanted to get his hands on the money quickly and that was to remove the obstacles that stood in his way, namely his niece and nephew, little Hermione and young Saul, with them gone Saul Solomon's estate would automatically revert to their parents. He would have to bide his time a little, a couple of months more would do it and after getting rid of them he could revert back to his original plan but this time, more aptly, as a grief stricken parent not a grief stricken son. Maybe he could even include the lovely Herodias in his plans, unwillingly of course, she could succumb to grief before him and with a little help from Jonathan decide that life was not worth living without her children, and then everything would go to him. It would be better if she took an overdose to finish her off, perhaps of the sleeping pills and antidepressants that were sure to be prescribed after such a tragedy. He had heard that a side effect of antidepressants sometimes led to a higher risk of suicide. As much as he would also have liked to have seen Herodias touch the live rail, better to not push his luck he thought.

Not that he would be staying long afterwards himself, there was just no excitement to be had in

Eden Falls and his brother would be getting warmed up at some point so that they could change places again and he could get back to his own life but somewhat substantially richer. Yes, with his mother, father, children and wife dead it would only add credence to his own apparent suicide on the tracks or rather that of his brother, and of the missing money, there would be no one left to ask. The irony was that anything that was left would pass to him anyway. Money grabbing solicitors would be searching for him to tell him the sad/good news.

If there were any holes in his new plan (and there were probably many) then Jonathan Cain was unable or just unwilling to see them, his arrogance was all consuming, the fact that he had so far been able to fool his brother's family and work colleges into believing he was Abel Cain only had the effect of making him more self-assured that he was in fact invincible. The small setback he had already suffered with the obvious ill ease of his farther and the sudden change in his will had however made him more cautious and so he decided that when the children met their fate he would need an airtight alibi and the only way to have an alibi was to have an accomplice. That accomplice would of course be Fredrick Frink.

When he was told of the role he was to play in the infanticide Frink was horrified and at first he flatly refused to have any part in it. It was not just the consequences of the repercussions of the crime should anything go wrong but also the thought of having the blood of innocents on his hands that frightened him after all Freddy wasn't a complete monster. Jonathan Cain however frightened Freddy more than the thought of killing young children and he was not being asked to do it he was being told. Cain used his full arsenal of manipulation, coercion and the promise of financial reward to get Frink to agree to do his bidding, Freddy was told that the plan was fool-proof, no suspicion would ever fall on him, he would be very well paid for his actions when all was settled and Cain had his hands on his father's wealth. It was also made clear that if he refused Cain would use the knowledge he had on his friend to bring him to his knees, no direct threat needed to be made Cain only had to allude to his intentions to again force his friends reluctant compliance.

So it was arranged that Freddy Frink would intercept the children on their way home from school. A ruse was to be put in place so that the twins would fully trust their would-be woodsman. Cain himself sowing the seed of the deception, it would appear that their own father had given his consent for the twins to cross the tracks with Freddy, a route that throughout their lives they had been forbidden to take. Cain knew which areas of track where covered by CCTV and more importantly those that were not and could be assured to be safe from prying eyes. The opening in the security fence designed to stop such crossings would be made in advance and after being introduced to Freddy beforehand the assassin Frink would lead the children to their shocking deaths. They would be told that the electricity had been turned off on that stretch of track, they would be holding hands, better for the conductivity, if need be at the last moment they would be given a slight push to ensure they made the connection needed all while Jonathan Cain sat on his slain brothers blood red leather chesterfield settee within eye line of their mother and listening to his brother's wife talk of her expectations and anticipations of the joint fourteenth birthday celebrations of her darling children, the apples of her eyes due to held the following day.

Cain once again looked toward the clock that sat on the mantle below the Malus wood plaque and noted that the children would have just left school and would be heading towards a point where he had arranged for them to be picked up. One phone call and it would all be up to Freddy. The cold blooded killer arose from the warm blood red leather seating.

"About time Abe'" Herodias complained. "I thought I was going to have to do it all myself"

"What" replied Cain?

"The cards and the party food"

"Yes, of course, I'm doing it now. Cards first, our room in the dresser, you say" Cain mounted the stairs, on the top step as if on cue, one of the two phones he had about him vibrated silently in the left hand pocket of his brothers borrowed chino trousers. He entered the bedroom and took the call. Young Saul was on the other end of the line. Cain spoke quietly so as not to be overheard "Yes...yes, sorry but I'm stuck here, fixing your mothers surprise, that's why I'm talking quietly so that she doesn't overhear...I know, that's why I sent Uncle Freddy to pick you up. He is there isn't he...good...I know he's not your real uncle, but humour him. Right do exactly what Freddy says, because you are on foot you will have to get back here quickly so let Freddy take you across the railway tracks to the back of the house and...Yes, I know what I've said in the past but you are with Freddy so you will be safe, I trust him with your lives and they have turned off the electricity today while they work on the line further down the track. So it's perfectly fine...Right be quick or you will miss the surprise we have for your mother and hold onto Hermione's hand. Put Hermione on the phone...Hermione, Do exactly as Freddy tells you and hold Saul's hand...just hold your brothers hand...yes, when Freddy tells you to. Oh, and you didn't mention anything to anybody in school like I told you…Both of you…good or it will spoil the whole thing…Yes…Yes, I love you too. Put Freddy on…Freddy, you know what to do!"

Jonathan placed the phone back into the same pocket from which he had taken it and opened the topmost draw of the dresser in front of him. He took out the two birthday cards distinctly different from each other but both equally bright and full of teenage symbolism and both with a splattering of stars. Their mother, even if only in some small way always tried to allude to their astrological lineage. Like the Dioscuri, before them, who's farther Zeus sired them in the guise of a swan, Caster and Pollux the original Gemini shared both their mortality and immortality between them spending half their time in the Heavens and half their time in Hades. The young Cain twins also happily shared everything and showed true love and affection for each other, born as the sun enters the northern constellation of the third sign of the Zodiac; they truly epitomized the Geminian spirit in more ways than they themselves knew.

Cain removed the cellophane wrappings from the neatly packaged cards and tossed the cards onto the bed, from the bedside cabinet he took a Mont Blanc pen and without reverence to its craftsmanship, threw that to join with the cards, finally from the pocket of a, currently out of style, wedding suit jacket that hung in a large gentleman's wardrobe he retrieved an imposing looking key and with it opened the Yale safe that had at different times belonged to both his father and his brother.

He had already become familiar with the safes contents in general and other than Herodias's jewellery box and some pieces of his brothers finery held nothing of great value. It did hold quite a few documents and Cain took out a bundle that contained amongst other things Baptism papers, birth certificates and a marriage license.

He took the bundle over to the bed and sitting down undid the string that held the documents together. Cain located the birth certificates of the twins and readied the birthday cards to write an appropriate greeting. He noted the name on the first birth certificate and in his brothers best handwriting wrote out a simple greeting above and below the pre-printed verse. Unsure of his brothers exact format style with regards to birthday cards he wrote it in the way that had been used by his own parents when giving cards to him and his brother.

He wrote; To Saul True Cain…Have a great day, Love, Mummy and Daddy.
XXXXXXXXXXXXXXX

Yes, he remembered well always using the childish form of Mummy and Daddy and adding one 'X' (kiss) for every year of life. He almost felt a pang of nostalgia, almost. He felt his brother would certainly have kept to the same style. He noted the absurdity of his nephew's middle name 'True' no wonder, he thought to himself that it was only used once a year on his birthday. Cain repeated the procedure for his niece.

He wrote; To Hermione Love Cain…

Jonathan paused without completing the remaining words. A feeling came over him which was alien to him, a singular coldness. Not coldness of nature of which he knew well, but coldness of spirit. The names, there was something about the children's names. Although Cain knew all of the dates in question he still had to see it on paper for it to fully sink in. He looked first at the birth certificates and confirmed, as if he needed to, that the twin's birthday was one day short of fourteen years. He then picked up the marriage license that lay on the bed with the other documentation and again although he knew it had been the night he had left Eden falls all those years ago he still had to see it in black and white. It had been the end of August when he had turned his back on his family and now it was May, Gemini was in its ascendancy.

Jonathan frantically worked back using his fingers to count the years and to count the months and the weeks. Was it nine months or forty weeks? He wasn't sure but however he worked it, it seemed impossible for the twins to have been conceived on or after their parents wedding night. It must have been a couple of weeks prior to their marriage that the twins were conceived. Cain could have dispensed with the mathematics altogether it was the children's middle names that, like a slap in the face or a knee to the groin, had awoken him to the reality of the situation.

True and Love the second names that had been given to the twins by their mother. True Love, the phrase that Jonathan had extracted from his inebriated sibling. Truelove the password that he had used to surreptitiously rape his future sister-in-law just two weeks before taking her wedding vows. He remembered it now, he remembered the whole sordid night. He had planned to get Abel drunk in the hope of getting the password and he had relished in pretending to be his brother.

Of course that was why Abel had without warning and totally out of character attacked him on the lawn on the night of his return, he must have known. He must always have known maybe from the moment they both discovered she was pregnant. Perhaps he remembered a drunken recollection of giving out the password, perhaps she told him when they were conceived and he just worked it out, women know that sort of thing; she must have known to have called the twins True and Love. He remembered that Herodias had said that they were supposed to be abstaining until after they were married on the night he had drove there in Abel's car and he doubted that their actual wedding night was very romantic after the trouble he had caused before leaving. Yes she must have known when they were conceived and that night could only have been it, but did she know that they were not Abel's children? Jonathan thought this unlikely; it would be just like his brother to keep the secret to himself, to love the children like they were his own and to never reveal the truth to Herodias for fear of hurting her. Cain could picture his brother rationalizing it; after all it was the same DNA that went into making them, just delivered by a different milkman. Still it must have killed him to have known for all those years but have said nothing and in the end of course it did kill him. Cain wondered what thoughts went through his brother's mind while his neck was snapping as he connected with the granite column.

Jonathan Cain scorned his dead brother's good nature; he, Jonathan Cain would not have brought up another man's children even with identical genes to his own. He looked at that part of the birth certificates that contained the father's name and saw Abel Cain's name written instead of his own name. How dare he, Jonathan raged, they, the children belonged to him, not Abel. At that moment he wanted them as much as he had wanted his brothers woman all those years before and yet he had sent them out like babes in some gruesome fairy tale to meet their gory end but weren't fairy stories supposed to end with a 'happy ever after'?

He would stop it; he would have what was his. Reaching into the right hand pocket of the chinos he took out the second mobile phone he had, his own phone, and dialled the number under the name of Freddy Frink. An uncaring generic voice informed him that the mobile he was calling was unavailable. It is well known amongst the criminal fraternity that the police can secure a conviction using mobile phone signals to put the accused at the scene of his crime any criminal worth his salt would guard against this and it was for this reason that Frink had turned off his mobile phone.

Still it wasn't too late he would stop them by the tracks. Cain frantically texted a message to the same number he had just dialled as he dashed down the stairs, passing Herodias and out via the patio door at the back of the house. >Freddy- abort the job- repeat abort job< he typed. As he quickly crossed the now slightly overgrown lawn he switched phones taking out his brother's phone from his left hand pocket and attempting to replace his own phone back into his right hand pocket. The transition did not quite go as planned and the latter device slipped out of its intended sheath and bouncing once on the recently neglected lawn came to rest on the base of a large granite sundial that stood like an ancient standing stone, a Neolithic timepiece guarding its history, silent, unfeeling. As Cain raced through the copse he called the number under the name Small Saul his intention to be passed on to Frink. The trees of the copse seemed to intentionally claw at him as he passed and once again he was informed that it had not been possible to connect his call.

Herodias was taken aback as her husband passed by her, rushed out of the house and across the lawn, she had expected him to enter his den to retrieve what she had been asking for all afternoon but when he passed the outbuildings and carried on she was confused. She followed him outside and stood looking on in bewilderment. She looked down at the lawn which had only had a single half-hearted cut all spring and lamented her husband's recent lethargy, and he still had not got the party food she had been asking for. Well she would just have to get it herself. As she was thinking this, her attention was directed to a slight buzzing sound, a vibration that came from the centre of the lawn not unlike a large bee in distress. Herodias approached the disturbance. At the base of the centrepiece that dominated the garden was a mobile phone similar to her husband's but an earlier model she knew this as she had only recently upgraded Abel's phone as a Christmas present. The phone intermittently danced then rested on the pedestal of the large granite sundial. As she picked up the phone the call ended but she did just catch sight of the caller's name, Freddy Frink. The unusual name rang a bell with her, wasn't the a Fredrick Frink in the same year of junior school as her whose friend had been electrocuted on the railway tracks shortly after starting their first year in same sex senior schools? She remembered the police visiting all the local schools in an effort to educate the children to stay off the tracks. Thank goodness she drummed it into her own children never to play on the railway. The thought of the poor dead boy sent a shiver down her spine and coldness permeated her very core.

Herodias composed herself and went towards the garage to collect the gateaux and other party food from the overflow freezer that was kept in the utility area of her husband's den. It was not her policy to enter her husband's personal space but she did have a key and she was tired of asking him without success to fetch the food. As she unlocked the door and approached the chest freezer the phone she held in her hand buzzed to alert that a text message had been received. The same name came up, Freddy Frink, and as Herodias reached the freezer she could not resist reading the contents of the text. The message was a short jumble of letters and numbers that seemed to make little sense it just read; >J0N02L8<.

I will get the party food and then write out the twin's birthday cards myself she thought, lifting the freezer lid.

Epilogue-

Jonathan Cain stood by the tracks the air around him bristled with energy and an old familiar smell greeted his senses, he looked at his legacy

Herodias Clayton-Cain stood in front of the large chest freezer its lid open wide, the refrigerated air greeted her with its cold embrace as she looked to from the phone she held in her hand to the freezers icy contents.

The gods in their heavens stood gazing down; already bored they looked to see what new game they could play.

A CHILD'S PRAYER

M Dainty

All around the houses,
Up and down the streets.
In and out the jiggers,
Eating penny sweets.
Wearing dad's old trousers,
Dragging mum's best sheets.
Secrets, smiles and sniggers.
Victories, defeats.
They'll pull this playground down one day,
And we will all grow old.
And the only place we'll have to play,
Are in the memories we hold.
Hold on to childhood laughter,
Let go of only tears.
For now and ever after,
Remember childhood years.
For when we leave this world behind,
And say our last adieu.
Another happy place we'll find,
And run in playgrounds new.

ANOTHER PLACE

M Dainty

Strong iron men, steadfast, look to the sea.
Trapped in sentient thought these guardians stand.
Through blind unblinking eyes watch endlessly.
Sentinels, set sure in shimmering sand.

Like silent souls froze in their locality.
Who dare hold breath at view of their command.
Secure in stilly awe of all they see.
Cast for the god hewn shore by mortal hand.

Fuglemen with purpose and grave gravity.
Hold fast their post o'er an ocean grand.
Fixed fair within beatific majesty.
Gaze 'cross unceasing waves to distant land.

Strong men grant me solace, love and quite grace.
Take me unbounded to another place.

BROKEN BOTTLES AND BROKEN BONES

M Dainty

Broken bottles and broken bones, for I-pod shuffles and mobile phones,
'quipped with essential apps and the latest ring tones.
Keep your hand on your sixpence and your eye on the ball,
'coz statistically speaking, you're in for a fall,
and you'll be 'had over' in no time at all.
So look over your shoulder when you're on your way home,
'though you're all on your lonesome, you may not be alone.
The times right for a muggin' and you'll be the mug,
had by adolescent assassins or some baby faced thugs,
and your 'last bus fare home' will help pay for their drugs.
So keep your feet in your trainers, put a step in your stride,
'coz if you get caught napping you'll lose more than your pride.
When the bastards surround you and you've no place to hide.

IN MEMORANDUM

M Dainty

I took an oak leaf from my father's grave,
and held it in my hand.
To warm November winters' win,
'gainst brave defeated autumns' stand.
I read once more the words carved through,
the cold Carrere stone.
The names of people I once knew,
I took the oak leaf home.

IRIS

M Dainty

A long lost seaman's daughter,　　with a deadly fear of water.
Went looking for her daddy,　　to discover just why had he.
Abandoned his own baby,　　in clear favour of the navy,
And why he would much rather,　　be a sailor not a father,
And chose the briny ocean,　　over parental devotion.
Could this early infant tear,　　be the cause of mal-de-mere?
Be the reason for her fear,　　her chronic hydrophobia.
She searched harbours, docks and ports,　　spoke to seamen of all sorts.
Boarded ship and boat and craft,　　looked port, starboard, bow and aft.
Till at last she found a man,　　on a sloop in Amsterdam.
An old salt, sat on a stool,　　from the port of Liverpool.
Fixing nets out in the sun,　　on the stool he sat upon,

And he looked just like her dad,   from a photograph she had.
His lined weather beaten face,   bore much more than just a trace,
Of her own sweet countenance,   so she seized upon the chance.
To approach the old Jack-tar,   who she'd searched for near and far.
She just handed him the print,   in his eyes there came a glint.
Then those orbs filled with salt tears,   as he wept for those lost years.
All his cries, his sobs, his wails,   were enshrouded by the sails,
And he dropped down to his knees,   as he swore by all the seas.
By the sun, the stars, the moon,   Nereus and great Neptune,
To give up his ocean ways,   for all his remaining days.
If she'd let him make amends,   and restart again as friends.
Just as shipmates, nothing more,   his old sea legs firm ashore,
And he kneeled there head bowed low,   as the sloop rocked to and fro.
She looked down upon the salt,   who was clearly the main fault,

Of her sea sickness and dread,   of all substances liquid.
In that moment came about,   an epiphany no doubt,
That her long nautical quest,   had put her fears to the test.
She had constantly to brave,   every eddy, swell and wave,
And could finally call avast,   on her phobia at last.
The lost mariner who knelt,   was relieved that he soon felt,
His child's arms about his neck,   as she kissed him on that deck.
Reunited finally,   father, daughter of the sea.

I have almost told my rhyme,   of this saga maritime,
But this tale is not yet done,   'till I tell you what become,
Of our reunited pair,   and the happy times they share.
They returned to their home town,   where they hap'ly settled down.
In a modern quayside block,   on the famous Albert Dock.
When the working week was done,   every Sunday they shared fun,
On the Mersey river tide,   with a weekend ferry ride.

Overlooked by Liver bird,   their long lost loud laughter heard,
And their love remains afloat,   on the Royal Iris boat,
And it's there for all to see,   from each side of the wide Mersey.

ODE TO THE GRAFTON ROOMS

M Dainty

Grab a granny, grab a gran.
Do the business, if you can.
Have a bevy, have a few.
Anything in a skirt will do.
Hit the dance floor, hit it fast.
Don't know how long the band will last.
One more shimmy, one more beer.
Kicking out times, nearly here.
Out the nightclub, off yer head.
Donner, Taxi home bed.
Grab a granny, grab a gran,
Do the business, if you can.

SONNET

M Dainty

Requesting only to write a sonnet.
Our homework given, we all now must toil.
Time to get cracking, to work upon it.
Until it's done our fuddled brains in moil.
No rest now for the poor wicked poet.
Dizzy with words as in a muddy sea.
And when it's full finished we must show it.

When we meet on Monday in room 2B.
Read our rhyme before our peers and tutor.
In yearning hope our leader we can please.
That our feeble offering's will suit her
Else with harsh words she'll bring us to our knees.
Rage 'gainst writers block, it's near completed.
Sonnet done! I will not be defeated.

ROS EMERY

A DICKENSIAN TALE

Ros Emery

It was some time before Nicholas began to wonder if Madeline Bray might not be quite the person he thought he'd married. Knowing a little of her recent unhappy life he had made allowances for her mood swings but now he seriously questioned whether there was possibly something amiss.

After she had been saved from a forced marriage to his uncle Ralph and following the sudden death of her father in the Debtors' Prison, Nicholas had been pleased to offer her his protection and she had accepted a temporary home with him, his mother and his sister Kate. Over the next few months she had charmed them all and, encouraged by the engagement of Kate and Frank Cheeryble, he had dared to suggest a double wedding. Initially she was reluctant to accept his proposal. He and Frank were both employed with fairly modest salaries by Frank's uncles, the Cheeryble brothers. They'd been instrumental in Nicholas and Madeline meeting. Her father was heavily in debt with all his assets sold but Madeline had some talent for painting and, as an act of charity, the Cheeryble's paid her generously for her pictures. Nicholas had taken the money to her in the Prison where her father was incarcerated. He'd been very impressed at how she had seemed so gentle and loyal to her father, who then virtually sold her to Ralph Nickleby to clear his debts. Surprisingly the loss of her father appeared to affect her more than her escape from matrimony.

After the suicide of Ralph Nickleby, who had faced various charges including defrauding his own son out of his inheritance and indirectly causing his death, Nicholas and Kate received letters from Mr. Jaggers the lawyer advising that they were now confirmed as Ralph's heirs and would each inherit a fortune. Frank and Kate announced their plans were unchanged. After their marriage Frank would continue to work for his uncles and Kate, with his whole-hearted support to use her money as she wished, would open a free school for girls where they would be taught a useful trade. Nicholas's idea had been to give up his work and fund a free residential school for boys (everything Dotheboys Hall had not been) staffed by himself and other like-minded teachers, but this plan had to be shelved because Madeline finally agreed to be his wife. Unfortunately she said she couldn't possibly live in the country and they must purchase a house in town, otherwise she would be miserable.

Nicholas understood that his wife had been forced to run and hide from creditors because of her feckless father and needed to feel secure and he was happy to give her what she wanted, though he was rather taken aback by the scale of house she envisaged. It had to be large and in a fashionable part of town.

The double wedding was a quiet affair. Madeline made no objections to this as she had no close relatives to invite. Nicholas was rather hurt when she seemed to deliberately ignore his good friends the Crummells, who had been so kind to him and poor Smike, but fortunately they didn't appear to notice. Frank and Kate enjoyed a week at the seaside and Nicholas managed to persuade Madeline that a month in Europe was long enough for a honeymoon. She was like a child, persuading him to buy trinkets and also expensive items to be shipped back for their new house.

When they returned to England the work on the house wasn't quite finished so they stayed for another month in an hotel. Nicholas had left the refurbishment of their new home to his wife, thinking it would give him time to rearrange his plans. He'd assured her she need spare no expense, and she took him at his word. He and Kate had now decided to join their resources and open a school for both boys and girls in town, with a broad curriculum and also some accommodation for pupils who had nowhere else to live. Nicholas would be the principal.

Kate's input continued to be considerable but, though they tried to involve Madeline, she made it quite clear her interests lay elsewhere. Nicholas had learned she could be extremely difficult if she did not get her own way and was not averse to making a scene in public. This was so totally at odds with the Madeline he had thought he knew he was at a loss what to do for the best, and generally he gave in to her whims. On one point however he did thwart her. She said it was absolutely essential for her to have her own transport and she wanted a carriage and a coachman. Nicholas finally agreed a contract with Barkis & Sons whereby they could be summoned at a moment's notice and would submit their accounts to him. This very successful family firm operated handsome cabs known to have reliable and sober drivers. Their horses were smart too and well cared for, and rumour had when they could no longer work they were sent to spend the rest of their days at a farm in Kent.

When they finally moved into their new home Nicholas was delighted to discover a kindred spirit next door. Mr. Brownlow was a scholarly man and immediately showed an interest in Nicholas's plans. Mr. Brownlow's ward Rose Maylie and her nephew Oliver lived with him. He told Nicholas something of Oliver's early life and explained he'd had a very poor education, though he was a bright boy and was quickly catching up. This opened up a new idea to

Nicholas and it was agreed he would tutor Oliver informally and once he found a suitable venue for the school and completed any necessary building work Oliver would be enrolled as a student and Mr. Brownlow would also take an interest in the establishment. Sometimes Oliver, usually with Rose, visited Nicholas for his lessons but generally they felt more comfortable studying in Mr. Brownlow's house. The house Madeline had produced was to be admired but it wasn't very homely.

Nicholas was conscious he was leaving her to her own devices during the day, but he always spent the evenings with her when she appeared very animated. In the mornings however she usually remained in her room until noon pleading fatigue. It was some time before he noticed a pattern in the accounts he was receiving from Barkis & Sons. Madeline was being taken to an address in Chelsea most afternoons and being picked up 2 or 3 hours later.

When he asked her about this at first she refused to reply, storming off in a temper, but then she relented and said she'd been having private painting lessons "to surprise you" but she had nothing to show him at the moment because her work wasn't yet "good enough".

Nicholas's immediate reaction was to forbid Madeline from going to Chelsea again but he checked his anger and just said "I'd like to go with you next time, my dear." Madeline turned pale and Nicholas thought she was about to faint, but she recovered herself and said she felt unwell and wanted to go to her room. Assisted by Marie her maid, Nicholas helped her upstairs. He was extremely concerned and asked if she would like to see a doctor, but that appeared to distress her even more so for the moment he didn't pursue the subject. Marie helped her undress and sat with her while Nicholas went downstairs to ponder the problem.

Half an hour later Marie reported Madeline was sleeping so Nicholas decided to see the house in Chelsea for himself, and the regular cab driver took him there. The house looked respectable and well-kept and when he knocked on the door it was opened by a neat maidservant. Nicholas took a chance and asked to see her mistress. He was invited into a nicely furnished hall and shortly a smartly dressed woman came down the imposing staircase. Her age was indeterminate and it was only when she came close to him that he realised she relied heavily on artifice. Although she spoke softly in a genteel manner he had the impression she was playing a part and he was reminded of the Crummells' theatrical group.

She introduced herself as Madam Mantalini and asked how she might help him. Unable to think of anything else, he blurted out "Mrs. Nickleby sent me." "Ah Maddie!" said the lady. "Though I don't quite understand." Nicholas improvised. "I was meant to come with her, but she's indisposed." "So you're here to relax anyway?" queried the lady. "Oh no" Nicholas replied "I just came to tell you Madeline (Mrs. Nickleby) can't come." Madam Mantalini smiled graciously. "Thank you" she said "but you're more than welcome to stay." Nicholas was getting an uneasy feeling and was anxious to depart, but he didn't want to alienate the woman or alarm her so he pleaded another appointment and promised to return.

Outside the house he found he was trembling. He hardly dared consider the implications of what he had discovered. Of course he was aware that private gentlemen's clubs existed but he had never visited one. Although his upbringing had precluded such excesses it was a fact that until recently he could never have afforded to frequent such an establishment. His first thought was that somehow Madeline had been drawn into the world of gambling and had been too ashamed to tell him. He knew he must rush home to reassure her everything would be alright, he would pay her gambling debts and they would think no more about it.

This wasn't immediately possible because when he got home, having been away for less than an hour, Marie reported her mistress was still sleeping, and Nicholas resolved to do nothing until the following morning.

However the next day Madeline was unable to leave her bed, complaining of exhaustion and refusing to eat. By the second day Nicholas was becoming extremely anxious as Madeline was alternatively too hot and then shivering and also complaining of stomach cramps. Money being no problem Nicholas was able to engage one of the Court Physicians, the fashionable doctor Sir Parker Peps, to visit his wife. The consultation was brief because Sir Parker was a very busy man, but he inspected her and tested her pulse before pronouncing she was just a little overwrought and needed a rest, with no excitement, and a tonic he would prescribe.

The tonic being duly delivered, after the first spoonful Madeline refused to take it, threshing about and upsetting herself, and Nicholas. Rose came from next door and her presence seemed to sooth Madeline. When Rose heard of Sir Parker's visit however she felt obliged to mention that he had attended the mother of her dear friend Florence Dombey prior to her death, and even now he was visiting Florence's brother Paul daily, and Paul was showing no signs that his health was improving.

While Nicholas was pondering what to do next, Mr. Jaggers called on a matter of business and hearing of Madeline's indisposition suggested Nicholas contact a young doctor of his acquaintance who was gaining a fine reputation, although not making a fortune.

Hearing Mr. Jaggers' name, Doctor Duncan came at once and immediately impressed with his quiet air of competence and pleasant manner. Madeline visibly relaxed when he spoke to her and Nicholas was persuaded to vacate the room, leaving Marie to look after her mistress. Doctor Duncan remained with Madeline for half an hour, leaving her with a smile and promising to return. She was obviously fatigued so Nicholas stayed just long enough to ascertain she desired to sleep and had everything she needed and then he went downstairs to hear what the doctor's diagnosis was and what was to be done.

The doctor wasted no time. "What can you tell me of your wife's former lifestyle?" he asked. His grave demeanour alarmed Nicholas who was nonplussed. At a loss how to reply he could only manage to indicate that she was a young lady whose father had fairly recently fallen on hard times and consequently their circumstances had changed. So far as Nicholas knew prior to this she had enjoyed high standards and had wanted for nothing. The doctor made no comment, collected his coat and bag and said he would return that evening.

This he did after Madeline had for the first time in days had a restful sleep. While with Madeline he was easy and charming and she responded to his pleasantries. Nicholas however had a feeling the good doctor was hiding something and when they were alone he demanded to know what was wrong with his wife. The doctor took a long time before he gave him some indication that the situation was serious. He began by stating that it had been necessary for him to prescribe a powerful opiate to Mrs. Nickleby and this was because she was used to taking the equivalent and her present symptoms were caused by the withdrawal of the drug. Nicholas was horrified, struggling to understand how she had first succumbed to the habit. He speculated her recent visits to Chelsea were the cause of her addiction, but Doctor Duncan said he suspected she had been taking stimulants for, maybe, the past 10 years. Nicholas was aghast. During that time she and her father had been living comfortably together, until her father had incurred debts he couldn't pay and been imprisoned prior to his death.

Nicholas was devastated, but worse was to come. The doctor warned him that Madeline's condition was very serious. He said her previous consumption had been sufficient for the effects to be masked as normal behaviour but a sudden increase in the quantity and quality had been catastrophic. Her body couldn't cope and she had collapsed. The treatment he proposed was to give her measured doses of the drug, gradually decreasing the amount, to stabilize her condition, but he warned it was a dangerous course of action.

During their conversation he had been keeping a close watch on Nicholas and it was evident that his diagnosis had come as a total shock to him. "I'll leave you to consider what I've told you" he said "and come back tomorrow morning when we can decide what we must do." Marie and Nicholas watched Madeline, who continued to sleep peacefully throughout the night. Nicholas was in a turmoil. Early next day Doctor Duncan returned as promised. He looked in on Madeline who had just woken up and then told Nicholas he had given her another dose of the drug.

During the night Nicholas had almost convinced himself there must be some mistake. He reasoned Madeline surely had no opportunity to meet suppliers of drugs and what the doctor was suggesting just could not be possible. Although reluctant to question the young doctor's expertise, he endeavoured to convey his misgivings. But the doctor reassured him and confessed he had foreseen Nicholas's apprehension and had taken the liberty of inviting someone else who would confirm his diagnosis. Much to Nicholas's amazement the visitor was Mr. Jaggers.

When the doctor left them alone Mr. Jaggers explained he had come in his capacity as a friend to both parties and he had no intention of discussing any actual event or circumstance. So far as he was concerned he was just passing on his way to his place of work and if he mentioned certain facts, possibly concerning deceased persons with whom he had once had contact, that would be because he was in the habit of thinking out loud. Virtually speechless himself, Nicholas could think to do nothing else but offer Mr. Jaggers some tea and once that arrived they both sat until the lawyer broke the silence.

"Now Nickleby" said Mr. Jaggers "put this case. Put the case that a young man from a very fine family, inheriting sufficient wealth, had expensive tastes and for a number of years was able to indulge them. He married an insignificant wife but she did produce a very significant child, a daughter. Time passed. He continued to keep ahead of his creditors, he borrowed occasionally from money lenders but mostly from his friends. Unlike many of his friends he wasn't addicted to gambling although he frequented gaming clubs. His addiction lay elsewhere. When he was a young man he acquired a taste for opium and it gradually took over his resources and his life. Mercifully for her his wife died, leaving him in sole charge of his daughter. He indulged the child, who contrasted him with her unhappy mother. He showed her off to his friends and, as a treat, he occasionally intoxicated her with magical vapours.

Then put the case that his creditors caught up with him and demanded their dues. Sure he would be able to recoup his losses he came to an arrangement with one of his friends to pay all his debts, at a price. The price was his daughter. But the debtor nullified the arrangement by dying. The daughter was saved. Good fortune smiled on her and she married a fine young man. However she now had untold wealth and a desire to forget recent events. She knew where to go for peace of mind and oblivion."

Nicholas was astounded. Of course he understood what Mr. Jaggers had been saying. It was all so horribly obvious. Mr. Jaggers got up as though his sole purpose had been to drink a glass of tea with a friend, shook his hand and departed.

Kindly Mr. Jaggers with his undeserved reputation for being always business-like and heartless didn't think it necessary to tell Nicholas that Madeline had been entirely in favour of her marriage to wealthy Ralph Nickleby initially to save her beloved father and had then been bitterly disappointed when that prospect was snatched from her by Ralph's suicide. She'd originally had no intention of accepting

Nicholas's proposal until, unexpectedly, he was confirmed as his uncle's heir.

Slowly Nicholas realised the inexorable path Madeline had been on and how wealth had played its part in her downfall. He acknowledged his desire to spoil her and give her anything she wanted contributed to the tragic situation she found herself in at the moment, but after Mr. Jaggers' departure Doctor Duncan's common sense appraisal of the circumstances forced him to consider she was her father's daughter and her outlook had been formed by him.

It has to be said that despite Doctor Duncan's best efforts Madeline could not be saved. Her passing was peaceful in the arms of her husband, surrounded by friends. Her sister-in-law Kate thanked God she and Frank had made the conscious decision to use Ralph Nickleby's money entirely for the benefit of others. Nicholas sold his smart house and reverted to his original plan to endow a school, and in due course he had the total support of his wife Rose.

A FAIRY TALE

Ros Emery

It might be said we found ourselves in such a terrible situation partly because of a good deed, but mainly I blame myself for being so naïve and stupid.

When I married Anthony Utley we were both orphans with fairly adequate resources, but young and foolish with no-one to counsel us. We therefore indulged ourselves and spared no expense to ensure our two lovely daughters enjoyed a happy carefree lifestyle. Anthony liked to gamble though he was not particularly successful while I couldn't resist all the latest trends and bought the girls whatever they wanted. We purchased a large family house in a fashionable area and loved our happy home.

Anthony's sudden death brought our world crashing down. Rather than face reality I initially ignored the circumstances I found myself in. It was more than a year later before I acknowledged that I virtually had no money and there were still debts to be paid. Even the house was of no value as Anthony had used it to secure a loan. I set about selling what I could, emptying the house prior to vacating it. At the time I had no idea where the girls and I would live or whether I would be able to support us, as I had no marketable skills.

This was when my good friend Marianne offered us the use of their house in Bath for three months while they were travelling abroad. Marianne was unable to help us financially as her money was controlled by her husband a Diplomat, but he was a kind man who indulged her whims. It solved my immediate problem and I was not offended when Marianne seriously suggested I use the time to maybe find a suitable husband to ensure our future security.

And that his exactly what happened. We had hardly settled in when I became aware of Baron Stanley Brook's interest. He was a hearty handsome man, a few years older than me, charming and generous. He told me he was a widower with a 16 year old daughter Eleanor – company for my Rose and Lily. He showed me a sketch of their lovely old house in the Yorkshire Dales. Nothing was too much trouble for him. He lavished gifts on us and refused to accept any payment in return. He said the pleasure of giving was enough. He refused to discuss finance. When I said I was forced to sell our house he misunderstood, implying I couldn't bear to remain there with my memories.

It is no excuse but I know now I was vulnerable and not thinking straight because before I knew it we were married and there seemed nothing strange that we went directly from Bath to North Yorkshire. I barely had time to arrange for our baggage, all our worldly goods, to be transferred from Marianne's house by a carrier. Rose, Lily, the Baron and I travelled in the Baron's own coach driven by his manservant Mr. Button, a taciturn creature, and we stopped just once overnight at a rather shabby inn. Until then the Baron had been extremely affable but his attitude changed noticeably and he spent the evening ignoring us and talking with Mr. Button. After our meal we retired for the night and didn't see the Baron until the following morning. My attempts at conversation were rebuffed and I could see the Baron was extremely angry, but he refused to explain what had upset him and lapsed into silence as we drove towards North Yorkshire.

It was dusk when we arrived but there was sufficient light to see the house was in far from pristine condition. Initially I told myself maybe it just lacked a woman's touch, but that did not prove to be the case. There was a woman in control of the Baron and his house – his mother. She stood on the top step and watched us as we stepped down from the coach. I was reminded of a snake, waiting to strike. "This is my good mother!" my husband said. "This is her home." She didn't attempt to make us welcome but after looking us over turned on her heel and walked back into the hall. In the shadows I caught a glimpse of a slight figure, scarcely bigger than Rose and Lily, and two anxious eyes which were quickly cast down. Suspecting this was Eleanor and wanting to lighten the moment I called to Rose and Lily who were waiting by the side of the coach to come and meet their new sister.

"Time enough for them to get acquainted." said the Baron. "Eleanor will show you to your rooms." With that he disappeared in the same direction as his mother and we were left in the hall with no alternative but to follow Eleanor upstairs carrying our hand luggage. She indicated three more or less identical rooms on the first floor, barely adequate for our requirements. I considered returning downstairs to confront the Baron but instead decided to find out what I could from Eleanor. Seeing how angry I was she shook her head and put her finger to her lips as if warning me not to act hastily. I therefore told the girls to remove their outer garments but do nothing further. We were all hungry so although I was loath to subject them to any possible unpleasantness after this long journey I suggested we go down to find something to eat. To my surprise downstairs Eleanor led us towards the back of the house and we ended up in a not too clean kitchen. But at least it was warm and Eleanor brought us some food, laying it out on the large kitchen table. After we had eaten and there was still no sign of the Baron or his mother I decided it was best to return to our rooms and tackle any problems tomorrow morning. As a precaution however the two girls remained with me. They slept soundly enough though I didn't.

Suffice to say the next day brought more shocks and some explanations. It transpired the Baron had thought he was marrying me for my fortune. His sole reason for going to Bath had been to find a wealthy wife. Unfortunately he had employed an unscrupulous (or maybe simply inefficient) marriage broker who had confused the name of the lady of the house – Marianne – with mine – Marion. The broker had made all the necessary enquiries regarding the lady who resided at my friend's address and been given details of Marianne's financial prospects. The Baron was furious when he discovered the mistake. I immediately said we would leave but he laughed, rather unpleasantly, and said it wouldn't be as easy as that. As he pointed out I was his wife and he expected me to obey him and, anyway, where would we go and how would we get there? We really were miles away from anywhere. He said we could all earn our keep for the time being, and there the matter rested.

Over the next few weeks we made friends with Eleanor. She told us the Baron had married her mother 6 years earlier, when Eleanor was 10. Eleanor said he had tricked them too and her mother was so unhappy she planned they would run away. But she had died and Eleanor was left alone to work for the Baron and his mother. Eleanor also warned us Mr. Button was a dangerous violent man not to be trusted and she suspected he had something to do with her mother's death.

All these revelations were frightening. I had no experience of such matters and initially could only think to instruct Rose and Lily, who fortunately at 14 and 12 were sensible girls, to be careful and keep out of the way of the three adults in the house, while I thought of a plan. Although I had no practical expertise I had run a well ordered house and instructed my servants in their various duties so I was able to lighten Eleanor's workload. Assisted by her, I undertook to work in the kitchen and, with trial and error, between us we produced edible meals and standards of cleanliness in the house improved. It was hard physical work I wasn't used to but at the time I believed there was no alternative but to placate the Baron and make him think I wouldn't cause him any trouble.

My husband was away a lot though back every night, maybe trying to replenish his fortune, and Mr. Button usually accompanied his master. The Baron's mother kept an eye on me and the girls during the day but seldom spoke and we tried to keep out of her way.

This uneasy life had lasted less than two months when Eleanor had a quiet word with me and said she had been spoken to by two men when she was hanging out the washing in the orchard. They had reassured her not to be frightened and asked her to tell me to meet them the next day in the same place, out of sight of the house. I thought I had nothing to lose and I also had another fear I hadn't shared with Eleanor, who was becoming a close ally. From some things my husband had said I believed he planned to find a husband who would pay him a dowry for Eleanor (and later presumably Rose and Lily) and I was determined not to let that happen.

I therefore wandered towards the orchard the following morning, complete with a basket as though I planned to collect some fruit. At the far side of the field my attention was attracted and I walked over to where two men were hiding. They quickly introduced themselves as Law Officers Daniel Dean and his assistant Bryn Chalmers, and said they were looking for Baron Stanley Brook in connection with the suspicious deaths of his wives.

They knew about me because Marianne had been concerned by our hurried departure and her husband had been persuaded to make some enquiries regarding our whereabouts. He then discovered the Baron was already being investigated with regard to the deaths of his previous brides. Apparently Eleanor's mother had not been his first wife to suddenly die. This information really astounded me. I had come to believe both the

Baron and his mother were unpleasant creatures, and witnessed their ill-treatment of Eleanor, but found it hard to credit they were anything other than vindictive bullies.

However I was anxious to help and answered all the officers' questions honestly, albeit with considerable embarrassment. When I explained how I met and married the Baron they were extremely sympathetic, especially Mr. Dean. They warned me they planned to arrest the Baron, his mother and also Mr. Button the following day, early in the morning. Until then it would be best to keep the girls out of their way.

While we were talking I'd already decided we would all pretend to be ill and would stay together in one of the bedrooms, and that is what we did. As a precaution during the day we hid some food upstairs and also moved some items of furniture to barricade the door if this became necessary. In the afternoon I told the Baron's mother that the girls were all unwell with suspected food poisoning and I had sent them to bed. I also hinted I might be suffering with the same problem. The Baron and Mr. Button arrived home about 7 o'clock. I had laid out a cold collation for them and, making my excuses, I went upstairs.

None of us slept that night as we anticipated the hammering on the front door and shouts to open up. Mr. Button slept downstairs and the Baron instructed him to delay the intruders. I could hear the Baron and his mother on the landing by our room debating what to do for the best. The Baron must have decided to bluff his way out because he called out "I'm coming" and apparently when he opened the front door he presented as the affable person I had first met in Bath. He invited the officers in and ushered them into the drawing room, which was quite presentable thanks to my hard work.

"My wife and daughters are abed." is what he said. "I'd rather you didn't disturb them. Women are such delicate creatures."

This had no effect on the officers who had painstakingly proved a case of multiple murder against the Baron, his mother and Mr. Button. It was believed two of the Baron's wives had been poisoned but one, Eleanor's mother, had met with an accident in suspicious circumstances which could only have been as a result of a violent assault, it was believed by Mr. Button. He had a reputation as a man to be feared for his uncontrollable temper and it was known there were unexplained marks on her body. Her death had prompted the investigations but it was only recently proof of their misdeeds was obtained. Messrs' Dean and Chalmers had been aware of Eleanor's predicament but unfortunately could do nothing about it. They had also been taken by surprise when the Baron returned from

Bath with yet another wife. That was when they decided the time had come to act.

In the end all three were found guilty of murder. The Baron and Mr. Button were hanged. The Baron's mother was declared insane and committed to an Asylum. It was actually thought she was the instigator of the fiendish crimes. As the widow the Baron I inherited his house and surprisingly quite a large amount of money. After discussion with my three girls (because of course Eleanor is now part of our family) we decided to remain in Yorkshire and restore the house. I have received much encouragement from Dan Dean but it's obvious when they visit us Bryn isn't coming to see me. Eleanor is blossoming. The future looks good and we all expect to live happily ever after.

COLIN AND BILL

Ros Emery

For three years Colin and I were inseparable. We spent all our free time together down by the river or exploring the woods. Colin knows such a lot about flora and fauna and he was happy to share his knowledge regarding the Latin names of plants and the habitats of animals and birds, which he said he'd learnt through reading the books in his grandfather's library. We'd pretend to be trackers or pirates, play hide and seek in the woods or would just lie on the ground watching the clouds scudding across the sky. So long as Colin wasn't late for meals no-one bothered. Various tutors came and went. It seems they generally felt uncomfortable as it wasn't a very happy household and none of them stayed long.

The large house they lived in had belonged to Colin's maternal grandfather. His mother never let her husband forget this fact. She came to believe he had married her for her position and wealth though when they first met she must have been impressed with his military bearing and air of authority. Now alas Clive was past his prime but still prided himself on his sporting prowess and thought of himself as a man's man. Colin's mother had long ceased to care for him but nevertheless she derived pleasure from goading him.

Colin was a disappointment to both his parents for different reasons. His father wanted a son who was an all-round sportsman he could show off to his friends at the various clubs he belonged to. His mother wanted a bright intelligent child who would entrance her friends at the numerous social events she attended. Colin was a dreamy bookish boy, shy and lacking physical co-ordination and painfully aware he didn't measure up to his parents' expectations.

Mrs. Palmer the cook did her best to make Colin's life a little happier. When his mother was absent, as she frequently was, she let Colin help her in the kitchen, though warning him not to tell his mother as she wouldn't understand. Mrs. Palmer never took any notice of me when I was in the kitchen. When Colin introduced me she just said "That's nice. It's good to have a friend." Generally I didn't go to the kitchen with Colin because I knew he was being looked after and enjoying himself. He didn't need me. Milly the housemaid did notice me but she would only smile and giggle. She never said anything.

I first spoke to Colin the morning after his 6th birthday. The previous day had been a disaster. Clive had given him a complete cricket set. Colin was used to receiving inappropriate presents from his father but unfortunately that day his father decided they should try out all the new equipment on the lawn. After setting up the wickets and marking out the crease he insisted on bowling a few "easy" balls, which of course Colin missed by a mile. As time went by, and with a sarcastic commentary from his wife, Clive's good mood evaporated and he lost his temper, yelling at Colin that he was useless and he didn't know why he bothered with him. The birthday meal was a miserable affair before Clive sent Colin to bed in tears and had yet another row with his wife.

Colin cried himself to sleep but when he awoke I was there and I know he was pleased to see me. "What's your name?" he asked. "What would you like to call me?" I replied. "Bill." he said. "That's fine. Call me Bill." So Bill I am.

We talked and talked, discovering so much in common. Colin had never had a best friend before and each morning he would plan our day together. He always asked me what I'd like to do but I was content to go anywhere with him. As I said, we did everything together. We were two against the world. We were so happy. We didn't need anyone else.

Then, when he was nine, Clive announced Colin would be going to his old school as a boarder. Colin was devastated and appealed to his mother but for once she agreed with her husband, and said it was about time he stopped wasting his time with dull books and learnt to mix with his social equals.

Colin and I made a lot of promises and had a touching farewell ceremony on the river bank. Colin even had the brilliant idea to carve our names on a tree nearby. He assured me he'd soon be back and everything would be as before.

It wasn't of course. I don't know how long it was before he came back. Although I know about seconds, minutes, weeks and months my concept of time is vague. Time is just how long it takes for something to happen then there is a gap until the next experience. That is how I can look back on the three years we spent together as one long event. So Colin came back from boarding school but he wasn't the same. He was busy making plans for his return to school, which he apparently loved. It was obvious he'd made some new friends and he was looking forward to seeing them again. That first time he didn't actually ignore me but he was preoccupied and I waited in vain for him to confide in me. The next and subsequent short vacations at home were even worse. Very quickly he avoided looking at me and eventually it was as if I wasn't there. He made it clear he had a new life and I wasn't included.

Now I wait, sometimes by the river but more often in the house, in his room. I don't really know what I'm waiting for. My life is over. I have no hope. I have no future. I did briefly think I might find a friend in Milly. I know she sees me. When she does she smiles, but never speaks. She has no imagination.

ALL'S WELL THAT ENDS WELL?
Sequel to "COLIN AND BILL"

Ros Emery

"You know Bill, don't you son?" The question hung in the air. Colin was completely taken aback. It was such an ordinary question, delivered in a matter of fact manner, yet that in itself was strange because his father hadn't said a civil word to him for weeks. He'd clearly resented what he perceived to be Colin's maliciousness forcing him to move against his will into a Residential Home of Colin's choosing and when his son visited him he either ignored him or ranted against his current circumstances. The Care Home staff who had also borne the brunt of Clive's anger assured Colin his father's attitude wasn't unexpected though so far no-one had been able to gain his trust. They reported this was rather unusual as, certainly after a couple of weeks, new residents generally became attached to at least one of their carers. But Clive had made it clear he hated everyone, most of all his son, and he refused to co-operate in any way.

Colin was reluctant to affirm that actually Clive's attitude was fairly consistent with the way he had spent his entire life. He'd neglected his wife and bullied his son. Muriel had long since gone her own way and now lived in a south coast resort with a young man not much older than her son. Colin, once he'd been sent away to boarding school when he was 9, seldom returned home but succeeded in carving out a very successful career for himself. Clive had continued to use the family home as his base. Because Colin's maternal grandfather had left the house in trust for Colin it couldn't be sold and Muriel had no wish to live in it. As the years went by Clive couldn't be bothered to deal even with basic problems so it had been slowly rotting away. Colin was alerted to the conditions his father was living in by the family solicitors, following a major structural collapse. Father and son hadn't seen each other for more than 10 years. They had never had anything in common and although Colin bore his father no ill-will he'd had no desire to spend any time with him.

He was shocked however as he drove up the overgrown drive towards the dilapidated house. Even more shocking was the rather grubby old man who initially mistook him for an official from the Council. Apparently they had been trying to gain admittance for some time and he'd refused to see them. When he realised who Colin actually was, Clive wasn't particularly pleased. He endeavoured to adopt his previous bullying tactics but Colin was no longer the shy impressionable youngster Clive had terrorised. Quickly grasping the situation he didn't stay long, and when he returned to his penthouse apartment he contacted the solicitors.

Over the next couple of months, having heard from his mother that she wasn't interested, Colin inspected various establishments with a view to providing suitable care for his father. Clive had no resources of his own, the family money emanating entirely from Muriel, but fortunately Colin was now a very wealthy young man and could ensure his father wanted for nothing. That said, it was apparent Clive didn't want anything that came from Colin but it was clear he didn't had a grasp on reality and obviously didn't recognise the dangers living alone in a structurally unsafe building.

The Elms Residential/Nursing Home won hands down when it came to suitability for Clive and he moved there three months later. Even before he moved Clive became increasingly morose, completely ignoring Colin and barely speaking to anyone else. Regarding the house, Colin employed a structural engineer and, following his report, authorised full scale renovations which commenced as soon as Clive had moved out.

Physically Clive had improved considerably over the past couple of months but his mental attitude was worrying. He was always so angry and obviously unhappy. On the face of it therefore it was gratifying to Colin, and presumably a relief to the Care staff, that Clive was conversing pleasantly, almost jovially. What perturbed Colin however was the reference to Bill. In more than 20 years he hadn't given Bill a thought. Surely Clive couldn't be referring to "his" Bill.

Without waiting for a reply Clive continued to chat amiably, saying how happy he was to be among such nice people. He couldn't speak too highly of the excellent staff, the food and the comfortable surroundings. Colin was aware of an enthusiasm about Clive he'd never seen before. Towards the end of the visit, Clive once again referred to Bill.

"Come back soon, dear boy" he said. "If the weather's nice I'm hoping we can go with Bill to the lakeside. He particularly likes it there. He's fond of the water, don't you know? We just sit on the bank and jaw or lie back and watch the clouds."

Colin made his farewells and went to find the Matron to ask if some stranger called Bill had been visiting his father. She was expecting him.

"You'll have noticed the change in your father" she said. "Of course unfortunately its not all good news. We think your father has a rare form of dementia. He sees things, or rather people, that aren't there. To him they appear real. Actually it's likely there's only one character. You could call him an imaginary friend because of course he doesn't exist. But your father is now much happier and content, and that's nice isn't it? We're very pleased for him."

All Colin's memories of Bill came flooding back. How happy they'd been. He felt a pang of guilt. When he didn't need him any more he'd conveniently forgotten him. He remembered the hours they'd spent on the river bank watching the clouds. How could Clive have known Bill was fond of water?

It wasn't long before Colin discovered his father's Bill and his own were the same. The three of them spent many hours together that summer, initially in the grounds of The Elms and later at the family home, now reduced in size and since renovation more suitable for a bachelor with frequent visits by his father. There were no recriminations from Bill. As he explained, time stood still for him. He had waited for Colin to return. He'd barely been aware that the house was deteriorating and because he was used to being ignored he hadn't expected Clive to notice him. Then Colin came back, focused only on his father's situation. Clive had also paid no attention to his surroundings until the very last minute when he was forced to move. His anger and frustration awoke Bill who, realising there would be disruption with builders in the house, decided to follow Clive to his new home. There he waited until one day Clive recognised him. They'd talked and Clive's life took on a new meaning. Bill told

Clive of his friendship with Colin and later they showed Clive where Colin had carved their names on the tree by the river before he went away to boarding school. Now Colin added Clive's name as a memento of their happy times together.

MEET THE FAMILY

Ros Emery

Thomas Walker was feeling particularly pleased when the family meal concluded without the usual bickering. Everyone seemed conscious that tonight was special and long standing disagreements were temporarily forgotten. Thomas sat back, brandy in hand, and surveyed his family. For once his wife Clare had made an effort, as she usually didn't deign to join him for dinner. She seldom spoke to him nowadays and then only to criticise or complain. And to think he hadn't believed his luck when the pretty quietly spoken daughter at the big house had shyly agreed to be his wife. How quickly she'd transformed into a sullen creature who made no secret she despised anyone she classed as inferior, and that included her husband. He'd long since become reconciled to the fact that she'd only married him for his money, though despite seldom missing an opportunity to belittle his background in trade she had no qualms spending the profits generated by his factory.

He took a moment to consider her consternation if she knew how close they had come to losing everything, including this house, but tonight when the engagement of their daughter Emma was officially announced all their financial problems would be over. Johnny Dawson had promised to invest some much needed cash into the business and had also indicated he wasn't averse to taking an active role in the running of the company. This was a great relief to Thomas as he had become aware that his son and heir Neil was never going to be an asset and in fact some of Neil's recent mistakes were contributing to the company's present parlous situation. He was much happier to know that his factory would be in the safe hands of his son-in-law.

Clare was also pleased her daughter's engagement was to be announced after dinner when Thomas's boring friends from the town council were coming for drinks and to meet Emma's fiance. He'd been expected to join the family for dinner but had been unavoidably delayed and promised to come later. Emma and Johnny had met at a trade dinner when Emma was accompanying her father. For some years Emma had gone with Thomas to official functions because her mother refused to have anything to do with "trade". Clare had actually never met Johnny and had evinced no interest in the blossoming romance. She and Emma were not close so tonight Clare's only feeling was relief that Emma would be leaving home soon and no longer be an irritation to her. She had always resented Emma and anything her daughter did was of no concern to her.

Clare's feelings for Neil her son were totally different. She doted on him, supporting him when his father insisted he spend more time at the factory and less on frivolous pursuits. Actually Neil was spoilt and easily led but his mother wouldn't hear a word against him. She lent him money and covered up for him when he got into scrapes. Neil resented her attention but tonight he was in good spirits because he believed his life was set to change and soon he would be an attractive assured man about town, like his best friend Charles. He thought they were about to make a fortune and would be moving into a smart apartment together.

At 30 Charles was ten years older than Neil and considerably more astute. He knew Thomas didn't quite trust him but Clare had been easily won over by his good manners and deferential attitude. She approved of him as a friend for her son, because she believed he came from a similar background to herself. Certainly when she regaled him with anecdotes of her superior antecedents he appeared to listen with rapt attention and she never guessed how he despised her and thought her a snob. It was true his early life had been privileged but, like her own parent, his father had spectacularly squandered the family fortune and Charles had been obliged to make a living by his wits from a very early age.

In effect he was a con-man, until now fairly successful, but his latest scheme showed signs of imploding very shortly. Charles was not too worried however because as usual he had a contingency plan. Unfortunately this meant Neil would he the one left to face the music and this time it was a criminal matter. But he just hoped Neil's father would be able to pull some strings and save his son from a lengthy prison sentence. Tonight he'd accepted the invitation to dinner in his role as family friend and, always on the lookout for another mark, he was also interested to meet Emma's fiancé. He had heard of him of course and was aware he was extremely wealthy.

After their initial meeting, Thomas had encouraged the friendship between his daughter and Johnny as he was desperate to find someone to invest in his failing company and Johnny had a reputation for turning failure into success, and their romance had blossomed as they discovered they had much in common. Emma, though anxious to leave home, also realised how fortunate she was to be marrying such an eligible man. Not only was he extremely wealthy and generous (she delighted in showing her envious girl friends the enormous solitaire engagement ring he had given her) he was also devastatingly handsome. He was known to be a self-made man, which she believed wouldn't impress her mother but her father didn't care where the money came from.

The diners at the table got up when they heard the maid answer the doorbell. Drinks were to be served in the drawing room and they made their way towards the hall where the guests were laughing because, despite the bad weather, they had all arrived together. Mayor Anderson had brought his wife. It was expected Thomas would succeed him, though the question of who would be Lady Mayoress with Emma leaving was problematic. Thomas hoped Clare would realise this role was sufficiently important for her to undertake. Until now Clare had shown no interest in his work on the council. She did not know the other two councillors Thomas had invited to share their good news nor their wives.

Clare was slightly ahead of the others but in the doorway she literally staggered back, her face ashen. "You!" she gasped before collapsing on the floor. In the split seconds before she hit the parquet she remembered the son who had been born when she was 16 in the discreet mother and baby home, which was later referred to as a finishing school. Even now after 33 years she could still recall how devastatingly handsome the gardener's boy had been.

THE VALENTINE

Ros Emery

Although Brendan had never actually spoken to Maureen he knew who she was and thought she was the loveliest girl he'd ever seen. In his dreams he imagined being part of her group of friends but he was painfully shy meeting people, becoming tongue-tied and inarticulate, so this was unlikely to ever happen. With people he knew, his work colleagues, he was popular and well-liked. His employers valued him because he was conscientious and efficient and his workmates enjoyed his dry sense of humour and good nature. He could always be relied upon. Nothing was too much trouble. The only failing they perceived was his lack of confidence and despite their best efforts he could seldom be persuaded to join in any social events.

Brendan lodged with Mrs. McIver, who treated him as the grandson she'd never had. He had been orphaned at an early age and there hadn't been much stability in his life until he met her and then there was an instant connection which had strengthened over the years. She fussed over him and worried about him, urging him to go out and make new friends, but he was more than content to help about the house and keep her company. He was clever with his hands and very artistic. Their home was a tribute to his talent and they were very happy together.

Maureen and her best friend Kate had planned a trip to the cinema but at the last minute Kate developed a sore throat and called off their arrangement. Maureen however decided to go to the cinema anyway and consequently found herself alone when the fire alarm went off and the audience rushed towards the exits. Maureen being small and slight was at a distinct disadvantage but she managed to make her way to a wall rather than be caught up in the middle of the crowd. That was how she stumbled across a small brown dog cowering in an alcove. Without thinking she scooped him up and clutching him to her managed to edge along the wall towards an exit into the street.

As she gasped for breath on the pavement Brendan rounded the corner and saw her. She was already on his mind because he was debating whether to post the Valentine Card he had painted for her, signed from "an admirer". He was confident she would never discover who had sent it but wanted to please her and let her know that someone thought she was special. Seeing her his dilemma was forgotten and his only thought was to do whatever he could to help. She was dishevelled and obviously shaken but he couldn't help notice close to she was even more beautiful than he'd imagined. She in turn recognised him as the young man she saw nearly every day who seemingly made a point of always avoiding her when she was quite prepared to acknowledge him and say hello. She had confided in Kate that she thought him rather standoffish but Kate pronounced "I think he fancies you!"

Now Maureen had the opportunity to look directly into Brendan's face and note that far from being shifty and evasive he had kind eyes and looked genuinely concern.

"What can I do to help?" he asked.

"I'm alright" she replied "but I'm worried about the dog. He's petrified."

"Here, let me take him and come with me." he said.

Cradling the dog with one arm, without thinking he supported her with the other and they walked the short distance to his home. Letting himself in he shouted for Mrs. McIver who came from the kitchen and immediately took charge of the dog, wrapping him in a fluffy towel and making soothing noises.

"There's some chicken in the fridge Brendan" she said "and then put the kettle on to make a hot drink for your friend and yourself. What would you like my dear? Brendan only drinks coffee but myself I like a cup of tea."

Maureen found her voice. "I prefer coffee too, thank you" she said.

The dog curled up on a cushion in front of the fire after tucking into a plate of chicken, introductions were made all round and soon the three of them were sitting at the kitchen table drinking coffee and tea and eating Mrs. McIver's delicious cake and chatting like old friends.

Maureen explained how she had found the dog. Once safely outside it had become apparent the fire was a false alarm but she had then been in a quandary what to do about the dog. Brendan, much to Mrs. McIver's surprise and later his own, appeared to have taken charge of the situation and came up with a solution which suited everyone, namely the dog would remain with him and Mrs. McIver but he would make enquiries at the cinema to discover what it had been doing there and if it actually belonged to anyone. It didn't have a collar.

Maureen and Brendan were so engrossed in their conversation a little later they didn't notice Mrs. McIver left them to get to know each other and busied herself in another room. The dog fell asleep, not realising he would never again have to find shelter wherever he could (which was what he was doing in the cinema) and scrounge for scraps.

The Valentine Card was not posted though Brendan produced it the next Valentine's Day when he and Maureen were on honeymoon in Venice.

Lucky and Mrs. McIver were at home eagerly awaiting their return.

LORAINE FELCE

THE STATEMENT

Loraine Felce

'What, our Eric a bomber! Don't be daft!'
Nevertheless Eric's family had to concede that initial investigations indicated that Eric had indeed been responsible for the destruction of a passenger plane.
Up until a couple of weeks ago, 56 year old Eric had never been on a plane before. Having lived with his mother all his life, Eric's only holidays had been with her in England.
At first living at home was convenient. For a small weekly amount Eric got all his washing, cleaning, ironing and cooking done. Him and his mum had the same interests both enjoying bridge and singing in the church choir.
As time went on and his mum got older, convenience turned to habit for him and necessity for her.
Then about five years ago, after his mum had a fall in the garden, Eric left work to care for her full-time. Holidays ceased and there was no more bridge or choir. Not that Eric had much to sing about.
He tried to enlist the help of his brothers but they always had the same excuse, that basically, they had a life.

Hard that it was, he had always promised his mum that she would not end up in a nursing home. When she died aged 89 peacefully at home, he knew he had fulfilled his promise.

Given the last five years, he was surprised that his brothers were shocked to hear that his mum had left him everything and when they bitterly said that he would not know how to spend it, he was determined to prove them wrong and booked himself a five star all-inclusive holiday.

'This is for starters' he said.

Secretly, he was nervous. He had never been abroad before nor was he an outgoing type. When he found an old self-help book on his mum's bookshelf called, 'Wake Up and Live' he was delighted. Apparently, it seemed that the key to not being a social bore were rules. Eric decided on the following:

1. No drinking before 6pm
2. Dress smartly for dinner
3. Never be the last in the bar.

As a measure of social success, the book suggested the obtaining of pen pals. Eric considered email addresses to be the modern equivalent and set himself a target of three including one from a member of the opposite sex.

The week went pretty much to plan. Eric stuck to his rules. He added a further one about giving tips as this seemed to ensure he got served before others in the bar. The one rule he could not control was the obtaining of email addresses. He had managed to obtain two, both from elderly German gentlemen but despite his best efforts, by the last day of the holiday he had not managed to secure one from a member of the opposite sex.

As Eric sat in the departure lounge waiting for his return flight home he wondered whether he might have one last chance to do this. It was then that she found him.

'Is anyone sitting here?' the woman asked flashing him a smile.

'No'. Eric blushed.

'Hard travelling on your own' she said sitting down.

'It is my first time alone. I have quite enjoyed it.' He omitted to say that all his previous holidays had been with his mother or that he had never been abroad before.

'Ren'

'Eric' he responded.

Eric thought that Ren was the most striking woman he had ever seen. He could not tell her age or where she was from. She was a mystery. Before he could explore further he was rather embarrassingly caught short. Regretting eating last night's devil chicken, only done to impress a young lady in a failed quest for her email address, he quickly asked

Ren to look after his case and hurried off in search of a bathroom.

When he returned Ren was gone and, there, sitting on its own was his case. Maybe she had been caught short too he thought. Anyway at least he had not caused a security alert and ended up with a blown up case.

Tinged with the embarrassment at what might have been he made his way to the gate. When he got there, to his surprise he saw Ren waiting to board the plane. He found himself smiling at her as she did him. 'Sorry' she mouthed.

Eric was sure his book would have advised him not to go over so he took a seat elsewhere. As boarding time neared, passengers including Eric formed a queue to board. It was only at that point that he noticed the sign saying that the airline had put in place additional security and that passengers could be requested to turn on electronic devices and have their bags checked before boarding.

Staff with bomb detectors appeared and randomly selected people from the queue. When the man with the detector got to Eric he waved him away meaning he could join the boarding card queue and get on the plane. Out the corner of his eye, he saw that Ren had no such luck and had to join the queue to be searched. Eric could not help but smile to himself.

Once on the plane Eric put his bag in the locker and sat in his chosen aisle seat. He was trying not to look for Ren but he could not help himself. Finally she appeared and sat two rows behind him on the other side of the plane. After takeoff, partly to take his mind off her, he decided to watch a film on his tablet. He got up and opened the locker but the tablet he pulled out of his case was not his. It was definitely much older and heavier.

Surely Ren had not stolen his tablet. He turned round and caught her eye. She gave him a wink. He might have got up and gone over to her but at that point the fasten seatbelt sign appeared.

He wanted to be annoyed with her but it was a long time since a female had winked at him, if ever. He was not sure what it meant but he was sure it was good. Then Eric had a sudden thought, maybe she had left him a message. Silly that it was Eric found himself switching on the tablet. He watched as the screen flashed on. There was no message but definitely a statement. Unfortunately the realisation of this came too late for Eric and all those on board flight TY7891.

NEW BEGINNINGS

Loraine Felce

Marcus had never been on holiday alone. As a child he went with his parents, then with his mates and from the age of 29 to the age of 45 he had gone with his partner.
Marcus had not been on holiday for three years. He had done very little since his partner died. He no longer went to the shops, making use of the Internet. He no longer went to restaurants or bars.
'I have eaten the best and drunk with the worst' he would say.

The only thing Marcus really did involving other people was work. He had declared himself fit for work soon after his partner's death. When the news of what had happened faded, he was left to get on with his job. He was good at work, enjoyed it and his change in lifestyle meant his savings had never looked so healthy.

When Marcus was invited to a wedding in *that* place, his friends said everyone would understand if he declined, but Marcus did not decline. To go back there with no reason might be seen as morbid, but to go back to celebrate someone else's beginning was surely allowed.

Friends urged him to go on holiday somewhere else. 'Forget the wedding. Create new memories' they said but Marcus wanted to stand in an old footprint.

When he arrived at the hotel, the receptionist stared at the empty space next to him. Marcus felt lost. He quickly escaped to his hotel room, but the superior room with king size bed and balcony with whirlpool seemed ridiculous. What was he doing alone in 5-star luxury? An in-room massage or the usual late night bottle of champagne felt out of the question.

Marcus took himself to what had been their favourite restaurant. Nothing had changed, not even the waiters. Marcus had always mocked his partner for having expensive taste, but tonight he ordered a large glass of the most expensive red wine on the menu. As he sipped it, he touched the seat next to him in case, then held the glass to his lips in case, before dabbing his lips slowly with his napkin in case.

The restaurant owner came over.

'On the house' he said plonking down the rest of the bottle of expensive wine.

'Only if you join me' said Marcus.

The owner sat down and poured himself a glass.

'Bastards' he said chinking Marcus' glass. 'Bastards' had been the preferred toast of Marcus and his partner.
Marcus laughed. Then cried.
'Bastards, Complete and Utter' he said through his tears clinking the owner's glass. Then he raised his glass to the sky.
'Whatever star you have ended up on, I hope they serve a decent red'.

Back in the hotel, Marcus ordered to his room a bottle of champagne. He also sent a bottle to the bride to be's room with a note.
'To new beginnings. Thank you for the invitation. Love M x'.

DYING TO LIVE

Loraine Felce

'Sorry my English' said the receptionist.
'It's great' said Alice. She was always amazed how apologetic people were for their English when she spoke not one word of their language.
'Taxi, me book.'
'No. I have already booked. We wait' said Marcus.
'Of course. Please seat.'
Marcus and Alice made their way to the sofas next to the fire.
'Why does it always go so quickly?' asked Alice.
'It's called a weekend away.'
'I know but I want to stay here forever, eating nachos and drinking beer. Who would have thought that Eastern Europeans would make such great nachos? And the hotel, I love these grand hotels. Fading beautifully like we will one day.'
'Stop now with your cheesiness' said Marcus grabbing Alice's hand.
They sat in silence. Going back was always hard. Back to work. Back to life.
As they stared at the fire, they did not see the taxi driver come in.
'Taxi. Marcus' he shouted.

'Barstard' said Alice under her breath. There was a bit of Alice who wanted to ignore him, but the less rebellious Marcus got up.
'Come on you' he said to Alice.
As Marcus shook the receptionist's hand, Alice whispered 'bye-bye hotel'.

As the taxi began its journey to the airport through the city and along the river, Marcus and Alice once again became aware of the beauty of the place. Lit by the moon, the castle on the hill dominated, as it had done all those years ago, when whoever lived in the castle was king in one way or another.
'Look at it. How can we leave this behind for Peckham?'
'We live in Peckham and our jobs in London pay for these holidays.'
'You mean yours. My job pays for nothing' said Alice.
'We are a team. We share.'
'I want to stay here forever' said Alice in her best child's voice.
'I love you' said Marcus.
At this the taxi driver, turned his head.
'Love' he said tutting.
Marcus half smiled but wished the driver would keep his eyes on the road.
'I was once in love.'

Marcus was willing him to concentrate on the job in hand but it was too late, a car came across their path. The taxi driver slammed on his brakes causing the taxi to skid and mount the pavement. Hitting the river wall, the taxi came to a halt.

The next thing Alice remembered was climbing out of the car. She was not sure what had happened. She remembered a crunch, then dark, then silence, then bright light but not much else. As she walked away from the car she saw people running towards it, they crowded round it. Alice could not see what was happening.
'Marcus' she said out loud.
She could see the wretched taxi driver staggering around and being assisted into an ambulance, but where was Marcus.
'Come on' she said making her way back to the car. She could see some people pulling at the car doors but everything was blurred and then she saw him lying on the floor. One man was kneeling next to him, trying to resuscitate him.
'Marcus'.
A man tapped her on her shoulder. 'Come away. You can't help' he said.
'I love you. Don't leave me' she shouted bursting into tears.

The man led her to a park bench where she sat, staring, waiting. The man held her hand. She thought him kind, but she wanted Marcus.
As she saw people shake their heads, her hope turned to despair and she buried her head on the man's shoulder.

When she could bear to look again she looked up and there he was in front of her.
'Marcus. Are you ok?'
'I have felt better. Mind you....' said Marcus pointing at the wreck of a car.
'I am glad you decided to join us' said the man.
'Jasper' he said holding out his hand. Marcus politely shook it.
'Not a firm handshake, but never mind for now. Welcome both.'
'Welcome to what?' said Alice.
'Death.'
'Death' they both repeated.
The man gestured towards the written off car.
'Don't worry it is not all bad. You are lucky. You get to stay on holiday. You see you die where you fall and there you remain. In your case, you were on holiday and so you remain as tourists. Forever.'
'Cool. I think. What about you?' said Alice.
'Me I was a diplomat, a civil servant. Ergo, I am responsible for all the ex-pats here. I will help you in any way I can. Right, good, so what do you need

to know before I take you back to your hotel? Ah yes, money. You are given what you brought and that will be topped up as you spend it.'
'I didn't bring any' said Alice.
'Ahh' said Jasper.
'I brought plenty so we can share, right?'
'Of course. This isn't prison. You can give Alice what you want for as long as you are happy to do so. Otherwise she would need to, well, urm, get a job.'
'No need. This holiday was my treat and will continue to be so.'
'If you don't mind me saying, this is all a bit mad' said Alice.
'They all say that. Right, your bags are in your room waiting.'
'But we checked out. Won't others be booked in?'
'This is death Alice. Think same space, different time. You will soon get the hang of it. Come on, let's walk.'

If Marcus and Alice had thought about it they might have imagined death to be silent, dark or eerie but what they saw was quite different. It was loud, colourful and animated. The streets were full of people. Some were dressed like Marcus and Alice. Others were in much older style clothing, ladies in long sweeping dresses with bustles and petticoats and men in top hats and long coats or in caps and breeches. There were cars, buses, trams, taxis, bicycles, horses and carriages and even the occasional chariot.

'Newbies and they are with me' said Jasper to anyone whose attention they attracted.

'Is he ok?' said one man pointing at Marcus.

'Not yet, but he will be.'

It was true that Marcus was feeling pretty rough. Alice on the other hand didn't seem to feel any different. She squeezed Marcus' hand.

The nice hotel receptionist from earlier was, of course, not there. Instead there was an old lady behind the desk. She spoke no English and made no attempt to converse with the couple. Jasper spoke to her and translated where he needed to.

Before he went, Jasper gave them his card. While they politely thanked him for his help, they were glad when he was gone and they were back in their room.

'I am glad we booked a five star now' said Alice.

'Forever is a long time. Imagine if we had died on a camping holiday.'

Marcus smiled. He loved her silliness.

'I could sleep forever' he said collapsing on the bed.

'You ok?'

'It must just be the shock. I probably just need a rest.'

In the morning, Marcus was no better but he was determined not to let it ruin things.

'Let's go to the bridge after breakfast. Then we can hit a doubles bar and see how long we last.'

And so they did. Marcus was not up to walking too far so they took a horse and carriage back from the bridge which dropped them off at the doubles bar. Marcus tipped the man handsomely knowing that there was plenty more where that came from. The doubles bar was a short walk from the hotel so nicely drunk they staggered back home at about 4.30pm for a late afternoon nap. Once back at the hotel they both slept. It was unusual for Marcus to sleep during the day but when Alice awoke in the evening, he was still asleep. She did not wake him.

The next day, Marcus was still unwell and rather pale, but again he did not want to spoil their fun.

'We can stay in. We are on permanent vacation so we have plenty of time' said Alice.

'No, shoes for my baby' he said. 'Those ones you packed are not suitable for long-term tourist life.'

So off they went. The main shops were not far but they stopped a few times for Marcus who seemed a bit short of breath.

'If you do not get any better you will need to see a doctor.'

'We are dead. I suspect the last thing I need is a doctor' said Marcus.

'Yes I suppose whatever you have got cannot kill you' Alice said with a smile.

But quietly she was concerned about him. Marcus was never sick. He hadn't had a day off work in seven years. It was her job to lie in bed with some flu bug or headache.

When the next day he was still no better and opted to stay in bed, she dug out Jasper's card and went to see him.

'I know this sounds daft but I think Marcus needs to see a doctor. He is definitely still suffering from the effects of the crash.'

Jasper scribbled a number on a piece of paper and handed it to Alice.

'Call this number. Mention me. We have everything in death. Remember doctors die too.'

Alice did as she was told. She explained to the receptionist the problem and was given an appointment the next day.

Marcus was not keen to go, but when later that day he coughed up a little blood, he agreed to attend.

The doctor's surgery was just like back home minus the patients. Despite this, the receptionist said that the doctor was very busy and would see Marcus when he could. Ten minutes later the doctor appeared at his door and gestured for Marcus to come in.

Marcus explained his symptoms and said how rubbish he felt. The doctor asked him if anything made him feel better to which the answer was 'no'. The doctor listened to his chest before slumping back into his chair.

'Am I OK?'

'Sort of. It depends what you mean by OK. To put it simply you are not dead. Or dying. You are still alive.'

'No I died in the car crash. I told you.'

'No you didn't. I suspect you came very close to it and that your heart stopped at some point, but somehow you were brought back to life.'

'I can't be alive. What about Alice?'

'There is always a dead woman involved. No doubt she was calling for you to be with her. I am sorry, but the fact is that you are alive. I am afraid the longer you stay here the sicker you will become until … well to be frank you will lose the use of your limbs and your speech will go and then it will be too late. You still won't belong here, well probably not for years and at the same time you will no longer have a role in life, just an existence.'

'Can't you assist me to die?'

'My dear boy, I am a doctor. You still have a life to live. You do not exist yet in death. It is important you understand the gravity of your situation.'

'What can I do?'

'Live' said the doctor handing him a prescription. 'Take the tablet before bed. You will go into a deep sleep and when you wake up you will hopefully be back where you belong, without too much damage done.'

As Marcus got to the door, the doctor said, 'she will understand.'

'How long have I got?'

'You are on the proverbial borrowed time now. Another day at best.'

Alice smiled when she saw the prescription.

'I knew a doctor would help.'

Marcus could not speak. Taking her hand, they slowly made their way out of the doctor's surgery. Nearby there was a bar.

'Let's stop here' said Marcus.

'But we need to get the prescription.'

'Not yet. Let's have a bottle of red. The best they have.'

The bar was dark and pretty much empty. Alice snuggled up next to Marcus.

'Did the doctor say what was wrong?'

Marcus did not answer. Instead, he squeezed her hand.

'Are you ill?'

'No. Not ill.' Marcus took a deep breath. 'I am alive. I am so sorry. I asked the doctor to help but he can't. He said that I didn't exist yet in death.'

'But the prescription?'

'Something to help bring me back to life, some sort of sleeping tablet. Maybe I should see someone else?'

Alice paused then shook her head. Neither of them had any words. Alice was fighting back the tears. She wanted to be brave but she could not bear to lose him. They were so good together. Everyone said that.

'I don't know what I will do without you' she said taking a deep breath. 'I'm sorry. I should be pleased for you. You are alive. It is just that being dead is not so bad, well not if we are together.' Alice started to cry.

'He said if I remain I may lose the use of my limbs and may not be able to speak. He said I could be like that for years, but if you want me to take a chance you know I will.'

Alice shook her head and wiped her tears. She knew now that she had to be strong for Marcus. Now was not the time to be selfish.

'Drink up. We are off to the chemist. Then more wine. Or maybe that doubles bar.'

'I have another day and I have things I need to do' said Marcus.

Alice insisted they got the prescription, just in case, but that evening much to her relief the tablet was not taken.

The next day Marcus got up early. He left Alice sleeping and took a taxi the short distance to Jasper's office at the embassy.

Jasper saw him immediately. Marcus recounted the doctor's explanation of his illness.

'Maybe I should seek a second opinion?'

Jasper shook his head.

'Did you know?'

'You never quite know but I suspected. Us dead are usually a healthy lot and so when you see someone poorly and getting worse, you suspect something is up.'

'I am worried about Alice. Not just that she will miss me, but how can I provide for her if I am not here.'

'You can't but we can do what we can as long as you are here. How long do we have?'

'Not long. Look at me. I feel awful.'

'Well let's cheat a bit. No one will know. Transfer your holiday spends into Alice's account. Your holiday funds will then be topped up, so you can do the same a few times. Let's say five times maximum. We don't want to arouse suspicion.'

Marcus logged onto an embassy tablet and did as he was told.

'Now do you have anything valuable you can sell? If you do and you are happy to sell it you must dispose of it now, otherwise it will disappear with you when you go.'

Marcus had his grandfather's watch. It was the most valuable thing he owned. He usually left it at home when they went abroad, but in the rush to get to the airport he had forgotten to take it off. He also had clothes and the usual iPad and iPhone.

Jasper made a list.

'Are you sure you are happy to let all this go?'

'Of course.'

Jasper drove Marcus back to the hotel. Marcus was relieved that Alice had popped out. They quickly gathered his belongings and drove somewhere out of town. They parked up at a warehouse and Jasper sent a text. A couple of minutes later a man appeared. Jasper got out the car and a discussion took place. Jasper pointed at the goods and showed the man the watch. After a time, hands were shook and an envelope of cash was provided which Jasper insisted on counting.

When he got back in the car, he handed the envelope to Marcus.

'Well done Jasper. On the way back we will stop at your bank so that you can pay the money into Alice's account. I am good' he said.

Marcus laughed.

'Will I remember any of this?'

'I don't think so. Probably not a thing' said Jasper.

Marcus was suddenly sad. He knew that Alice would be ok in time but he would not remember any of it. In fact not being religious, he might even think she no longer existed once he was told of her death. He would never forget her though.'

'When we stop to go to the bank, can I buy Alice a gift?'

'My advice, keep it small, she needs hard cash to keep her going until she gets a job. I might even be able to swing an assistant job at the embassy once she has learned the language. We could do with some young blood. I jest you not, some of the older members of staff are still using quill pens.'

'Will she be able to come to England and see me? Even if I can't see her.'

'No. I told you when we met, you die where you fall and there you remain. The days of spirits roaming the earth are long gone. Border control. Otherwise it would be chaos.'

What Marcus didn't know was that Alice had called Jasper earlier and asked him the same questions. Jasper changed the subject.

When they stopped Marcus went into the bank then to a small gift shop. Jasper dropped him back at the hotel. Jasper got out the car and shook Marcus' hand. He promised to look after Alice. Marcus thanked him.

'Even though I won't remember any of this, it has been a pleasure meeting you.'

When he got back to the room, Alice had decorated it with candles. She had pulled out the small round table from the corner and had put a gingham tablecloth on it together with some bread and pate.

'Remember that French bistro where we had our first date. I was so nervous that I kept dropping the knives and forks. Then I ordered the pig's cheek because I thought it was French and you said which cheek is it and put me right off.'

'They got closed down by health and safety the next week' said Marcus laughing.

'Now don't be mad but I sold a few of my things today, well pretty much everything. I paid the money into your account. I needed to know you would be OK until you got yourself sorted.'

Alice could see he was not wearing his watch but she did not comment. In truth, she was grateful for his help. She had no idea what was going to happen to her.

'I bought you a gift. It's only small' said Marcus handing her the little packet.

Alice opened it. 'Pumpkin man' she shouted taking out the small figure dressed as a pumpkin. Where did you find him?'

'Some random gift shop. Who would of thought that they would have made a model of me? Remember that party.'

'How could I forget? I had just told the whole office that I had met the man of my dreams and then you turned up to the Halloween Party dressed as a pumpkin. I was mortified. I swore I would never speak to you again, but then your little orange face smiled at me. Everyone in my office called you pumpkin man for the next year.'

She squeezed the small orange figure tightly. She would have done anything to be back at that party.

Marcus looked tired. It had been a long day and while he wanted the night to last forever, he was finding it hard to breathe.

Alice got up from the table. She came back with a glass of water. She took the tablet out of its container. They both knew that once he took it, there would be no going back.

'Please' she said.

Marcus ignored her.

'Please' she said again pressing the tablet into his hand. 'Do I have to ask you again? Take it. You have a life to live and I have a death to enjoy.'

Alice looked away. Marcus wanted to be strong and resist but he had no strength left. He did as he was told. Taking her hand the couple stared into space. Breaking the silence, Alice said 'make sure you feed next door's cat. You know the old lady forgets.'

'You are so random, so perfect' said Marcus.

Alice got up. She held out her hand and for the last time they got into bed together. They kissed and then held hands. Alice lay awake listening to the sound of Marcus' breathing. She fell asleep thinking how there must be away for her to get to England to see him.

When she woke it was light and for one moment she expected to see Marcus, but he was not there. On her pillow was Pumpkin Man. He made her happy and sad. She knew she had so much to sort out but today was not the day. Hotels had mini bars and she intended to indulge.

ANN GALLAGHER

SNOWBOUND

Ann Gallagher

Mary, a lady in her sixties, lived alone in a big old house in the country. She was looking forward to having visitors to stay with her over the festive season.

It had been snowing steadily all day, some of the snow was already in deep drifts and it was a worry whether or not her friends would arrive. Then Mary had a phone call to say owing to the bad weather, her friends couldn't make it. Oh, no! The thought of being on her own all over the Christmas holiday, and not even being able to go out because the house was already becoming snowbound, filled Mary with dismay.

Still, she reasoned, she was fortunate that her house was warm and cosy, and she had plenty of food in. There was the television to watch, and she had lots to read. Mary decided she'd settle in and make the most of it.

About seven o'clock that evening, the front door bell rang.

"I don't think I'll answer it," she thought. "It can't be my friends, or anyone I know on a night like this!"

The ringing persisted, so Mary cautiously went to the door. She was now beginning to feel quite nervous about this unexpected caller.

"Sorry to bother you, ma'am," the man began politely. "My car has broken down in the snow, and as this is the middle of nowhere, I wonder could you ring the nearest garage for?"

"It'll be shut for the holidays." replied Mary, considering her visitor carefully. He was a middle-aged man of slim build and smart appearance, but he looked cold, tired and very miserable. "You'd better come in, until we can sort something out."

She really didn't have any other choice. She couldn't leave him standing outside in the snow. He was frozen, and wouldn't be able to get any transport because of the awful weather conditions. But just the same, Mary naturally felt uneasy.

"I'm sorry about this," he said, aware that as Mary was evidently on her own, she must be feeling apprehensive about inviting a stranger into her home.

"I'm expecting friends for Christmas. They may even be on their way now" Mary said, but they both knew there wasn't any chance of that.

Looking through the open doorway, it was a beautiful night. The snow looked very deep, and everywhere was so quiet. The stars in the sky were in abundance, and not a sound could be heard.

Mary made something for them to eat, and then they sat by the fire. She didn't want to ask too many questions, and she certainly didn't want to leave the stranger alone in the room. It was going to be a long night.

She decided to introduce herself. "I'm Mary."

"I'm Edgar," he replied, explaining he had checked into a hotel for the festive season and could he phone them and tell them what had happened?

Mary agreed, Edgar made the phone call, and as the evening wore on, they were feeling more comfortable and relaxed and even watched the carol service on the television together.

Mary didn't want to go upstairs to bed, but suggested to Edgar he could use the settee in the front room if he wanted to rest, while she was going to sit up all night in the armchair here. He agreed.

Gradually, sleep overcame Mary and she awoke at dawn. At first wondering where she was. Going to the door of the front room where Edgar had spent the night, she knocked and listened. No answer. She knocked again. Then looked inside, and found Edgar wasn't there.

His coat and hat weren't hanging up in the hallway, and when Mary looked outside, there were no footprints in the snow and no sign of Edgar's car.

"He was definitely here!" she thought, mystified. "He used the phone and stayed all night."

Mary phoned the hotel. No one of that name had booked in, the hotel told her, or cancelled their booking.

Was it a dream? Or had it really happened?

"I might never know," thought Mary with a smile. "But at least I had some company on Christmas Eve – and what a tale I'll have to tell my friends when I see them!"

CHILDHOOD MEMORIES

Ann Gallagher

I was born in Walton Hospital, Liverpool, on the 27th December 1938. I was the second born of twins. My twin sister, Catherine, arrived ten minutes before me.

As a child I lived in Seaforth, near to the docks. There were eight in the family. Mum, Dad, two brothers and four girls. My dad worked on the docks whenever work was to be had, which in his case wasn't very often. So it was a struggle for my mum, who didn't go out to work until we were all old enough to be left.

I was the fifth born of the family. I didn't have many responsibilities and quite a lot of freedom to go to the park and Seaforth shore, mostly with my twin sister. Catherine and I were very close and went everywhere together.

We earned our pocket money by doing messages for a neighbour in the street. This lady didn't have children of her own, so her treat to us was to take us both to the grotto at Blackler's every Christmas, a veritable Fairy Land to us, and then to a pantomime in the New Year. The memories of those outings have stayed with me ever since.

My brothers didn't have chores, in fact they were both evacuated to Llandrindod Wells for four years during the War. They were strangers to us when they came back, talking posh and being bossy! It took quite a while for us to accept them back, and also a long time for them to settle back at home. We never ever played games with our brothers, and I can't ever remember playing family games.

Christmas was a bit different in that we actually got a chicken for dinner. There was very little meat in those days. We had a maiden aunt living next door and she did her best to help Mum and Dad out, and made sure we got home-baked scones and casseroles with tinned stewing steak inside and a pie crust on top. I remember us all sitting around the table eagerly awaiting the "pie crust" coming out from the oven.

Our Christmas toys would be maybe a rag doll with a china face, an apple, orange, a new penny and some sweets. One year the doll fell out of the stocking hanging on the bed post on Christmas morning. The doll had a cracked face before hardly anyone saw it.

One year, my mum got the girls a second-hand pram to share, but we all fought over it so much that she had to get rid of it! At Easter, we had boiled eggs done with colouring to come out of the pan dyed yellow.

We never ever felt deprived, everyone else in the area was practically in the same boat. We had a three bedroomed house, no bathroom, just a tin bath hanging outside on the wall. God help the one on the Saturday night who was bathed in the last water! Hence the saying "Throwing the baby out with the bath water!"

Mum and Dad slept in the large front bedroom with my youngest sister. There were three of us in the middle room and the two boys later on had the small room. My eldest sister organised singing sessions when we were in bed. We took it in turn to sing "Dublin's Fair City", "Knick Knack Paddy Whack, Give the Dog a Bone" or "She'll be Coming Down the Mountain When She Comes". We all had nicknames for each other, but they weren't very nice so I won't repeat them!

We didn't have many family outings. There wasn't the money for them, but now and again one of the neighbours in the street would arrange a coach trip for the children out to North Wales. There were many children in the street, and we'd always love those outings and take a picnic with us.

We didn't often visit relations, so we were never close to our cousins, but I did love going to visit my Aunt and Uncle who managed a pub in New Brighton, which was a hive of activity in those days – New Brighton, that is, not the pub! There were two fairgrounds, a swimming baths, a ballroom and taking the ferry over the water was a real treat in itself. I preferred New Brighton to Southport.

We lived in a good community where everyone knew each other, and would help each other out. My mum was always sent for when a baby was due. She used to help the midwife, and also help with the other children in the family. A lot of babies were born at home in those days.

We mostly played in the street. Our games were hopscotch, skipping, two balls and rounders. We had street parties for the Festival of Britain in 1951 and the Coronation of Queen Elizabeth II in 1953. Both events were memorable with all the neighbours helping out with the preparations. I can still remember my dad helping to put up the flags for both occasions, and see all the mums setting the tables with the cakes, sandwiches and jellies they'd made.

We had a lovely park in Seaforth, situated off Seaforth Road. We spent many happy hours there playing on the swings, roundabout and American Swing. The American Swing could get to a great height, and sometimes I felt a bit scared in case I fell off – but I never did.

I attended Star of the Sea school. It was a Catholic school. In the infants and juniors, we were in with the boys, but later on in the senior school it was girls only. We went to mass each Sunday and Benediction every Thursday afternoon. We were taught by nuns, who were very strict and stood no nonsense.

If we did P.E. we had to wear shorts, which came just below the knee. Games consisted mainly of netball, and physical exercises in the school yard. I consider we were taught well by the nuns, but we were very wary of them. I joined the Girl Guides for a while, but that didn't last long.

I wasn't evacuated during the War because I was too young. My mum lived in Bootle at the time, but she had to keep moving because of the heavy bombing there when hundreds of homes were damaged or destroyed. She moved from place to place, then up to Southport and over to Wales.

The War didn't affect me a lot. I was too young, but I can remember going in and out of the air raid shelters in the street, and my mum had a shelter like a wire construction in her front parlour. My twin and I and our other sisters were sometimes put into this shelter at night.

After the War, we would play games building play houses with the bricks left over after the air raid shelters were knocked down.

I would sum up my childhood as very happy and content. My mum was always there for us. We didn't have a lot, nor did we expect it. If I had the chance of growing up then or now, I would definitely say "then."

It wasn't perfect, people had poverty and heartache, but they also had time for each other, and cared for each other, and that feeling of community spirit has stayed with me for Life.

POSTCARD HOME

Ann Gallagher

Dearest Jack,

The sea looks great, but I've not tested it yet.
As you know, I've been here for three days. The weather's lovely, and the food and accommodation very good.
I couldn't believe it when you suggested separate holidays this year. I'm aware we have different tastes, but you know I've always loved you.
I work long hours, so when going away I just want to sunbathe, swim, relax and enjoy the hotel facilities and meet other people.
You enjoy an activity holiday. Sightseeing, visiting old ruins and travelling all over Malta on the little old British Leyland buses, visiting markets and so on.
Having had time to think, I've decided since we haven't anything in common anymore, now can be the time for us to part.
We've been married for twenty years; we only have one life, and we're still young enough to start again. Maybe in time, meet someone else.

I'll call you when I get back to make arrangements. Sorry about this, Jack, but please remember – Being separate was your idea in the first place. Think about it. You have most probably done us both a favour.

With love from Lorna.

SECOND CHANCE

Ann Gallagher

They called it Second Chance
It came at the right time for me.
Having finished work the year before,
Didn't want to stay at home
I needed more.
A friend said "Why not go to college?
There's so many courses you could do!"
So off I went, in 2002.
Spoilt for choice, so much looked good.
There were many like me
All eager to learn –
And around my age.
What was more, the lessons were free.
I'd left school at fifteen,
And went straight into work
I was one among many
But always had regrets.
Now here was the chance to learn again.
"History of Liverpool" – we were taught so much
About people and buildings, and how life was
tough.
The Slave Trade made merchants rich
From the misery of others – yes, life was a bitch.
There was Creative Writing, poetry and plays

Our tutors were good, we had outings too.
To Albert Dock, the ancient chapel of Toxteth
The cathedrals and places I'd never been.
In St Nicholas church at Pier Head,
I sat having lunch and watched the service below.
So for anyone retiring
For somewhere to go
Try your Community College
There's something there for you!

THE CONFESSION

Ann Gallagher

Dear John,

This is so hard to write, but for a long time now my love for you has turned to pity. I can't keep matters to myself any longer.
We have known each other for six years. The first five years were great. We were both so happy and I thought I'd finally found my soul mate. Then you started to get depressed. The doctor put you on tablets, and we would talk for hours about what brought the depression on.
I know that you've had a rough childhood and there were many family problems. Since the first time you tried to commit suicide by taking an overdose, I've really wanted to help you get well again.
You were twenty-six that first time, and then when you tried to do the same again, it was just awful. It left me living in fear. You are now in a place of safety, and are on more treatment, but what happens when you come out and are home again?
I think about the future. In time, I'd like to get married, but I know that I can't make any plans now – perhaps never – while I'm still with you.

I've thought long and hard over this. Worried if we break up, will you try suicide again. There doesn't seem to be any right time to tell you – I can't live my life this way anymore, John, wondering and worrying about the future.

I will always have strong feelings for you, but the time has now come when we must part. I'm so sorry, but please understand that I want a future, too. And I really hope and pray that you will get better, find peace and in time, you can have a good life.

Life is so short and precious, please God you will realise this and with help, will in time pick up and get on with living.

We all *have to*.

TITANIC - SHIP OF DREAMS, QUEEN OF THE SEA

Ann Gallagher

How proud we were to build her
Belfast, the chosen city
Blood, sweat, tears and even deaths
Before the launch took place.
My son and I worked
Side by side.
Happy to help create
White Star Line's pride.
The most powerful ship on earth
Could not compete
With that huge iceberg.
Foundered on the 15th April 1912
Her maiden voyage tragically complete.

FIRST FOOTING

Ann Gallagher

A dark-haired person to bring in the year
The first visitor to my home, made welcome here.
What a year it's been, right from the start.
A sequence of events, to touch my heart.
It's been all about family, so dear to me.
There's been sickness and loss
And happiness too
The birth of a babe.
She's made us so happy
She fills us with joy
I know others have all got their share
I want them to know, that I truly care.
So on New Year's Eve, I'll drink a toast
Out with the old,
In with the new
May the New Year
Be good for each of you!

LAST OF THE MOHICANS

Ann Gallagher

That's got to be *me!*
Won't learn the computer
And Facebook? Don't want to know!
I'm content as I am
Won't go with the flow.
I do have a mobile
My family insist.
But learning to text,
I simply resist.
There are too many other things
I'm eager to do.
So many books
I have to get through.
So many places
I still haven't seen.
And while I'm still able
I'm living the Dream.
I'm not calling technology –
It's a wonderful tool.
The little ones use a computer
Before they start school.
I'm sure it will help them
In their future careers.

They get every chance
And that's the main thing.
I was happy enough
When I was at school
Reading, writing and arithmetic
The main subjects I learned.
I left at fifteen, my living to earn.
Now, I'm happy just plodding along
So please - bear with me
We're not all the same.
I learn from you all
And that is my aim!

ENDLESS NIGHT

Ann Gallagher

Andy worked in a restaurant. He was tall, slim with blue eyes and black hair. He was twenty-nine, had a pleasant personality and was a waiter, working mostly in the evenings. Andy was charming, confident, very smart and got on well the restaurant's customers – especially the ladies.

Evenings at the restaurant were long, and because Andy worked until very late, he didn't have much time to socialise so would sometimes save up his nights off and then enjoy a long weekend.

He'd dated many girls over the years, but so far hadn't got too deeply involved, preferring the single life. His motto being "Love them, and leave them" – That is, until he met Tina.

Tina was a customer. She was married, and started coming into the restaurant with her husband Derek on a regular basis. They were a handsome couple, both with successful careers and they appeared to be very happy together.

Andy was smitten.

He couldn't take his eyes off Tina, and did everything to try and capture her attention. The rest of the restaurant staff soon noticed this, and warned him not to get involved or cause any trouble. The couple were valued customers, who paid and tipped well for the service they received at the restaurant.

Andy was smug enough to believe that Tina fancied him as much as he did her. One night, while Derek was in the men's room, Andy approached Tina.

"You're looking lovely tonight!"

"Thank you," she replied. "You don't look so bad yourself!"

Taking this as encouragement, Andy decided to go a step further. "How about us getting together sometime?"

"That's a good idea," said Tina. "As you work late nights, how about you come around to our place for lunch one day?"

The day was fixed.

Andy couldn't believe his luck – It was all so easy!

He spent a week wondering what to wear. Casual – or a lounge suit?

Andy was impatient to be alone with the girl of his dreams and the night before their lunch date seemed endless. The restaurant had been particularly busy, so he got home even later than usual. He set his alarm to make sure he didn't oversleep – But Andy found it difficult to sleep at all, he couldn't stop thinking about tomorrow. And being with Tina.

When the day finally dawned, he got up bright and early. Taking time to have breakfast, shower and then set off on his way. He arrived at the apartment block right on time, and was very impressed. It was a modern apartment, set in a lovely building with each apartment having its own private entrance.

"Good!" thought Andy. "Complete privacy!"

When the door opened, Tina was standing there looking more beautiful than ever.

"Come straight in to the lounge," she smiled, leading the way.

To Andy's surprise, Derek was sitting there.

"Hello, Andy," he rose to greet their guest. "What a great idea of yours for us all to get together.

"Welcome to our home!"

THE BOOK CLUB

Ann Gallagher

Joining a Book Club
Isn't for me.
Thrillers, crime and mysteries
Are not my cup of tea.
Family situations, adventure and romance
Books about animals
Autobiographies and biographies
Historical novels and poetry –
I've plenty of choice.
Reading "Jane Eyre"
Just makes me rejoice.
The Bronte sisters
Were all so clever
Despite their problems
And illness to endure
The books they have written
Will be read evermore.
There are so many writers
I've yet to discover
Keeping me keen
From cover to cover.
The authors of yesteryear
Didn't have computers
Their love of writing just spurred them on.

How lucky are we
That they persevered
Their work, for me
Will always be revered.

GHOSTS

Ann Gallagher

Ghosts? No such things!
Is what they say
Then why do I feel
At the end of the day
In my big old house
With its massive rooms
All on edge, as darkness looms.
I think of families
Now long gone
Who have lived in this house
Perhaps with a spouse
Lots of children
And domestic servants
Nanny, cook, maids, gardeners
The list is endless
Expenditure tremendous!
Cosy kitchen always busy
Cook permanently in a tizzy
Master out all day at business
Mistress left to supervise,
Entertain and socialise.
I feel a presence in every room
Is it all in my mind?
My heart goes BOOM!

Children's laughter and their cries!
Each tick of the clock signifies
That soon I too
Will be part of the past
But my presence here may surely last . . .

THE JOURNEY

Ann Gallagher

The wind wailed
The ship sailed
The cargo juddered
The passengers shuddered
The fear was endless
The storm stupendous
The waves got higher
The people did tire
The end of their world seemed nigh
The wind abated
Peopled were elated
They said
Next time we're going to fly!

FIRST LOVE

Ann Gallagher

First love can be awesome, exciting and kind;
attraction of two people with romance in mind.
It can also be cruel, selfish and unkind.
Someone will get hurt and it will take time to
'trust' again.
First love can be for 'someone' who isn't aware;
for a teacher or doctor or someone out there
Who will never know the person is longing for
them.
A teenage crush, to them it's so real; only that
special person knows how they feel.
One thing's for certain and for sure; there can
only ever be one first love for 'Evermore'.

THE BOSS'S DAUGHTER

Ann Gallagher

Geoffrey worked in a large department store in Manchester.

He was a salesman in the menswear department, good at his job and well-liked by the other staff and his boss.

Geoffrey was aged twenty-five and single, although there was no shortage of suitable girls working in the store itself. Every year the store held a big party for the staff, which was very popular and looked forward to very much by everyone.

Geoffrey was introduced to a young girl called Ruth, who had just joined the company. The pair got on well and were very attracted to each other, but when it was pointed out that Ruth was the boss's daughter, Geoffrey realised he would have to tread very carefully and ask his boss if he could take Ruth out.

The answer was "No!" The family was Jewish and Geoffrey a Christian, and he wasn't what they were looking for, even just to take Ruth out on a date.

Because the couple felt so strongly, and against all the advice from work colleagues and family, they decided they were still going to see each other, outside of work.

The boss found out and promptly sacked Geoffrey, who was so miserable and torn between loving this girl and losing a job that he was good at.

Ruth was also miserable. She had the wrath of her family to put up with, because all of her life they had brought her up to marry someone of her own faith and customs.

Eventually, Geoffrey got work in another store. He couldn't bear not to be seeing Ruth all the time, and it was likewise for her. The couple eventually got an apartment together.

Ruth had been cut off by her family, and told by her father never to get in touch with them because they didn't want to see her again.

As time went on, a child arrived and Geoffrey and Ruth informed their families. There was no response. So the little one was brought up not being involved with the rest of the family.

Geoffrey and Ruth were bereft. What a price they had had to pay just for loving each other, and they were still paying it even after all this time and trouble.

There was a phone call from Ruth's family to say her father had died.

How terrible she felt, that they never made up their differences. The funeral took place very quietly, and Geoffrey and Ruth decided to attend and take their daughter, Lilian.

When the family saw them there together, with a lovely daughter, they decided to welcome them back into the fold.

All the bitterness was gone, just a great deal of sorrow that life could have been so different and so much happier.

Ruth's father had missed out on so many years and of the joy of seeing his grandchild. It had taken an awful lot of heartache for them all to realise that life was so short, and it was best from now on to make the most of every day.

THEN AND NOW

Ann Gallagher

When I look back upon the past
Such memories I have.
Childhood days while war still raged
Bombs falling, gas masks, uncertain days.
We had shelters in the streets
Also in our homes.
These were for the little ones
To help keep them from harm.

Then came the celebrations
VE Day, I was aged six
But remember it all so clearly.
Our soldiers, sailors, airmen
Who had paid so dearly
So our children could have a future.
Free from fighting, and peace at last.
Long may it continue,
Long may it last.

EDNA GRIFFITHS

CHARLIE TED

Edna Griffiths

A Bedtime Story
In the children's hospital there was a teddy bear who came to life whenever there was a very poorly child in the hospital. His name was Charlie Ted.
When Charlie Ted was put into the arms of a sick child, he came to life whenever the nurses were away from the ward. Only the child cuddling him knew Charlie Ted was real.
Charlie Ted would whisper. "Come, little one – Let's go and play!"
The child would not respond at first, but Charlie Ted wouldn't give up. He'd gently rub his soft nose on their face - but as soon as somebody came into the ward, Charlie Ted would lie still until the nurse or doctor had gone.
Charlie Ted would go from bed to bed, whispering to the children to come and play.
One day, a little girl told the nurse about Charlie Ted getting her up to play. Then an awful thing happened. A cleaner was sorting out the toys and throwing the old or broken ones away. Charlie Ted was one of these toys!
That night, a very poorly young girl was brought into the hospital. A nurse went to fetch Charlie Ted

to give to the girl to help her settle down to sleep – but Charlie Ted wasn't there! He'd gone!

"Have you seen the teddy bear that was kept in this ward?" the nurse asked the cleaner.

"Yes," said the cleaner. "I threw him out."

"Why?" cried the nurse. "Charlie Ted is old and ragged, but the children love him! Where have you put him?"

"In the basement," replied the cleaner.

The nurse hurried down into the basement to find poor Charlie Ted!

She found him, and took him up to the ward – all the children were very pleased Charlie Ted was safe and back with them!

Then the nurse found out why Charlie Ted was so very special – She watched him come to life and play with the poorly children!

So Charlie Ted stayed on the ward for always – and he was given his very own bed!

LADY IN RED

Edna Griffiths

When I first met my husband Jimmy, I was only sixteen. I was wearing a red dress and I was coming out from work. He started singing Lady in Red. I was as embarrassed because my dad was standing beside him and I had some friends with me. Jimmy and my dad had been mates for a long time and they worked together. A few months later, my dad and Jimmy were laid off when the firm closed down. Jimmy and my dad were at the top of Moorgate Road waiting for me, so Jimmy could say goodbye to me. He also said "One day we'll meet again, Edna. I don't know when, but I know we'll meet again. Until then, be safe."
We didn't see Jimmy again for a very long time. Then one day, Dad and I were out with the church just before Easter, when Jimmy walked into the club where we'd gone in for a drink. I didn't see him at first. My dad was at the bar getting our drinks, and when he spoke to the barman, Jimmy tapped my dad on his arm. "I know that voice!" he said.
They got talking to each other and my dad forgot that I was with him, until I went up to the bar and

asked him if he had been served yet because he'd been by the bar for a very long time! Dad gave me my drink and then turned back to talk to Jimmy. I took my drink and went back to our table. I still hadn't recognised Jimmy, because it had been years and years since I'd last seen Jimmy. I was now thirty-seven, a single Mother of two children.

That night, I had on another red dress. Jimmy asked my dad "Is this your daughter who worked by us when she was only young?" "Yep." my dad replied.

Jimmy came over to where I was sitting, and I stared to blush because he'd asked the DJ to play Lady in Red. He remembered I had also worn a red dress on that day long ago when we said goodbye to each other. That song became our song.

A year later we got engaged, and a year later we married. Sadly, my dad had a stroke and wasn't able to come to our wedding. Jimmy and I had twenty years of married life before he died five years ago and I still love hearing our special song.

The Lady in Red will always be my favourite song. Jimmy even bought me a new red dress for our anniversary. I had that dress for a long time, and loved wearing it when we went out together because I was his Lady in Red.

JUST LIKE OLD TIMES

Edna Griffiths

Jill was born in Liverpool, she lived with her Mother, Father and two older sisters. When she was six years old her mother became ill and was told that she needed to move to a warmer place for her health. A few months later the family moved to the USA. Her father was a banker and got a job over there with the help from his boss here in Liverpool. Jill's mother started to slowly improve as the months went by. Within a year, her health was better and she was to do much more with her children.
Jill didn't like the U SA and wanted to come back to Liverpool. Her father said that she couldn't as she was too young to fly home alone, and there was no one to take her. She was unhappy and didn't do well in school. Jill missed her gran and all her friends back home in Liverpool. Jill gradually became very subdued. She hardly ever played out, and just stayed in her room. She hardly ate anything and was so sad and homesick that eventually her parents wrote to her grandparents to ask if Jill could go back to Liverpool and stay with them. Her grandparents

agreed and within weeks, Jill's granddad went over to the USA to collect her.

Jill came home to Liverpool and was much happier. She settled back in her old school, worked very hard at her lessons and made a lot of new friends as well as being reunited with her old friends. Her gran helped her to write letters to her mum and dad in the USA. Jill told them how she was doing in school and about her classmates and that she missed them and loved them lots.

When the school closed for the summer holidays, Jill's mum asked her to come and stay with them in the USA, but Jill was scared she mightn't be able to come back to Liverpool again. Her mum and dad promised she could come back home to Liverpool – Her mum even said that now that she was feeling well again, she would bring Jill back to Liverpool herself! Jill was now nearly eight years old, and she did go to visit her family in the USA that summer, but it was so hot that she couldn.t sleep and she missed her grandparents very much. Jill asked her mum if she could go back to Liverpool, but her mum had changed her mind and wouldn't let her go. Jill was very upset, and every day she asked if she could go home.

Three weeks went by and her mum still wouldn't let her go. Jill decided she'd run away, and try to make her own way home to Liverpool. One night she packed a few clothes and some food, found her return ticket and went to the airport. She tried to get on a plane for England, but as she was only eight the airport staff said she was too young to go to England alone. Jill asked them to ring her grandparents and ask their permission, and if they would meet her off the plane. Her gran had been worried about Jill and was overjoyed to hear from her. She and Jill's granddad arranged for her to travel back and promised they would be there waiting to meet her in Liverpool.

When Jill arrived home with her grandparents, she said "This is just like old times - being here with you again, and going back to school with all my friends!" Jill often wrote to her parents in the USA, but her mum never phoned or wrote back to her. When Jill was eleven, her mother died. Jill's dad wrote and told her that he and her sisters where coming back home to Liverpool.

Jill was very happy to have her dad and sisters back with her, and their family together again "Now it really is just like old times," said Jill to her gran and granddad.

LONG LOST FRIENDS

Edna Griffiths

On Friday 25th of September, I travelled from Lime Street on the 7 15 to Chester.
I was on my way to meet an old school friend called Lyn. I hadn't seen her since I left school at 15. Lyn went abroad to work as a nurse to help the needy. I kept in touch with her family, until her dad took ill. Then they moved away to a warmer climate for his health, and gradually our letters stopped.
Lyn has been travelling around the world helping the sick wherever she was needed, and we haven't seen or written to each other for many years. A few months ago, Lyn saw a photo on Facebook. She told her daughter that she had seen a photo on Facebook that looked like a girl she'd gone to school with. Her daughter Mary asked to see the Facebook page, and said she'd take the photo of the woman and try to trace her.
That's what Mary did, and when a friend of hers, called Joan, saw the photo she told Mary. "This woman looks a bit like someone I work with! Can I borrow this photo and take it in to work to show her?" Mary agreed. On Monday morning at work, Joan took the photo out of her bag and showed it

to her workmate. "Doesn't this picture look like you, Carole?" she said.

"Let's see," replied Carole, and was shocked when she looked at the photo. "Oh my god, Joan! This is my mum!"

Joan phoned Mary and said. "I've got a name for the woman in the photo you gave me!"

When Joan explained to Carole about how she'd got the photo, Carole said. "I'll ask my mum if she knows anyone called Lyn."

Carole phoned me and asked if I knew someone called Lyn Banister – And I told her that I'd been to school with a girl with that name, and we'd been great friends!

Carole gave Joan my number and address, Joan passed them on to Mary, who passed them on to Lyn! We got in touch with each other, and I've now had a great weekend with Lyn and her family in Cardiff.

It was 48 years since we had seen each other – Two long-lost friends reunited by a photo on Facebook!.

THE NIGHT BEFORE CHRISTMAS

Edna Griffiths

It was the night before Christmas and Zoe and John were putting the presents under the tree.

The house was quiet and the children were asleep so John went to get him and Zoe a glass of wine and put out some treats for Santa.

Suddenly, there was a thud and Zoe shouted: "What was that!"

"Maybe it's Santa come early" replied John.

"No!" Zoe said, "it's only 10.30 in the evening, he wouldn't be here yet."

John went outside to see what the thud was and to his surprise there was a helicopter on his roof.

"Zoe!" he called, "come and see this!"

She went outside to see what John was shouting about. "WOW," she said, "I thought Santa came on a sleigh, not a helicopter."

John said, "It's the 21st century, maybe he's changed with the times and upgraded from a sleigh to a helicopter to get around faster?"

Zoe looked at him and replied, "Are you mad? It would not be Christmas without Santa and his reindeer."

John got a ladder and put it against the roof and climbed up to see if the pilot was ok. When he opened the door, he saw a young boy was flying the helicopter and he was dressed as an elf.

The boy asked John where he was.

"You have crashed onto my roof. Are you ok?"

"Yes, I`m fine. I just bumped my head."

John helped him out of the helicopter. "Who dose this belong to?"

"My dad."

"Who's your dad?"

"David Beckham."

"Does he know that you have been flying this helicopter?"

"No, sir. He'll kill me when he finds out!"

"No," John said kindly. "He`ll just be glad that you are alright - and there's nothing wrong with the helicopter!"

They climbed down the ladder and Zoe took the lad into the house and gave him a can of Pepsi . The boy phoned his dad and told him where he was, and could he come and get him. David asked him how he got there.

"I borrowed the helicopter, Dad, but I lost control and landed on some bloke's roof in Liverpool!"

CINDERELLA

Edna Griffiths

A long time ago there was pretty young girl called Cinderella who lived with her mother and father. When Cinderella was five years old her mother became ill with scarlet fever. She was ill for a short time then she died. Cinderella and her father moved away from the home where she was born.
When she was 12 years old her father met and married Isabella who had two daughters. Isabella and her daughters didn't care for Cinderella. They made her life hell. Two years later, her dad was killed in an accident. Isabella made Cinderella do all the housework and clean all the fires in the houses, her two stepsisters bossed her around and she was made to sleep in the cellar.
One day Cinderella was sitting by herself talking to the mice. "One day," she told them. "I shall leave this place and marry a prince. I'll live in the castle and be very happy!" Isabella shouted for her to come and iron her clothes. Cinderella hurried to her stepsister's room, but she was covered in ash from cleaning out the fires and Isabella was fuming when she saw her.
"Get out you dirty girl! Get cleaned up before you touch my beautiful clothes!" Cinderella fled from

the room and ran downstairs to her own little room in the cellar. It was dark and cold, but it was her very own place where she could sit and dream of better, happy times.

A few weeks later a letter came inviting all the family to a grand ball at the palace so the king and queen could choose a bride for the prince. The stepsisters were so excited, and they ran up the stairs to choose what they should wear and how they would do their hair. Isabella told Cinderella the invitation didn't include her. "But it says you and your daughters," Cinderella replied. "Yes, it says me and my daughters," said her stepmother cruelly. "But you are not mine!"

On the night of the ball, Cinderella helped them all get ready for the ball. After they left, she had to start cleaning their rooms ready for when they came home again, but while she was all alone down in the cellar, suddenly there was a flash of brilliant light!

A strange lady spoke to Cinderella and asked her to fetch a large pumpkin and four white mice.

"What for?" asked Cinders.

"You'll see, my dear!" smiled her fairy godmother.

Cinderella fetched the things and put them by the lady. She waved her magic wand over the pumpkin and it turned into a coach and the mice into horses. Then the fairy godmother turned to Cinders and waved her wand again. Cinderella couldn't believe her eyes! Her old ragged clothes had turned into the most beautiful dress she had ever seen!

"Cinderella, you shall go to the ball!" said her fairy godmother. "You must be home by midnight or everything will turn back and you'll be dressed in rags again!"

Cinderella danced with the prince until the clock struck midnight. Then she fled from the palace, but lost one of her shoes. No one knew who she was, but the prince was sad that she had run away. He began searching the whole town to find the girl that the shoe would fit. When he came to Cinderella's house, her stepsisters tried on the shoe on but it didn't fit.

"Is any other girl here in the house?" asked the prince.

"No, just my two daughters." replied Isabella, then Cinderella came up from the cellar.

"What about this girl?" asked the prince. "She must try on the shoe!"

"The shoe isn't hers," said the stepsisters together. "It can't be - She wasn't even at the palace last night!"

But the prince insisted Cinderella try on the shoe – and Isabella and the stepsisters were very shocked and surprised when it fitted her perfectly!

So Cinderella's dream came true. She married her prince and they lived happily ever after!

BLACK COFFEE

Edna Griffiths

Early in August, it was a very hot day. Sally was out for an afternoon walk in Hyde Park, but it was too hot to walk far, so she found a café and sat down by a table outside. The café a waitress came out and took her order.

While she was waiting, a crowd started to gather on the park. They were pointing up at the sky. From where Sally was sitting, the sky was blue and she couldn't see what was wrong. But behind the café, the sky was as black as night. In panic, the crowd all stated running away from the park. The waitress came out and asked Sally to come and sit inside. The café was closing its doors, but they would still be serving any customers who came inside. "Why would I come inside?" asked Sally. "What's wrong? What's happening?"

"Haven't you noticed the sky? It's so black over there. It's blue here because it hasn't change yet. but it will soon!"

Despite the warning, Sally stayed where she was and had her black coffee. She had a book and had just started to read it when a few drops of rain hit the page. Sally grabbed her coffee and went inside the café just in time. The rain came so heavy that you couldn't see through it. Outside was so dark you would think it was night and not 2pm in the afternoon. Two hours later it was still raining and then it started to thunder and lighting. A young man came running into the café and asked for a black coffee. Sally was the only customer still there. He introduced himself, and asked if she would like another coffee, because it could be a while before the weather cleared up and they could go outdoors again.

Sally nodded, so Richard brought over their coffee and sat down at her table. They talked and talked while outside the storm went on. An hour and half later the rain stopped but it was still very dark Richard and Sally made their way to the café's entrance to see if they could get a cab to share. A while late, they hailed a taxi and Richard dropped Sally off at her home. He asked if he could see her again for another coffee, and she accepted! A few days later the sun was shining and she and Richard met in the same café and had several black coffees!

This happened several years ago, and was the start of a relationship that began with a storm and a cup of black coffee! Richard and Sally married and regularly went the same café for black coffee. They had two children Sally's first child was born in a middle of a thunder storm. Her second baby was born in the café, where she'd popped in for a black coffee after she had done some shopping for

Christmas. She had called Richard to tell him she needed to get to the hospital, but although he'd rushed to her – he was too late! The baby had already arrived in the very same café where he and Sally had met years before.

The café's manager told Sally and Richard, "From now on, whenever you come into my café - Your black coffee is on the house!"

A NIGHT ON THE TOWN

Edna Griffiths

Fay was on a night out from work with some of the staff, when she got a weird text on her phone. It was an unknown number. Fay told one of the girls she was with.
"Take no notice of it." May said.
 The evening was great! They had a few drinks in the Penny Farthing before going to Mathew Street. Fay got another text. It said "Be careful. Watch your back. You are in danger. Watch your back"
Fay stared at the text. May said "It must be someone playing a trick on you - Or have had a disagreement with someone? Someone who would scare you like this?"
"No," said Fay.
 "Stay close to me and the rest of the girls," said May. "You'll be ok - We're all here with you"
At 11pm another text beeped on her phone, it said "You are in danger here. Get out. Get out or you'll get hurt. Get out."
Fay ran out off the club, with May racing after her.
"Fay! What's wrong?"
Fay showed her the phone message.
"What are you going to do?" asked her friend.
"Go home!".

May made sure she called a taxi, saw her safely inside and driving away. But even before Fay had finished telling the driver the address she was going to, her phone beeped again. The text said "Get out. You are not safe in the cab. Get out."

In terror, Fay shouted for the driver to stop the cab. Paid him, and leapt out into the street. She looked around to see if there was anyone watching her, but couldn't see anyone. How had somebody known she was in a taxi cab? Hurrying home, she kept looking over her shoulder to see if anybody was following her – but the street was empty. She was all alone. The phone rang, and Fay nearly jumped out of her skin.

It was May. "Are you ok, love?"

"No, I'm not!" cried Fay, and she told her friend about the text she'd received just after she'd got into the taxi. "I'm not even home yet!"

"Tell me where you are," replied May. "And I'll come and get you right away."

"Ok," sobbed Fay. "Hurry up – Please come quick!"

When May got to the place where she was to pick up her friend, there was no sign of Fay. Just her phone lying on the pavement.

Hours later, Fay was found. She'd been beaten and raped and left in a park not far from her home. She didn't know who attacked her or why. Who had been watching her, sending her texts? Was that person trying to warn her and keep her from harm? Or was it her attacker, texting her and telling her she was in danger to separate her from her friends and get her out of the taxi onto the street alone? Fay never found out.

She never goes out on the town now, not even with her friends close by. Fay stays at home. And when her phone beeps, she never reads the text message. Just in case it's from that same person.

EYE WITNESS

Edna Griffiths

Mark was walking along the High Street in Manchester when he saw a car speeding along the road towards Barclays Bank. There were three men inside the car.

The car mounted the pavement a few yards from the bank. One man stayed in the car, the other two leapt out and pulling on face masks, ran into the bank. Once inside, they took sawn-off shotguns from beneath their coats and ordered the bank staff and customers to lie down on the floor if they didn't want to get hurt.

Mark noted the car's number, but carried on walking along the pavement as though he hadn't seen anything. When he passed the bank, he glanced inside and saw the people lying on the floor. Quickly, he took a picture on his phone, turned around and photographed the waiting car, and hurried around the corner to dial 999.

He'd just finished the call, when the two masked men ran from the bank into the car. The car screeched down the road at speed, and disappeared from Mark's sight. He could already hear the police sirens approaching.

Police cars tore down the street and Mark showed one of the officers the photos he'd taken of the robbery and the getaway car. The police gave chase, and the robbers were caught a few miles away after a stinger had been thrown across the road to burst their car's tyres.

The three men were arrested and charged. The police thanked Mark for all he'd done. Nobody inside the bank had been hurt, and the bank got all the money back. Mark was offered a reward, and he asked for it to be donated to the Roy Castle Fund for Cancer.

MAKING DO

Edna Griffiths

Mary Jones and her husband John struggled to make ends meet because of the war. Food was rationed, and in short supply. It was very hard to get things like milk, eggs, sugar, butter and fruit.
Mary had five children, Sandra, May, twin boys Tim and Paul, and then came baby Joan. The older ones were all at school and growing fast. Clothing was on coupons during the war, but you could get clothes and food and plenty of other things on the illegal Black Market – If you could afford it. Mary made all of her children's clothes, passing them down from one child to the next, and she also took in sewing to earn a bit of extra money.
John worked on the docks. It was very dangerous because of the air raids. Cargo ships at sea were torpedoed, and ships in the docks bombed. The Liverpool docks were very badly hit, so were the warehouses where food, munitions and other goods were stored. Thousands of houses were also bombed, and destroyed or badly damaged. Lots of families lost their homes. One of Mary's neighbours who lived a few doors down the street was bombed-out.

There was a really bad air raid one night, and it seemed like the whole docks and buildings all around were on fire. John was working in one of the dockside warehouses when an incendiary bomb fell. Not many men managed to get out from the burning warehouse, those that did had serious burns. The others all died. John was one of the men who was killed that night.

Mary's sewing work only brought in coppers to the household, and so she had to go out looking for even more work to pay the bills and keep the children clothed and fed and a roof over their heads.

Sandra, who was the eldest, was nearly 14. She left school to look after the other children so Mary could go out and work long hours, doing two jobs as well as her sewing. It was a very hard life for Mary, but she kept going for John and her children's sake. The most important thing was to keep their family all together.

PETER HEATH

JENNY McCRACKEN

Peter Heath

Old Kemps Orchard

The five young lads had had a fun evening. It had been a relief to get out again after several days of unseasonable heavy rain. They had been scrumping apples, in old Kemps orchard, swilling cider, and now, their bellies full to aching; they went back for one more scrump before the light failed.

'Give me those apples and the cider,' said Campo his arm out stretched, beefy fingers snapping.

'Hey, there mine, Andy,' said Stu.

'Yeah? What's mine is mine and what's yours is mine. Now give.'

'That's not fair.'

'I'll give you–'

'Oi,' old man Kemp yelled, and shaking his staff at them, broke into a run.

'Scarper,' Campo said, struggling awkwardly to his feet. The lads hurled insults as they took off through the orchard.

'Head for the graveyard,' Campo yelled at them, 'then we can split.'

He was the heaviest of them and with his shirt, tucked into his shorts, and stuffed full with apples; he was almost twice his normal size. He had to make it to the churchyard before old man Kemp and his swinging staff caught up. They all knew from bitter experience, that Kempy wasn't afraid to use it.

A mist began to rise as the sun went down, the warm evening had suddenly become chill, and had drawn the late summers evening in, early. The branches of the apple trees looked like skeletal fingers in the gloom and Andy Campion, in his haste, came too close to one. The branches clawed at his face, drawing a foul-mouthed curse. The light was fading fast, he would never admit it, but he didn't like the dark.

The others fitter and less burdened with ill-gotten gains had run on ahead, leaving the lumbering Campo behind, to make his oxen-like-way up through the orchard. The half-light and the rising mist cast strange ever-moving shadows. Campo couldn't see his mates, his gang.

'Hey wait for me,' he called. Even to his ears, it sounded lame, weak. He would pummel Stu, the runt of his pack, later. Yeah, he was due a good thrashing; teach him to hog the cider then run off with the others, leaving him to face the old man alone.

The churchyard, sloping towards the cliffs, bordered the orchard. The spire, rising starkly in the gathering gloom, cast a long menacing shadow over the deep pit behind the church that was the graveyard dumping ground, an ancient rubbish pit. The plan had been to go through the churchyard but the Reverend Percival was there, talking to members of his flock. The 'gang' had taken the only detour - through the dump. They knew Campo hated the pit especially at night. It gave them a secret glow of pleasure.

Campo was panting hard, sweating with the effort of the uphill run, but the broken fence was just ahead. Just as well, his chest was tight and his legs burned with the effort. He was a big lad for his age in every respect, tall, large and now with a shirt stuffed full of apples, even heavier.

'We're here,' Campo heard their cries of relief as his gang slid down into the slimy pit. They splashed one after another into the rainwater pond.

'Come on Campo,' they cried out to him.

A grunted 'all right,' was all Campo could manage between panting gasps. His shirt had loosened and he had lost the apples as he ran. It didn't make him any faster.

'Hey, where the fuck did this water come from,' said a dripping Stu surfacing.

'It's been raining for day's moron, where do you think,' said Barnsy? The gang waded through the chilling waist high water before they climbed and slithered up the far side. Jem, Spiky, Stu and Barnsy fell to the ground panting, waiting to see if Farmer Kemp would catch Campo, and maliciously, to watch Campo slither and slide his way through the hated, now darkening pit. 'Let's go,' said Barnsy rising.

'Quiet,' hissed Stu still smarting from the loss of his cider. 'Keep still and watch.'

Campo hated the pit. When he was younger, he and his mates had tumbled into the pit; he had slipped and slithered in the slime of the rotting flowers and grass cuttings as he had tried to climb out. His mates laughed at him and as his panic rose, he'd cried and Spiky had come back down and hauled him out. He was angry in his shame, his humiliation and lashed out wildly beating them with his fists. It was the day he became gang leader and bully.

At last, the rubbish pit, his salvation was at hand. Campo turned to taunt the old man only to find that Kemp was on him, the staff flying. Andy fell to his knees stunned, his head exploding with pain. 'That'll teach you,' panted Kemp.

'You bastard,' Campo snarled and came up fast, head butting the Farmer, before he could raise his staff again. Old man Kemp cried out, lost his balance, and fell.

'Campo, come on,' yelled Spiky, Stu and Jem, in unison.

Reverend Percival and the parishioners, alerted by the sounds of the altercation were making their way through the graveyard. The boys all knew to stay well out of his slimy clutches.

Campo kicked the old man. 'I'm not afraid of you.'

'Leave him Campo,'

'Percival's coming,'

'Don't kill him Andy.'

His attention wavering, Campo didn't see old Kemp swing the staff. It took him by the knees. The crack of staff and bone connecting rang out across the pit and the churchyard. Campo on the edge of the pit yelled his pain, staggered and tumbled down into its stygian depths. He came up spluttering in waist high water. The pit; even filled with years of rotting flowers, grass cuttings and who knew what else, and now flooded with a pool of stinking stagnant water; was a welcome sanctuary. Farmer Kemp stood at the edge, breathless, supporting himself with his staff, blood trickling down his face.

'I know you Andrew Campion and your cowardly friends. I'll find you and when I do woe betide you all.' Campo opened his mouth to curse the old man but cried out in surprise and terror as the ground rumbled and the pit opened under his feet. He fell into the blackness, along with the mud, rock and the stinking water.

Andrew Campion looked up, to see the darkening sky and the silhouette of the old stooping man with his staff disappear into the mist just, as the now; unsupported graveyard wall gave way and collapsed on him. The boy was carried away in the avalanche. He was tumbled, scraped and bounced against what felt like rock. The ground shook and the earth itself seemed to convulse. He didn't feel the crack as his head collided with a rocky ledge.

When he came too, all was dark; he could only hear the sound of trickling water. Cold, wet, disorientated and half-buried under soil and rock, he was frightened; he screamed or would have done, if his mouth hadn't been stopped with soil. He spat the filth out.

Kemp, Percival and the parishioners stood looking with horror, into the pit. Percival, called out to the boys. 'Come here now, I know you can hear me.'

The gang of lads were shaken by the collapse of the pit and the disappearance of Campo. They had seen Kemp hit Campo and they knew all about Percival. 'Let's scram,' said Barnsy 'we'll meet here later, and get Campo out.' They had snuck away. Word quickly got back to the families and the boys were questioned. When the story was out, the families all congregated and the Barnes. The parents as one forbade their sons to leave the house.' You're not going anywhere near the church or that pit. The rescuers will get Andrew out. You will stay here. Sit have some supper.'

'No Dad, we have to go back.'

'You're not going anywhere until PC Ainsdale has had a word.'

PC Ainsdale knocked on the Campions door. 'Your son Andrew was in the churchyard pit with his, friends. The rubbish pit seemed to open and the church wall collapsed… Nobody knew… We're doing all we can,' said the usually avuncular local police officer grimly. '
'Is he hurt, injured? Is he…'
'We don't know. He disappeared when the church wall and mud bank collapsed on top of him.'
Mrs Campion sobbed her hand to her mouth.
'I'm terribly sorry Mr and Mrs Campion.'
A short while later there was a frantic hammering at the Barnes's front door and a distraught John Campion stood there.
'Mr Barnes they told me your son was with Andy, can I see him; can you tell me what happened?

Welcome

'No, no, noooooo. Barnsy,' he called 'Jem, Spiky, Stu.'
He knew no one could hear. The sounds he made were dead. The earth swallowed all sound just as it had swallowed him. He knew too that he was trapped. God only knew how much rock or earth was over his head.
He struggled to free himself from the fall of rock and soil. He moved gingerly testing, each leg. His knee hurt from the blow of Kemps staff but nothing else hurt, not badly anyway, no broken

bones, his head thumped, he felt the trickle of blood.

'Welcome.' the word seemed to echo.

His heart stopped. 'Who…who said that?'

He turned and felt something touch his face, he all but screamed as he brushed away the spider's web. Inexplicably, suddenly he could see and looking round, Campo saw an ancient storm lantern glowing dully.

The storm lantern flared, and in its eerie light Campo saw that he was in a tunnel or a cave, carved out of the rock. He saw the rough floor that led away into the darkness; water flowed along an old watercourse. He saw too, in the light, pools of water, soil, rock, and things gleaming white. He stooped to look and stepped back in horror, he had nearly picked up a bone, even he, knew enough to realise it was human. Something crunched underfoot; he looked down, and saw that he had stood on a jawbone. Now that he looked, there were scattered skeletal remains everywhere. His heart pounded in his chest, not just from the gruelling run or the lucky escape–

'What are you talking about Andrew, what lucky escape? You are trapped underground like us,' said a whispering voice.

He looked around quickly. 'I know you're there,' he said with just an edge of panic in his voice. 'You don't scare me. There are no such things as ghosts. Hey Barnsy,' he said a note of relief creeping into his voice, 'got it, nice one. Your pulling my plonker right. Hey, Jem, Stu, Spiky, how did you get down here, get me out, get me out,' he said arrogantly. They would pay for the fright - but not yet Campo, let them to get you out of this hellhole first, and then you can make them pay. 'Hey, come you bunch of tossers, get me out of here.'

'Stealing from Farmer Kemp, not that he doesn't deserve it,' whispered a gruff voice.

'Rude and brutal too, if you hadn't stopped to confront Farmer Kemp you might have got to the pit earlier and been out the other side,' said a softer voice.

'You bully the others in your 'gang' and at your school, just like all Campion's,' said a commanding voice, the more menacing for the hushed tone.

'Who is our guest,' a coarse whisperer asked?

'Meet Andrew Campion, great, great grandson of the Lord of the Manor, Matthew Campion. Lord of all you survey, but you're not lord of the manor are you Andrew? Your father, John, lost the house and the estate – gambling and drinking,' whispered the soft voice.

'Did you know your friends laughed at you, behind your back?' whispered the commanding voice. 'They were waiting tonight to see you snivel in the pit, like you did all those years ago.'

'They didn't... they wouldn't laugh, they wouldn't dare, but if I find out they did I'll... they'll be sorry.'
'Campo, is that what they call you,' asked the gruff voice. They have no idea how much you hate that, do they, but they pay every day with your sly comments and your vicious fists.'
'You are a very nasty boy Andrew Campion, greedy, selfish, rude, a glutton, a thief, a bully; but under it all, you are just a scared little boy, a coward.' said the coarse voice softly.
The old storm lantern flared, casting an eerie light. 'See, your friends they have all run home. They are having supper. They are not worried about you; they couldn't wait to get away, to leave you here.' As the soft voice died away, the lanterns iridescent light dimmed, and it seemed to float up to the roof of the cavern. Campo felt panic rising, he didn't know what was going on, but he knew he had to regain the advantage. 'Snatch the advantage every time boy and pummel the opposition,' his granddad's words rang loud in his ears.

Storm

The gale force winds lashed the rigging; they had torn the sails to shreds. Where she had been a graceful lady flying proudly on her course, now without the driving force of her sails she was a sow, driven on, at the mercy of the elements. There was precious little mercy offered that night. She and her crew were in the worst of all possible situations, an onshore wind, and a rising tide that was running them onto a rocky lee shore. The fierce jolt as the ship hit the rocks was a terrifying moment, all on board heard the timbers ripped asunder – they knew in that moment, that they were no longer masters of their own fate. The grinding of the hull on the merciless rocks filled them all with dread as the sea ripped the heart out of the once proud ship. Orders, shouted, were snatched away in the night. Some heard and obeyed; others looked to save themselves and jumped or clambered down onto the rocks, only to be swept away in an instant, by the merciless, dark, rushing sea.

'We have to abandon ship Captain,' the first mate said, fear making him reckless.

'You will pay for you insubordination Mr Gardener,' yelled the Captain through the teeth of the gale but he knew his First Mate was right. 'Cut the helmsman free,' he snapped. Deck hands scurried to cut Henry Martin, the helmsman, from the ships wheel. He was lashed, as much his safety as the ships. Captain McCracken knew that as close as they were to the shore there was little chance of survival. Giving his crew the *only* chance they had, he gave the fateful order to abandon ship. His unmanly tears lost in the driving rain.

Captain McCracken knew his ship was lost. He saw the lights of the storm lanterns and friendly figures on the shoreline and ordered the crew to jump to seaward and swim round the rocks to shore and safety. They had seen the plight of the other poor souls smashed on the rocks. He went below to his cabin, his wife Jenny and son George were huddled together.

'We have to leave,' he said. His wife crossed to him and wiped the tears from his eyes.

'I'm so sorry,' he began.

'It was our wish to sail with you James. You named your ship for me. I'm so proud of you. There will be other ships,' she said.

'But none as fine as this,' he replied.

'Mother is right father,' said George, 'there will be other ships and I... I am proud too.'

James McCracken led his wife and son up to the storm lashed deck, he hugged them, and watched as they plunged into the broiling sea. He surveyed his once proud ship one last time and followed.

Cruel Sea

If the sea was cruel, the waiting figures were nothing less than evil.

The shore party waded out to the struggling sailors. They, the sailors, who made landfall, raised their arms to their rescuers to offer thanks and found only death.

Others watched in horror as their shipmates begged in vain, for mercy. The crew of the Jenny

McCracken were slaughtered to the last man on the rocky storm swept shore. Their bodies would bob in the sea for days.

'You couldn't tell the men from the women. They looked alike in their long heavy coats and trousers tucked into sea boots.' hissed the course voice of the helmsman Henry Martin.

'If you looked for an angel of mercy you only found the eyes of the devil itself. Their knives rose and fell faster than those of the men. The devil rode out that night with its murderous, merciless horde,' Nathan Gardener's gruff voice whispered.

'It was only the imminent arrival of the dragoons from the garrison that prompted the conspirators, the Lord of the Manor, Matthew Campion and the Reverend Percival, to bring us ashore and then to hide the ugly crime they had instigated. The 'rescue party,' were the very same men and women who had butchered us in the shallows, three days before,' the soft voice of Jenny McCracken whispered.

'The final indignity,' whispered the commanding voice of James McCracken, 'was to be thrown into this pit, this un-consecrated ground.'

The soft voice, his wife whispered, 'The creatures of the sea gnawed us for three days before the devils hoard, hauled our sightless, rotting carcases ashore. They threw us down here without compunction, without Christian burial, and to hide their shame, they covered us with quicklime. We were unshriven. I feel the burning of the quicklime still.'

'Your family,' hissed the gruff voice of the first mate Henry Martin, 'know the truth of it, and deny the crime to this day. The *Young* Reverend Percival - you *know* him, don't you Andrew, just as he knows you; has his congregation throw their rubbish on us - to bury our memory ever deeper.'

Rich Pickings

'Do you remember William Pearce Andrew, you should, your great, great, great, great, great grandfather Josiah ran with him, Pearce was hanged when he was eighty, in the year of Our Lord, Seventeen Hundred and Sixty Nine,' whispered Captain McCracken.

'It would have been better for you boy if Josiah Campion had hanged beside him. He would never have sired the whelp that passed on your race memory. Your great, great grandfather, Matthew was the Lord of the Manor who led those ghouls to the shoreline that night, who saw to it there were no survivors, no witnesses and it was he and the Old Reverend Percival who led the wreckers to plunder my ship.'

'No it not true.'

'You are cast in the same mould,' hissed the First Mate, Nathan Gardener.

The lantern flared again and Andrew Campion saw and heard, ghostly voices, noises, shouts, faint echoes of screams. Howling winds, a ship, driven onto the rocks and in the lashing rain, hooded figures - waiting.

He saw clearly the storm lanterns, the ship floundering, the rocky shoreline, the vultures descending, the blades stabbing, cutting, killing, the murder of half-drowned sailors struggling towards shore and safety. He saw a woman, fighting, first one, then two harridans. The knives flashed and, in a moment, the woman lay dead her throat cut, her dark blood washing away in the pounding sea.

'No,' Campion screamed, but he knew it was true. He was there or a part of him was. A new voice echoed in his head. 'Yes my boy, a fine days killing that were, and rich pickings to boot.'

'Pity about the woman, she would have been – a roistering entertainment,' said a salacious voice.

'Enough of your carnality Percival, the boy is too young.'

'I like em young, Campion.'

Solemn Charge

'My first ship, the Jenny McCracken,' said James McCracken, 'My first command, Captain James McCracken, Master. When I gave the order to abandon ship, it was in the hope of rescue by the strangers on the shore. We saw the welcoming storm lanterns and dared to hope salvation, was but ours, we offered our prayers, but to whom, to what, on that night. We didn't know it was the Grim Reaper's fiends - waiting to harvest our souls. I saw the lantern swaying as I came ashore. "God bless…," I staggered into the arms of a woman, I think. She gutted me and cackled at my surprise. In horror, I pushed myself away and staggered back to the sea and saw my poor wife lying tossed in the surf, her throat cut, and the harridans that passed for women, rending her clothing looking for – the Almighty alone knew - spoils, trinkets? My crew lay dead around me; some saw their fate and turned back to the sea. I know not all that happened that dreadful night, but we are joined together now, in this god-forsaken hellhole, man and wife, master and crew. I know the fate of every mariner on the Jenny McCracken save that of my son. Thank the Almighty; he didn't come ashore that night or any night since.' The catch in his voice might have been a sob. 'We are all so tired now. You have the watch Master Campion. This solemn charge, I now lay upon you, witnessed by my wife, my first mate our helmsman and my crew. Our son George, may cease his wanderings at the end of time and if he does, you are charged to offer him safe passage, a safe haven and guide him home.'

Degenerate

The new young Master cried out in terror, despair, teetering on the edge of reason and comprehension. 'No you can't, I can't. I have a life. I'll find a way out, my friends they… they will rescue me, you morons.' I am not waiting for your f– your son, to come ashore. I am getting out I'm going home. I am going home.'

In the soft glow of the lantern, he saw sea creatures, of every shape and size, swimming through the rock walls, floating around him nibbling, biting, gnawing, at his flesh. He felt the pain of every bite. He brushed them away but they returned again and again.

Thud.

He raised his arm to ward of a fearsome looking predator. The skin wrinkled and shredded as the muscle and sinew fell away. He looked in horror at the bleached bones that had been his arm, his hand. His burning flesh dropped from him but now his bones felt the fire.

Thud.

When the new Master raised his hand to wipe his snotty, streaming nose, the flesh of that hand too, fell away. The flesh had fallen to the floor of the cave landing with a dull thud, suddenly he realised, somewhere in his deepest consciousness, that the thudding had been going on for some little while. His bony hand scraped his cheek, the flesh fell away to the hard rocky floor, he went to scratch his nose – it wasn't there.

'No,' he cried. He looked but couldn't see. His eyes melted and ran out of their sockets, dripping over his cheekbones.

'Do you understand now Master Campion,' said Jenny's soft velvet voice, 'you are home.'

His innards, dripped in globules splashing his skeletal feet.

He staggered to maintain his balance as his thighs and mountainous buttocks sagged heavily and tore from his frame, dropping to the floor with a sickening squelch. The creatures, rudely disturbed, regained their hold on his rancid flesh and feasted. His pendulous gut peeled from inside, a rat poked its nose out and jumped with a squeal of fright, as his belly slithered to the ground dislodging the host of devouring creatures.

'The worms and the rats will feast well tonight, fit company for a Campion,' whispered Nathan Gardener, the first mate.

The grey rain of his brain spattered his ribs, and oozing down his thighbones, pooled at his feet.

'They,' whispered Jenny McCracken, 'walked the walk of life, now you, Matthew Campion's great, great-grandson, the new Master, will walk the walk of death.'

His clothes, once tight now hung loose on his skeletal frame. When he staggered forward in the near dark his shorts fell to the ground; he tripped and fell into the broth that had been his living body. When he stood again, his fouled shirt slipped down over his bony shoulders and fell with a soft sigh to the floor.

'Can you feel it burning, the quicklime? It never stops, never,' said Henry Martin, the helmsman.

Eternal Guardian

'It was the night of thirty-first of August in the year of our Lord eighteen hundred and seventy four, one hundred years ago this very night. No one kept watch for us that night; but you will keep watch now, whilst we sleep the sleep of the damned, through all eternity. Keep a sharp watch,' commanded Captain James McCracken, 'farewell Master Campion; Guardian of the Dead.'

The boy began to scream. The howl was the last sound heard by those so frantically searching and digging.

His throat tore apart; his naked skeletal frame collapsed. Andrew Campion, Master, could only rattle and hiss in his prison as he watched eon follow eon, the Eternal Guardian.

GIRL UNSEEN

Peter Heath

A girl walked along the beach, the waves lapping at her ankles.
Monique wore a pale summer dress with splashes of vibrant colour. The dress hugged her to the waist and then swirled freely around her legs.
Her dark hair danced carelessly caressing her bare shoulders.
The wide brimmed hat shaded her eyes from the sun and any admiring glances and Monique took many an admiring glance.
They looked at her; they wanted her; a few even tried, before she crushed them with a look or a word.
It amused her.

The beach was sparsely populated the silvery sands stretched away for what seemed like miles.
A light breeze whipped up the surf and the sea splashed her legs as she walked in the shallows. Monique enjoyed the solitude. She led a busy life; the demands on her time, her attention, and her intellect were, both exhilarating, and exhausting. This holiday had been long overdue. Simon, who

passed for personal entertainment, had begged to join her on the ten-day break.

She had flown alone, happily, apart from an overweight bore in the seat next to her. He had salivated at the capture for a couple of hours, of the attractive woman, who was Monique.

She had crushed him with a cruel comment when his hand grazed her knee.

She roused from her reverie at the sight of a man lying on the sands ahead of her.

She looked, ready to dismiss him, but in truth, she was a little bored with her own company at that moment. It might be fun to entice him, to see if she still had it. She knew, damn well, she 'had it.'

As she approached, Monique gathered the dress, raised it clear of the teasing sea, and swirled it provocatively, revealing long tanned legs, and her sumptuous curves.

In moments, she was past him.

He was aware of a soft splashing as the waves gently lapped the beach and he just caught a hint of perfume or lotion on the breeze.

He was Hugo. He had decided to spend a few hours working up the tan.

There was a patina across his broad chest where the sand had adhered to his wet skin as he lay soaking up the warmth of the sun, after a tough workout in the sea. The sand was warm under his skin.

He had been totally alone on the beach for five days, until now.

She threw a glance, albeit brief, over her shoulder. Monique was stunned, he had not turned his head at all, not rolled onto his side, to rest an arm under his head to enjoy the view – her. Monique walked on. She turned her head slowly to look again. He was as she had left him, asleep or just enjoying the solitude and the suns golden rays.

Men, all men, looked at her. It was her right. She was the consummate master of the putdown and she wanted to play that cruel game now.

She walked on, turning and walking backwards to watch as the guy turned over, not towards her for a sneaky look, but away, flattening himself prone on the beach. She turned and walked on again, her interest piqued. He hadn't even noticed, not turned his head, raised himself, or tried to catch her attention with a crude line or two.

Monique her temper rising at being ignored, turned and walked back towards the recumbent figure.

She walked past him again in the shallows. He didn't stir. She walked on a hundred metres or so, turned, and retraced her steps.

He had turned his head.

Ah, a bite.

She flicked her dress high and let her legs, and she knew the curves of her thighs, and beyond show, but the man hunk didn't stir.

She stopped by him.

'You're back again,' a deep rich voice said. It was like a bolt out of the blue.

'Urm, yes, no, yes,' she said losing the plot. He had not moved.

'You could try moving out of the shallows,' he said, 'it would save your dress.'

'My dress,' she said.

'It wouldn't get wet.'

'Oh.'

'Hugo,' he said

'Oh, erm, uh–.'

'Let me guess,' he said.

'Blonde.'

'No,' she said.

'Ah, dark then. Tall?'

'Yes,' she said.

'Educated, perhaps in Europe.'

'I was born in France,' she said, 'and grew up in England.'

'Used to getting your own way,' he said.

'It's not... I don't...'

She was nonplussed. No one ignored her, turned their back to her.

'Arrogant?' He said.

'I am not arrogant,' she snapped.
'With a bit of a temper,' he said, teasing her now.
'You could turn and look,' she said.
'Where is the fun in that, let me guess, golden tan.'
'How would you know that, you haven't–?'
'There is only the hint of France, not African, or Asian in your voice,' he said.
'So you know a bit about me.'
'Nothing at all,' he said. 'Not even your name; so, rude too.' Before she could respond, he said, 'Would you like to join me,' and so saying at last deigned to sit up.
It didn't help her, his eyes, like hers, were hidden behind sunshades, and gave nothing away.
'I can see you're tanned, more recent,' she said noting the lightness.
'Yes,' he said, 'four or five days now.'
'You tan well.' *(Hello, what?)*
'You're dark, not blonde.'
'You're cheating,' he said.
'What do you mean,' she almost snapped?'
'You're looking.'
'Well you're obviously thick, a pleb,' she said with a sneer.
'Ah,' he said, 'you could be right.'
'No education, just plain boring English.'
'Guilty,' he said

She was struggling. Usually men fell over themselves to gain her attention, and they hoped, a little more. This prick wasn't interested.

'Am I disturbing you,' she said archly.

'Yes,' he said, 'you are. I was enjoying the tranquillity of the sea and the warmth of the sun until you poured rain on my parade.'

'That's not true, I didn't…' but she knew she had. The moment she had laid eyes on him, she had been intrigued. From what she could see, and she could see a lot, he was fit.

Whenever did fit, matter to her. Get a grip Monique.

'Like to join me,' he said once again.

He had drawn his legs up and resting his arms on his knees stared at the sea, at the sea, not her.

She looked down at him - he seemed to ignore her.

She sat. He drank in her perfume mixed with sun lotion.

'Well,' she said with a note of exasperation, 'you might look at me.'

'Why would I do that, is looking at you going to tell me anymore than I know now?'

'You don't know me at all,' she burst out.

He was so infuriating - she was in the outfield. She snorted with self-derision; she was never in the outfield.

He turned to look at her at last and removed his shades.

She gasped, in shock - his eyes: he had no eyes his face was scarred.

'Sorry,' he said, 'a bit of a fright for you.'

She stood and backed away.

'What happened?'

'An accident,' he said.

'When,' she whispered?

'Couple of years ago now,' he said. 'They did what they could but I didn't give them much to work with.'

'How, I mean where - what happened?'

'I don't talk about it to my close friends or family, why do you, imagine for a second, that I would talk to a stranger and an arrogant uncaring one at that.'

'I'm not, I'm not.'

'You have given a good impression of self-obsession in the past few minutes. Perhaps you should leave the poor blind sod in peace.'

'God you're bloody impossible,' she said.

'I'm blind, not impossible, not now,' he added the last softly.

'I can see that. But...'

'That is, what you're thinking isn't it,' he said sharply.

'No,' she said.' Yes,' she said quietly, 'that is what I was thinking. I'm sorry,' she said.

'For what, did you throw the grenade, cause the explosion?'
'Oh God. No,' she said. 'No, I'm sorry. I… interrupted you. It was a game.'
'I know,' he said. 'I heard you fifty metres away splashing in the shallows. Best go now,' he said and stretched out on the beach.
She stood looking at him. She saw now, under the skein of sand, the marks on his chest.'
'You were badly injured,' she said
'I'm alive,' he said harshly, 'others aren't.'
She backed away from him towards the sea, turned, and ran, tears unaccountably streaming down her face.

  Her beach chalet was a mile away; she ran the whole distance.
She liked her solitude, just like the guy – what did he call himself. Damn she never listened. *You never listen;* her mother's words rang stridently in her ears.
She slammed the door shut and sank onto the divan sobbing. Her tears dried. Why was she crying? She didn't know the man, didn't feel sorry for him, didn't care about him, so why?
She stripped off the dress and her bikini and stepped into a cold shower washing out the sea, the salt, and the sand.
How the hell did he get to the beach? How was he going to get home to the hotel or wherever he was

staying? He was out in the sun, no shade and as far as she could recall no refreshments, water, food or clothes to shield him from the sun's rays. She dried herself, pulled on tee shirt and shorts, grabbed some cold beers, from the fridge, stuffed fruit, sunblock and some, long gone lover's clothes, into a bag and set off along the beach. To her relief he was still there.

She hallooed him and he sat up and turned to her.
'It's getting busy on the beach today,' he said, 'you're the second person to come over and chat.'
'Sorry,' she said, 'it's me again, Monique.'
'I know,' he said, 'your voice, your perfume.'
'I brought beer, fruit, sunblock and some clothes, to cover up.' she said sitting beside him.
'What are you my mother,' he snapped at her.
She stood up. 'You call *me* arrogant and rude,' she stormed at him.
'No,' he said rising. 'No sorry, totally out of order, not called for. Please,' he said, 'sit.'
'If you sure,' she said and sat slowly.
'You said something about beer.'
'Uh, oh yes, here,' she said passing a can.
He pulled it open and raised the can to his lips.
'Ah, larger, good enough,' he said. 'Cheers,' he raised the can to her and heard the ring pull on hers.
'Monique,' he said, 'French.'

'Yes, clever b…,' she stopped dead. 'Yes,' she said. 'French I was born in Lyon.'
'When,' he said.
'Twenty six summers.'
'Twenty-six summers,' he said, 'I like that.'
'Here,' she said, 'an orange, I can peel it.'
'I'm blind, not an invalid,' he said with a flash of anger.
'No of course, sorry,' she said and passed the fruit to him. Her hand just grazed his in the exchange.
'Were you in the army,' she said.
'Yeah,' he took another slug of beer, 'yeah.'
'When?'
'Until two y… two summers ago,' he said.
'I'm sorry,' she began. He cut her off.
'If you say sorry again, you can go. I've done with pity,' he said bitterly, 'first the army, then friends and the family… My mother, oh dear god, the tears. Dad was silent, didn't know what to say, only…,' he trailed off.
'And you,' she said.
'Yes, me most of all, then Sal left.'
'Sal?'
'My wife.'

"I want to see your beautiful grey eyes smiling at me. I want the man who scored touch down after touch down, to hold me. You haven't touched me since… You're not him." she had said and walked out.

'The pity started again. I've done pity,' he said fiercely.

'Now it's just the anger,' she said, he started up but she rushed on. 'I don't do pity, and anger is a waste of energy unless you channel it, use it. You're a strong man, intelligent, arrogant, you can do so much when you put your mind to it.'

'Not exactly thick then or a pleb,' he said with a tease in his voice.

She coloured.

'No,' she said, 'I was...that was out of order.'

'So who are you Miss Arrogant, but soft Monique?'

'Soft!'

'You're sitting on a beach with a blind man, sharing a makeshift and very excellent picnic,' he said.

'I'm head of corporate affairs for a finance company.'

'Ah,' he said, 'the bad boys.'

'No,' she said rising unwittingly to the bait. 'We grease the wheels of commerce.'

'And line your pockets in the process.'

'No, I don't, but yes,' she said diffidently, 'some do.'

'It was ever thus,' he said. 'Business drives the government, the government, rank amateurs, cock things up and send the military to sort it out and restore the norm. Then open for business as usual, after clearing away the debris.'

'Debris?'

'Us,' he said.
'Here,' she said, 'a banana.'
'Are you going to–, sorry crass.'
She tossed it to him. It fell into his lap. He was surprised for a moment and then laughed, 'serves me right.'
He slugged the beer, 'cheers,' he said.
'I'm not very good at listening,' she said.
'Oh?'
'I didn't catch your name.'
'Hugo,' he said, 'Hugo Powell'
'Monique Du Bois.'
He held out his hand and found hers.
'Pleased to meet you,' he said.
'Me to,' she said.
'That's stretching it a point,' he said, 'isn't it?'
'No,' she said. 'I haven't enjoyed talking to someone, without side, for a long time.'
'Side,' he said, 'you make me sound naïve.'
'Not naïve, most people want something either from the company or...' she hesitated.
'Or from you.'
'Yes,' she said a catch in her voice.
'And you don't encourage that in any way at all.'
'No,' she said indignantly.
'But you walked up and down in front of me several times, swishing your dress.'
'I... urm, yes, I did.'

'Now,' he said, 'no dress, but I would guess you're not naked.'
'No,' she laughed, 'tee shirt and shorts.'
'Ah.'
'Look,' she said,' it's getting on for lunch, why don't you come to the chalet, I'll make us something.'

'That would be great,' he said and hesitated. 'Look, you've seen me in all my gory, sorry glory. Will you let me see you?'
'I don't understand,' she said.
'It is difficult for a first timer,' he said, 'I understand that.'
'What,' she said.
'Can I touch your face,' he said, 'feel the contours, the outline.'
'Oh, I… I… don't know.'
'You shake hands with people all the time don't you?'
'Yes,' she said.
'You don't always know where their hands have been?'
'I have never considered that,' she said.
'If it helps, I'll put my hands in yours and if; when; you're ready, raise my hands in yours, gently to your face. I'll need your help anyway, I wouldn't want to gro… misplace my hands.'
'No,' she with a hint of a grin. 'Here,' she said, 'give me your hands.'

He laid his paws in her delicate hands.

'Just rest them for a moment then if you're happy, raise them to your face.'

Slowly she raised his hands in hers and turned his palms to her cheeks.

He traced the outline of her head, felt the texture of her long dark hair. Traced her hair line, her forehead, floated his hands lightly over her eyes, found the line of her nose, her cheeks, her mouth, traced the softness of her lips, her ears, her chin, the graceful column of her neck, all the while sensing the softness of her skin.

'Hugo, Hugo. Ah, there you are. Oh!'

He felt the change in Monique instantly. She was on guard, on the defence in a flash. His hands fell away.

'Hi sis,' he said.

'Hello,' she said walking towards them. 'Rebecca,' and held out her hand to Monique.

Monique relaxed a little and said, 'Hi, I'm Monique.'

'You've been feeding him,' Rebecca laughed.

'You make me sound like a monkey at the zoo,' he grumbled at her good-naturedly.

'Just come to see how you're doing, making sure you're not roasting in the sun.'

'He is doing just fine little sis,' Hugo said. 'Two glamourous girls on a deserted beach, what's more—,' he paused, mid-flow. 'Tell me,' he said in a stage whisper, 'does she have all her teeth; is she covered in warts.'

'Hugo, behave,' admonished Rebecca. 'For the record, yes she does have all her teeth and no she is not covered in warts. How do you manage it Hugo? You can't see a thing and you find the prettiest girl.'

'Pretty,' said Monique bridling, 'pretty.'

'Well,' said Rebecca, walking around her inspecting her with a cheeky grin.

'If not pretty, then down right beautiful. That do you,' she said laughing as she skipped away from Monique's feeble slap.

'You two are going to be friends,' Hugo said.

'Oh we are,' said Monique.

'What about poor me Hugo whined,' both girls wacked him around the head, lightly.

'Ow,' he said.

'Serves you right,' said his sister, giving him a hug.

'I'll leave you two – to get to know each other,' she said looking at Monique with sparkling, mischievous eyes.

'I saw that,' Hugo said,' in your voice.'

'It's strange the first time isn't it,' Rebecca said to Monique, 'the feeling by hands.'

'Yes it is, but I liked it. I felt something of your brother as his hands wandered.'

'No too far,' said Rebecca making large eyes at Monique.

Monique blushed and grinned, 'not this time.'

'He may be blind but he is all man. You look after my little brother,' Rebecca said. 'I'll come back for you later Hugo,' she called.

'No, don't worry,' Monique said, 'I'll bring Hugo back.'

'Hugo behave, be good.'

'Oh!' He said with a wide grin, 'I'm always good.'

Rebecca barked a laugh. 'Monique come to supper and tell me how good he's been.'

'Don't you dare,' Hugo said turning to Monique, but she had gone.

Monique threw her arms around Rebecca and said softly, 'I don't know where this is going; I'm out of my depth.'

'So is he. It may go nowhere,' Rebecca said, leaning back from Monique to look at her, 'but be good to him, he needs it, deserves it.'

'You mean!'

Rebecca's fingers were on Monique's lips. 'I mean be good to him, whatever you want that to mean. Bring him home to us when you're tired of him.'

'What if I never tire of him?'

'Bring him home anyway and meet the rest of us.'

'Us?'

'Mum and Dad, me and his brother and baby sister.'

'Don't know if I can do "us",' Monique said.

'Do him, and worry about the rest of us when you feel comfortable.'

'Hey,' Hugo cried, 'what nefarious schemes are you two hatching?'
'Nothing,' they replied and hugged.
'Come 'ere little sis,' he said gruffly. He pulled her into a bear hug, towering over her and kissed the top of her head.
Rebecca strode away up the beach smiling for the first time in more than two years.

'I'm going for a swim,' Monique said.
'But you said you only had…'
He heard the soft thunk as she dropped her tee shirt and shorts to the sand.
'Oh,' he said. 'Is anyone around?'
'Only you,' Monique called back. He was on his feet lumbering down the beach in her wake. He felt the cool wet sand under his feet and shrugged his trunks down to his knees, then let them drop. As the water hit his thighs, Hugo dived, Monique squealed.

ONE FINE DAY

Peter Heath

I must collect my pension. Mary scrabbled around looking for her pension book. 'Ah, there you are,' she said quietly to herself. Mary walked out into the early morning sunshine and ambled the short distance to the Post Office. Her head felt fuzzy; a breath of fresh air would help it clear. She hoped it wasn't the start of a cold.

'Hello Mary, what can we do for you this morning, are you keeping well?'

'Yes, yes fine – thank you. I've come to collect my pension.' *God what was the woman's name* – it was on the tip of her tongue.

'Mary, you collected your pension yesterday,' the startled woman said.

Veronica, that's her name.

'Oh, did I, I don't remember.'

'You're in a bit of a tizzy I expect,' said the woman, Veronica with a gentle smile.

A tizzy, me in a tizzy! Stupid woman; she doesn't know what she is talking about.

Mary walked out of the post office in a confusion of embarrassment. She started back towards her home;

everything seemed floaty, the house almost hidden in a mist, her eyes felt unfocused.

Olivia, Mary's oldest friend saw her fall in the street and crossed to her hurriedly.
'Mary! Mary, are you all right?'
Olivia helped Mary to her feet. The look on Mary's face frightened her. It was one of bewilderment, of fear, of incomprehension. 'It's Olivia, Mary, Olivia Meredith.'
'I'm not Mary, – I'm Rose – Rosemary,' she said harshly.
Rose-Mary shook off the 'intrusive' hand fiercely and wandered down the street she knew she ought to know, as a kaleidoscope of noise, fleeting thoughts, flashing images and scraps of speech whirled in her head.
She turned into a gate, once so familiar, but now only a vague recollection, limped up the steps, and opened the door.
Feeling giddy again, she grabbed for the wall, catching at a picture. Her world went black; she didn't hear the crash when the picture fell.

What am I doing on the floor; have to get to the armchair, then a nice hot cup of tea, that always does the trick?
Mary's skirt tangled around her knees. Clumsily she hoiked it up and crawled on all fours – *my knees hurt.*

Olivia was confused and worried. Mary, her closest friend of thirty years hadn't recognised her. She followed uncertainly, then hearing the crash and a cry ran to Mary's still open door. She saw the broken picture on the floor, the glass shards scattered, and the blood. Olivia, full of concern, called out and followed the bloody trail to find Mary in the sitting room crawling towards her armchair, sobs wracking her.

'Mary, let me help you.'

'Don't need help,' the old woman snapped. Mary grabbed the arm of the chair and staggered to her feet, her knees bloody.

Voices came at Mary; soft, loud, images flooded her mind but before she could grasp them, make sense of them — they were gone.

Derek her husband was laughing with a little girl.

Little girl?

'Emily,' he said.

'Emily? Who's Emily, Derek? I don't know an Emily.'

'Mary,' said a voice close by, 'I'm going to call Doctor Brewis and then make you a cup of tea.'

'Yes dear, a cup of tea - that would be nice.' Mary seemed to be having trouble with her mouth. The words wouldn't form properly.

Olivia returned with a bowl of water and started to bathe Mary's knees.

'What are you doing? Leave me alone. Who are you?'

When she had called Doctor Brewis, Olivia told him of Mary's confusion, non-recognition, odd speech, and the seeming loss of movement in one side.

'Her mouth,' he said, 'is it drooping to one side?'

'Yes,' said Olivia, 'yes it is.'

'Can you stay with her Mrs Meredith?'

'Yes of course Doctor Brewis.'

'Good, I'm on my way.'

As the ambulance was leaving the Doctor turned to Olivia, 'is there anybody to be contacted.'

'Only her married daughter Emily, she lives in Birmingham. I'll call her.'

'That's a good couple of hours even on a good day, nobody nearer?'

'No, no family, only her friends.'

'Don't alarm Emily…?

'Brady, Emily Brady.'

'Don't alarm Mrs Brady but she needs to be here,' said Doctor Brewis.

'Is it a stroke Doctor?'

'I can't be absolutely certain until we have the results,' he said and paused, 'but the signs do all point that way.'

'Hello Emily, its Olivia Meredith.'

'Oh, hello Mrs Meredith.'
'Emily, it's your mum—'
'Oh god, what's she been up to this time,' Emily said with a laugh.
'She's had a fall. Doctor Brewis thinks she might have had a stroke. He thinks you should come, now.'
'You know mum, Mrs Meredith, strong as an ox.'
'Not this time Emily. She is very confused; she didn't know the doctor or me. Mary is on her way to hospital even as we speak.'

Emily Brady is mother of two and holds down a job. Her husband is often away on business.
Her life is complicated; a lover, her children, her job, her too often absent husband, and now her bloody, bloody mother.
'I've got the children home, snuffles, and a cold.'
'Your mum needs you Emily, she needs you now.'
'Oh God…I'll see if Molly can look after them for a while.'
'That would be a good idea. Don't rush Emily; I'll keep your mum company until you get here. You might want to—' started Olivia, but Emily had already gone.

'Oh mum, mum what have you done,' Emily said sitting at her mother's bedside, a couple of hours later. Her mother's frightened face looked back at her, incomprehension in her eyes.

'Who are you?' snapped her mother and who's that old busybody who's just left?'

'MUM,' Emily cried in an almost panicked shout.

'Mum, that was Olivia and I'm Emily, I'm your daughter. Look, look,' she said feverishly reaching into her bag and dragging out a photograph. 'Look mum, the twins, your grandchildren, Rosemary and Robert.'

'Don't be stupid girl, how can I have grandchildren. I would have to have a child of my own. I don't... I don't know where I am. Where am I?'

'You're in hospital Mum.'

'Why do you keep using that word? Who are you? Where's Derek?'

'Mum, Dad died, four years ago.'

'Don't be stupid girl; we're getting married on Saturday.'

'No Mum, no you're not. You married Dad - Derek - forty years ago.'

'Go away I don't want you I want Emma. I want my daughter Emma.'

'Mum, there is no Emma. I'm your daughter, Emily,' Emily said tears starting in her eyes. 'I'm Emily.'

'Of course you are child. Of course you are. Now run along and make a nice cup of tea for me and bring one for Emma, she'll be here soon to take me home.'

ERIC McEVOY

AMSTERDAM IMPRESSIONS

Eric McEvoy

A City of sensations with sounds, sights and smells that assail your brain.
Haunting, lasting.

From the aircraft, strips of coloured bulb fields mingle with the fresh green of emerging winter wheat like a giant's mosaic.

Dykes and canals crisscross a landscape of precisely ploughed fields that sport model shaped farmhouses. Windmills, like ancient wooden sentinels guard the land from flood.

Keurkenhof bulb gardens with breathtaking polychromatic displays of tulips, hyacinths and daffodils, bright enough to stun the senses, after a grey dismal winter.

In the city, sunglasses and windows reflect ever moving masses of people, trams, bikes and cars in choreographed mayhem.

Ever moving crowds of diverse race and face. Clothing strange. Unfamiliar spoken languages. Stimulating, exotic.

Whizzing trams with harmonious clanging bells compete for space with cars, trucks and jaywalkers, nervously crossing the roads.

Flowing packs of bicycles with tall riders in an endless stream caterpillar over arched bridges in almost synchronized formations.

Riotous colours shout from flower beds and concrete sidewalk planters in stark contrast to the muted shades of building frontages.

Buildings, strange but familiar. Like constant Déjà vu. Striking architectural facades with crazy leaning sides and precisely mortared uniform bricks.

Spicy smells of burning hemp mingle with fast food aromas of fries and smoky meat. Heady stuff.

Sunlight sparkles on mud brown canal water and foam that forms from their frothy wakes as glass topped tourist craft ply their trade endlessly back and forth.

Vondelpark joggers compete for space with bicycles their riders with bouncing windblown hair all under a canopy of emerging green and aerial blossom.
Like snow in summer.

Red lit Windows with shapely bodies that beckon, sinuously move, or stare into the distance. Always on the phone.

Coffee shop youth in earnest conversations, surprised their ideas suddenly gain drug induced clarity. Damascus epiphanies.

Restaurant touts accost the crowds, imploring entry to their establishments with the pervasive smell of barbequed meat. Salivating delights.

Open air cafes serving coffee, beer and a myriad of tempting cakes and cookies while customers laugh and relax. People watching.

Hurdy-gurdy man tends his orchestra of tinkling bells and wooden animated marionettes who mechanically produce the haunting melodious notes that coalesce into a sidewalk symphony.

The Amsterdam Hilton hotel with canal basin views. Home for a week to John and Yoko for Vietnam peace from an untidy bed. Nostalgia revisited.

Merchant's houses display their opulence from ancient trade in spices, silks and all things exotic from the other side of the world. If only buildings could talk.

Model windmills, clogs and football size cheese in shop windows, compete with back street head-shop displays of drug paraphernalia, magic mushrooms and seeds. Promises of heaven in a package.

Fast train to the airport through uninviting concrete blocks of offices and apartments that sprawl alongside canals and motorways. Unattractive modern carbuncles.

Enduring airport processing, your seat awaits in the overheated aluminum tube. Climbing to great heights over the old brown city, ochre in the sunset, a russet fading picture.

THE TRUTH WILL OUT

Eric McEvoy

Charles rather enjoyed dining with the Bensons even though he thought them tediously provincial and Clare, the lady of the house, was such an outrageous social climber, a trait that greatly amused him.
'Tell me Charles, do you still minister to the Royal Family?' She asked in a slightly patronising tone, eyes glittering in expectation of a juicy titbit of gossip.'
'Yes, I help occasionally with therapeutic ministrations as part of the Royal Medical group of practitioners. We work together by consensus to ensure any malaise is efficiently dealt with in line with current knowledge. Indeed, there is rapid progress in nineteenth century medicine and who else but the Royal family deserve the benefit of the most modern treatments available.
He saw the disappointment in her eyes as he guessed she wanted an insight on any of the Royal family's business, especially anything to do with their wellbeing so she could share this information with her cronies.
How tiresomely predictable.

'Now then, said her husband Tom, stop interrogating Charles, you know full well he is governed by Doctor patient confidentiality, especially anything to do with the Royals.

Claire gave her husband a withering look of distain.

'I was only asking if he was still involved with the Royal family out of interest. At least I have some curiosity as to what goes on in the world outside your damn ironworks.'

I smiled to myself at this petty family squabble as I gazed at the daughter, the delectable Emily and wondered what she would look like naked, unconscious and tied to a table.

He enjoyed these normal family interludes unlike the dysfunctional fracas that regularly occurred at meal times within his own family.

From a young age he remembered the sarcastic, cutting exchanges at the dinner table between his Father and Mother and the shocked but stoic look on the servant's faces when the arguments became exceptionally heated.

When old enough, he realised Father suffered from constant frustration due to lack of conjugal access because of mothers refusal to have any more children. His, was a particularly difficult long and painful delivery and consequently Father never again slept in the marital bed.

The family were landed gentry and his upbringing ensured he received very exclusive private education along with all the character forming brutality the system imposes on a young impressionable mind.

After leaving school he entered University to read medicine, where as a budding Doctor he excelled at surgery and the relatively new science of anesthesia. Graduating with a first class honours he moved to London to practice his talents in the large teaching hospitals. This was quite a culture shock as it brought him into contact with the poor, a group to which he had never been exposed in such numbers before. It was an unfamiliar experience to see the wretched lives they led and for the first time, a strange, unfamiliar emotion of compassion was triggered in his brain.

This had a profound effect upon him and a close friend and medical colleague was shocked to hear him say

'Giles, my friend, I feel sympathy for these wretches but I do not much care for that emotion. Most of them would be better off dead instead of our ministrations trying to prolong their miserable existence.'

Giles knew about his upbringing, they had talked on many occasions, but was shocked at this revelation particularly as it came from a person who should be professionally compassionate.

Recalling this moment in the future it became part of the enigma that was Charles Ormsby-Winnterton.

XXXX

The feelings are back with a vengeance, a yearning to be assailed by the coppery smell of fresh blood. It happened so long ago, that evocative, heady scent when our gamekeeper slit the throat of a fox he had caught in his trap. The initial spurt of blood, a crimson fountain that slowed to a congealing ooze as the spark of life slowly ebbed from the animals eyes had a profound effect on a young impressionable mind. He taught me how to quickly dispatch a wide variety of game and vermin from deer to crows and I began to enjoy the use of my new found skill. It probably influenced my decision to become a medical doctor and eventually a surgeon but I was told, on many occasions, that I lacked empathy and not to look at my patients so dispassionately. Of course I paid lip service to these recommendations but saw most of my subjects as convenient collections of tissues and organs on which to hone my surgical skills.

As my reputation for style and flair spread, I was noticed by the elite group of medical men who ministered to the Royal family and their hangers on. My speed and skill with a scalpel was outstanding and most patients made a full recovery from my surgery with minimal blood loss, a most important factor when dealing with Royalty.

Around this time my interest was aroused in the relatively new technique of chloroform anesthesia, not as a vehicle to reduce pain, but to keep the subject immobile while I happily cut away.

To me the feeling of scalpel slicing through flesh is extraordinarily erotic and the way the wound grows, opening slowly under the blade's path is thrilling to the point of priapism.

I would go and find relief from this painful condition in certain establishments in London's east end dedicated to gentlemen who desired erotic distraction from their stressful or tedious lives.

It was on a visit to one of these places that I espied my Father going upstairs with a particular lady whose specialism included bondage and asphyxiation, using a garrote to enhance sensation.

I rapidly left the building without being spotted by my father. Unfortunately, this was the night she chose to apply her strangulation techniques a little too enthusiastically.

The funeral was a prestigious affair, attended by the titled, the rich and some minor Royalty. Circumstances around his demise were elegantly and fastidiously concealed so as to avoid the ensuing scandal.

In case of recognition, I never again visited these pleasure palaces but was forced to seek relief with the ladies who inhabited less salubrious areas of east London nearly leading to my downfall.

I had acquired the services of a streetwalker who rented a room a short distance away from her patch on the corner of Mason Alley

'Come on dearie, be careful where you step in those fancy shoes, rubbish is a nice word for what's thrown on the streets around here she said with a cackling laugh.

I was already regretting my decision to visit this retched place but my body yearned to be released from the more basic demands of procreation.

We entered a filthy room, lit by a smoky oil lamp which exposed a grubby bed and bucket used as a latrine. The smell of human waste and cabbage assailed my nostrils.

I was used to strong odours in the hospital but these were acrid, foul from age and reeked of the desperate poverty these people endured. It convinced me that death would be a merciful relief from this, their God forsaken existence.

I quickly performed the conjugation and was hastily on my way home to my West end apartment by means of a handsome cab. Subsequent visits became easier but I began to notice there were more ruffians who looked at me as a possible source of revenue so, for defence, I began to carry a sword stick and a surgical steel operating knife.

Then it happened.

It was a foul night, raining heavily with a squally wind ensuring most ladies of the night and their customers were muffled up against the stinging rain. In the dim light, I was beckoned by a woman whose face I could not see and guessed she could not see mine as we adjourned to her hovel.

After removing my hat and muffled scarf she said, 'Ere, don't I know you? You're that Doctor in the poor clinic at the hospital. Good heavens above, wait till I tell me mates I looked after you tonight."

I panicked and almost instinctively reached for my knife and slit her throat, severing the vocal chords and simultaneously stifling a scream.

The warm blood gushed out of the wound and the claret coloured fountain spurted in time with her rapid heart beat until she became unconscious. I lowered her cooling body into the floor and my nose detected the faint odour of copper and the sharp tang of urine as her bladder released it contents. I watched her eyes become unfocused as the life force left her body.

I was intoxicated, dizzy with orgasmic delight. This was like no other experience I had ever encountered and knew from that moment, I wanted more.

I quickly exited the building without seeing a soul. On a night so foul, the elements seemed determined to assist my disappearance. I walked against the wind and rain to find a cab located a safe distance from my encounter.

Nervously I scoured the newspapers for the next few days and it appeared on the second page of the

Telegraph towards the bottom, written almost as an afterthought. It mentioned that a common prostitute had been murdered by an assailant, or assailants unknown, in the Whitechapel area of London's East end.

I would be better prepared next time.

****

I continued with my medical ministrations to the poor and researched the effects of a newly discovered chemical compound called Curare. It was described as a paralysing agent in poison arrow darts used by some South American jungle tribes to hunt primates. My investigations focused on its potential as an anesthetic and to formulate a dose range that could be adjusted so as not to cause death by asphyxiation. In higher concentrations the respiratory muscles would paralyze leading to suffocation. I was becoming more competent modulating the dose for animals such as rabbits and dogs and not injecting a toxic amount with terminal consequences. With the optimum dose, the creatures came around for their paralytic stupor with no apparent ill effects.

However, so far, the sub- lethal dosage had never been determined in humans.

The feelings returned in an almost overwhelming tsunami of emotion, constantly occupying my waking hours. I felt as though it was best to subvert these passions by directing my energy into furthering my research.

My plan was to visit Whitechapel, select a subject, render her unconscious with Chloroform or Ether and then inject her with a sub-lethal dose of Curare just as she was gaining consciousness. Once the ensuing paralysis had begun, then surgery would proceed and observations on the subject's reactions recorded and entered into my journal. On finishing, the subject would be quickly dispatched and steps taken to disguise my surgical procedures from police investigation.

The night chosen obligingly provided very inclement conditions to conduct my experiment.

London fog, most unusual in August, was colloquially known as a pea souper, and was ideal to conceal my movements. The acrid sulphurous taste from coal smoke sent people coughing indoors to escape the fog's suffocating blanket and left the area almost deserted.

She was standing on the corner of an alleyway, some distance from my previous subject and chosen as a precaution not to be too close to the site of my previous encounter.

'Ello luvvie, want to show a girl a good time?'

She was young, between her late teens and early twenties but her occupation and poor diet had taken a heavy toll on her young years.

I nodded and we hastily left for her lodgings a short distance away. My heart was racing in anticipation of my evening's ministrations and my small leather Portmanteau bag felt heavy in my hand as we entered her decrepit room.

With her back to me she started to remove her clothing and I quickly poured chloroform from a bottle in my coat pocket onto some thick folded cotton waste.

"Ere what's that funny smell' she said slightly alarmed but I swung her around and clamped the pad over her nose which muffled the screams and caused her to deeply inhale the chloroform. She struggled for a short time before succumbing to the narcotizing effects of the anesthetic vapours and I lifted her onto the bed. Preparing the Curare injection, I closely watched for signs of her coming around from the chloroform before injecting it into her Cephalic arm vein.

Her eyes fluttered then stayed open wide as the paralysis blocked the function of the motor nerves which cause muscle contraction and the sensory nerves that transmit pain signals.. The object of this study was to maintain a paralysis dosage at a level that did not cause the respiratory muscles to stop working. The heart is not affected by the drug as it essentially has its own self-contained nerve supply and would keep beating for a short time even if it were removed from the body.

I made the classic pathologists longitudinal incision from the neck to the pubic bone plus four lateral incisions, two on each side to fully expose the chest and abdominal cavities. The heart beat strongly, the lungs rhythmically inflated and deflated and the wave of peristaltic contraction could be observed in the intestines, writhing like a huge coiled snake. The smell of blood and abdominal contents assailed my senses and caused my heart to race. As was habit during this procedure, I gave commentary in the same manner as if my medical students were present. I looked into the wide open eyes which stared at the ceiling and for a moment, imagined they flickered but that was not possible.

'Thank you my dear, your contribution to today's experiment will benefit thousands in the future but now I must say goodbye, as you go to a better place. I severed the main blood vessel in the abdomen and she slowly bled out, life fading from her eyes.

In order to disguise my fine surgical skills, I butchered the cadaver, making it look as though a maniac had disfigured the corpse.

Time was pressing and looking out through the dirty curtain, the fog was slowly dispersing, thus making my exit more observable.

Leaving quickly I made my way back home without incident, wrote up my journal and reviewed my next objective, to thoroughly examine the dorsal surface of a body, and in particular, the spinal column.

It also would be an advantage to use an older subject, in order to see if there was any difference in the efficacy of Curare as an anaesthetic.

Waiting until early September, as the seasonal autumn fogs rolled in from the Thames, I carefully chose my next subject. My *Modus Operandi* remained the same and I was able to leisurely remove a kidney for further study. However, it happened again, the eyes flickered and for a moment and thought I saw a look of terror in their focus. Very curious and disturbing.

Once again I mutilated the corpse to disguise my surgical abilities and managed my escape without incident.

The newspapers were full of stories with gory details in order to sell copy and were speculating about a madman stalking the streets of London's east end.

Having seen the eyes flicker on my last two subjects, I decided to test Curare on myself to see how effective the drug was at blocking the pain of surgery but how was I going to be able to induce pain in my body when paralysed? It came to me after an excellent meal with my trusted friend and medical colleague Giles Devereaux. We dined at the Connaught club, a Freemasons venue which assured privacy and elegance for its members. An oasis of calm in the bustling capital city of London.

The table candles provided a solution. I would induce paralysis by injection, then position a lit candle to drip wax onto my arm.

'Charles, he enquired, how goes your research? You seem to be keeping it very secret. Are you going to tell me or be a bore and leave me speculating as to what hideous practices you are up to?'

I mumbled some excuses and talked in general terms of my efforts with anesthesia but obviously could not reveal the contents of my scientific studies.

'All will be understood, once I have thoroughly completed my investigations, I muttered, and the world will benefit from the sacrifices of the few.'

He looked puzzled but seemed content with this answer and did not pursue me for any further information.

The following day I made preparations for my self-administered medication with Curare using the small laboratory in the basement of my house.

I dismissed the servants for the afternoon and set up the operating table, candle holder, and hypodermic syringe. Lighting the candle, I positioned my arm under the dripping wax and proceeded with the injection. The paralysis begun within a minute of injection as a wave of muscle relaxation spread over my body along with an increased difficulty in breathing as the respiratory muscles and the diaphragm became less efficient.

This caused me to panic a little but I had specifically reduced the dosage so there was no possibility of asphyxiation and the effects of the drug will cease after two hours.

To my horror, I became aware of a burning sensation as the hot wax dripped on my arm.

The pain lessened as the wax droplets congealed on my skin effectively acting as an insulating barrier but the realization dawned that my subjects would have felt the full excruciatingly painful effects of my surgery.

What have I done?

After what seemed an endless time, the effects of the drug diminished and I gained some movement, enough to extinguish the candle and lay back on the table until the complete cessation of paralysis.

The burning sensation and patch of redness on my arm, caused by the candlewax would dissipate in a few days but the realization that my subjects suffered overwhelming pain without analgesia was indelibly etched on my mind. I am not a monster. Admittedly, my compassion for these people is zero but the solution to effective, safe anesthesia outweighed all my misgivings and the benefits to humankind would be immeasurable. It then dawned upon me. The Curare blocked conduction of electrical impulses in motor nerves but had no effect on the sensory nerves. I concluded that although nerves, they must work in totally different ways. I then decided to mix Curare with Laudanum and Cocaine. This I thought an elegant solution to blocking pain because Laudanum contains ten percent Opium. Also, adding Cocaine to the mix would increase breathing counteracting the depressive respiratory effects of both Curare and Laudanum.

I needed more subjects to test my idea and adjust dosage according to efficacy.

Reflecting on my achievements so far, it has been, and still is a difficult problem to induce a safe state of anesthesia and maintain a sufficient and effective level of analgesia. During the process of anesthesia the body is worryingly close to death and a critical reaction to an overdose of narcotizing agents can lead swiftly to the demise of the subject.

A perilous frontier between life and death.

I managed to find further prostitutes to test my different formulations of the paralyzing agent and the narcotics to block the pain. The results were quite successful but the police and press involvement became intrusive, therefore, I decided to temporarily suspend my research before I was caught.

xxxx

So now it was time to leave the great city of London and off to further opportunities in other parts of Great Britain. All major cities needed Doctors and each had its red light area where I could practice my anaesthetic arts. This time I would restrict my experiments to limited numbers of subjects in order not to arouse the suspicion of the local Constabularies. People, especially prostitutes, frequently go missing, so their loss may not trigger extensive investigation.

For the next twenty odd years I travelled the country practicing medicine in various towns and cities. For a few years I became a country Doctor, a pillar of the community, if they only knew of the monster in their midst!

I continued my research trying different formulations of mixtures but mostly only used small mammals and the occasional piglet in my experiments as their anatomy and physiology are remarkably similar to humans.

On occasion, I made a foray into the red light district of the larger cities to obtain a human subject. I would sedate them and transport their supine body by covered cart to various isolated barns rented from local farmers.

Once my work was complete, I would bury them in a conveniently private place and quickly move on.

I was satisfied for a while but wanted to travel abroad as my research had reached a critical point where I needed more subjects so, I decided to visit the Americas. My reading of the scientific journals had uncovered the use of another type paralytic toxin by some other South American Indian tribes. They smear the poison obtained from the skin of brightly coloured frogs on an arrow, or blow dart, which they use to hunt monkeys for food. I understand once the animal is shot, it rapidly becomes paralysed and falls to the ground from high in the tree canopy.

What is interesting, from the aspect of my work, is the monkey can recover, apparently unharmed, if the dosage is too low.

Very exciting stuff.

I arrived after a long steam train journey at Lime street station in the City of Liverpool. Although sorely tempted to visit the notorious dock lands that stretch along the magnificent waterfront and seek out the many prostitutes inhabiting the port, I think it prudent to postpone my tour for another time.

The continuation of my work in the Americas is vital to pursue my goal of effective, safe anesthesia and although my subjects may suffer and will die, the knowledge gained will make significant progress, in pain free surgery, for the benefit of all. No doubt my ministrations will classify me as a psychotic serial killer but eventually, the truth will out.

After a short stay in the splendid Adelphi Hotel, I booked passage on a ferry to Ireland. Journeying to the south, my arrival at the small port of Queenstown was without incident and I eagerly awaited the arrival of my steamer to the new world where my research would continue with gusto. This journal I am preparing will be recognised as a work of genius, a medical wonder, each snuffed out life recorded in graphic details along with descriptive data of the procedures before life ebbs away.

I will complete my studies on many different races to see if they respond in the same fashion as Caucasians or do they hang on to the spark of life for a longer or shorter time.? Unfortunately, so far I have no data on male subjects. Although I am now in my early fifties, who knows I may remedy that omission during the rest of my hopefully long life of research

****

April the eleventh had arrived and the RMS Titanic looked splendid in the early morning spring light. It was moored at Roches point on the outer anchorage of Queenstown Harbour. With my medical qualification and links to the Royal family, I was able to secure comfortable accommodation in first class and looked forward to the party atmosphere which appears to prevail throughout the vessel.

It was bedecked with bunting and once all were boarded, it sailed for New York to the haunting strains of Erin's Lament played on bagpipes by one of the third class passengers.

All is not well, I was awoken around eleven forty five on April the fourteenth by the ships alarm. I was relaxing in my cabin after a splendid dinner when a shuddering vibration shook the ship. Shortly after a klaxon began to sound. I quickly dressed in warm clothing as the temperature had plummeted from earlier in the day and made my way up onto the promenade deck to see almost mass panic as people dressed in life vests were running about. I ascertained from a crew member that we had struck an iceberg and were taking in water. I had to save my journals so returned to my cabin and am now packing them as best as possible to prevent water damage. All is now done so must get up on deck.
This was the final journal entry of Charles Ormsby-Winnterton.

****

DAILY TELEGRAPH
Obituary for Charles Orsmsby -Winnterton Doctor and Surgeon to the Royal Court by Giles Devereaux
It is with great sadness I have to report the death of my friend and colleague who is amongst the missing, presumed dead, on the maiden voyage of the RMS TITANIC.
Memorial service details to follow.

****

'Doctor Devereaux, there is a young lady, a Miss Elise Bowerman who appears rather anxious to see you said Grayson, the dour head porter at the Connaught. As you know females are not allowed in the club so I have escorted her to the small library to await your presence.'
'Thank you Grayson, did she say why she wishes to see me by any chance?'
'I understand she has a package from Doctor Orsmsby–Winnterton and she insists on delivering it to you in person.'
I almost run down to the library, passing some older members on the staircase and their tut-tutting disapproval at my quick pace in the sedate atmosphere of the club.
I opened the elegant oak doors and she sat demurely in a winged arm chair clutching a large bag. I estimated she was in her early twenties and had an honest open face. I crossed the room and shook her gloved hand.

'I'm Charles Devereaux, pleased to meet you Miss Bowerman'
She smiled and said, 'very pleased to meet you as well and to discharge my responsibility for this.'
She handed me a large oilskin package with an almost sigh of relief as she passed it over.
'I am a survivor of the tragic sinking of the Titanic and your friend asked me, no, begged me to deliver

this parcel to you, and only you, at the Connaught. He gave me a hundred pounds which I tried to refuse but he insisted, said the package contained vital medical research of immeasurable benefit to mankind. He was convinced that his end was near as only a few lifeboats were left and these full of women and children.'

'Thank you for this, I will ensure it will be looked after. Did he say anything else?'

'In the circumstances, he said that I was his best option for personally delivering it to only you. He looked stoic, almost resigned to his fate as if it were divine intervention. He did say tell Charles not to think badly of him but to use the journal as you see fit.'

As his best and possibly only friend and colleague, I am tortured by the uncertainty of what next to do, should I publish the discoveries obtained in such a horrendous way or is this best left alone, buried along with his sunken bones?

Only time will tell.

****

Note from the author

Although this is a work of fiction, a synthetic form of Curare is now in regular use for surgical procedures, particularly for abdominal operations as it relaxes muscles and reduces tissue trauma but with one important factor. The anaesthetist needs to carefully monitor the depth of unconsciousness as it is possible, and has happened, on very rare occasions, when the patient has become conscious and are unable to communicate this fact, due to paralysis, but can feel the pain of the procedure.

THE RIDE

Eric McEvoy

It all started like most ideas after a good session in the pub.
Why don't we do a sponsored charity cycle ride in Europe? Perhaps some part of the Tour de France, say in the Alps, nothing too hard.'
These words of wisdom were uttered by Oscar, the youngest member of our amateur, weekend only, very exclusive, cycle club of five, him and four other semi-intoxicated friends.
We met in our village local every week to plan our next regular outing, normally cycling around fifty miles or so through the country lanes around Oxford.
Our village, Primrose Heath, is recorded in the Domesday Book and ideally situated for the London commute. Our members Dan, Henry, Tim, Angus and of course Oscar all worked in the City. By that, I mean the stock exchange. We were all in our mid-forties, comfortably financed, fairly fit, and always up for an adventure to escape our stressful work and to keep from under our partner's feet as they so often complained.

So, in the cold, sober light of day, it still seemed a reasonably good idea and as always, up to me to organise the logistics of the journey.

We all were very fond of Gourmet food, vintage wine and constantly competed to discover exciting and obscure restaurants in order to earn respect and accolades from our peers.

We met in the pub that Friday night after the proposed idea in order to discuss the planning to date that I had researched so far.

'Right Dan, what have you come up with? Said Oscar.

'Well, so far I've discovered a circular route in the Alps of around two hundred and fifty miles that will take a week to complete. I realise it's under forty miles per day but there are some steep uphill sections to contend with. We also need a support van to carry our luggage, spare wheels and tools. Finally, we need to fly with our bikes to Grenoble and after a day's ride we should reach the foothills of the Alps, ready for the hard bit.

The route I propose heads us North East towards Chambery and Annecy near the Swiss border then West towards Premillieux and eventually South back down to Grenoble. Here are copies of the route so you can all go away and research the best places for our overnight stays and of course special places to eat. As we are all members of the Rotary, they will organise sponsorship and all funds raised will go to local charities.'

There were nods of approval of the plan so far and Henry offered the use of his handyman Fred to drive his van and the equipment as support.

'I'm sure he'll jump at the offer of a free holiday and a hundred quid a day if we all chip in.' Once again, there were approving nods around the table.

'Tim, didn't you know a guy who could arrange a flight for us?

Wasn't he an ex school friend?' Asked Angus one of our founder members.

Tim looked a little uneasy. 'Well, he is sort of a friend but we lost contact.' Tim could be economical with the truth, prone to exaggeration and tended to go off on his own when we were out on our weekend rides.

'Not to worry, said Oscar my uncle owns an air charter business and I'm sure I can arrange something that meets our needs.'

Finally, in a moment of madness we all decided to have our bikes painted primrose yellow and we bought yellow cycling jerseys printed with the words PRIMROSE WHEELERS CHARITY CYCLE TOUR. In addition, to cement our commitment, we agreed to have a small primrose flower tattooed on our right buttock cheek, much to the amusement of our partners.

So, three months later in glorious sunshine, we touched down at Grenoble-Isère airport ready for our charity ride. Quickly clearing customs, we unloaded our bikes and were on our way towards Chambery.

Physically, it was very demanding and the hill climbs torture but this was more than compensated by the spectacular Alpine scenery of tall pines, sparkling blue lakes, and wild flower meadows like jewelled carpets.

We often strayed off the planned route to find some obscure village restaurant that one of us had researched. This is when we found the small village of Caché and the restaurant recommended by Tim.

It was a pretty village and our restaurant Le Cochon Rose was easy to find at the end of the main street next to Swinettes, a hairdresser, beautician and massage establishment.

We arrived early enough to book a table for lunch in a fairly crowded dining room. Patrons must have come some distance as the car park had numerous expensive vehicles with number plates from many countries confirming the exceptional reputation of the establishment. The lunch was outstanding and Tim basked in the reflected glory.

'I knew it would be good, he said in a patronising tone, one of the best kept secrets in this part of France. My friend Giles knows a top restaurant critics and he shared the information with me as long as I didn't tell a soul.'

'Good to know he can keep a secret.' I whispered to Henry who laughed out loud, much to Tim's annoyance but we all agreed it was one of the most memorable meals so far.

There would be no further cycling that day which didn't matter as the afternoon was a designated a rest stop.

Tim told us he was going next door for a massage and would meet us at our evening accommodation a small B&B located two miles out of town.

That evening he came in with a silly grin on his face explaining the massage was as good as the lunch and Madame, a very shapely lady had commented on his exceptional physique and the firmness of his buttocks which, he went on, she tested with a few hard slaps. Eyebrows were raised, shoulders shrugged, and no comments were needed.

At breakfast the following morning he was missing.

'Tim on his travels again! Remarked Henry to no one in particular.

'Well, he's a big boy now and will have to catch us up unless we find him on route.

Don't know about you guys but I really fancy an evening meal in that place tomorrow night. We all enthusiastically agreed and booked in for an evening meal at the Pink Pig on the way back through the village of Caché

As we parked our bikes in the wall rack next to the entrance a peloton of riders sped past and I glimpsed one bike in the middle that was almost the same primrose yellow as our own but I could have been mistaken.

As we sat down in the restaurant Tim was still absent and we agreed to wait another day before instigating a search as he was frequently prone to go off on his own for a few days.

The Chef a Monsieur Toddé came to our table and said in passable English 'Welcome back my English friends, I am so glad to again see you. When I see you re-booked I prepared a very special meal to honour our English friends.

'I hope you will like my Ragôut Anglais it is robust, full bodied and with herbs to die for.' And he laughed out loud and long. Enjoy!'

The salad arrived, a magnificent platter designed like a union jack with chopped red peppers, white onion and the spectacular blue of mountain gentian flowers. It made us feel very patriotic.

The stew was just heaven, the meat could be cut with a fork with a herb gravy like no other we had ever tasted

Towards the end of the meal, the Chef came to the table with his arm around a very attractive woman with sparkling eyes and full red lips. She smiled at us with an almost mesmerising stare.

'Gentlemen, may I introduce my wife Madame Swinettes who runs the salon next door.

We were all a little taken aback but stood up and shook her dainty white hand with its crimson nails. The same hands that had smacked the bottom of our friend Tim.

'Bloody hell I whispered to Angus, it's his wife, no wonder he's gone is missing.

I had eaten enough but was further tempted by the last few pieces of meat in the dish. I greedily helped myself.

Suddenly my gorge began to rise in the back of my throat and the room started to spin. Just before my knees buckled and I hit the floor the horror struck me.

Tim had joined us at the table, for there on the plate, on the back of a neatly cubed piece of meat, was the unmistakable pale yellow tattoo of a primrose flower.

WAR

Eric McEvoy

What happens if they want a war and nobody came?
Would the Field Marshals feel stupid, Politician's shame?
Fighting for peace is the propaganda they spread
But deny responsibility for the mountains of dead.

They just want to conquer, as quick as is possible
'Just stick it to them son, you can do the impossible'
Some mother's daughter, some father's son
The country's on God's side of us all, everyone.

So victory's in sight with collateral damage to pay
But the injured and orphans will soon fade away
To memories consigned to the back of your mind
The pain doesn't matter, they are not of our kind.

Their land is ours and we can raise the flag high
And we crush and bleed them until they are dry
Deny them their birthright, their riches, their land
Soon speculators will arrive, rubbing their hands.

But what of the arms dealers, was it profitable for you?
Did the poison gas work, were the bullets so few?

Do they support you with fervor and political spin?
Do lobbyists ensure that the money rolls in?

And when it's all over you can make lots of money
Organise lecture tours, words spoken like honey
Blame others, for the misinformed intelligence you had
Your self-deception complete, look serious, look sad.

Make lots of cash and accolades galore
Forget about coffins at Wootton Basset for sure
How do you sleep at night with blood on your hands?
We voted for you, the fools of the land.

Looking for excuses is what to expect
Clergymen, Generals, politicians circumspect?
Liberation, not food, is what you'll receive
With God, the regiment and voters deceived.

They think it's enough for a poppy to wear
For the rest of the year do they turn a blind ear?
So remember each daughter, remember each son
For the battles lost and the battles they won.

So let's aim for a war were nobody came
When we all say enough, and there's no one to blame

If they insist on a war, with mountains of dead
Send in the politicians, to do battle instead.

THE PHOTOGRAPH

Eric McEvoy

It was an old black and white photograph of a snow covered path in a city park. On a wide pathway alongside a park bench, a single set footsteps disappeared into the distance.

Donovan was deep in the underground lab when the first nuclear warhead struck the city.
His job was to check the cosmic particle detectors buried deep in the earth as part of the government funded research programme into the formation of the universe. Later when he realised how ironic, these particles had travelled immense distances over millions of years to reach a planet whose life may now slowly end due to self-inflicted nuclear radiation.
MAD, it was called, **M**utually **A**ssured **D**estruction as the superpowers emptied their nuclear missile stocks on each other.
Philosophers and scientists had speculated that human life would be wiped out by a plague or a comet striking the earth because, after all, nuclear weapons were under control weren't they and no world leaders stupid enough to use them.
Donovan wasn't concerned how it started, or who the protagonists were, Russians, Chinese, Iranians,

Israelis, all as bad as each other. His main objective was to stay alive as long as possible. How many people had survived, how long did they have before succumbing to the deadly effects of radiation? These, and lots of other thoughts occupied his mind as he prepared his underground home for a long stay.

A nuclear shelter for the good and the great of the city. Initially, this was going to be the primary use of this resource but as the superpowers appeared to reduce their capacity for nuclear annihilation it was deemed superfluous and could be put to better use. Donovan speculated that after six months the radiation levels would have abated enough to venture outside for short periods. He could then discover what had happened, how many survived and see if he could travel to an uncontaminated area and find a place to live.

Luckily, the lab had living accommodation plus six months power reserve from a bank of Hydrogen fuel cells. Due to the depth from the surface, the bunker design engineers had included a self-contained water supply from an underground aquifer and a filtered air system to keep the facility as uncontaminated as possible. It also included a six month supply of died food, edible but not exciting

Fortunately, the facility had a good library, including a significant quantity of pre-recorded video entertainment and a computer system. Unfortunately, this was now not connected to the internet but nevertheless had its own server containing a huge amount of programmed information on post holocaust survival in order to help the occupants cope when they emerged from the shelter.

His main objective was to mentally prepare for six months in total isolation and not to speculate what has become of his family and friends.

Not an easy task.

After nearly six months, he was counting down the last few days before his first surface visit. He had taken iodine tablets and anti-radiation medication that would hopefully mitigate the effects of radiation exposure.

The unobtrusive surface door was embedded in a rock wall and opened into the City Park. His heart was racing in anticipation of what he would see. A landscape destroyed, bodies all over the place, fires still burning but what he hadn't expected to see was snow.

It reminded him of a favourite print he had framed of an old black and white photograph showing a snowy park.

The lab Geiger counter he carried gave off irregular staccato ticks but to his relief, did not enter the red zone. Donovan could risk moving about for a few hours and needed to find food as his supplies were rapidly diminishing also, he desperately wanted to find out if there were other survivors.

As he walked through the cityscape he was surprised there appeared to be little damage and fewer bodies than anticipated. What had happened? The answer was presented to him when he entered a shopping mall.

It was full of decaying bodies, people had dropped in their tracks.

It was a Neutron bomb. An enhanced radiation weapon this horrific device was developed by all nuclear superpowers but they had agreed never to use them. So much for empty promises.

The hard radiation emitted, killed life but left property intact. Donovan wondered what warped minds could conceive of such an instrument of death that snuffed out life without the accompanying destruction of property. This was why the background radiation was relatively low. Once a city had been cleansed of its human population by irradiation, the protagonist's forces could then move in and seize the undamaged assets. Providing of course, they aren't destroyed in the conflict.

He collected tinned food from the supermarket in the mall and tried to shut out the horror of the bodies in the shopping aisles. Men, Women with babies in pushchairs little children all sprawled on the floor as if asleep.

He managed to collect a portable radio and batteries in the hope of hearing there may be someone still alive and broadcasting.

He limited his wanderings to a short fifteen minutes to reduce radiation exposure in case of any 'hot' spots in the vicinity. There were lots of abandoned cars and trucks some crashed into each other or protruding from broken storefront windows. Bodies caught in the open when the airburst occurred were horribly burnt and contorted into shapes unrecognisable as a human being.

Struggling with his food he made his way back to the bunker through the park.

As he entered the snow covered path in the park, his heart skipped a beat.

Footprints, two sets.

His, barely visible prints covered by the snow and another set, fresher and more defined.

He was not alone.

WHAT'S GOING ON IN THE SLEEPY TOWN OF STORFAIRY?

Eric McEvoy

AN EXPOSÉ
By our investigative reporter
Noah Fable

In the archetypical English country town of Storfairy, not is all what it seems, certainly when it comes to town planning and building regulations. Readers may remember my recent report about this place regarding the shocking kidnapping and enslavement of seven persons of restricted growth by the notorious Ms S. White whose sexual proclivities included small men and in particular diamond miners.
No readers, this is not the same as that ghastly tale but nevertheless, other misdemeanours I expose, will have major implications for the building industry and social services throughout the land.
The town is a perfect example of our rural heritage with an imposing tree-lined high street, Pubs, churches and schools all built from the locally quarried sandstone giving an air of cosiness and warmth. A quintessential English enclave.

Unfortunately, this vista may be ruined by an aggressive construction programme proposed by the Hamm Brothers who lead a consortium of companies including Beanstalk developments known to flaunt building and design regulations.

They plan to use novel building materials to erect affordable housing in record time. Superficially, this seems a good idea in times of housing shortages but using these untested materials to construct houses could be disastrous as they are likely to fail in windy conditions.

When asked to comment, the chief town planner Mr Onceuponatime replied 'We are not at all happy with these proposals, The Hamm brothers have tried to do this before in other towns using this novel straw and sticks construction to create very unsafe buildings. Indeed, our chief structural engineer Dr B. B. Wolf has used a wind tunnel to test the design and integrity of these new materials which quickly failed in a puff of wind. The proposed model for the house constructed of brick is yet to be tested.'

The Lord Mayor Alderman R. U. Sitingcomfortably commented, 'The
Hamm brother's attitude is cavalier by turning this place into a testing ground. It's a right pigsty of a mess.'

When asked, the three brothers refused to comment but their spokesperson told me they were awaiting the results of wind tests on the brick house before taking any action.

Whilst on the subject of novel building materials, a court hearing due next Tuesday is to hear a case of child cruelty regarding the Hansel and Gretel twins. Their mother, Mrs Oldwitch, has been accused of neglecting her two children and causing unnecessary suffering.

At first, this seems unconnected with the issues around the Hamm brothers and building materials but this reporter has uncovered a potential catastrophic time bomb, which, if left unchecked, could be disastrous for all young people.

It all began when Mrs Oldwitch inherited a holiday cottage in Dark wood from her grandmother Mrs Lupine. The cottage was left in disrepair ever since the infamous incident with Ms Hood and the Grandma impersonator. However, it was an attractive cottage in a lovely wooded glade and Mrs Oldwitch who ran the local bakery decided to render the house with a gingerbread compound produced in her shop. She regularly made this confectionary and used the surplus to redecorate the cottage.

This new interior was very attractive, smelled of cinnamon and studded with candies in a colourful pattern.

The Hansel and Gretel twins spent a lot of time in the cottage during school holidays, in fact, it almost became their prison as they often refused to come home. They became addicted to eating the gingerbread plastered walls and also consumed large quantities of the embedded candies.

Mrs Oldwitch had noticed the children's weight gain but did nothing about it. Only when they visited the dentist was the full horror of the children's tooth decay revealed.

Commenting on this situation Dr Wewillbegin said 'I've not seen such extensive tooth decay as this in young children. It's disgraceful. I was obliged to contact social services as I suspected these children had been severely neglected.

Ms H. Evereafter, the head of Social services stated,' this type of neglect is unacceptable in modern society. Tooth decay and childhood obesity are increasing problems and I hope this court hearing will send a message to Mrs Oldwitch and others it is not acceptable to treat children this way.'

The case continues and this reporter will keep the readers updated.

BREAKING NEWS from the Editor

Our investigative reporter Noah Fable is missing. He was on his way to interview Mr Jack Beanstalk at Fefifofum Farm situated just outside Storfairy. Once again, he was investigating a report about the use of unapproved building materials, in particular an unusual tower construction that has mysteriously appeared on the farm.

Mr Beanstalk was at the cattle market earlier in the week and was last seen walking home alone clutching something in his hand.

THE LAW AND THE LADY

Eric McEvoy

Blind justice she is called, reaching with her scales
With wisdom, mercy and authority that prevails
To evenly balance man's good and evil doing
Or, blindness, if truth and lies are brewing

Lustitia her name, in ancient Rome
For her impartial justice, universally known
With her double edged sword she wielded power
Over nobles and poor and the guilty who cower

She stands alone, proud, on many a justice hall
For liberty, law and fair retribution for all
Lawbreakers in their droves come under her spell
Lawgivers expect her to give miscreants hell

Is true justice blind, is justice the truth?
An eye for an eye, a tooth for a tooth
Is hanging justified for stealing a sheep?
To feed hungry children who bitterly weep

Miscarriages of law and the fallibility of man
Serve warning to us all, to do what we can
To ensure the rights of the innocent are heard
Do the lawyers ensure the truth is not blurred?

When Judges, our servants, are called to the bar
Do they interpret the law to apply from afar?
Far away from the reality of everyday life
Immune and cosseted from everyday strife

In their chambers so opulent and their outfits so grand
Do they detach themselves from the poor of the land?
Or do they distance themselves away from us all
To ensure objectivity in judgement doesn't stall

Most of us will never be judged by our peers
But fairness and truth is the sum of our fears
When the verdict is in and the judgement agreed
Will the law and the lady judge every deed?

JIM McGUIRK

ROBERT FROST –
WRITING BETWEEN THE LINES

Jim McGuirk

Whose woods these are I think I know
As children we both watched them grow
His house is in the village though
Bereft of care and full of woe
He will not see me stopping here
No meeting up to bring good cheer
To watch his woods fill up with snow
He never knew I loved him so

My little horse must think it queer
For us to take a breather here
To stop without a farmhouse near
And chill beside the frozen mere
Between the woods and frozen lake
I pause awhile for old time's sake
The darkest evening of the year
Cannot hide my falling tear

He gives his harness bells a shake
His torso writhing like a snake
To ask if there is some mistake
And see if I am still awake
The only other sound's the sweep

If one discounts my stifled weep
Of easy wind and downy flake
Blowing on the solid lake

The woods are lovely, dark and deep,
This winter does the sun out leap
But I have promises to keep
For I have sown and now I reap
And miles to go before I sleep
To kiss the earth as mouldered heap
And miles to go before I sleep
No more to love, no more to weep

THE FUSTARD BIRDS
by Colonel Oblivion, RSPB, BTO, WWT.

Jim McGuirk

Being one of the world's greatest ornithologists, I felt duty bound to accept, without question, the commission offered by the Global Bird Management Organisation. They wanted me to find out if the Amazonian Fustard bird actually existed, or was it just another well-perpetuated myth, similar to that of the Oomygoolies bird.

It was once reported by certain ornithologists of sound reputation, that the indigenous tribes of Outer Mongolia claimed that the male of the Oomygoolies bird had no legs, and that its strange name was said to be derived from the loud cries it made on landing, but as most modern day twitchers are now well aware, all tales and sightings of this bird turned out to be a complete hoax.

Armed with state-of-the-art surveillance equipment and a small, enthusiastic team of fellow ornithologists, I set off for the dense rain forests of the Amazon Basin.

As there are no photographs of the Fustard bird in existence, we had to rely on drawings composed from various verbal descriptions given by those who claimed to have caught a glimpse of this supposed creature.

We battled daily through dense undergrowth for three months solid without success, then, when we were about to give up on our mission, we broke through into a lush grassland plateau. To our utter amazement, this unadulterated plain was densely populated by Fustard birds, easily recognizable from the drawings we had.

The most surprising thing though, was that there was a marked diversity between the Fustards and they seemed to have branched into two separate species. One had colonised the prairie and the other had made its home in the forest.

When threatened by a predator, the birds which had adapted to life on the prairie simply turned away from the danger and flew off in the normal fashion, whilst those that had evolved in accordance with dense forest conditions and overhanging canopies, engaged their predators in a hypnotic gaze and slowly backed away on foot until they had enough clearance to take off and gain sufficient height to enable them to fly over the heads of their would be captors, thus making good their escape.

In order to distinguish between this and the prairie dwelling variety, I decided to catalogue the first as Fast Fleeing Fustard, and the latter as the Backing Fustard. When I informed my colleagues of my decision to name the birds thus, they looked in puzzlement from one to the other, and, for some reason I was unable to comprehend, they were chuckling and seemingly amused.

Although the Backing Fustards were difficult to catch by conventional means, we eventually caught enough of the creatures, twelve in all, to bring back with us in order to further our research.

The voyage home, as ever, seemed to take such a long time and we lost one of the birds which had escaped at feeding time. As we approached it with the nets, it backed away in its usual manner, but it had overlooked the relatively small size of our ship and plunged overboard, only to be eaten by a hungry shark.

Eventually we docked in Liverpool, my home town. Suddenly, it dawned on me that I had forgotten to tell my good lady wife about the trip. I had just upped and left one night after finishing my evening meal. I am wont to do such things when preoccupied.

I'll bet she's wondering where I am, I thought as I knocked sheepishly on the front door of our home.

She opened it and stood glaring at me for what seemed an eternity, after which she finally spoke.

"Where have you been you fucking bastard?" she screamed.

Hmm, I thought as I stared into her angry face and backed away, *I'll have to change the names of those birds.*

THE TIME MACHINE

Jim McGuirk

Jeremy Foreshaw stood back and admired his handiwork. At last, he had completed his dream. It had taken more than three years, but now, his decision to immerse himself in the study of quantum physics had paid off. There, on the bench before him, was the world's first time machine.
It bore no resemblance to time machines of the science fiction stories he read avidly as a child. The fact that it interfaced directly with the quantum world meant that perceived size was irrelevant. He had long since discovered that in the quantum world, size was an illusion and did not really exist. The infinitely large looped back seamlessly to the infinitely small. The box of tricks before him could be attached to anywhere on his person, and it would give him the ability to travel to any moment in time.
A tapping on his workshop door distracted him.
'Come in'.
The door opened and Jeremy's wife Elizabeth walked in carrying a tray.
'I've made you a cup of tea and a sandwich darling,' she cooed, 'you must be hungry by now.'
Jeremy took the tray and placed it carefully alongside the time machine on his workbench. He

took Elizabeth in his arms, hugged her tightly and kissed her hard on the lips. Elizabeth drew back in surprise and laughed.

'It's only a cup of tea darling.'

'I know,' he replied, 'it's just that I don't thank you often enough for all the little things you do.'

'It's my pleasure,' she smiled, 'I do it because I love you.'

His eyes moistened and he felt the wet heat of a tear escaping down his cheek. He turned away so she wouldn't see it. He knew he would be leaving her soon.

She kissed him again.

'Don't work too late,' she said, then turned and left the workshop, closing the door behind her.

Jeremy inhaled the residual traces of her perfume. The large workshop suddenly felt empty and he wondered if he would ever see Elizabeth again.

He took a sip of his tea and cursed the obsession that brought him to this impasse.

He had, so far, led a very successful life. But Elizabeth had been the backbone of that success. It was she who shaped the path he had taken. When they met, Jeremy had been working on a farm picking potatoes and drifting aimlessly. She saw his potential and encouraged him to study and go to university. He had a particular liking for physics and took to higher education like a duck to water. Within ten years, he was head of atomic research at Cambridge University and was one of the few people in the world who could almost make sense of quantum physics. His forte was understanding how time fitted neatly into quantum structure. He was the first person to know for sure, not only that time travel was possible, but how it could be achieved.

Now that his machine was completed, he could rid himself of his irrational obsession about Sheila Jackson, the girl he had fallen hopelessly in love with when he was fourteen years old.

His mind drifted back to those school days when he used to follow Sheila around without daring to speak to her. People who knew him said he had a crush on her, but he knew that so called crush would be the strongest love he would ever feel in his life - and he was right. This overwhelming young love was Mother Nature's way of ensuring that couples would pair up and procreate, but nature's rules had now been overwritten by man's.

Jeremy's plan was to travel back in time, meet and befriend his younger self, and encourage him to ask Sheila out on a date. Of course he'd miss Elizabeth, but the fact that his new life would take a different path with his first love would mean he wouldn't meet her, and if there were any problems, he could use the time machine to put things right.

He picked up a bag of gold sovereigns, put on the retro mid-eighties clothes he had gathered together in preparation for his trip, and drained his teacup. Taking a deep breath, he set the date on the time machine to his fifteenth birthday, Tuesday, 2nd of April 1985, strapped it around his waist and pressed the button to activate it.

In an instant he was standing in a grass field. His house or workshop had not been built yet. This was no surprise. He had made sure he knew what was on this site in 1985. He did not want to materialise inside a tree, a brick wall or a block of concrete.

He walked to the high street, cashed in some of the sovereigns and booked into a hotel; after which, he set about seeking out his younger self.

He flagged down a cab and gave the driver directions to his old school. Pleased at the accuracy of his time machine settings, he arrived at his old Secondary Modern school at 3pm. Half an hour before the pupils finished their school day.

He bided his time by taking in the sights. He marvelled at the fact that, although he was actually present in 1985, he was still steeped in nostalgia.

Shortly after 3.30pm, the double doors burst open and the children started to stream out. He saw his fifteen year old self leaving the school gate. He was slouching and seemed to be in an unhappy daze. He put his hand on young Jeremy's shoulder.

'Look Jeremy,' he said, 'you love Sheila Jackson, do something about it, ask her out or something. Don't be such a wimp.'

Young Jeremy was shocked to the core.

'Who are you?' he said, 'how do you know my name?'

'Let's just say I'm your guardian angel,' old Jeremy replied as he turned and hurried away.

Back at the hotel Jeremy considered his obsession and wondered if he'd done the right thing. He felt a sudden movement on his waistband and watched with horror as his time machine disappeared before his eyes and he started to lose consciousness.

When he awoke he was in a dirty bed with unwashed sheets. He jumped up and looked at the clock, it was 10am. Somehow, he knew where his clothes were and dressed himself. He wondered why he was so familiar with these strange surroundings and made his way downstairs.

He entered the lounge. It was dirty and untidy. There were dirty, overflowing ashtrays dotted around the room, but the biggest shock of all was the unkempt, obese woman stretched out on the sofa nursing a large glass of wine. This was the focus of his obsession, Sheila Jackson aged forty-seven.

As the memories of his two lives intertwined and jostled for position, each trying to merge within his ill-equipped brain, he realised that Sheila was now his wife. His obsessive dream had been fulfilled, but that dream was now a nightmare.

He remembered his happy years with Elizabeth and how much he loved her. How much he loved a woman he had never met and would never see. He also remembered the strange man who had met him outside school when he was fifteen. The man who had given him the advice that ruined his life. He also remembered giving that advice when he was forty-seven years old.

Such are the paradoxes of time.

HITCH HIKER'S GUIDE TO THE LOONEY BIN

Jim McGuirk

John mopped up the remains of his full English breakfast with his last piece of toast and wedged it into his ample mouth. Taking care not to spill anything onto his new tie or his crisp white shirt, he glugged down what was left of his tea and looked around. Burping quietly, he wiped his lips with a handkerchief, stood up, and made his way out to the car park. *They always do a good breakfast at Lil's Cafe*, he thought, feeling replete.

As he drove off, he checked his mirror, signalled, and edged out from between the other parked cars. Within seconds he slammed on his brakes as someone banged heavily on the roof of his car and called out loudly in a blocked nasal tone.

"Oi mate, are you goin' anywhere near the menkle hospiggle?"

He reached over and wound down the passenger side window.

"St Austin's? Yes I am sir. That's where I'm heading. Why?"

"Can y'givvus a lift there please."

The stranger's saving grace was the honesty in the way he said the word please.

"Ok, get in," John replied, giving him the benefit of the doubt for the thumping his car roof had just had.

The stranger's large, hairy, oaf-like hands snatched at the passenger door. As he clambered into the car, he loomed over John, blocking out most of the daylight from the passenger side. John was taken aback. The stranger was huge. He looked up into deep-set, staring eyes which seemed to pin him to his seat. The reason for the nasal-sounding voice became obvious. The stranger's nose was completely flat and spread, like a huge 1940s ladies coat button, right across the middle of his face.

The car rocked wildly as he bounced heavily into his seat.

John took a deep breath.

Thank God it's only nine miles to St Austin's, he thought.

"Thanks matey," John's new found friend bellowed, "my name's Bimbo, what's yours?"

John hesitated. Feeling a bit scared, he tried to gather his thoughts and make sense of everything. "Err, it's John, err, yes, that's right, John Culshaw. How come you're called Bimbo?"

"It's my nickname. My mates made it up for me. They call me, Bimbo, the Big Bad Ballcrusher."

"What's your real name?' John asked.

"I can't remember."

John put his foot down. *The faster I go the quicker we get there*, he thought.

"Why do they call you that?" he asked, hoping Bimbo wouldn't be angry at such a question.

"I used to be a wrestler." Bimbo answered calmly, "that's why I'm on my way to the hospiggle. I kept gettin' knocked out in the ring an' I got a few dents in my skull. Everyone says I've never been the same since but I can't notice any difference. They must be right though, 'cause one day I forearm smashed my missus right through the bedroom window when she set the alarm too early. That isn't normal is it? Well, everyone keeps tellin' me it's not, but I can't see anything wrong with it. Why didn't she just set it at the right time?"

John gripped the wheel tightly and sped up even more.

"There's somethin' else as well, when I try to play chess or do crosswords, I get a thumpin' headache. Thump, Thump, Thump". Bimbo screamed banging his clenched fist hard on the dashboard. "Just like that. Thump, thump, thump."

John started to panic and tried to talk Bimbo down. "Were you good at chess then - before the injuries?"

"Oh no," Bimbo said, switching instantly back to calm. "I'm not clever enough. I don't know where all the pieces go … but it's even worse now … if you know what I mean?"

"Err, yes I think so." John replied nervously.

They drove on in silence, then all of a sudden Bimbo shrieked loudly and started to pull out clumps of his short, patchy hair.

John was stricken with terror. "What's wrong, what's the matter?" he asked.

"You're goin' too fast!" Bimbo screamed, "we're gonna crash."

Later that day, the police were attending an incident reported by a passing motorist. The witness said he saw two people struggling violently in the front of a car, outside the main gate of St Austin's Mental Hospital. When the police arrived at the scene, the medical staff from the hospital had already been out and recognised the mentally unstable aggressor as one of their out-patients. They sedated him and he was now safely interned at the hospital. Unfortunately, there was little they could do for the other person; he had already died from severe head injuries sustained in the struggle.

Detective Inspector, David Cusack, who was in charge of the crime scene, walked over to the car and peered through the open car door.

"Good Heavens!" he exclaimed, "I Know that man. It's Bimbo the Big Bad Ballcrusher. He's a famous wrestler … at least he was"

PAT McGUIRK

A QUIET PLACE

Pat McGuirk

This is my quiet place
Snug and cool and shady.
And quiet.
At least it will be soon.
It shouldn't be long now

At last!
A place where I can get my head together.
I would have tried it a long time ago
If I had known it would be so peaceful here.
That's the best thing about it
Nothing to do here

Just BE

Do not disturb!
That's what it should say on the plaque outside.
No interruptions.
No responsibilities
No appointments
No work
Just time.

Time for ME!

Well it sounds like they've finished out there
The digging has stopped
They're all drifting away
Just the headstone to place
Then I'm alone
Ah!

ANOTHER FINE MESS

Pat McGuirk

Cuthbert Oliver Stanley was instructing Johnathan his apprentice in his small office at Grimes, Slater and Bell, Funeral directors.

'You must always be polite and accommodating to all clients,' he said, 'and you must fulfil their wishes to the best of your ability.' He got up and closed the door. 'That will do for the senior partners,' he continued, 'but what I'm going to tell you now must not leave this room.'

Johnathan pricked up his ears. He knew he was going to be let in on some of the perks of the job.

'The thing to remember,' said Cuthbert, is that lavish funerals are a result of the mourners' pride and guilt, and a misplaced sense of duty. It wouldn't do to voice this opinion widely but a simple pine box should be sufficient for anyone. After all the deceased will not know any different and the money that's wasted on trimmings can be used for better purposes. There are ways, if you are discrete, of making a tidy sum for yourself. For instance, if the mourners choose a fully lined padded coffin, you just pad the top half where it will be seen. Nobody ever checks the bottom. Or if they pay for gold handles you use gold plated ones. It's seen as bad taste to examine the coffin while the deceased is lying in it. If there are going to be few mourners and none of them very close to the deceased, I see no harm in taking the money for an expensive casket and then substituting it for a much cheaper pine box and pocketing the difference. Who does that hurt? The mourners go away happy in the knowledge that they have done their duty, the deceased won't know or care what they are buried in and you have a small windfall that the tax man does not need to know about.'

Johnathan looked doubtful. 'But what about when you have to face them on the other side?' he asked.

'That's all twaddle and claptrap!' Cuthbert exclaimed laughing. 'This is 1850 not the dark ages. Don't you go worrying about all that superstitious nonsense. This life is all there is and you have to make what you can of it. Once you're dead, you're dead.' How wrong he was.

'Take this client for instance,' he said handing Johnathan a letter. It was addressed to Mr Cuthbert Oliver Stanley, c/o Messrs Grimes, Slater and Bell. Johnathan took the letter and read it through. It said:

'Dear Mr Stanley

You have been recommended to me by your superior, Mr Grimes as being a conscientious and discrete individual.

I am writing to you in the hope that you will fulfil my wishes to the smallest detail. I require the utmost discretion in the performance of this task. I have unfortunately but a short time to live and as I am alone in the world I must necessarily make arrangements for my own funeral. The details I leave to you except that the coffin must be at least seven feet long and three feet wide at the shoulders and be made of the finest polished teak, lined with silk, padded thickly for extra comfort. The only other stipulation is that you should draw as little attention as possible to my passing. Paid mourners will not be necessary, nor will a church service. In fact it would be better if you carried out the necessary duties alone.

Please find enclosed my card and the key to my home. Upon my demise you will receive a note whereupon you will proceed to my address to begin your preparations.

A cheque has also been enclosed which, I am sure you will agree, will more than adequately compensate you for your trouble. Thank you.

Yours sincerely'

'This is a prime example of what I have been saying,' Cuthbert said when Johnathan had finished reading.

'If we cash this cheque and then bury him in the cheapest coffin we have, who will know or care? We could dig his grave ourselves or pay the gravediggers a pound or two to keep quiet and we could make a fortune.' And that was precisely what they did when, a few weeks later, Cuthbert received a note to say that the client had died.

That night Cuthbert was awoken by a strange musty smell in his bedroom. As he sat up he froze at the sight of his latest client sitting at the end of his bed. He rubbed his eyes and looked again. The apparition shook his head mournfully as he stared at the coffin that was wedged tightly between Cuthbert's bed and the wardrobe. Then he turned to Cuthbert and said, 'I came to you in good faith and had your assurance that my wishes would be carried out exactly, to the smallest detail. You failed me dismally, and now you will face the consequences of your action. As he glanced forlornly through the bedroom window the moonlight shone on his pale face, glinting off his very pointed teeth. When finally he turned with an accusing look on his face Cuthbert was mesmerised by his piercing eyes that seemed to pin him to the bed, allowing no possibility of escape.

'What is the world coming to?' he sighed, 'there was a time when professionals took pride in their work for its own sake. Now everyone is out for what he can get without concern for the service they should be providing. You let me down sir, in the worst possible way. You are by no means the first person to have played this particular trick on me. The others are all dead now of course, as you soon will be. You have only yourself to blame, Sir. Your dishonesty is inexcusable.' Pointing at the coffin he said, 'You assured me you would provide the finest, most comfortable casket your company could offer, and this . . . this abomination . . . is what you gave me. I find it absolutely unacceptable.

  You cannot possibly conceive of how furious I was when I woke to find myself in this inferior box instead of the luxury one I had paid for. Look at it! That's another pine chest you've put me in to Mr Stanley.'

BROTHERLY LOVE

Pat McGuirk

Horace strolled along at his own leisurely pace, enjoying the sunshine and looking forward getting home and kicking his shoes off. Work had been awful and all he wanted to do was vegetate in front of the telly with a cool drink. He had no idea that Don his younger brother was at his house waiting for him to get home. He had no idea what his brother had in store for him.

'I'm gonna get my revenge tonight,' Don thought to himself. 'All my life he's made a prat out of me. He always has to go one better; make me look a fool. What he did last week was the last straw. It makes me cringe just thinking about it. In front of Susie too, she was laughing as loud as everybody else. Now I'll show him. I've put up with him for long enough. He's gonna pay tonight, I'll see to that. Ha ha, I can't wait. When he walks through the door he's gonna get the shock of his life.'

Obviously he couldn't turn the light on but it was nerve-wracking sitting there in the dark listening to the voices telling him his plan would go wrong.

'You can't fool him, he'll know.'

'He'll be ready for you, wait and see.'

He had to shut them up somehow.

'Be quiet! I'm not listening,' he said, but they just laughed even louder.

Don tried not to listen, to shut them out, but they were getting to him. 'Just sit quiet and still', he told himself, 'He's got to be home soon and then . . .'

He imagined his brother's shock in that moment – that first split second – when he realised what was happening. It wouldn't go wrong, it mustn't. He had planned this for days, checking and re-checking to make sure he had everything ready.

'It won't be long now,' he gloated to himself, 'I can't wait to see the look of shock on his face when he sees what I've got planned for him. That will be bliss. This time I will be the one in control. Hee, hee, hee. He's really gonna be sorry he messed with me.'

'You're going to look a fool when it falls flat,' one of the voices said and the others all laughed again.

'Shut up! Shut up!' He whispered urgently, 'there's his key in the door.'

'Get ready,' he thought, 'stay calm and don't make a sound. Don't give the game away. Ha ha won't he be shocked - they won't be quiet, he's gonna hear them. '

'Be quiet, you'll ruin it,' he hissed

'Any minute now!' he thought. 'You're gonna pay Horace, hee hee. Stay calm, can't jump up too soon and ruin it now. No! That would be disastrous. He always manages to come out on top somehow. I can't let that happen this time. Breathe slowly; deep breaths. Ha HAA! He doesn't suspect a thing poor slob - they're laughing again.'

'Why won't you be quiet? He's outside the door, SHUT UP!' He hissed.

'Here we go,' he told himself 'it's payback time.'

Don got up slowly and quietly and stood next to the light switch. Then he heard Horace's hand on the doorknob, turning it, opening the door. Thankfully the voices had quieted for the moment. 'Deep breaths,' he reminded himself, 'get ready to switch the light on. . . . Now!'

'Surprise! Happy Birthday to you, Happy Birthday to you.'

GONE!

Pat McGuirk

Absently Ada polished the china cup although it was already perfectly clean and shining. The clink as she placed it onto the saucer echoed in the silence of the kitchen. After pouring some hot water from the kettle into the pot waiting on the kitchen worktop, she swirled the water around to warm it and tipped it into the sink. Then she carefully measured two spoons of tea into the pot and poured on the now boiling water. Outside the rain was so heavy it had made the kitchen window opaque. The wind threw a squirl of damp leaves that hit the window and stuck to the glass. Shivering slightly in the chill air she put the single cup and saucer onto the tray with the pot and milk jug and carried it through into the living room. All her movements were automatic, almost robotic as she sat on her usual chair by the fire. A lump came into her throat as she glanced around the room settling on Stan's empty chair. 'Empty' doesn't really convey the acute physical absence of someone who should be sitting there. His slippers were placed neatly on the floor beside the chair with the book he had been reading placed on top of them. His chess set was on the table as usual; still halfway through the game he had been playing with their twelve year old grandson Tom. Stan used to love these games, pondering for ages over his next move and chuckling with delight when Tom surprised him.

Pouring her tea she felt the need to stop herself asking if he wanted one. Placing her cup down carefully after one sip she sat staring into the fire. The pop and crackle of the coal fire should have been cosy in contrast to the rattle of wind and rain on the window but it only kept the chill from the room. She gazed around, not really seeing the many things they had chosen together. Colours seemed faded and drab, souvenirs trite and pointless.

The parts of her accustomed to responding to him seemed suspended; dead with him. Yet the expectation of seeing him or hearing his voice, never noticed before, was acutely tuned so that she had a sensation of his presence; as though she could almost reach out and touch him. If she could just turn fast enough she would see him sitting in his armchair as usual, his head nodding over his book. Everything she did was a fresh reminder of her grief. Lost in a radio or TV programme she would turn to him to make some comment on it, or to read out an interesting item from the paper, and her throat would ache from the renewed absence of him. Taking another sip of her tea she glanced at his medication on the floor next to his slippers.

Reaching for it she said, 'You won't be needing this anymore will you?' She opened the bottle and poured the contents into her hand then sat clutching the bright blue pills, listening to the hypnotic tick-tick-tick of the mantle clock. Her eyes glowed with reflected firelight on unshed tears, while she sat and tried to decide what she would do next.

'Are you coming tonight?' Shocked, she raised her head, listening for more. The deep, gravelly voice outside her window had sounded so much like his that it instantly transported her back to the first day they had met. She was a new starter at the paint factory and she hadn't yet learned to hear the others talking over the thumping noise of the packing machine engines and conveyor belts. But she heard him perfectly.

'Are you coming to the dance tonight?' She nodded, smiling and he said, 'Great, I'll see you there.' Winking he turned away and carried on loading the finished paint cans onto the pallets at the end of the line. The memory was so strong it was as though she was back there. The air was thick with smells, from the acrid, warm rubber of the conveyor belts and the sharp acetone of the paint in the vats, to the smoke on the clothes and breath of the girl showing her the ropes. Being new she was only folding boxes for the others to use as they packed the finished tins ready for stacking onto the pallets. She remembered the smooth feel of the waxed cardboard as she bent each box flap, and the dust that flew off every time she picked up a new box to fold. In no time at all it was in her clothes, her hair and her nose. She must have sneezed constantly that first day. Looking up in a quiet moment she could see the dust floating in the air, glinting in the shafts of weak sunlight through the high, dirty windows lining the white painted brick walls of the factory. She must have looked a sight and she would never know what it was that made him ask her out.

The annual Christmas dinner and dance of the paint factory was held in the local school hall. Home-made paper garlands in rainbow colours hung from the walls and ceiling and there were balloons everywhere. The sad Christmas tree in the corner was already shedding its needles on the polished wood floor and a faint lingering smell of beeswax and school dinners combined with the stale smell of the school gym kits in the lockers near the entrance. The tables had been set at either side against the brown walls in long lines, leaving the middle of the floor clear for dancing.

She thought of that awful yellow dress she had worn with the stiff lace bodice that scratched and itched, with five stiff underskirts under the billowing satin skirt that meant she could not sit down, only perch on the edge of a seat. She had thought she looked beautiful as she danced and, thinking back, she probably had but she had vowed never to wear it again.

He had been there when she arrived, standing outside talking to a group of the other lads from work. She watched him in the light from the open doorway as she walked across the playground. Tall with short dark hair he carried off the evening dress well and his slightly too-long nose suited his face perfectly. She liked the way his mouth always turned up at the corners, even when he was working, and the amused glint that seemed to be a constant feature of his eyes. As she drew near he separated from the group and approached her.

'Can I walk you in?' he asked as he took her arm. He smelled of fresh soap, she loved that. There was a different look in his eyes then as he gazed at her,

'You look beautiful,' he said and her heart leapt. She loved dancing and so did he. It seemed that they never stopped all night. And he had made her laugh. She couldn't remember what they had talked about but she remembered that first kiss when he had walked her home. The cold December air had been pleasant after the heat of the hall and they had walked slowly, looking at the stars and the bare branches of trees silhouetted against the sky. He had his arm over her shoulder and she could still remember the warm, safe feeling it had given her. Her hand was around his waist feeling the thick weave of his overcoat. They had compared the windows they passed, decorated for Christmas, and argued about which was the best. When they reached her front door they had stopped and gazed at each other for a long time, not speaking, listening to the silence all around them. Then he had kissed her, or rather they had kissed each other. She had never felt so close to anyone before in her life. He gave her a last hug and said, 'Good night.' As he walked down the path he turned back and said, 'I'm going to marry you, you know.' Then he grinned and walked off.

The glow of that memory made her smile despite the ache in her throat. She sat for a while longer deep in thought before getting up to take the tray out to the kitchen. As she rinsed the cup and teapot and left them to drain, a shaft of sunlight burst suddenly through the window, glinting brightly off the pills she had placed on the window ledge. Sighing she gathered them up and threw them into the bin thankful that his pain was over at last. Then she walked into the living room and began to tidy his belongings away. She would give the chess set to Tom, Stan would like that.

RESOLUTIONS

Pat McGuirk

This year I'm going to do it
I definitely mean it. I do.
I'm going to pack in smoking
No addiction no lungs filled with goo.
I'll throw away this packet and I won't buy any more
And I won't give in to temptation as I did each time before
No more packets to open
No more lighters to buy,
No more fags poking out of my mouth
No more . . .
No more warm smoke or tang of tobacco easing down my throat soothing and smooth and relaxing and . . . NO!
Definitely this time.
I'll lose two stone by summer
My figure will look divine
Twice a week at the gym, and jogging
Out early rain or shine
Covers off, jump up, a warm up routine
No more dozing my life away
No more . . .

No more five minutes more snuggling down under
the duvet wrapping it around my neck and feeling
the warmth and sticking my toe out and pulling it
back in and . . . NO!
Definitely this time.
I've put on some weight over Christmas
Well it's allowed then, isn't it?
I'll cut out the crisps and the chocolate
In no time I'm going to be fit
No more pizzas, or curries or pies, or ice cream
No more . . .
No more bread with lashings of butter, filled with
chips and the butter melting and dripping out of the
sides and licking it off my hands and ... NO!
Definitely this time.
I might as well go the whole hog
I'm giving up drinking as well
I think my brain is shrinking
And my liver has started to swell.
No more being sick in the gutter
Or waking up feeling like hell
No more . . .
No more nice warm glow in the back of my tongue
and the cosy way that it makes me relax and the . . .
NO!
Definitely this time.
This year I'll stick to my promises
A New Year, new start, new me
Slim and fit, and bright as a button

That's what I'm determined to be.
Starting tomorrow - After tonight's party - It IS
New Year.
Definitely.

ON THE MOUNTAIN STANDS A LADY

Pat McGuirk

Four young people sat at a table in the White Lady pub waiting for other friends to arrive. They were discussing their planned camp out in the woods. It was Halloween and they had chosen that area because of reported sightings of a so called white lady in the area. The pub had been named after her. With the cynical arrogance of the young, none of the group really believed this story but they had met here to walk up and camp out at the bottom of the hill. It was Halloween and they wanted a good scare.

Katy said, 'How far away is this camp site?'

'It's not far,' John answered, 'We should be there before its dark if they're not late . . . Get a room you two.' This last was aimed at the couple opposite. Sally and Kevin both stopped kissing and laughed. They had been together for a while now and they were becoming embarrassing, always grabbing and touching each other, when they weren't arguing at least.

The door opened and Andy walked in with Liz.

'At last!' John said, 'I thought we were going to have to walk up in the dark.'

Andy laughed and went to the bar to order another round of drinks 'Just get ready for the scariest night of your life,' he said sitting down at the table. 'I've got "Cabin in the Woods" and "The Blair Witch Project" on my iPad to watch later. Who's up for a race to the top of the hill at midnight?'

They all grinned at each other, each taking courage from the others, none prepared to admit that they had a small gnawing doubt about going through with this.

'If you need to call anyone do it now,' Andy added with a grin, 'You won't get a signal at the bottom of the hill. We'll be completely cut off from civilization.'

The locals who had overheard their conversations and, mostly with tongue in cheek, told them tales of people who had seen the ghost and then died in their sleep the next night. One old man sitting by the fire, glared over at them seeming to take it more seriously.

'You shouldn't toy with these things,' he told them. 'Some things are best left alone. He took a sip of his drink before continuing.

'Men have gone up that hill and never come down again. You should keep well away from there, especially tonight.

'Does anyone know who the white lady is supposed to be?' John asked.

'Don't encourage him,' the barmaid laughed, bringing their meals

'There'll be no stopping him now. He just loves the chance to tell his stories to anyone who will listen.'

The old man settled himself in his chair. 'She is said to be the ghost of Annabel Croft who was hanged as a witch in the 17th Century,' he began. The group were delighted. This was just what they wanted, a scary story to build up the atmosphere for their camp out.

'Annabel had been promised in marriage against her will to Edwin Symes, a middle aged farmer who only wanted a wife and sons to help him run his farm. But Annabel was in love with Thomas, a young lad from the village and had been planning to marry him. They had been meeting secretly in the woods, in an old cabin at the top of a hill. When Annabel told Thomas she was pregnant though he had had second thoughts. He told her he had no plans to settle down yet and then moved on to a young dairy maid from the farm up the lane. Times were different then. Women who got pregnant outside of marriage would be ostracised by the community. Devastated, Annabel decided the best thing for her to do would be to go ahead with her marriage to Edwin and pass the baby off as his.' He finished the last of his ale and pushed the empty glass towards their table.

'Hang on, mate,' Kevin said, getting up to order another round of drinks. He came back with the drinks, putting a pint of bitter on the table for the old man who took a large gulp of the beer before carrying on with his tale.

'Annabel became reconciled to the idea of being Edwin's wife and had begun to think it might not be so bad. He wasn't a romantic man but he was a hard worker and didn't drink. Plans went ahead for the wedding but on the day, when the priest asked if anyone knew of any reason why they should not get married a group of village women shouted from the back of the church that she was pregnant.

'Fuming with anger, Edwin stormed out of the church. Annabel followed, sobbing. Deeply ashamed she had nowhere to go but the old cabin she had shared with Thomas. For a while she lived alone on the hill, only going down into the village when she had no other choice. Before long, whenever someone had a run of bad luck, or an animal died, or a crop failed, the villagers began to murmur her name. When she lost her baby it was rumoured that she had killed it in some sort of sacrifice. It was only a matter of time before she was openly accused of practicing witchcraft and arrested. She never made any attempt to deny it, in fact, during her trial she had been so furious she had shouted that the devil could have her soul if he would allow her to remain on the hill and have revenge on the village people and their ancestors. Soon after that everyone who had been involved in her trial and execution had either died or disappeared.'

One of the men at a corner table shouted over to Andy, 'You want to be careful out there mate, she likes redheads.' Most of the locals laughed at this and, looking at Andy's bright orange hair his friends joined in.

'Whooo!' Katy said waving her fingers at Andy who grinned sheepishly, his face bright red.

The barman came over in a quiet period knowing the old fellow was entertaining the locals as well as the visitors. He asked them if they had ever been in the woods at night and then started to set the scene.

'Trees have a way of changing at night time into contorted, tortured shapes, like strange creatures, frozen in the throes of agony. Black branches take on the form of tossing, writhing limbs, stretching and straining to catch the unwary. It's no good telling yourself then that they're just trees. You won't believe it when you're standing there alone, your mouth dry and your heart pumping, listening to those strange creaks and pops that sounds as though the trees are trying to wrest their roots from the earth. 'Is that just a trick of your mind?' you ask yourself 'or are they really whispering secrets to each other.' You feel as though there are eyes staring at your back, like a physical touch on that spot below your neck, watching; waiting? Did that branch just blow in the wind? Or was it guided by an intelligent awareness that knows you're there and wants to trap you? You sigh, trying to get control of your breathing, but the shaky breath rasps in your throat.

He looked at the nervous faces around the table as the visitors leant towards him. 'Mist makes it worse. You enter a clearing, relieved to be out in the open. But then you see in the distance, surrounding you, the grey writhing forms of wraiths straining to reach you. Are they getting closer? Surely they are.

"It's just your imagination," you tell yourself, and you might pretend to believe it for a while, you might even laugh out loud, as though there is someone there to hear you. But there is no one; only the living, writhing trees, and you. What do you do now? Will you stay in the clearing, waiting for them to reach you? Or will you go back on to the narrow path where they can scratch at your face and pull at your feet. You have to decide.

"Go on" you tell yourself then, "They're only trees." But you know different.'

The locals were in an uproar and the group thanked him then laughing a little too loudly they left the pub and headed towards the forest, jostling and teasing each other. The first thing they did when they arrived at the campsite was to go up the hill together marking a path to the top with white rags cut into strips and tied to the branches of the trees. It took them half an hour to reach the top. On the way down they discussed the legend, laughing and pushing as they tried to scare each other. When they got back to the camp site they all busied themselves with putting their tents up before it got dark and lighting a fire.

Then Katy whispered, 'Did you get it?'

Liz laughed and said 'Yes, we'll have to get the lads to let us go up first. We'll say we need a head start.' They grinned at each other, anticipating the trick they would pull later on. 'It'll be freezing, she said but it'll be worth it to see their faces.' They all laughed again, just as the fire burst into life. Around them it was already getting dark although it was only teatime. Sitting around the fire with some bottles and cans of beer, they spent the early evening engaged in light hearted trivia that was important to them at the time. They felt safe then, all together, and the alcohol helped to mask the tiny trickles of fear that were invading their thoughts. After wolfing down the food they had brought with them they huddled together in the biggest tent watching their films. They were scared then, but it was the nervous, fun fear people get watching horror stories.

This group, like most young people of today, with their mobile phones, tablets, laptops, TVs and other gadgets, had never truly been alone. With street lights shining through their bedroom windows at night they had never truly been in the dark. They would soon find out that being in total darkness, away from all contact with others, their primeval fears, so close to the surface in all mankind since the dawn of time, would emerge. Overcome by that terror of being alone and scared, while some unnamed entity lurks in the shadows, just out of sight, they would be more frightened than they had bargained for as their pagan natures took over.

Midnight came. The girls refused to go up alone and said they should get a head start, reasoning that they could time the boys' arrival at the top. It was agreed that they should go first and then the lads would follow, staggered at five minute intervals. Though they would never have admitted it, by this time the boys would rather not go up alone either. The girls ran into the woods together, laughing as they went, picking up the parcel they had hidden earlier.

As planned, John followed, running as hard as he could, intent on reaching the top in the shortest time possible. Then he entered a clearing. The woods had looked totally different in the day time. Like an impenetrable fence the trees seemed to surround the clearing. Gasping for air he stood a moment to get his bearings. He looked around to find the rag that would lead him out of the clearing and back on to the path. He couldn't help but think of the barman talking about the trees as though they were malevolent entities. He tried to dismiss the thought and laugh it off. But it lingered there in the back of his mind. His heart beat faster. As he stood there, sucking in great lungsful of air, he glimpsed something white moving off to his left. Turning he could just make out the figure of a woman dressed in a long white dress. He froze on the spot, a dry, hoarse groan escaping from his throat. The blood drained from his face. Then with his heart pounding in his throat he ran to what he hoped was the path. Hearing a laugh behind him he turned to see the girls pointing at him and calling

'Got you.' Katy said.

Liz was wearing a long white dress and they were doubling over laughing at him. He laughed himself then, and called 'Good one girls,' before sprinting across to the marked path. By the time he reached the top of the hill he had just about convinced himself that he had known all along that it was the girls.

Kevin was the next up. He wasn't far from the top before panic began to set in. He was trying to avoid looking at the trees telling himself he was nearly there. When he caught a glimpse of a woman dressed in white his scream came out as a strangled squeak. He ran for his life, throat tight, his body charged with pure adrenalin. He was gone before the girls could let him in on the joke. They were hysterical by this time and couldn't wait to see him at the top.

Andy came running up the hill and almost ran into a woman in a white dress. Just for a second he froze and then peered at her through the thickening mist. She just stood, glaring at him. His skin prickled and he could feel beads of sweat running down his spine. His heart drummed against his ribcage as he gulped in air, trying to breathe.

Forcing a laugh he called 'Come on girls you didn't expect to catch me out like that did you?' She just stood motionless glaring at him.

'I'm going to the top,' he said, voice trembling, 'come on its freezing I want to get back to the fire.' As he tried to pass her, she blocked his way, her dead eyes locking onto his. Then he screamed.

After Kevin had passed, the girls waited for Andy for a while. Deciding they must have missed him they eventually made their way up to meet the others. When they heard his scream they looked at each other and laughed.

'Come on Andy' Sally shouted, 'we're waiting to get back down. You don't think we're going to fall for that one do you?' Then they heard the laugh; a mocking, chilling screech of a laugh like nothing they had heard before. It chilled their blood and froze them where they stood. They glanced at each other and without a word they all turned and ran, panting and gasping for breath until they found

John and Kevin at the top of the hill. Nervously they called out to Andy saying that a joke's a joke but they were freezing now. After a while they all agreed that he must have gone back to the fire and was probably sitting there in the warmth laughing at them. They decided to go back and followed the marked path down keeping close together and jumping at every noise and shadow. In the back of all their minds the old man's tale about the white lady nagged at them. They tried to dismiss it as just folklore, but it would not go away. There was no sign of Andy at the camp so they called out to him again, starting to worry that maybe he had fallen and hurt himself and that the scream might have been genuine. There was no point in looking for Andy until morning they agreed. In the mist and the darkness they could easily walk right past him or get hurt themselves.

'Anyway,' Liz said, 'He'll probably make his way down sometime in the night.' They all agreed readily; none of them felt ready to brave the hill again. Sitting around the fire amongst their tents, normality began to reassert itself in their minds. They couldn't accept the possibility that the white lady might be real. But neither could they rid themselves of the nagging doubts that lingered in their thoughts. Their eyes spoke of it eloquently when they looked at each other. No-one got any sleep that night.

It was a much more sober party that took the unused tents down the next morning. They kept glancing into the woods and calling for Andy. Without stopping for breakfast they decided that the best thing would be to go back to the pub and see if he was there. If he wasn't they would have to get the police to help them search for him because he might be still out there hurt.

Andy stood rooted to the spot, unable to take his eyes from hers. She stared into his soul laughing. He felt his heart drop in his chest as she approached and walked around him, teasing and running her fingers through the hairs on his chest. He screamed once before his voice gave out. Pointing to the trees around him in turn she gloated, 'This one was my lover before he betrayed me and now he is mine forever. This big one here was to be my husband but he rejected me. That skinny one was a village lad, married, but coming into my woods with another girl to cheat on his wife. This was a soldier, hiding so that he wouldn't have to go to war. This one thought he was taking a shortcut home. All of these people have invaded my woods. There have been many more over the years, too many to relate. And now I have you.' He could feel a straining in his body as though his skin would split. His toes broke through his shoes, digging deep into the ground, anchoring him to the spot. Without volition his arms rose, straining up as though begging for mercy. His head became warped and deformed while his whole body twisted and writhed in agony. Unable to speak he could hear his friends call his name as they walked right past him. Later he could hear the calls of the searchers who totally ignored the trees they passed. Who would notice one oak tree in the middle of a forest? Every part of his being felt only pain. His arms and head continued to stretch, impossibly high while his torso twisted in agonizing contortions. And he knew that there he would remain, totally aware, unable to move, for all the hundreds of years of the tree's life. After that he could not guess, but he somehow knew it was something he would dread through all those long years.

TIME'S ARROW

Pat McGuirk

Looking out of the window, his face frozen with horror Mick could not accept what he was seeing. How could he have been so stupid? How could he have made such a basic mistake?

Mick looked up from his desk and glanced around the room. 'Three years of University for this,' he complained to himself 'stuck in a dead end job with a pittance for pay, I deserve more from life.'

Brought up in a string of foster homes from a very young age, he had determined that he would be rich one day. Never an easy child to love he was always solitary, rejecting the offers of friendship from the other children until finally they stopped trying. He was so quiet and unresponsive to them that, after a while, they didn't even tease him anymore. Generally everybody just ignored him. He supposed that was why he had not made an impact on any of the couples who came looking for children to adopt. He had learned that he could not rely on anybody but himself. Coasting through school and college he had never really stretched himself to reach his full potential. He always got average marks in everything he did and ended up with a mediocre 2.3 degree and an enormous debt.

While at university he had resented the fact that he had to get a loan that would leave him in debt for a very long time. On top of that he would have to work part time while the more affluent students would be studying or socialising or just lazing about, their tuition and keep all paid for by their parents. Although this undoubtedly had some effect on his final score, his resentment made him blame the system alone for his general failure to shine. Throughout his time at university, he had done the bare minimum of study that would get him his degree, constantly putting in late work. When those same privileged students tended to be the ones who took up all the plumb posts, that strengthened his conviction.

He had finally found work in a third rate university and now here he was doing mundane calculations and filing while all the exciting work was being done elsewhere. He hadn't worked for his degree to do routine, admin work. Somehow, he determined, he would fulfil his ambition to be rich and he wasn't going to be too particular how he did it.

Andrew stood gazing through his window into the main office, deep in thought. He wasn't really looking at anything in particular just taking in the general bustle of the daily routine. He was nearing the culmination of his life's work and that scared him just as much as it excited him. There were just a few more calculations to do and if it all worked out as he thought, he would be ready to go in a month or so. Overwhelmed by that thought he reached for the chair behind him and fell rather than sat onto it. Breathless and heart pounding he forced himself to do his relaxation routine. Closing his eyes he listened to the sounds around him, the slow steady tick of the clock on his office wall, the muted murmur of voices and footsteps from the main office, the occasional ring of a telephone and the beep and clatter of the printer outside his office window. Sitting there quietly while taking slow deep breaths, his mind began to drift. 'Won't be long now, love,' he murmured, 'if this works we can be together again.' He stood, still feeling shaky and decided that he would go home. He could work on his calculations there as well as he could at the lab.

Mick watched as Andrew came out and locked his office door behind him. He wondered, not for the first time what was going on in there. If he ever got the chance he would get in and find out. How that opportunity was going to materialise, Mick wasn't sure, but if it did, then he'd be ready.

Andrew was very secretive about what he was doing; never leaving the office, even just to go for a cup of tea, without locking the door behind him. He was only human though, Mick thought, and he was bound to make a mistake one day.

That opportunity finally came one Friday afternoon when Andrew was locking up. He had come out of his office looking flushed and disorientated. Then he had collapsed, leaving the key hanging out of the door. Mick hid his grin, and leaping to his feet shouted, 'call an ambulance!' He quickly locked the door and slipped the key into his jacket pocket. In the panic that followed Andrew's collapse, none of the other office staff spotted his little piece of subterfuge.

After the ambulance had taken Andrew away Mick sat back at his desk. He couldn't concentrate on his work but then neither could anyone else. As they began to drift away early he bided his time, waiting for the last of them to leave. Looking around nervously he turned the key in the lock and walked in, closing the door behind him.

He was in a typical, medium sized office. Every available surface and half of the floor space were covered with books and files so that there was not much room to move about. The room was painted in a nondescript colour that could have been grey or green. On his left stood an old fashioned desk and chair next to a filing cabinet, and the wall to his right was completely hidden by a huge bookcase stuffed with dusty books. The wall directly opposite the door was made of toughened glass with a glass door in the centre leading into a lab of some sort. Blinds were drawn down allowing only a small amount of light to filter through into the office. Mick edged his way around the floor, being very careful not to disturb anything in the dim light. He tried the door to the lab but it was locked. Then he noticed the combination lock on the wall. Wiping sweat off his hands on his jacket, he wondered how many combinations he would have to work through to unlock the door.

Peeking through the cracks in the blinds he could dimly see tables running the length of the room on either side, filled with various instruments and gauges he couldn't make out in the dim light. A large curtain cut off the back of the room completely. Mick had to see what was behind there.

He searched the office looking for some indication of what the combination might be. Wondering how long Andrew would be in hospital he hoped it would be for a while so he would have time to find the code and see what was hidden in the laboratory. Then after a fruitless search he locked the office door and left before the cleaners arrived.

Mick's modest flat was furnished with the bare minimum of furniture, bought for practical use rather than aesthetic value. It didn't matter to Mick, and nobody else would be likely to see it. He had no time for other people, generally finding them to be vacuous and boring. After eating a microwaved ready meal he sat down think. Dismissing the idea of writing down all the possible combinations of the numbers and letters as impractical he tried to get inside Andrew's head to figure out where he would keep it hidden.

Over the next month he visited Andrew's office every day to search for the code. He finally found it written on the inside cover of an old diary on the bottom shelf of the bookcase. Mouth dry he tapped it into the pad. He tried the door but it was still locked. 'Of course,' he told himself irritably after a few moments, then he took the key from his pocket and unlocked the latch. When he tried again the door opened. Closing it behind him he went straight to the back of the room and slipped behind the curtain.

Dominating the curtained off area was a huge cylinder that looked like a pressure chamber. The round door had a wheel obviously used to release or tighten the seal. Through the window in this door he could see what looked to be a smaller cylinder. He could only guess at its exact dimensions because it seemed to shift in his vision and he couldn't quite focus on it. He put that down to an optical illusion caused by the faint glow coming from the machine itself. He guessed it was slightly more than his height and around a metre in diameter.

Beside the machine was a desk with a draft of a paper on the mechanics of time travel. It went into detail about the specifications of the machine and the materials used in its construction. The paper referred to the machine being held in a 'superposition' where it was both there and not there at the same time. It went on to describe a supposed multiverse of infinite possibilities that, when measured would collapse into one reality. Mick had heard of this in the paradox of Schrödinger's cat that is both alive and dead in its box until the box is opened. But that was an illustration normally applied to particles on the quantum scale. The paper went on to point out that these effects are evident on a macro scale too but are infinitesimally small and not noticed in everyday life. Apparently Andrew believed he had developed a method by which he could 'fool' the system into behaving on the macro scale as if it were the quantum world. This would mean that once the machine was sent to a specific time its position would in effect be measured, collapsing the superposition, and the machine would be stuck in that time.

Mick didn't understand all of the notes. There was something about anomalies and strange behaviour of quantum particles in time and space and how some of them are apparently able to travel through time. There were other notes that seemed to Mick to be flights of fancy, describing the nature of time and speculating on the possibility of time travel.

'Is he a nutter?' Mick thought. 'Or could this work?' That was when he got the idea that gradually developed into an obsession. While Andrew was away in hospital he would examine the machine in detail. That was where his strength lay, in more practical, hands on engineering. He wasn't happy with what he called 'pseudo magical theoretical physics.'

As an idea time travel appealed to him even though he didn't really believe it was possible. He had no ties and his life here in 2016 was mundane and boring. He allowed himself to speculate about going back into the past. It would certainly open up new opportunities for him. He could study the financial times to see when company's shares rose and fell, or even study the pools and lottery numbers. Knowledge is power and he could make himself as rich as he believed he deserved to be. Pondering on the idea of time paradoxes he decided that it would be prudent to avoid meeting himself or any family members, but he decided that wouldn't be a problem for him. He had never missed what he had never had.

Outwardly Mick acted like any of the other office workers. He enquired about Andrew's health and contributed to the office collection to buy him a card and basket of fruit, but he drew the line at visiting the hospital. Each day after work he would let himself into Andrew's office studying the papers and notes relating to the machine. Andrew had had a heart attack. It had not done any serious damage to his heart but he had been advised to recover his health before even thinking about going back to work. It would be at least two months before he returned to the lab.

Still not really believing this could work Mick began to think about what he would need to know to live in the past. He decided the early seventies would be the best time to aim for. Smiling he thought about attending live concerts of groups that no longer played together. He had always had and affinity for the music of that decade. The money would be more or less the same as the present. He just had to be careful about dates. The clothing would be readily available from one of the many vintage shops around. He would only need one outfit to start with, once there he would be able to buy more. This was before everyone's identities were held on computer so it would be easier for him to establish a new identity then. All he would need would be a copy of a birth certificate.

He had heard that back then it was possible to have a new job every day, cash in hand, no questions asked. He couldn't really imagine that but if it was true it would be possible to choose a career. He could even take some exams to get the certificates to build up a profile. With his maths skills he would be able to establish a career and get into a lucrative position where he could earn a good salary. The wages were a lot lower then but that was relative because everything cost a lot less as well.

This became a new pastime for him. He spent hours in the local library scouring back issues of the national and local papers. At home he watched hours of old newsreels, films and television shows to get a feel of the zeitgeist. Wading through the early Carry-on films he raised his eyebrows in disbelief. Did people really laugh at this rubbish? Then he checked out old maps of the area. The lab building had once been a warehouse that had been derelict for a time so it should be easy enough to slip out of the machine and either dismantle it or dump it in the nearby canal.

Every night after work he would go into the lab, studying the machine until he thought he knew how it would work though still not completely convinced that it would. Two months later he believed he knew how to operate it. When the time was right, if it didn't work, what harm would there be in trying. He had nothing to lose.

Andrew lay in his hospital bed crying. After all these years building his machine, had he left it too late? He remembered as though it were yesterday the day that Helen had died. It had been his fault. He was always chivvying her along, complaining if she was late. She had been rushing to meet him for lunch that day when she had stepped out into the road without looking. The car had thrown her to the ground before crushing her under it. She had died instantly. Andrew had built his career on the idea that someday he would go back to that moment and stop her. Instead of this lonely existence he would have the life back that he had wanted; with her.

For two months he did everything in his power to get well enough to return to the lab. In his condition he didn't know whether a time trip would kill him but neither did he care. If he couldn't make it work he would rather be dead than live one more day without Helen.

Still not entirely convinced, Mick had actually bought a suit on impulse when he had been at a car boot sale and it was in the lab with a wallet full of money in the jacket pocket. He couldn't quite bring himself to try the machine though; he kept putting off the moment because he felt he needed more time to research the era. The decision was finally made for him while he was in the lab one night when Andrew walked in on him.

Shocked Andrew demanded 'what are you doing here?'

'Isn't it obvious?' Mick answered, laughing, 'I'm taking your machine.'

'You can't' Andrew said panicking, tears glinting in his eyes, 'I have worked all my life for this. I need it to go back and save my Helen. I need her.'

He sobbed, tears flowing freely down his cheeks. Ignoring him Mick grabbed his suit and the shoes he had bought to go with it and walked toward the machine. 'It's not ready yet', Andrew shouted 'there are still some vital calculations to be made before it can be used.'

'Do you really expect me to believe that you old fool?' Mick growled 'You're just trying to delay me while you call security and have me thrown out.' He pushed Andrew roughly out of his way, causing him to fall and hit his head on the side of the desk. Then he changed his clothes and stepped in to the machine, locking the doors behind him.

He could see Andrew's agitated face through the chamber door blood oozing from a cut on his temple. He was saying something that Mick couldn't hear. 'It doesn't matter,' he told himself with a sneer; 'there's nothing he can do to stop me now.' He set the dials and flicked the switch and everything went white for a split second before coming back into focus.

After a moment of disorientation Mick looked out of the window, his face frozen with horror. How could he have been so stupid? How could he have made such a basic mistake? The stars were all there in their familiar constellations and the Earth, in its slow, convoluted and complicated journey through the universe, would be with him in forty years' time.

ROUND ROBIN COLLABORATIONS

IN THE WOOD

LIZ BIGGINS & PETER HEATH

The snow started falling in the early afternoon; the air had been chilled all day. Gradually the sky darkened with heavy clouds hastening the dusk. Leaving school, I left my friends, feeling the need for solitude before returning to my large bustling family.

The wooded area drew me into its midst, the downy snowflakes growing larger by the minute. Steadily and relentlessly falling, it provided me with a crisp white carpet underfoot. As I plodded though the snow, the darkness deepened. I gradually became aware of the soundless world I now found myself in, and the depths of the woods that had been so lovely in summer now seemed a little menacing.

Suddenly, ahead of me, there was a clearing, where there had been no clearing earlier in the year. "What has happened to the trees?" I asked myself. Puzzled, I looked across the opening and was startled to see, for a moment, a girl. She was clad in strange clothes and appeared smaller than I, but a little older perhaps. "Her clothes are not really suitable for this weather," I thought. Yet her appearance reminded me of someone. "It cannot be Maid Marion? Or can it?"

The tinkling of a bell floated in the air, it could only have been a small bell as it was so light, and then there was another and another. I didn't feel uneasy, just curious. The young girl emerged from the bushes encircling the copse, and placing one foot carefully in front of the other led her pony to the far end of the clearing. Before I had a chance to call out to her, they were disappearing into the depths of the woods. "No one is going to believe this." I thought, and decided to follow them. The snow was now deep enough to cover my shoes, and my socks were getting wet. I shivered. The girl was a long way ahead; walking in the deepening snow was laborious. Yet ,I was drawn to follow! Looking around, slowly and scarily, realisation dawned on me that I was now in a part of the woods that I didn't know.

Fear rose up threatening to choke me. Every warning Mum and Dad had ever given me, rang loudly in my ears.

"Don't go into the wood alone or at night." What *had* I been thinking?

Then the bells tinkled again. Somehow, the sound was comforting. I felt safe and then, out of nowhere the girl and the pony appeared again. There was a sort of misty light around them and I noticed with a start, that where the girl and the pony now stood, the ground was free of snow. She was standing barefoot on grass, the pony champing lazily, close by, in a sunlit glade.

'It's scary isn't it?' said the girl by the pony. 'Don't be afraid,' her lips hadn't moved once.

'You spoke without moving your lips.'

'We don't need voices. Your lips didn't move either.'

My hand flew to my lips.

'What's your name,' I said startled. I heard the words and the pony girl smiled. The pony cast a look at me and went back to grazing.

'What's yours?'

'My name is Mary-Ann,' we said together.

The me Mary-Ann from the schoolroom with soggy socks gazed in wide-eyed amazement.

'Look at me,' said pony Mary-Ann, 'you thought you recognized me earlier as Maid Marion.'

'But how did… how could know…'

The 'Maid Marion' smiled. 'I am you and you are me.'

'How can that be?'

'If you like, think of it as a dream. We dream of having a pony.'

'I've always wanted a pony,' I said wistfully.

'*We've*, always wanted a pony.'

'But you know I can't,' I said, tears threatening. 'Mum and Dad won't let me - *us*. The farm is struggling and with so many of us - things are too difficult - that's what they tell me, over and over.'

'Us,' said the other girl. 'We cry all day on Christmas Day when we don't find a pony, in the stable. I - you - we, get over it, until our older brother Jake gets a new motor bike for his birthday in the summer and we...I had a tantrum and shouted horrible things at Mum and Dad. They sent me to my room but that night, I snuck out of our bedroom window, still in my nightdress and clambered down into the yard. I ran away, came here, as we have tonight and then got lost in the darkness. I tripped over a root and hit my head on a rock. They didn't find me for days. Zarhin – it's not his real name - that's Russian and unpronounceable, was nuzzling my face. I pulled myself up and clambered onto his back he took me back to the farm. I saw the search parties, the police, Mum, Dad, and the rest of them all crying. I tried to tell them it was OK, that I had Zarhin. Then the world spun, and the police were knocking on the door again and Dad cried "Noooo," when they told him Jake had been killed on his motorbike.'

'If you know all this why don't you do something, tell them?'

'I can't, not easily, but I can tell you.'

'Because we are me,' we said together.

'I have to go soon.'

'No don't, I can't find my way back.'

'Yes you can, Zarhin will take you.'
'But you know what Mum and Dad will say.'
'They won't, not now,' said pony Mary-Ann.' I did something last night that we Sprites aren't supposed to do, I showed Mum and Dad our future, yours and mine and Jake's, in their dreams. The Queen of Sprites is very cross with me and I have to go soon but she let me draw you here today and to see you.'
'Is that why Mum and Dad were funny this morning, odd?'
'I expect so.'
'Won't they be worried about me now?'
'Not yet, they know we are talking and they know about Zarhin – I don't know how he got up the stairs to their room, frighten the life out of them.'
We both burst out laughing.
'And you didn't.'
'What?'
'Frighten them.'
  'I have to go now, Baby Mary-Ann.'
'I'm not a… Oh. I moved towards the older Mary-Ann.
Can I… can we… hug?'
The light in the clearing intensified suddenly, hurting my eyes. I scrunched them tight shut.
'Just this once,' said a serene voice. A tall woman with in a flowing emerald gown held out her hands. Each Mary-Ann, squinting, took her hand and she brought them together. 'The Winter Solstice is the

most magical of days, a time when, for a brief moment, the veil is lifted between our worlds. You are not ready for our world yet Mary-Ann,' she said as the light faded. 'When your time comes, you will be most welcome. Go now,' the final word, was no more than an echo.

I opened my eyes to find myself alone in the glade with Zarhin. He pushed his nose into my face. 'All right, all right, Mr Impatient' I said, as he nudged me to a log. I jumped up, gripped his mane and hauled myself onto his back. Even as I settled, Zarhin was heading out of the sunlit glade into the snowy darkness of the woods.

THE 10.40a.m. TO OBAN

JOHN COLLIER, ERIC McEVOY & ROS EMERY

The School Master was leaving the village, and everyone seemed sorry including the crowd of school children and many other locals, who were waving their much revered 72 year old Master 'goodbye` on his final trip back to his retirement on his beloved Isle of Barra.

Like many other essential professionals, Steve Manley had been persuaded to come out of his planned post-war retirement, and return to his pre-war teaching role in the small West Scotland village. Returning to school after his arduous wartime years in the Intelligence Service had seemed like a wonderful break. His legendary pre-war reputation had preceded him as a firm but inspirational disciplinarian.

In another village away across the Minch his wife Emily loyally waited for his 'final return home`, as she described it in her daily long letters to him.

The 10.40 a.m. Oban train steamed importantly into Crianlarich Lower. That March 1947 morning was crisp and bright, and a few spring tourists were also waiting on the same platform, as they all headed west towards Oban.

"Sir, how wonderful to see you again!" An eager face smiled from across the carriage. "Jimmy Glover. I hardly recognised you there in your uniform." "Yes sir. I'm going back to Barra on my first leave. I'm doing my National Service." "Please Jimmy, less of the sir. You are well out of school now. Please call me Steve. Come over and join me."

Jimmy stood up and walked over. "Oh sir, sorry I meant Steve, it's such an honour to see you again, especially after all the news about your recent Military Cross Award for your work in Occupied France. All the lads with me were so made up."

Captain McTavish was looking worried. He hated being delayed by 'those unreliable B.R. Trains`. The McBraynes Ferry RMS Claymore had to wait for the Glasgow train to arrive, however late it was. His First Mate tried to console him. "Captain, it was snowing heavily on those hills overnight, so anything may have happened."

Emily Manley picked up her 'phone and Mary the Barra 'phone operator answered. "Hello Emily. I know what news you are after, and yes the Ferry will be very late. We have just heard there has been serious trouble on the Glasgow Train near Falls of Cruachan". Emily started weeping. She had been through so much already whilst waiting during those long wartime years alone on the Croft for news of Steve. "What trouble?" she cried out to Mary. "I can't take much more". Mary went on. "Don't worry Emily. I'm sure they will quickly sort things out and Steve will soon be home".

Steve was lying semi-conscious in the damaged carriage after the explosion occurred. He had been day-dreaming about his time in France before and during the war. His fluency in French and German had singled him out as ideal to become a spy in occupied Europe. His training had been intense and although not a young man he was fit and exuded an air of authority. With the correct forged documentation, this ability to command respect enabled him to establish himself as a feared member of the German Gestapo which opened many doors. It was not healthy for anyone to question his orders given to the local military commanders and he managed to cause massive disruption to the local German army troop deployments wherever he travelled. He smiled at the memory of ordering a tank commander and his men to protect a disused factory site while the British SAS destroyed an active ammunition factory on the other side of the town.

He realised this deceit could not last forever and he would soon get caught so with the blessing of his UK controller he boarded a train for Calais and a clandestine route out of France to Dover. As the train, a German troop carrier, barrelled through France bellowing steam and sulphurous smoke it was targeted by the French Resistance, who managed to bomb the engine and the first two carriages. As a precaution, and knowing French Resistance tactics, Steve always chose the last compartment in which to travel.

Once again his decision to travel in the last compartment had saved him though he was trapped, pinned down by wreckage. The impact of the collision with a goods train brought to a standstill by an obstruction on the line, because of snow, had slewed the engine and first two carriages sideways and overturned the third, which was now straddled upside down across the tracks. All the fixtures and fittings had therefore fallen on top of Steve.

Although unable to move, Steve's mind was crystal clear and he mentally assessed the situation. He could smell smoke and hear, above the sound of escaping steam, shouts and cries for help. As it was early in the season there had been only a few tourists, though unfortunately they had been in the first two carriages. The only occupants of this last carriage had been Jimmy Glover and himself. Where was Jimmy? Steve became aware of a movement to his left. Jimmy? That might mean Jimmy was near the window and possibly could escape.

"Is that you Jimmy?" he asked, surprised his voice sounded so firm. His companion coughed, spluttered and grunted "Aye." "Are you alright? Can you move?" "I think so. What about you?" "Not so good I'm afraid. I seem to be trapped. I can't move."

There was a pause, then more scuffling. Someone outside was screaming but the sound ceased abruptly and Steve realised it had been the train's whistle. More ominously there was a distinct smell of burning and although Steve couldn't move he could see, which was worrying for although the carriage was pitch black there was a flickering glow presumably coming from outside.

He could hear Jimmy's laboured breathing fairly close by and then intermittent noises and panting. "I'm by the window, what's left of it" Jimmy said. "I'll try to clear this debris off you and get you out."

Steve had the presence of mind not to add to Jimmy's problems by entering into a discussion. After all Jimmy was in the Military same as himself and could be expected to know what he was doing. Steve just hoped he'd be quick about it because he'd seen the aftermath of train crashes and it didn't take long for the situation to go from bad to worse. "Tell me if there's anything I can do to help" was the only thing he said. Then he closed his eyes and concentrated on Emily and their plans for a new life together on Barra. It seemed like forever before he felt a slight movement and was able to shift his position. He appeared to be lying in a pool of water but once the weight was removed from his legs he realised he had a nasty gash just below his femoral artery and it was bleeding profusely. Another inch higher!

"I'll need a tourniquet" he said, and efficiently Jimmy attended to the problem applying pressure before dragging Steve out of the broken window which he had padded with his jacket. The snow cushioned their landing and Steve was able to take notice of his surroundings. By this time locals had arrived and the fires were being dowsed. A few people had escaped from the first two carriages but the driver, fireman and six tourists were dead.

Steve was extremely grateful then to Jimmy but it was only later he learnt how heroic his rescuer had actually been because Jimmy, though himself injured rather badly, had moved a ton of rubble to get Steve out of danger. At the hospital where all the casualties were taken it was acknowledged Jimmy's first aid had undoubtedly saved Steve's life.

During their stay in hospital Steve and Jimmy became good friends and Steve said he regretted putting 'could do better' on Jimmy's school report all those years ago.

On his discharge from hospital Steve was reunited with Emily who had been obliged to remain on Barra because of the dreadful weather, waiting for him though reassured daily regarding his progress. Then they could finally settle down to enjoy their retirement.

Captain McTavish's ferry did sail that March day, though considerably behind schedule.

GILVIN

JOHN J CULKIN, LORAINE FELCE & ROS EMERY

It was the best of times; it was the worst of times ….

….but on balance Gilvin was happy with the cards that life had dealt him. His fingers flickered through the pages of yet another passport. "All in order." Gilvin smiled at his good fortune. Everything was going to plan. Why wouldn't it be? He was a perfectionist. Each contract he had ever taken on was planned meticulously.

There was however something crawling about in the dark corners of his brain, in the depths of that analytical mind there was a spider weaving a web. Maybe just a little oversight. He shook his bald head. "You're getting too old Gilvin son." He spoke out loud, confident in his isolation. Everything according to the book. The book he had written.

He checked the CCTV monitors. Green lights at the bottom of each screen comforted him. His equipment was telling him "You have got it right again Gilvin old son, no intruders." He smiled and picked up the cheap mobile 'phone, which would be discarded later, into the river Mersey.

Gilvin dialled the number for the Swiss account. He didn't wait for an answer. He turned his head in the direction of the Laptop. "You have got mail." Green words zipped across the screen.

Two hundred and fifty thousand pounds sterling will be deposited into your account at Zurich Switzerland tomorrow, at 09.00 hrs GMT, April twenty first two thousand and fifteen.

He checked the TV monitor again. Just soothing beeps. Grinning he made his way to the toilet. Gilvin was actually whistling whilst washing his hands. It made him wonder if it was time for him to quit the business. Whistling did not fit in with the violence of his art. The beeps halted, the harsh sound of the intruder alarm that was linked to the CCTV hurried him from the bathroom.

His eyes went to the TV monitor, the little niggling worry that had invaded his thoughts earlier now a full blooded crisis.

A smiling face gazed up at the camera. It was the face of a young woman. Even with the woollen football supporter's hat pulled down over her ears, Gilvin knew the woman. She was accompanied by a black Labrador that was sitting obediently at her side. The dog confirmed his fears.

When he had stepped out of the shadows two hours earlier, on to what he believed was a deserted country lane, and after plunging the blade deep into Hartson's chest, he had smiled grimly at the completion of his task. He caught sight of the dog; it was sniffing at the carcass of a long expired rabbit. He knew who the woman was now.

His hand went to the shoulder holster. The coldness of the Glock pistol reassured him, but only temporarily. His earlier thoughts were confirmed. He was getting soft.

* * * * *

Maybe Gilvin should have ignored her but he found himself buzzing her in.

He knew it would be a couple of minutes before she reached him. The building had been designed that way to limit the risk of attack. It consisted of one long corridor which ran from the entrance door to Gilvin's office.

While he was waiting, Gilvin took out the Glock from its holster, and shoved it behind the solitary cushion on the couch. He thought how he would never have done that before, not even for her.

When she reached him, Gilvin smiled.

"Rona. Long time. I like the hat."

He gestured for her to sit but she did not.

"You fool." she said. "Why did you kill him and in my lane? The lane where I live."

"It was the job. You know the deal. Target identified. Passport secured."

"He was bloody blind you fool."

"Blind? Hartson wasn't blind."

Rona pointed at the big black Labrador sitting obediently at her side.

"Rona, when you are about to eliminate a target, you don't hang around."

"Research. Don't you do research?" "You are out of touch." said Gilvin.

This was true it had been a few years.

"I have a DNA app which tells me if someone is the target I am looking for. It is 100 per cent accurate. Once I get the nod, I do the job. I walk away and bag the prize. You remember how it was?" Gilvin could not believe he was bothering to explain himself.

As for Rona she barely remembered. She had only been part of the business for a short time. It was fair to say that she was as outraged as any other person would be at such a crime.

Gilvin found himself smiling.

"This is not a joke. Someone has lost his life. Does nothing matter to you?"

"You have changed. I think I preferred the couldn't care about anyone Rona."

Rona tried to keep her composure but he knew he had found her chink.

She had left the business before she had really got started. She was very young and had met Gilvin on a training course and had fallen for the older Gilvin immediately. She had no choice but to leave having found at least one person she was not prepared to kill.

The business never knew who her love interest was. Gilvin told her in no uncertain terms what he would do to her if she mentioned him.

"You have not lost those instincts. You tracked me down" he said.

"That is because you are sloppy. I tracked you down so I could look you in the eye and tell you what I thought. You don't scare me anymore. I will blow the cover on the whole lot of you."

Rona turned and left. The dog minus his master followed her. As she began the walk up the corridor, Gilvin knew what he had to do. He took the Glock from behind the cushion and opened his office door.

* * * * *

Gilvin's suspicions that Rona was still not to be trusted had been confirmed. When she was infatuated with him all those years ago the intensity of her passion had disturbed him and with hindsight he had to admit he was relieved when she went out of his life.

The ending of their short-lived affair precipitated her withdrawal from the training and, while he had been unable to share his concerns with his employers at that time because of the nature of their relationship, as her mentor he had submitted an adverse appraisal which was accepted without question. Her involvement with the TASK (Tactical Action & Specialist Knowledge) FORCE was brought to an end and she was moved "sideways" where she could be kept on the radar, but generally she was not considered to be of much significance.

Gilvin however did not under-estimate Rona. He had continued to keep an eye on her, initially because she appeared to take their break-up very hard, but soon he noted how her life now followed a pattern involving multiple sexual affairs. What became increasingly obvious to him was that she seemed to select the men and she was the one who ended the affairs. As he had personal insight he could sympathise with the men who succumbed to her undoubted charms but he became aware that her targets were invariably in a position of trust within the organisation and inevitably were in possession of secrets and could be open to blackmail.

Her parting shot "I will blow the cover on the whole lot of you" confirmed she was about to take her revenge.

Rona had wrongly assumed he was no longer meticulous in his planning. It had taken him some time to grasp that, for her, their brief affair had been truly significant unlike her recent relationships. That is why he was fairly sure she would not harm him after he set tonight's trap.

Hartson had been a fairly recent conquest but Gilvin knew Rona had already moved on to another lover, much to Harton's regret as he was totally smitten with her. It had been known for some time that Hartson was dangerous to the organisation and it came as no surprise to Gilvin when he was told Hartson was to be his next target.

Accordingly Gilvin sent a message to Hartson, purporting to come from Rona, asking him to visit her at home that evening with a view to resuming their relationship. Gilvin knew of Hartson's doubt life as a con-man, sometimes pretending to be blind with his guide dog Jet, and so did Rona though she had deliberately lied about the dog. Gilvin had been surprised to see Jet but knew the dog, running free, was "off duty".

Gilvin ambushed Hartson outside Rona's house, confident when she found his body virtually on her doorstep he could expect her to turn up at his office, but maybe not as quickly as she did.

Now he knew what he must do. He followed her up the corridor, the Glock in his hand. Hartson's body would inevitably be discovered tomorrow and, after investigation, suspicion would fall on Rona, whose DNA would almost certainly be found at the scene of the crime, and Rona would be missing. She and her secrets would be buried together.

Until he had seen her again this evening Gilvin had wondered whether he was in fact getting soft and it might be time to retire. But he still took a pride in his work. It was his whole life. Meeting Rona face to face had confirmed the error he had originally made becoming romantically entangled, a mistake he was determined never to repeat, though he was looking forward to having the companionship of a well-trained black Labrador.

THE SCHOOLMASTER

ROS EMERY, PETER HEATH & JOHN J CULKIN

1
The schoolmaster

The schoolmaster was leaving the village, and everyone seemed sorry. Regretfully George Scott realised that he had played his part all too well over the last few months. He had used his considerable talents to become a much valued member of the teaching staff at the local school, and he had succeeded, so much better than he had hoped for.

Consequently, although he had requested leave of absence, only that morning, Mrs Dodds the caretaker's wife had managed at short notice, to produce a modest buffet after school, so his colleagues could wish him and his ailing family well.

He had stated that he'd been called away unexpectedly, because his sister, the sole carer for their invalid mother, needed an emergency operation. He said that he expected to return after the summer holiday, but it would be helpful if he could leave now. His colleagues believed that he was going home tomorrow, but actually his luggage was already in his car, and he only intended to pick up a few things from his locker, before departing, for good.

Now for two hours he had been obliged to parry the kind, but no less intrusive questions regarding the family that no-one had known he had. He was anxious to be gone, but he had a strong desire to preserve the character of George Scott.

The credentials for George were impeccable. He had used them before, and intended to do so again. Mrs Barnes, the Headmistress had been sympathetic to his request for him to miss the last few days of term, and she had assured George, as she had referred to her favourite member of staff, that there would be no objection to his request.

She had been immensely impressed with his testimonials, and she couldn't believe how lucky the school had been to secure the services of such a competent and popular teacher. She did not want to lose him.

Tactfully he had extracted himself from the effusive good wishes, promising each of his fellow staff members that he would keep them all informed about his sister's and mother's progress. Privately he had already decided that his "make believe sister" would die on the operating table, so it would be with a heavy heart that he would have to terminate his current employment, to care for his ailing mother. He grinned behind splayed fingers as he thought of the sad faces when they received that particular phone call. But best of all, George Scott would live to fight another day, and if the truth be known, he had grown rather fond of his alter ego.

All that remained now was to check his mailbox in town, one last time, and then he would disappear, forever. He pressed the button on his car radio, and grinned again as the Stones belted out, "This could be the last time."

The Nissan Qashquai seemed to glide down the hill, and George Scott, happy as a sand boy, put his foot down on the accelerator. The car reached the first bend on the hill, and he applied the brakes to check its increasing speed. Except, the brakes were not working, and a little knot of panic snatched at his stomach.

2
The Township

The Township was pitch dark, and hidden within that African night, an old man was dying.

He screamed in agony, as masked thugs went about their business. No-one stirred in the houses as the old man was very slowly beaten to death.

His screams were a warning to those who heard, and many of his tribe did hear those terrible and final wails of agony, as he begged for his life, that It did not pay to cross the DeVere family.

The single bulbs of light that lit up the sparse rooms were switched off. The occupants of those overcrowded houses, huddled in their beds, and shivered, locked in a silent terror, as one of their own was murdered by DeVere henchmen.

*

The old man had hidden the rock. He had known the second that he picked it up, that it would change his life. It did, but not in any way that he could have imagined.

The rock turned out to be a diamond of magnificent intensity. It wasn't the largest, but it was pure blue. When you looked into its heart, you felt the urge to dive into its flawless centre.

Scottie had been buried quickly, the next day. It was his tribe's custom. The police were there, sjamboks, the wicked rhinoceros hide whips, being swished through the hot African air by an eager police force, watching, not to investigate, but to ensure there was no civil disturbance.

A young boy cried on the rough grave of his father, helpless in the face of an evil society.

That was where it started. The crying boy was my father, the murdered old man, my grandfather. His death had broken the family, the shame, and the fear of retribution through association, drove my family from the Township.

We had been poor, now we were destitute. My father managed by taking menial jobs, to save enough money, which would secure us passage on a ship bound for England. It would be the start of a new life.

My parents did not take to well to life in England, but they worked hard to put me through school. Every year, on Scotties birthday, and his death day, we told the story. Once a thief always a thief, Isn't that what they say. It must run in the blood.

*

I finished my education, getting passable marks in all of my exams, but nothing to write home about. In my family, however I was the brightest star. I had an English education, and I eventually boasted an English accent, but I had the distinctive dark complexion of my African race.

My father got sick and lost his job, so to keep body and soul together, I helped myself to some of the necessities of life, until alas I was caught, and I served a short spell behind bars for my sins. That was when I met D.S. Roquefort.

I had learned to be quick and silent, and being young and fit, I found I had the natural ability to climb trees, and scale the steepest of walls. Those activities had always been fun at school and, they grew me a circle of friends, who otherwise would have been my bullies.

Pa eventually died from his illness, and with four younger siblings, I developed my skills and began to visit the posher side of town. An open window was a gift not to be sneezed at. I fenced the proceeds of my crimes with some old cronies. They ripped me off for sure, but I made enough to feed the family. If mother suspected she said nothing.

Then I got cocky and careless. I fell into the waiting arms of the newly promoted Detective Inspector Roquefort. He was a bigger bastard than I remembered.

'Well, well, well' he said, 'Scott Masters. You're looking at a long stretch this time Scottie old son.'

I bridled at the name. 'Don't call me Scottie.'

'Oh, touched a nerve, have we? His grin was sly. 'I know all about your grandfather, Scott.'

'He was bloody well murdered, and no-one lifted a finger to help; not the police, or our friends, no-one.'

'Yes well,' he harrumphed, 'he was a thief.'

'It was just a rock, a useless piece of rock.'

'No Scott it's more than just a useless piece of rock. That rock is the DeVere blue old son.'

'The DeVere what?'

'It's one of the world's most valuable diamonds. It's not the largest, but it is the purest, Scottie.'

'Okay so you know about a rock and my grandpa.'

'What I know, my friend,' he said leaning close to me, 'is that the DeVere daughter, Charlotte, is at a private school here in England, and that her doting, but seriously deluded father, had given her the diamond as a sixteenth birthday present.'

'And that's my problem because...?'

'Well it gets you a share of the proceeds, or a long spell in the Scrubs old chap.'

'I don't underst...Aah, now I get it, you want me to steal it.'

'Well done Scottie old son, you've finally got it. But it's not for me, just for some friends of mine, you understand.'

I nodded, absolutely understanding him. 'And in return?'

'In return, you get a cut of the profits, and this case disappears forever. You walk away scot free so to speak.' He laughed at his feeble little joke. 'A new identity and a clean slate old son. How does that sound?'

'So, how?' I was trying to see his angle, Roquefort was a shifty bastard.

'It'll be Christmas soon, and I am reliably informed that there will be a vacancy at Charlotte's school, you know some kind of accident will occur during the holiday. You will be the replacement teacher.'

I know that people with power can make things happen. I thought back to my grandfather's death, and this bent copper turned my stomach. 'Me, a bloody teacher?' I said incredulously.

'You're bright Scottie, good results at your school. You could have gone to college. In fact you still can.' He winked slyly at me.

'I have to support my family Inspector.'

'Yes I know, but you can't do that from a prison cell, can you old son?'

I was sold on the idea, why not? It sounded like there was easy money to be made. Somehow, George Scott was born with an impeccable CV.

A phone call was made, and Miss Barnes, the head at St Bartholomew's Academy for young Ladies called and offered me the job.

I remember driving up that treacherous hill, in the winters snow and ice. Mrs Barnes hid her shock at my colour quite well, as I stepped out of the car. My perfect English accent had obviously thrown her when we had spoken on the phone.

'Welcome Mr Scott, I hope you will be very happy at this Academy.'

I settled in to the routine quickly, and to be honest I enjoyed "working" for a living.

Charlotte was an out and out De Vere. Arrogant, rude to everyone, and offensive, particularly to me. It was going to be a pleasure relieving her of that rock.

When colleagues, who were, in the main friendly, asked, I skirted around my back ground. My colour though could not be hidden. My home is South Africa, and I still had the lilt, which fascinated teachers and students alike, and the colour, everyone it seemed was complimentary about it, at least to my face. Other than that, I steered the conversations around to the teachers and students. It was during these casual conversations that I garnered little nuggets of information about the life and routines of a certain Charlotte DeVere.

As winter turned to spring, the schools sporting itinerary moved on from winter sports to summer stuff, and for several afternoons during the week, the school was almost deserted.

I had to be careful. I had no place in the student's accommodation, but as I said before, I was quick, silent, and now, bent on revenge for my grandfather's brutal death, I was very careful.

Once a week, whilst in town, I sent reports to Roquefort, and picked up any letters at the mailbox.

As the end of term approached, and the exams were over, there were more outdoor activities, which resulted in the staff and pupils being away for a day, or on some occasions, for few days at a time. I used this time to scout out the DeVere girl's room. I couldn't afford to leave any trace of my visit; so it was slow painstaking work looking for the stone, and covering my tracks.

Roquefort and his "colleagues" were becoming more and more anxious as the term rolled onto its conclusion. Soon Charlotte DeVere would be returning to South Africa, and the gem along with my freedom would go with her.

The school sports day arrived, and whilst it was in full flood, I was in her room, removing the rock.

God it was beautiful, but it was tainted with my grandfather's blood. I had searched the room for days until I found its hiding place, in her bloody jewellery box for God's sake. She either didn't know or didn't care. I smiled, soon someone would.

I lifted the jewel with shaking fingers, my grandfather had held this very piece of African rock, and had died, in agony for it.

I slipped it into my pocket, and replaced the small, but now empty velvet lined case back into the much larger jewellery box. I left her room quietly, and just made it to the stairs, as a voice drifted up toward me from the floor below. It was a man's voice. It had no right to be there, but I recognised it.

'Come on Charlie.'

'I hate that bloody name.'

'Let's get into your room; it's nice and cosy in there.'

'For what?' Her voice was filled with the usual arrogance.

I didn't hang around to find out about the "for what" Eventually an opportunity presented itself, and I crept down the back stairs. My heart was hammering in a tight chest. That had been too close, and I cursed my carelessness. It wouldn't happen again.

*

Clair Barnes had looked a bit miffed, when I told her that my sister had been admitted for an emergency operation, and that now I had to leave to take care of our invalid mother, pretty much right away. I needed a good story and that was as good as any. Beautiful Clair eventually became quite sympathetic to my plea, and I smiled my thanks at her. Then she raised her lips to mine. We knelt together on the plush carpet in her office, and loved as only passionate lovers can. Then I told her I had to pack, and needed the rest of the day off. That was another lie, but I was getting used to lies now. I had already put my stuff into the boot of the car.

Today was my last day, but to be honest I felt like a bit of a shit. Clair was becoming a nice part of my life, but I pushed her to the back of my mind. That guilt soon passed, I was about to change my life forever, and that was all that mattered.

There had been a call from Roquefort the day before, he sounded a bit pissed off. 'Our friends are getting twitchy old son. The school term is nearly over and they want their goods.'

'I'm getting it tomorrow.'

'You'd better be right Scottie old son, because if this goes wrong, then I'm going to be the least of your troubles.' He coughed nervously. 'Our friends will tell De Vere that you lifted the stone, and you know how thorough they are, don't you Scottie?'

'They can't do that.'

'They won't if they get the rock.'

'How do I know that I can trust them or you for that matter? I don't even know them for God's sake.'

'Then all you have got to do is get that bloody stone to me, pronto old son.'

'What?' I said incredulously. 'What guarantee do I have that you'll come through?'

'There are no guarantees in life Scottie, but you had better get that stone to me by tomorrow.' Roquefort's voice had a tinge of desperation in it. I smiled into the phones mouthpiece, his fear was becoming obvious. His life was in as much danger as mine.

'Yeah okay, but I want a passport and ten grand.'

'Don't be bloody stupid, I can't get hold of that kind of money at short notice.'

I barked my anger at him. 'Listen Inspector, you're getting a rock worth millions at bloody short notice, so sort it.'

'Okay, okay Scottie old son, keep your hair on, I'll get it done.'

*

I endured the questions from colleagues, at my farewell party. All of their questions concerned my poor mother and sister. I extricated myself eventually, and tried to keep my walk to the car slow and casual. I had turned my back on the lovely Clair Barnes, and that was my only regret.

The Qashquai engine hummed into life, and I began my journey down the hill, probably a bit too fast, but what the hell, I'd done it. George Scott had the De Vere Blue in his pocket, a new, and very rich life, was about to unfold.

As the car approached the first bend I touched the brakes, finally aware that I was going too fast. There was nothing there. The brake pedal went all the way to the cars floor. I was in deep shit.

3
Charlotte De Vere

The journey from the school took you through the village, and eventually down to the coast road about a mile below. But before you reached that wild and beautiful part of Column Bay, you had to negotiate a tight and viciously twisting gravel covered road. Most drivers, including myself, would make this descent at an old man's pace, about 10mph.

Those people who poo pooed the danger and roared down the cliff road, usually with a belly full of alcohol, or a nose full of coke, ended up ricocheting off the cliff face on the opposite side of the road to the big drop, and were to be found smashed on the rocks 200 feet below the village of

Column Bay. Their bodies might eventually be recovered from the jagged rocks, except sometimes; when the English Channel was in a rage, it became a terrifying stretch of water, and unfortunate drivers were often swept from those rocks, never to be found.

Sweat ran in rivulets down my spine, soaking my shirt. Was that to be my fate? I stamped hard again on the brake pedal, but to no avail, panic took over, and this wasn't supposed to happen. I'd over estimated my driving skills, and had gotten careless, again.

The Nissan Qashquai skidded on the gravel, and picked up speed. Then it slammed into the cliff face on the left hand side of the road. My head cracked into the steering wheel, and I felt the cartilage in my nose snap, blood cascaded from my damaged face onto the windscreen.

*

'Well Charlie.' Roquefort grinned at her obvious annoyance. She always got a bit snotty when people referred to her as Charlie. 'It should be all over now, I watched the black fucker as he drove onto the gravel road.' The detective smiled in triumph. 'He must have gotten quite a shock when he hit that brake pedal. I heard the squeal of tyres from where I was standing. I'll take a little stroll down to the beach in half an hour, before the tide comes in and he eventually gets washed away.' He stroked

Charlottes arm, she responded with a little smile, and her tongue glided provocatively across already moist lips.

The policeman continued. 'When that happens, and if the sea creatures haven't picked his bones clean, then the propellers on the ships that plough through the busiest shipping lane in the world will ensure that there is not enough of him left to identify.' The detective grinned maliciously. 'I'll find the one rock in his pocket that really matters in this little drama.'

His voice took on a serious note. 'My contact will get us a really good deal for the diamond Charlie, he said it's worth twenty six mill, we'll get a third of that, and your father will claim the bloody lot of it on his insurance.' He gave her a hug and whispered to her. 'The only loser in all of this Charlie my little foxy lady, is George Scott, and in a couple of hours no-one will know that he ever existed,'

Superintendent Roquefort was happy in the knowledge that when George Scott disappeared from this world, Scott Masters would join him, and the world will be a safer place, well for him at least. His smile was dark and sinister. Two black men dead and only one corpse, if it was ever found. Life was getting better all the time for a copper who would be handing in his resignation letter in a couple of months.

Charlotte slid an arm around the detective's waist, then she smiled at the man who a year earlier, had busted her for smoking Crack Cocaine. She had wriggled out of that little spot of bother with a weekend of passion in Roquefort's flat. It was during those couple of days of mind blowing and drug fuelled sex sessions that she had persuaded the smitten detective to help her with the plan to have the "De Vere Blue" stolen. She had dangled George Scott's spare car keys in front of him, and outlined her plan.

Now that plan was about to bear fruit. They were lying fully clothed, for a change; on the bed in her single roomed accommodation that she had convinced the headmistress, she absolutely had to have to maintain her privacy. 'How gullible can someone be Ashley?' He smiled, slightly bemused, as she referred to him by his Christian name for the first time. 'That damn fool Scott didn't realise this whole thing was a set up, and you had even set up a video camera in here.' She smiled again, and clicked the television set off, having just watched a recording of George Scott slipping the diamond into his pocket. Her hand found its way under the waistband of Roquefort's trousers. 'Have we got time, before you go?'

'Best not Charlie, I need to keep my wits about me, besides its getting dark now.' Then with a sly smile he added 'That gravel road can be dangerous at night.' The detective extricated himself reluctantly from her searching fingers. 'See you in about an hour Charlie, then you can have your wicked way with me'

Roquefort left the luxurious little room on a cloud of expectation. After he'd gotten his share of the proceeds, and he had given her one for the last time, then little miss rich girl could just fuck off. He was pissed off by her snot nosed attitude anyway, and soon he could have whatever took his fancy. Eight million plus, buys you a lot of whatever you fancy, he thought.

*

The detective stifled a laugh as he came across the skid marks on the gravel, and he couldn't avoid the triumphant "Gotcha you bastard." Roquefort punched at the night air. The marks in the gravel, and the gouges in the cliff wall opposite the 200foot drop onto jagged rocks below, convinced him that little miss smart arsed De Vere's plan had worked.

Looking over the edge of the road at the scene below, it took a few seconds in the fading light, for him to make out the wreckage of the Qashquai. The wind was freshening. Little white horses were appearing on the crest of growing waves.

Just half an hour 'til the tide turns, he thought. Then he shouted his triumph to the English Channel. 'Bloody perfect, it's going to get stormy around here.' Then he was sailing through the air, arms flapping wildly. His final words whipped away by a shrieking blast of wind.

*

Charlotte De Vere's mobile chimed. She snatched it up and whispered excitedly at the mouthpiece. 'Hello Ashley. Is he dead? Did you get the diamond?'

'Sorry to disappoint you bitch.' I tried to picture her face. Was it full of fear? 'Your boyfriend is dead. He didn't survive the flight.' Even I smiled at that little gem.

'I...I ... I don't know what you mean, what flight. Who is this anyway?'

I answered her with a laugh. 'Don't you play the innocent with me bitch. You and Roquefort tried to kill me. Well your lover boy is dead, lying on a rocky beach that was meant for me. I wondered where my spare car keys went to, you bloody thief.'

I heard as she sucked air in noisily. Then in a voice that was flat calm. 'Okay Kaffir, so he's dead. There is no reason why my little scheme can't go ahead as planned. You bring the diamond to me, and I'll contact Roquefort's friends, we can still do the deal. You will get a hundred thousand English pounds'

I stared unbelievably at my mobile, her casual dismissal of the coppers death, and her disgusting putdown of my race, made me boil in anger. This is one cold hearted bitch I thought. But then that's how some white Afrikaans are. Blacks should do as they are told. Blacks are expendable so long whitey gets the lions share. I growled at the phone. 'No, you listen to me Charlie.... that's how your pet copper referred to you isn't it, I have got the De Vere Blue, and I'm keeping it.'

'Now you just wait a fucking minute boy.' Again she riled me, and I struggled to stay calm.

'Don't call me that bitch; my grandfather was beaten to death by De Vere's henchmen because of that diamond. So I'm claiming it back.' Then I added solemnly, 'It's for my family you understand, don't you Charlie?' She tried to interrupt me, but I snarled at the phones mouthpiece. 'Just shut up and listen. You and that bloody copper thought you were so smart with your video tricks. Well let me tell you something little girl, I've robbed lots of places that had video surveillance; I can spot them a mile off. So I just carried on with my own plan. When I'd gotten what I wanted, I left a recording device hidden under your bed.' I heard a gasp from her, and I laughed again. 'I knew the next time you were in bed with lover boy, that you would talk about it. Pillow talk bitch, it's always the best way to get info. So when you had your next sports day at school, I just went to your room and retrieved my little gadget. And by the way I heard you and Roquefort on the stairs that day. You make a fine pair of fuck ups.'

'So what happens now?'

I waited for the derogatory remark, but she was obviously learning. 'You can carry on with your little plan to defraud the insurance company, and hope that I'll keep my mouth shut, up to you whitey, do you trust me?'

'How did you survive the crash?' Her voice was still matter of fact.

'It was just pure luck Charlie babe.' I could feel her bridle at my words, 'When I stamped on the brakes and nothing happened, I panicked, and the car hit the cliff on the side opposite to big drop. Bust my frigging nose. I was bloody, but safe, and after getting out of the car and checking that your diamond was still safe in my pocket, I just gave the car a little nudge over the edge. Half an hour later Sherlock turns up to admire his work. I made sure he got a close up. The rest, well..... You know the rest don't you?'

'We can still do this you know Mister Scott, I'll up your share to a Million.'

'Fuck off whitey, this gem is worth twenty six million, and I have my own contacts.'

I smiled at my mobile as Charlotte De Vere's voice screamed at me. 'You fucking black bastard Masters.

4
India

A month later I was strolling along a white beach in Kerala southern India. I dialled Clair's number on my new I phone. 'Hello Claire, it's me.'

'George, George Scott, can that really be you; you're supposed to be dead?'

'Ah no Clare, George Scott has gone, it's me Scott Masters. I'm in India. How do you fancy teaching English to some nice kids for a change?' I took a deep breath. 'Listen Claire, I'm in a town called Cochin, in Kerala. The local school here is crying out for a good English teacher. The salary isn't brilliant, but you don't need to worry about that, I've got plenty'

'I heard about George's death Scott. It seems that he was involved with a Policeman who had stolen a diamond from that awful De Vere girl.'

I could sense the happiness in her voice, she knew who I was. 'That gravel road going down to the beach, has now claimed two more lives Scott. They found the Policeman's body, broken on the rocks. George's blood was splattered all over the windscreen of the Qashquai. His body was probably washed out to sea; they don't expect to find it. I think, apart from some paperwork, that they've closed the case. So yes Scott, I do need a change of scenery, and someone who appreciates me. As for the salary, I can get by on very little. See you in a week, love.'

An old fisherman, who was sat cross-legged on the beach repairing his nets, grinned toothlessly as I let out a whoop of happiness. Would my old Granddad be happy now? God knows. Clair and I will be though. The "De Vere Blue" has made sure of that.

THE SCHOOLMASTER

ANN GALLAGHER, ROS EMERY & JOHN COLLIER

The schoolmaster was leaving the village, and everyone seemed sorry.
John is a good man, a man of integrity. He is married, with two children, a good husband and father. He is aged forty, popular with most people and very successful in his career. The family live in a school house located in the grounds of the school. We can't understand why he would want to leave.

Rumour has it that John's wife and children won't be going with him. We don't know what will happen to them if they stay, because the house goes with the job. John is a good looking man, gets on well with his colleagues and, more important, with the children at school.

It's not a big community, but it's close knit, where most people know each other. A lovely rural village, one hardly hears of any trouble. The family have a good social life and have many friends. The children, a boy and a girl, are involved in sport, school clubs and are both promising scholars.

John and his wife Jenny seemed to be very happy together. They've lived here for over ten years and have been asked to numerous events in that time, and have also organised many.

The parents of the children in the school get on well with John. They feel at ease when talking to him but now the question has arisen in their minds. Just where will John go to and why'?

John didn't particularly want to go but it seemed he had no choice. Insidiously over the past couple of months his whole well-ordered future had been turned upside down. It had begun innocuously enough with vague unformed dreams, he could barely remember the following morning. He'd not been inclined to mention them to Jenny, because really there was nothing much to say about them. It wasn't as if he'd had a restless night. In fact each morning he awoke refreshed and strangely content.

The dreams occurred every night, gradually taking a more tangible form, and he began to hear voices, though the words at first were indistinct. It was after more than a week that he thought someone said "We need you John. John we need you." This continued to be repeated before it faded away and he woke up at the usual time when the alarm went off.

Once he was certain he was actually hearing "we need you". He thought he should mention this to Jenny. After all, they'd always shared everything and never had any secrets from each other. Try as he might though, he couldn't articulate his thoughts. The words just wouldn't come out. Jenny didn't appear to notice anything was amiss, and as that day progressed the desire to share his experience lessened.

He felt no qualms as night-time approached. He would drift into a deep sleep and when he awoke his dreams were pleasant memories. There was no reason for him to worry. After a few more nights the message became "John you must prepare." He took this in his stride, and commenced talking openly to friends and colleagues about moving on. They in turn looked to Jenny to explain, but she couldn't as she had no idea what John was talking about. At first she genuinely believed John was referring to their future together when the children had completed their education. Because she loved him, she would have considered any scheme he proposed but then, frighteningly, she became aware he was planning an imminent move without her and the children.

On the face of it he was the same John- steady, reliable. loving. So she was astonished when he said "I've given in my notice." While she was reeling from the shock he then went on to mention some trivial events that had happened in school that day, but omitted to tell her how astounded the headmaster had been when John told him he would be leaving in less than a month's time. The headmaster had been completely mystified by John's complete incomprehension that anything was out of the ordinary.

When she got her breath back Jenny's first thought was that John had some terrible illness, but he assured her this wasn't so and he'd never felt better, fit for anything in fact. Other than this reassurance he would say nothing further on the subject except he would be going alone, and she couldn't get him to discuss it. She ended up in tears, which John seemed to find puzzling. Later efforts by friends and colleagues to get to the bottom of these out of character announcements were equally unsuccessful. No-one had any idea what he planned and he seemed impervious to the problems he was causing, not least the welfare of the family he was proposing to leave homeless. He refused to say where he was going. Actually at that time he didn't know.

Two nights later he received his instructions. On the evening of the 31st he was to leave home, telling no-one his destination, and make his way to the forecourt of the local Railway Station where he would be picked up at precisely 23.55 hours.

That November Evening was dark, damp and dismal, as the winter mists begun to rise up from the valley fields.

"The last train to Nottingham left at 23.15 hours." John muttered into the gloom, as he stood there waiting for further orders from his unknown voices. The station car park was now empty except for a dark unmarked van. John knew most of the local Villagers and was puzzled.

The Village Church clock had just struck midnight, and nobody seemed to be about. John wandered over to the Van and knocked on the driver's door window, as he could see the shadow of a person slumped over the steering wheel. Nothing moved or stirred when John knocked more loudly. John gingerly opened the driver's unlocked door, and a body fell out towards him. "Oh my God, what's happening to me ....." John screamed into the darkness as he slammed the van door shut. Then John just stood there petrified for a few minutes, before his former military training began to kick in.

"They told me not to bring my mobile phone" John kept stuttering into the Station's Public Phone. The 999 operator at the other end gently asked for the 3rd time "Where are you calling from Sir, and what's your name?" "I'm Private John Jones no 234538 Mam" .

"John, we know where you are now, and I'm sending assistance to you. Please stay in the Station phone box" the reassuring voice said. "There's a dead body nearby Mam" John, still shaking, with fear whispered down the phone.

"That's OK John, we are sending out an ambulance and the Police to assist you. Please just stay where you are".

The Emergency Services found the terrified man still clinging onto the phone, as the 999 Operator's voice continued to try and keep John calm.

"John, it's Jenny and Chris & Janice are here too to see you". John gazed confused and dazed at his loving family sitting around his hospital bed. "What are you doing here, and why am I here" John murmured to them. Janice reassured her husband with a gentle touch on his hand. "It's OK John, we have been told you have had a very frightening breakdown. Your voices were all from the past from when you were in the Falklands, and now you are well on the road to recovery".

Chris broke into the conversation "It's OK Dad, we all understand, as we have been studying about PTSD during our History lessons, and the effects it can have years later. You are still our Dad, and we want you home soonest." They all hugged him, good bye as an anxious Nurse felt her patient was getting very tired.

"What about that body in the Van, who was it ?" John asked the CID Officer sitting close to his Hospital Bed. "It's OK Sir, it was one of ours, Detective Sergeant James Johnson, and he owes his life to you. He had been working undercover, and had been badly beaten up when discovered by the gang he was investigating. He is recovering well."

The Hospital Chaplain dropped by as usual to greet John. "Father can you explain all that's happened to me. First the voices, then me waking up here being hailed as some sort of hero".

The Old Priest smiled gently and said "Do you know John, sometimes life is stranger than fiction, but l believe there is greater plan, which you have just become a wonderful part of"!

THE SCHOOLMASTER

PAT McGUIRK, ERIC McEVOY & ROS EMERY

The schoolmaster was leaving the village and everybody seemed sorry. Not me though. I couldn't wait till he was gone. I hate him! Why couldn't the others see what a monster he is? It made me sick to watch them, all gathered around the coach in the gloomy evening, ignoring the wind and the constant drizzle. They were all crying and hugging him and giving him gifts and enough food and drink to last him to London and back ten times over. If they found out I was the one responsible for him leaving they wold all hate me. Then it would be me leaving and I bet there wouldn't be one person there to see me off. They wouldn't understand that I had to do it. I couldn't allow him to stay, not after what I saw. As I watched the lights of the coach turn out of sight around the bend in the road, I wondered when I had first begun to suspect what he was up to. I think the first inkling I had was last summer, just before school closed. I ran back to the schoolhouse because I had forgotten my books. That was the day my life changed forever although I didn't realise it at the time.

Mr Taylor seemed agitated when I walked in on him that day. I now know that he was trying to hide something from be but it wasn't until the following Sunday that I knew for sure. As I walked back from church I noticed that the schoolroom door was open. I went to investigate thinking Mr Taylor had forgotten to lock up. Then I saw him.

The vision still haunts me to this day. He was standing in the empty classroom in the middle of a six pointed star chalked on the dusty wood block floor. I came in behind him and the noise of my footsteps was masked by his chanting in a strange incomprehensible language. I froze as he turned around and to my horror, noticed he was holding a pigeon in one hand and a knife in the other. Its throat had been recently cut as blood dripped onto the chalk lines in large crimson drops.

'Charlotte, he exclaimed, what are you doing here?' I couldn't answer him and just stared transfixed at the bird, its feathers matted in blood. He held up his hand and gently muttered some words and my panic subsided. I felt almost sleepy as he guided me towards a seat near a desk, and the light in the room appeared to dim.

'Look at me closely Charlotte and listen carefully to what I say. It may look strange to you but witchcraft can be used for good as well as evil. This schoolhouse stands on an ancient site used by druids and witches for thousands of years. It is steeped in magical powers and I need to tap into these before leaving for London.'

I tried to scream but my throat had seized. I just wanted to get away, as far away as possible from this monster. The idea of this popular teacher being an evil wizard, or so I thought at the time, left my mind in conflict.

He raised his hand again and his deep voice penetrated by head as if all other noise around me had disappeared.

'You will remember this Charlotte but you won't be able to tell anyone until after I am gone.' He was so right about that but then he was gone and I was standing there watching the coach lights fade into the distance. What was I to do?

Watching the coach lights fade into the distance I felt my whole world was disintegrating. All the promises that everything would be okay meant nothing. Had they just pretended to believe me? Was I expected to walk away as if nothing had happened? Mam and Nan were tense I could see but they were obviously still waiting for something to happen. And happen it did. The coach returned, escorted by two police cars with flashing lights and I also noticed Barbara in her smart R.S.P.C.A. uniform. The crowd of well-wishers were still standing around and immediately the coach was again the centre of attention.

Barbara walked over to the coach door which opened. The crowd gasped to see Mr. Taylor in handcuffs. Behind him were tow plain clothes policemen but it was D. I. Paula Mitchel who publicly arrested Mr. Taylor for a number of offences, mostly connected with animal cruelty, including unnatural practices involving killing and mutilation, plus extortion and blackmail. Barbara and Paula had assured me they intended to shame and embarrass Mr Taylor as a deterrent to others. If he had been apprehended at home it certainly would not have had the same impact.

After I saw Mr Taylor and the pigeon, forgetting my books, I'd raced home and would have liked to go straight up to my room. I knew what I had seen but at that time I was convinced there was a spell on me and I wouldn't be able to tell anyone about it. Neither Mr Taylor nor I had bargained for my Nan with her sixth sense however. She knew immediately something was wrong and it took her no time at all to persuade me to tell her why I was upset. My Mam was also listening and at first I thought she didn't believe me 'cause she was saying, 'but he's such a nice man. Everyone thinks the world of him.' Nan though had never succumbed to his charms and his elaborate compliments had been like water off a duck's back to her. 'Of course Charlotte has seen something evil,' she said, 'and we must report it right away.' She never doubted me for a minute, which gave me the strength to see the whole unpleasant matter through.

Much to my relief that evening when Paula and Barbara came to our house they were dressed informally. I'd feared police cars and flashing lights but they were very friendly and reassuring. They asked me to relate what I had seen, with particular reference to the image on the floor. As I'd not wanted to look at the pigeon I'd focused on that and I was able to describe it in some detail. Though they didn't say much then it transpired there had been a number of atrocities locally concerning animals, and Barbara and Paula had been working together. Although there was plenty of forensic evidence they had no suspect. Now they had just that. They had more than enough to arrest Mr. Taylor but wanted to make sure the case received maximum publicity. Hence the public arrest. There would be no need for me to appear in court and no-one need know I had anything to do with his apprehension.

At the trial Mr. Taylor eventually pleaded guilty on all counts, saying in mitigation that he had only made the sacrifices to appease his demonic master.

This didn't go down very well with either judge or jury and had I been called to testify I could have confirmed that, despite what he thought, he didn't possess any powers stronger than my Nan. He was sentenced to a lengthy term in prison and will of course never work with children again.

TAKE ME TO ANOTHER PLACE

THE AUTHORS

LIZ BIGGINS
RITA CHEMINAIS
JOHN COLLIER
MICHAEL CREAN
JOHN J CULKIN
M DAINTY
ROS EMERY
LORAINE FELCE
ANN GALLAGHER
EDNA GRIFFITHS
PETER HEATH
ERIC McEVOY
JIM McGUIRK
PAT McGUIRK

YOU HAVE BEEN READING ROTUNDA WRITERS

Made in the USA
Charleston, SC
28 November 2016